Half Worlder

Poppy Thruman

Contents

Chapter 1-The universe conspires against me

"I don't see why you're going."

Mom turned her back to me like she would our old dog when he'd misbehave. Ignore that dog for any length of time and he'd tuck his tail and whine for forgiveness. But I was no dog. We could argue about this all morning, but I was going to school. No matter what. At the very least, I was going to finish my junior year with my butt in a chair in a classroom, not parked in the old recliner in the living room waiting for another phone call.

'You've already got an A in Latin." Mom interrupted my thoughts. "He said you could exempt the final."

"I know, mom, but I want to go. I've got to get out of this house." Sucking in a quick breath, I tried to inflate my lungs. Instead, they felt like popped balloons. We were doing a better than average job of using up all the oxygen in the house, even with only the two of us home. "I know you're worried, but everything's going to be fine."

I said it as much to myself as to her.

She pinched the bridge of her nose and wiped at her eyes, finally turning to me. "How is everything going to be fine, Gil? Your father's been missing for two days."

There. She said it. Someone finally said it. Out loud.

Watching her face cloud over like a summer storm, even fake eating my cereal no longer appealed to me. Still, I continued pushing it around in my bowl making little hills of soggy mini-wheats. "I don't know, but it has to be. It just has to be. Otherwise, I don't know what we'll do."

It was as close to an admission of fear as I'd come since the call came from Palenque two days ago, when we'd learned dad and his grad student had gone missing at the Temple dig. When everything normal, even having an archaeologist for a father, crashed into abnormal, making a wreck of what I thought a storybook life.

I pushed the bowl away and went to stand with mom at the sink. I wanted to be strong for her, but a knot of fear was growing inside me too. One I could barely ignore anymore.

"I just can't take another minute in this house. Everything reminds me of him. You can understand that?"

I twisted the silver ring on my finger that dad and I unearthed together last year, but the reminder was too much. I pulled it off and stuffed it in my pocket. I wished I could do the same thing with my emotions, except I needed a deeper place for those. Staying numb was the only thing keeping me sane.

Mom took my face in her hands, looking closely at me. She brushed the bluish circles forming under my eyes with her fingertips. "You're not sleeping," she stated, transitioning in three seconds from terrified wife to mother. "You're still having nightmares?"

It was a harmless enough question, but the truth would only make her more uneasy. She hated when I had nightmares. I thumbed the ring, now in my pocket. Bad habits were hard to break. "No." I pulled at it harder and attempted a fake laugh, one I didn't think she bought. "Unless you want to count my defective alarm clock. It went crazy this morning and started to smoke. That was kind of a nightmare. It's been on the fritz for days though."

At least it was an ounce of truth, weird as it was.

She sniffed the air then, the acrid smell barely perceptible, and narrowed her eyes at me. "Wait, your alarm clock?"

"Yeah, you should have seen the red numbers spinning before it went—"

"Policía Palenque!" The digital voice of our caller ID struggled to pronounce the Mexican police station investigating the disappearances. My stomach sank. Not now. My butt wasn't even parked in the recliner. More than anything, I realized I didn't ever want to take that call. I didn't want to hear if dad and Elaine had been found. I didn't want to learn dad would be coming home in a body bag. Dad was probably coming home in a body bag! My heart thumped and the electric voice warbled, almost in response

Mom frowned, hesitating between me and the phone like she was dancing, then ran for it, decision made. It was then my bus rumbled outside the house. Thank God. I had to get out of here. I ran for my backpack, the side door and escape.

"Gil, don't go! Maybe they found him."

"Found a body, you mean."

I winced at my own mental betrayal. Mom didn't deserve that.

"Wait! Gil!" she called from the door. She held her hand up, imploring.

The bus stopped on the curb and I bolted up the stairs, pretending not to hear. Her voice was muffled by the closing door. I kept my eyes down and walked toward its middle trying to drown out her words and my thoughts with the familiar smell of pleather and Jenny Miller's perfume. I fell onto an empty bench and searched my bag for my iPod, crushing papers as I dug for it. A minute later, the bus stopped on a familiar corner and Simon Stillwell ran up the steps. No time for reprieve. His eyes zeroed in on me, and he made his way up the aisle, throwing his backpack on the floor against my feet. His jeans hung loose on his scrawny frame just as they had in kindergarten.

"What's up dude?" Simon plopped down, too close and gave his curly brown mop a flip. Even after a cut, Simon's hair was always in his eyes. "You're back?" He arched an eyebrow in surprise. I'd texted him as soon as I knew dad was missing.

"Yeah." I scooted over. "Last day and all. Thought I'd give it a try."

He nodded and glanced at my iPod. "What're you listening to?"

"Journey, I think. Dad downloaded it." The words were out of my mouth before I could stop them. I choked to shut myself up.

Simon noticed. "Cool man."

"It's okay."

"No. I'll let you back at it."

He reached into his bag and pulled out his sketch book, quiet for once. I tried to smile at the feat. It was better than breaking down. If I let myself think much more about him, I was pretty sure that's what I'd do. Why did everything come back to dad? Maybe I was crazy for coming to school?

I closed my eyes and concentrated, pushing dad's image out of my mind. It took a minute, but with the numb feeling back in place, I glanced back at Simon. His fingers were already stained black with charcoal, his drawing nearly complete. Yep, another disaster. A tsunami this time. The sketch showed the aftermath – palm trees everywhere.

Simon had a thing about disasters.

His eyes met mine. "You have to watch out for tsunamis, dude. They hit when you least expect, and if you don't find high ground, you're toast."

"I'll keep that in mind." I made my characteristic, 'what you said was weird' face, and stuck my ear buds back in. Still, I risked another glance after he went back to it. The detail was incredible. I tried to focus on the thousand little sweeps of his pencil that made up the sketch. Disasters in life, disasters on paper. Sort of a theme lately.

I shifted in my seat and my iPod slid off my thigh. My hand jerked unexpectedly toward the movement and I snatched it as it fell, but as soon as I touched the metal, the darn thing jolted me like I'd stuck my hand in a wall socket. I shook my hand in the air trying to get the sting out.

"You okay, man?"

"Yeah, but it feels like I got stung or something."

"Killer bees?" A grin caught the corner of Simon's mouth.

"Maybe ... oh, you're kidding me."

Simon rolled his eyes at me as Everclear's Father of Mine started playing. I groaned but not from the ache in my hand. Oh man. I forgot this was on here. I clenched my fists, closed my eyes, and got lost in the words, hitting replay when the song came to an end.

Father of mine Tell me where have you been You know I just closed my eyes My whole world disappeared

"Dude. Your face is red. Did you seriously get stung by a bee?"

I cracked my eyes and pulled out a bud. "I doubt it," I said over the song. My eyelids shuttered again as I popped the bud back in, trying to ignore the fact that my iPod screen was whirling like my alarm clock, all while the lyrics rolled over me, making my head pound.

The fear crept up easily as the music dug in, conjuring everything I couldn't ignore. It made me sick. Dizzy even. My hand tingled where my iPod had nailed me and I felt short of breath. The bus raced my beating heart, climbing the hill to Mountain View High.

It was early yet and the street lamps flickered as we drove up to the bus circle. It felt like forever before the yellow behemoth lurched and came to a stop at the curb. My vision blurred into a sea of colors punctuated by green pleather seats. It wouldn't let up. I was going to be sick. I put my head against the seat and closed my eyes, willing it to be over. Did I taste metal? The song went silent. I hadn't even noticed it playing after the world began spinning. And then, just as quickly as it all started, it stopped.

I could breathe again. I tried to swallow, but couldn't. Instead, I coughed and sucked the air. Kids stood and Simon handed me my bag, but I could only mumble my thanks as I stumbled for the door. I barely registered how the sky was changing, deepening into colors more suited for twilight than morning.

Simon patted me on the back, perceptive as ever. "Do you need to go to the nurse's office?"

"More like the psychologist," I muttered.

School was a bad idea.

Trying not to drag anyone else into my mental breakdown, I stuck my ear buds back in and ambled down the steps to the curb. Then like a moron, I hit replay for the third time. Pressure built up in my brain like it was going to blow and I grabbed my skull, trying to make it stop. As soon as my hands hit my temples, the electrical transformers on the power lines near me exploded in a shower of sparks and spent electricity. My body lurched and I stumbled to the curb landing hard on my butt.

For a brief second, I thought my head had exploded. My iPod went dead and all was silent in my mind. Smoke reached my nose from the dying embers bursting off the transformers. Kids ran for the school.

Even Simon took off and left me behind, ducking under his book bag as the transformers sent down a scorching red shower. I barely noticed the little stings on my bare arms, but a few other unlucky students shrieked from the falling embers. Teachers yelled and ran too, but I sat where I fell.

What was that? Did I do it?

No. I laughed out loud. Really, Gil. You are going mad.

My head was a bigger mess than I thought. I basically had the worst migraine of my life and now big things were blowing up around me. And it was only getting worse: the sky above darkened in serious swirls of purple and red, and I smelled rain mixed with smoke in the air. Coach Harris and a few other teachers were busy scooping up the handful of kids who hadn't run into the school. The wind whipped at his windbreaker, and his voice sounded stressed above the gusts. I sat there dropped jaw. Lightning cracked too close.

"Get in the building, Gil," Coach yelled at me, eyes wide. I swallowed hard and picked myself up off the ground to hurry in with the rest of them, dusting ash off my arms as I went. Small charred holes speckled my gray shirt. Rain fell as I dove for the doorway.

Emergency lights lit the dim hallways and kids whispered excitedly as we made our way to class.

"You okay, man?" Simon was already in homeroom.

I nodded and stopped in the doorway, staring out the window.

"You were so close to that thing when it exploded."

"Take a seat," Mrs. H. interrupted, pausing only briefly to stare at how disheveled I was. I was a mess – my hair tussled from the wind, my shirt wet and smoky from the storm's first gray raindrops and the red shower of sparks. "Gil." She motioned again with a double flick of her wrist toward my seat, but I didn't move. The room was eerily dim in the emergency light, but the storm outside churned fiercely. She eyed me again, but let it go.

Dad, I thought. The word emerged unexpected from my brain. A sudden volley of lightning sounded outside and rain came down in sheets. I couldn't get him out of my head. I pictured him getting drenched in a storm like this one somewhere in the jungle, lying soaked and helpless, tangled in a heap of twisted vines, one of his legs twisted just as miserably.

One of the school secretaries poked her head in, startling me. "Assemble in the gym please. The power may be off indefinitely, so we're centralizing everyone. We're expecting early dismissal." She winked at Mrs. H. and spun into the hall toward the next class.

So no Latin final.

Lightning hit again and the branches of a nearby tree slapped violently against the window. The wind was getting dangerous. Mrs. H. jumped back as the glass shook with the roar of thunder and the sound of angry branches. That was motivation enough for the class. We quickly packed up and made our way down the gray hallways to the gym. Simon caught up and we sat down on the bleachers. I felt so on edge, and it was only getting worse.

I need to go home. This was a terrible idea.

"Students, students?" Principal MacIntyre called out. I barely heard him, and no one attempted to listen. Around me, people shouted. He tried to yell over the noise, but his voice didn't carry. Short and squat little man that he was, Mr. MacIntyre could only waddle around looking for help to gain control of the students filing into the gym. That is, until Coach Harris's hulking figure made its way across the shiny wood floor. Harris found the bullhorn he used to lay into us during gym class and handed it over to our mild-mannered principal, which quickly took care of the volume problem.

The whole situation struck me as so absurd. I felt a jolt of amusement course through me and all the broken lights in the gym sprang to life so brightly they blinded everyone. Simon yanked up his hoodie, and the bullhorn fell out of our principal's hands. The entire room fell silent as the gym was plunged into complete darkness.

Lights don't work without electricity.

Something felt suddenly, horribly wrong. And wrong with me. Wrong inside me. A mix of panic and dread settled in me, tightening my chest. What was happening to my body? The room began to tremble. The pit of my stomach felt hot and I couldn't breathe. Metal. I could definitely taste metal. And dirt. Was that dirt?

My stomach lurched as the earth rumbled. Stadium seats shook and rolled in giant waves like they were responding to my wrenching guts. Was this even happening? Nothing felt real. Yet something inside me was more alive than I ever knew possible. Little electric pops began in my head. Pop. One of the gym walls shifted. Pop. Another wall. Pop. Pop. Another and another.

If the walls came down, we were going to die.

"No!" I cried. I wrenched down everything inside me and the walls froze solid in place. I couldn't believe I was doing it, but I knew it then: My alarm clock. The iPod. The transformers. The storm. The gym lights. The earthquake. All me. I was doing it all. A knot of energy solidified in my gut at this knowledge but then the walls groaned again and I panicked. My stomach jerked and an outside wall started crumbling in slow motion like someone had time in a headlock.

Time had crawled to a near halt. Like my nightmares.

If I can stop them once, I can do it again. A note of hysteric laughter escaped my lips at the thought, but I concentrated on keeping the falling wall together anyway. It seemed to obey me, yet I had trouble holding it back. All around me, kids lay unconscious. It was as if the entire school had fallen into some kind of deep sleep. Every one of them a rag doll being tossed around to their doom. I watched Simon's pencil fall out of his limp hand, still in slow motion, and roll across the floor. His head cracked against the bleachers, and he rolled to the side, only to be banged again with each shift of the earth.

Then I saw her.

Mom ran across the gym, rain dripping down on her through the cracks spreading in the ceiling.

She made her way through the growing rubble and unconscious kids like she was a windstorm blowing through the trees. She touched nothing, yet I felt the force of her. When she got to me, she grabbed my shoulders and shook me. "I tried to warn you." Before I spoke, she slapped a gold bracelet on my wrist that closed around like a mouth taking a bite. The inside of the bracelet whirled around and locked down with a click, piercing my skin with a thousand tiny needles. Instead of pain, I immediately felt a flood of relief. And I lost the solid ball in my gut holding back the wall.

It took no more than a second or that would have been the end of us. But when I looked up at my mom, something in her eyes took my breath away, terrified me, numbed me and enlivened me all at the same time. They were like molten pools, whirling eddies of shining kinetic energy coursing through them. She locked them on me in that second and threw her arms up and out with such force that her hair whipped in her face.

The crumbling cinderblock wall lifted up and fell back into a semblance of its former place; though it was cracked and shattered and broken open in places, it held. Smoke and dust whirled in great clouds around us too. I hadn't left mom's gaze. She had never seemed so sure of herself or as strong as she had in this moment. It was like she was alive for the first time and every other time I'd seen her throughout my life, she'd been in some waking coma. My breath caught in my chest. When I finally released it, I crumpled to the ground in unconscious oblivion, like the rest of them.

I woke with everyone else.

Great clouds of dust choked those who wereremembering to breathe. The gym filled with coughing and moaning, shrieks and crying. Principal MacIntyre and Coach Harris held each other and MacIntyre sobbed. People tried to get their cell phones to work, but everything electronic was dead. I remembered thinking, "I must have hit my head pretty hard." But then I caught my mom's figure standing under an exit sign that hung on its hinge. She locked eyes with me and silently left unnoticed – but for me.

Chapter 2-Origins

Simon was too still.

"Hey. Hey, man! Simon!" I knelt and shook his shoulders. Even at his weirdest moments, he was still my friend – but my friend felt like a limp dish rag at the moment, which worried me after watching him slam his head. I yelled even louder and shook his shoulders again, not sure whether that was actually a good idea. "Hey! Wake up, I said! Wake up!"

His eyes fluttered and he tried to focus.

Oh, thank goodness.

"Oh," he moaned. "Oh man, my head. What happened?" He sat up shaking and reached for his forehead. His hoodie fell back revealing a mop of damp curls that fell forward into his eyes as usual. Bright red blood coated his fingertips and some of his hair and he choked back a strange gurgling sound. I gave him credit for not screaming. His head fell forward between his knees, and he went silent, though his steady breathing showed he was at least okay for now.

Mrs. H. was already up and moving from person to person, though she limped. She caught my eye and I saw a flash of recognition. I nodded back to show her I was fine.

"You okay, Simon?"

"I think so." He wiped again at the blood, but it was slowing. He turned green and swallowed something back. "How are we still alive?"

"I don't know." I lied, gulping for different reasons.

Simon's eyes darted around like the ground might start moving again.

Could it? An aftershock, maybe?

I stuck my hands in my back pockets to hide the bracelet. I had a sneaking suspicion the jewelry I sported suppressed my inner freak-ishness. I had caused all this somehow, hadn't I? There was blood on Simon's head. I touched my own, but it was clean. No injury to blame this on.

This. All this was real – like Simon's sketches came to life. If he hadn't already imagined this in his notebook, he'd draw it later for sure. Twisted rebar, cracked cinderblocks, chalky ceiling tiles, and splintered stadium seats littered the floor which was scattered with hundreds of bodies in different states of consciousness.

"I can't believe that happened." This time I spoke the truth. It was nearly impossible for me to accept. "It's like a bomb went off." My heart whammed against my chest and my eyes darted around like Simon's – fearful of what might happen. The last time my heart pounded like this, I started the quake.

"Can he walk?" Mrs. H. tapped my shoulder and I jumped. Simon gave a weak thumb's up, but that was answer enough for her. She moved on to another group, continuing on until she was done with her methodical inspection. Then she stopped and stood with her hands on her hips commando-like. "Those who can, follow me. We're getting out of here." She pointed to a broken wall with daylight streaming through. The door mom had left through collapsed after she left. The exit sign now lay on the ground. Mrs. H's low wall was gonna have to do.

She walked toward our escape, but she wasn't limping anymore. She carried her black heels in one hand, one of them missing its tall spike. Mrs. H. noticed me staring. "They're Jimmy Choos. You didn't think I'd leave something that important behind?" The thought seemed to exasperate her. I shrugged my shoulders at her, but it made me remember. I scanned the ground and leaned over to pick up Simon's missing pencil.

He eyed me. "Thanks buddy. Imagine finding that in all this."

"Well, you know?" I gulped and went silent.

Why did I do that? Does he know now? How could he?

I ignored him like it was nothing and made my way around a smashed metal chair. I caused this, I thought, touching the bent frame. My heart tried to break free of my chest again, like my ribcage was its prison.

Stop thinking about it.

But I couldn't. I stepped over a chunk of ceiling tile that blocked my path, careful to make my way around an unconscious girl.

This is all my fault. That girl there. She's hurt and it's your fault.

Stop it, I yelled mentally. Stop it!

I knelt down and moved her hair off her face.

Jenny.

She groaned and her eyes opened slightly. At least I could help her. Simon must have had the same idea. We lifted her up by the arms together. She stumbled along with us, leaning heavily on my shoulder, growing more conscious with each step.

Still, the thoughts smoldered. With her leaning on my arm, the more I considered what had happened, the heavier the pressure in my chest got. I took another deep breath and tried to relax, but it wasn't working. I thought I might lose it, but the bracelet seemed to do its job.

Simon stared. He didn't miss much.

"Let's get out of here," I told him under my breath. "This place is freaking me out."

"Agreed."

We walked until we reached a mangled set of bleachers where the outside wall had broken open, leaving a gap where we could escape.

"You two first." Mrs. H. pushed us forward, taking Jenny into her arms.

Being voted the first ones out either meant we didn't look so good or we looked expendable at this point. Either way, I crawled the mangled bleachers to the gap and my shadow Simon followed. Jenny smiled at us lazily as we made our way.

From my new perch, I saw emergency responders waving and running in our direction. They hadn't even gotten the ladders off the truck, but I still swung my legs over. A fireman ran up to catch me from below, but I didn't wait for him to get into position either. The distance didn't seem too bad.

I jumped.

And my flesh ripped open on a truss hiding in the brick.

"Aa-agh!" I cried out as the metal cut deep. Still I managed to land on my feet.

The officer's mouth fell open, more shocked than me. He immediately waved for help as if his arm moved without his brain's direction. Simon came down next, avoiding the shrapnel I had found. Simon stared at my arm. My eyes followed his and I realized why the officer looked the way he did.

"You didn't feel like you'd been through enough?" Simon grabbed me by the other sleeve and pulled me toward an EMT who was running straight for us. Dried blood caked Simon's hair, but bright red blood streamed down my elbow.

The tech's eyes went wide as he inspected my arm, and he yanked me too, this time toward his ambulance, applying pressure as we went. "Come on kid. We gotta stop that bleeding." He waved off a stretcher, rushing us back on foot. "He may have nicked a vessel," the tech told his partner, pushing me up into the ambulance.

My arm was bloody with crimson, but the other tech paused and blinked at my arm, confused. "God that's ... wait, it's clotting."

The original tech frowned and hopped up. His nametag read Robby Shari "But it was a lot of blood?"

"It was." The partner pulled Simon into the ambulance as well.

Robby took a closer look at my arm, his eyes narrowing as he cleaned and wrapped it, only a haze of pink soaking through the gauze as it twisted around. He shook his head, then took a quick pulse. "Did you hit your head? Your pulse is fast."

"Nope. He did." I pointed at Simon.

"You sure?" Robby ignored me and got out a blood pressure cuff.

"Yeah, I'm just freaked out." Even though I knew exactly why my heart was pounding, I wasn't about to tell him. Mentioning I caused the earthquake would get me a one-way ticket to the Psych Ward.

Robby took another reading and rubbed the back of his neck. "It's beyond high." He tapped the gauge.

Simon's head was already bandaged. He scratched happily with his rescued pencil, a small white dressing adorning his forehead. "Check his hand. Something stung him earlier."

Yeah right, I thought. This was caused by a bug bite. How very Spider Man of me.

When the tech turned over my hand, he mumbled "electrical burn" to his partner and bandaged it, but got me a dose of Benadryl anyway. After 10 minutes, Robby checked my blood pressure again, then put his hands on his knees thinking. "I'm not sure I should let you go after all that, but it's normal now. Probably something wrong with the cuff." He wrapped the stethoscope back around his neck and opened the door.

"Alright, well." He glanced at my wrist, satisfied, and stood, gesturing out the door.

I was a little surprised at his abrupt dismissal, but it was easy to see why when the door fell open. Kids were being wheeled away to ambulances that drove screaming from the parking lot as soon as they were loaded. The KRCR News van was already parked on the curb, its satellite uplink raised to the sky, Stephanie Montano readying her microphone for an interview. A med tech was evaluating Principal MacIntyre who had collapsed on the sidewalk nearby. He was probably having a nervous breakdown – though Coach was holding up pretty well, considering he was chatting up a smiling Ms. Montano before she went live.

Our school grounds were in chaos.

I scanned the growing crowds for mom, only to find Simon's.

She saw us and ran. Her eyes flooded with tears and she grabbed her son, folding him up in a bone-crunching embrace. Simon seemed to disappear in her ample bosom. I winced in sympathy. When I walked over, she hugged me too, but I thankfully didn't get a face full of her like Simon. I'd had enough trauma today.

"Oh, Gil. I'm glad you two are okay. I can't believe this is happening." She touched Simon's bandage timidly.

"Yeah, it's crazy." I shielded my eyes from the sun. It was so high now it blinded me. "But Mrs. Stillwell, you should take Simon home. He hit his head pretty good. My mom's here somewhere. I better go find her."

She didn't argue, but dabbed at her forehead with a floral hanky she had produced from somewhere on her body and inched backward. "I promise I'll ring her as soon as we're home. Tell her you're safe."

It was a kind offer. For some reason, cell phones still weren't working.

"Thanks."

She reached out and closed the gap once more, hugging me with a big sigh. Once she released me, she turned for the parking lot, motioning for Simon to follow with her thick fingers. It was sometimes hard to believe she was Simon's mother, as skinny as he was.

"See you later!" Simon ran to catch up with her, but turned back to me. "I can't believe we lived through that."

"Me neither."

He waved, but then stopped, yanking a crinkled, folded-up piece of paper from his jean's pocket. He pressed it into my hands. "This is for you." The sides of it were smudged with black charcoal. The picture he had drawn in the ambulance. He hesitated before adding, "It's for the last day."

It was probably a drawing of the gym collapsing, yet another disaster from his collection. I didn't need a reminder any day soon, but I waved at him in thanks anyway. And then I stuffed it in my back pocket.

I watched him leave before turning to look for my mom.

I found her on the soccer field where parents were gathering. We just stared at each other. There were no tears, no hugs and no words exchanged. We would have seemed strange to other people, had they

not been busy hugging their kids and laughing at finding them alive
and well to notice.

"Come on, mom, let's go. We need to talk about this."

I started for the parking lot, but she grabbed my elbow and steered
me back to the pedestrian path. "I didn't drive. I ran here. I followed
your bus."

"You followed my bus?"

"Yes."

We walked for a while in silence, until we had passed by the crowds
of people and cameramen surrounding the school. "Look, I'm sorry.
I tried to get to you before it started. All those kids..."

I tried to drive the images from my head and swallowed.

"Was it really me, then?"

She nodded and kept walking.

I stopped dead in my tracks. "Wait. Really?"

She turned, her eyes confirming it before her words. "You may have
started it, but you saved them all too. I can't even comprehend it,
Gil, how mature your control was. If you hadn't held back the walls,
then ..." She shook her head free of what could have been. "You were
incredible, son."

Considering what I had apparently just done to my high school, I
wasn't sure "incredible" was the right word.

"To just wake up one day, and at 17," she went on. "We've never had
one turn so late."

Had one turn? What was I, a vampire? Wait. At least the fact I was
standing in sunlight ruled this out. Not a vampire, apparently.

Despite my mental gymnastics, mom kept rambling. "When you told me about your alarm clock, I was stunned. But the electric forces are the first sure sign. And then of course you ignored me and got on that bus before I could explain. We haven't seen that kind of life force since Alexandra."

"Mom!" I stopped and grabbed her by the shoulders. I couldn't believe she was so casual. "Do you realize I just destroyed part of my high school with an earthquake?" Thankfully no one was around to hear that.

She did a quick scan around us, probably thinking the same thing as me.

"I blew up the transformers." I threw my hands up in frustration and felt grateful I hadn't lifted any homes off their foundations.

"I summoned this crazy mega storm." I made a twisty motion with my finger, even though there actually hadn't been a tornado. Thank goodness!

"I totally toasted my alarm clock and I have no idea what's happening to me, and you are rambling on about life forces and vampires and all this crazy stuff. What is going on with me? What just happened?"

Mom smirked, showing a hint of her old self, the one before dad disappeared, and softened. She had been so off lately. "I didn't say anything about vampires."

"Well, I know that," I conceded, "But mom, what happened?"

"Let's go inside."

I looked up. We were home.

The kitchen side door still swung on its hinges.

Mom banged it shut and sat across from me at our oversized oak table. The planks were stained with little flecks of paint from when I was little – a shred of normality infused into the wood.

"We've made lots of memories at this table." She knocked on the old boards. As if an afterthought, she reached for my hand. "We should make one more."

I nodded for her to continue.

"How do I say this? I've never had to tell a teenager before. Mom pulled her hand away and bit at her fingernails. I didn't think I'd ever seen her at a loss for words. It wasn't her style.

"I'm saying this all wrong." She took a deep breath. "But you're my son. You're as strong as I am. You'll be able to handle it, okay?"

I never thought of my mom as strong before. I did now. She shook her head at me waiting for my approval to go on.

"Okay mom. I can handle it."

Crossing her arms, she leaned in. "The short answer is we're not from around here."

She paused to let that sink in, but I sat there dumbly.

She tried again. "Well, technically, you are from here, but also, not from here. Me, well I am definitely not from here."

I cocked my head at her and raised an eyebrow. She didn't make sense. "Everyone knows you're not from Redding, mom." Although I'd never met my grandparents, mom was the daughter of a British nurse and an Egyptian soldier, even raised in the shadow of the pyramids the first half of her life. "You have that weird accent to prove it."

"No. Gil, darling. I am not from here." She pointed down and nodded her head at me like I should understand. Her eyes even lit up a little at the revelation of this "secret."

This secret I still didn't totally understand. Yeah, I know. Sue me. I scratched my head because nothing sunk in. "Not from here. O-K." I drawled out each letter.

Mom began drumming her fingers on the table. The wood bubbled and rippled away from them like surf rolling back from the shore. Her eyes locked on mine and she cocked her head at me, grinning

Whoa.

"Mom!" I snapped. "If you're not from here." I pointed down. "Where are you from?"

Mom smirked again. And that's when she pointedup.

Chapter 3-The Knot of Isis

Complete darkness surrounded me but for the colors that floated around me too – colors I'd never seen before and didn't think humans could see. An absurd memory tried to surface – I wasn't one, a human, I mean. It was a strange thought, but in my dream state, it made my head hurt and this place was doing enough to give me a migraine, so I let it go.

But then the vision shifted and I found myself in a long room carved from bedrock. A wet dirt and moss smell filled my nose, and it was so warm, sweat soaked through my shirt. Near me, a blanket twisted sloppily on a sleeping cot, a loaf of bread sat half-eaten on a table, and metal boxes stamped with the word "rations" littered the room. The only light came from a lone monitor that idled in the corner, and it was deathly quiet but for the ragged breathing of the girl crouched beside me. The girl from my nightmares – of course.

Who else should I expect?

We knelt together on the hard ground, backs pressed against one of the boxes. There was a scratching noise and her head perked up. She swallowed hard when she found the source, and her breathing started coming in such ragged bursts I thought she might hyperventilate. My heart joined her panic, beating in my chest like it knew what to expect. I didn't have much time to consider this before there was louder scratching and sparks lit the dim room not 20 feet away. Someone was cutting a ventilation grate from the wall, trying to get in from the other side.

The scream of a handsaw pierced my eardrums until it stopped abruptly and the intruder kicked out what was left of the wall. The grate thudded the floor staccato, the sound whipping off each wall in the room. The girl threw her hands to her ears cowering even lower. My hand pressed hard against the box, steadying myself as the man worked his way out, his light flashing erratically as he brought his bulky frame through the opening. But then he steadied himself and his light flashed back and forth in a studied grid, no doubt looking for us.

I leaned down to whisper to the girl, but she ignored me and took a fleeting glance around the corner at him instead. Going still like some paralyzing numbness struck her, she fell against the box again. Her chest rose and fell with quick hard breaths – the kind that hurt with every suck of air. Her cheeks flushed and her eyes darted back and forth searching for any means of escape. I wondered if she'd start shaking with fear and scream out and reveal us, but she stayed quiet and kept her body still.

The man was getting closer though with every second and I knew we needed to run. The girl bounced on her legs in anticipation, and I saw the moment her face stilled; resolve finding its way into her panicked eyes. Even then, she made a little sound like a whimper and looked rapid fire around before sprinting to the nearest box the moment his light fell away.

"Wait," I hoarsely whispered and ran, clumsily diving down behind her silent figure to avoid the light. Instead of stopping, my body went straight through her and she flickered like an old TV on the fritz.

"Whoa," I said.

The girl ignored me still.

My brain attempted to wrap itself around this, but time wouldn't pause for my reflection. My eyes snapped back to her. She had collapsed onto her knees and sat staring at a simple gold locket resting on a braided chain. Her eyes were sad, and when she pressed her lips hard against the metal, they closed on heavy and unspoken memories. Then she relaxed her rigid posture, slumping to the ground. It looked like the girl from my nightmares was finally done running.

A tear formed in her eye and fell upon the locket, but the moment the tear hit the metal, light flashed with such brilliance, my eyes went blind for a second. The locket flew open and out burst a pinprick of crushing light, the pressure of its containment evident in its awesome release, its tiny light growing and swelling and catapulting into the air above the girl.

This light became the very image of a small sun, with all of its terrible energy but none of its burning fire. The energy that coursed through it churned like rough oceans captured in a bottle, trying to pound the shore, but instead finding itself beating against a prison of its own walls. It was brilliant and awful all at once.

The girl stood up then, our pursuer somehow forgotten, mesmerized by the thing that hovered above us. Her square-cut bangs hung in her eyes, and she pushed away the black hair from them like it was an old habit. Her eyes were black too with smudged makeup, staring at the arms of light extending from the orb's body towards her. They were rays of light, yes, yet arms nonetheless with nearly literal hands, and when they reached down, they embraced her, brushing me but leaving me alone.

Then it took her. Right from my side.

The girl rose up in the air, hovering above the floor. She was like a fly caught in a spider's web, except she didn't struggle. She floated unmoving in its tentacle arms. Even her eyes were locked in place.

New fear gripped me, and I tripped over myself to get away, but the other man's movement brought me back to reality. Unfazed by the levitating girl, he ignored me and sprinted for her. With one motion, he pulled out his weapon, the orb turning only slightly as if noticing this new situation. Its reaction was impassive, bored even, but pronounced in the end. Out shot an explosion of energy that evaporated the man as he raised his arm to strike. The orb's light brightened, then dimmed at this expenditure of energy. Still, the girl in its arms didn't move.

My heart nearly fell out of my chest watching the man with the knife crumble to the dust he was made of, yet the sun-like thing wasn't done. With calculating efficiency, it turned and pulsed again. There was a cracking noise and rock fell in some hidden recess of the bunker, a whoosh of air rushing over me as dust filled the cavern.

My tongue went dry and rough like sand paper, but my skin stayed damp with sweat. It was all I could do to steady my breathing and make myself small and motionless in hopes I'd survive long enough to escape this nightmare.

My heart sank.

I wasn't going to make it.

The light-sphere sensed me. I could feel it. It paused and spun on its axis, seeking me, taking inventory of the space. The frozen girl turned with it too on its slow path of rotation. I noticed the pile of ashes that was the would-be assassin and held my breath as it stopped and faced me. Its strange arms reached out and I jerked, terrified and ready to run, but the orb touched the girl's cheek instead, turning it down until her eyes were on me.

This time, a low thrum echoed.

The unseen shackles that held her frozen were released. Her body trembled awake. Her eyes focused and lit up in recognition, seeing me for the first time I now realized. "Boy," she addressed me, even though she wasn't much older than me, her eyes darting around wildly before they fell back on me. "Listen fast, for you must follow the path we have laid for you or there will be blood. Surely, I tell you, there will be blood but it will be this Earth's, and she will bleed until she is no longer." Her eyes darted again, and her breathing came faster. "The time is short. I can only sustain it for so long," she said looking up, wincing at the light. "You must watch for the path Gil Scott. Watch for it. Please Gil, I beg you." She stretched her arms to me in her appeal, then abruptly froze yet again – the only sound left the echo of her strange statement fading away to nothing.

Unaffected, the orb pulsed again and dimmed, then strange, almost liquid lights filled a transparent vessel that formed and surrounded the girl as the liquid traveled up from her feet. She hovered quiet as death while the strange egg of molten swirling colors slowly closed around her, her hands still outstretched, her emerald eyes still pleading in desperation.

I tripped backwards in fear but caught myself. The room began to change. Time accelerated. The metal storage boxes filling the room rusted. Her blanket frayed, fell apart, and turned to dust. The bread molded, bugs ate it, and it disappeared. But all the while, the girl with the pleading eyes stared at me unchanging.

■■■■■

It was then I woke up. Terrified, of course. But this felt rather routine for me.

"Oh, man," I said aloud and opened my eyes to darkness. My head felt foggy. Another nightmare. They were all so real, so unnerving. My body ached.

I rolled over, stretched my stiff limbs, and reached blindly for my side table. What time was it? I fumbled in the darkness, my fingers tapping the surface. Where did I put my alarm clock? I stopped suddenly and sniffed. Burned plastic still lingered in the room.

Yesterday came flooding back.

For one thing, my alarm clock didn't work anymore.

And for another, I wasn't human.

■■■■

I stumbled down the stairs in the darkness. There was a low voice, so I stopped short, remembering my Boy Scout training. I tiptoed around the corner but mom didn't notice. My old scout leader would be proud.

She leaned on the hall table with the phone to her ear, talking in whispers. "I know. I know." She cupped her hand over the receiver. "Yes, Benton Field. Two hours. No, I already started packing. We'll be there."

When I walked up and revealed myself, she nodded at me to stay quiet. I leaned against the wall alongside her where moonlight from the front door's side lights cast strange shadows off the hall clock's hands. Apparently a lot had gone on after I walked catatonic-like from our kitchen table yesterday, straight into my bed.

Benton was that little one-runway airport right outside of town. It was so small, they didn't even have an air traffic control tower, but still, lots of private planes were in and out of there. And we were going to be on one of them – at 2 am.

A low voice spilled from the phone. Most of it unintelligible, but I caught the last part. "It will be fine, Helen," it said.

"I know. Okay, Morty." She hung up, tucking her hair behind her ears. She hadn't slept based on the state of her clothes.

"We going somewhere mom?"

"Yes. Uncle Morty has a plane in the air heading our way." She checked her wrist watch and tugged at her sweaty shirt to cool herself. "We're supposed to be on it in two hours. I've already started packing you, but check if there's anything else you want to bring. We're going to the ranch in Montana."

"You mean the one I've never set foot on?"

"Yes, and for good reason. You hadn't turned." She seemed to catch herself, but a little late. Her guard was down for once.

"Okay. What exactly does that mean?"

She put her hands down on the hall table and talked down at them. "When your powers suddenly turned on yesterday and you transformed your high school gym into an active fault line, that's called turning."

"Powers, huh?"

"That's your only takeaway?"

"Yep."

"Figures. Okay superman, your suitcase is on the sofa. You've got 30 minutes to grab what you can while I get a shower. And, uh, maybe you should too?" She wrinkled her nose at me and opened the basement door.

"Mom, the shower is upstairs." I grinned. Man, she must be tired.

"Oh, ha, no. I just have to grab some things for our trip."

"Like from 'up there' kind of supplies." I pointed up and her eyes lit in response. Her secret was mine now.

"Yep, the kind I keep in my super-secret vault in the basement." She snickered and descended a few stairs. "Oh, and your Uncle Morty is more than an old colleague from the University." She poked her head back up with this information. "We've been colleagues much longer. We crash landed on Earth together nearly half a century ago."

She said it so matter-of-fact, I didn't have time to blink. She turned on her heels and went back down.

Wait.

She crash landed here? How long ago? What was she, three years old?

"Don't even try the math," mom called up. "I'm 3,600 years old Gil, and your great-great-great-great grandfather lived to be 19,028, well, in Earth years anyway. I suppose there's a lot of strange things you're just going to have to accept." She paused, and I could almost feel the weight of her breathing, even so far down the steps. "And, just so everything's on the table, the Egyptian gods, they were from my home planet. I came here to find them. They were missing – still are."

"They were aliens?" I ran over to look down into the basement. She stood in a recess that wasn't there yesterday. There was a soft glow coming from it. So, she wasn't kidding.

"We are aliens," she corrected, grinning up at me. "Your dad's and my work's starting to make a lot of sense now, huh?"

It did. My parents the Egyptologists. My mother the alien. My dad the ... then it hit me.

"Mom, but gramps died when he was 72?"

"Oh, uh ... hmm." She went silent for a moment. "Gil, that's because your dad is human. You get the alien superpowers from my side of the family."

Everything about her sentence gave my brain pause, then my 17-year-old mind rerouted to one word in particular. "Superpowers." I turned it over on my tongue. Then, "Alien."

I couldn't get used to that word. Alien. But that's what she was. And even though I'd been born here on Earth, that's what I was too. "Half alien only though," I whispered.

"Hybrid," mom answered from downstairs. She had Vulcan hearing.

With all this churning in my already over-full brain, I walked toward the bathroom, stopping to strip off my dirty jeans in the darkness of the living room. I had fallen into bed earlier without so much as changing. They were pretty gross, but I could wash them later. I yanked my ring from the pocket back to my finger and chucked my jeans in with the rest of it. Still shaking my head in disbelief at everything that happened, I headed toward the shower in my boxers.

Chapter 4-Area 53

The pilot announced our descent into Gardiner Public Airport, then began a steep drop onto the valley runway. I peeked out the window while the pilot put down the flaps. A swath of mountains rose high around us on all sides and an expanse of brown grass ran from the asphalt all the way to the foot of those mountains. It was like we were landing in a fish bowl made of peaks and scorched grass.

The little jet vibrated as the wheels rotated out of its belly and mom's hands flew out of her lap to clench her armrests. She never liked to fly and now I knew why. It took her crew 200 years just to get here, only to crash on arrival. The irony was great, considering they came here searching for another lost starship.

I took mom's hand and felt tension knot her muscles as we came down and sped along the airport's one runway, then relax as we slowed. My stomach twisted but for different reasons. My mind kept replaying the dream from last night. Out my window, the scene outside blurred as we roared to the end of the strip, never really stopping. Our pilot was in a hurry.

We slowed only long enough to make a wide U-turn and head back toward the motley group of buildings that sat off to the side of the runway. He nosed in to one of the few private hangers that sat amongst the airport's buildings. It was old and gray and made of molded metal. It had seen weather, but it was free of rust and had a fresh coat of paint.

Uncle Morty waited by the open door of his black Humvee, parked at the back. His arms were crossed over his chest and he tapped his foot like a drummer going hard on the pedal of a bass drum. He stood there straight and tall, yes, but I got the impression his body was coiled like a spring and near ready to snap. He waved impatiently at the plane, unaware of us waving at him from inside.

Mom wasted no time when the door opened. She grabbed her purse and left me to follow alone.

When I emerged, Morty called out to me. "Gil, my boy. You've grown up since last I saw you."

"You could say that," I answered.

Morty laughed and walked over to clap me hard on the back. He caught the eye of his steward as he did, who quickly sped up off loading our suitcases. Morty had that effect on people. The steward brought them to the back of the Hummer and slammed down the gate, downshifting his eyes.

"You're ready to go sir."

"Thank you, Tom. That will be all."

The steward bolted and Morty motioned for us to get in.

"Buckle up," he said from the front. "I'm going to make good time back to the ranch."

He gestured with his hands on how to connect the clasps of my harness-like seatbelt. I guessed Morty liked to off-road on his ranch, but who wouldn't if they owned nearly 2,000 acres of land along Yellowstone National Park?

I should have gotten the message then.

The engine revved and Morty bolted out of the garage, barely pausing to see if any other traffic was on the airport road. I tumbled across the seat and slammed my shoulder into the door. Mom didn't notice, but I caught Morty grinning at me in the rearview mirror. I went to work on the straps. The way he drove, I thought I might die otherwise.

The two fell into a hushed conversation, so I kept quiet. I wished I could catch a quick nap, but every time I closed my eyes lately, the nightmare-girl was there. My exhaustion wasn't enough for me to offer her another invitation back into my head by falling asleep. I was almost positive she'd be back, and I couldn't shake the feeling that settled into me after I woke this morning already. Her words held such weight, they practically pressed my mind into believing it was real. I hated dreams like that.

I tried to shake the feeling again, keeping my eyes peeled for the ranch. I'd only ever seen it in pictures and now that I knew it was off limits to me until now, I was pretty curious to know why. But the feeling was still there. She said the earth would bleed. Something felt really wrong.

Yeah, dad's missing and I'm a half alien. Why else would I be worried?

True, I thought. But I wasn't falling asleep either.

■■■■■

When we finally pulled up, it was just as I imagined it. Gray rough-hewn logs, all knobby where the limbs had been cut off, framed the three-arch plank head gate. A similarly rustic plank in slightly warmer tones hung down from the taller center archway that crossed the drive. The words GRIZZLY CREEK RANCH in all caps were burned black into the wood. A wooden fence lined the property as far as the eye could see and a dirt and gravel driveway plunged into the valley below, seemingly ending at the foot of a mountain range that bordered the back of the property. The farm road meandered down into this lush valley, stopping briefly at the ranch's heart, a 10-acre compound which housed several homestead cabins constructed in old-west log and timber frame construction. The buildings looked miniature from my view on the ridge.

Morty stopped the car outside the gate and put his arm on the back of my mom's seat so he faced me. "You're going to want to take off the amulet now." He pointed at the gold bracelet on my wrist. "I think you'll want to see this and that band is constraining your abilities." Morty's stare was hard. "However, after your experience yesterday, you can imagine how important it will be to keep your emotions balanced until we can teach you how to control your abilities. Getting emotional can make them uncontrollable, and that can be bad indeed."

I totally understood.

Morty grabbed my wrist.

I was seconds away from this thing opening like the mouth of a Pac Man and my freakishness would be back. I was a nervous ball of eager energy. I mean, who hasn't wondered what it would be like to have super powers? This was going to be awesome, but I still worried what kind of damage I might do to that spectacular mountain range framing Uncle Morty's property. I had a propensity to cause earthquakes. I held my breath.

"Now, when I take this off, at the very least you'll feel a buzzing at the center of you. That is your Bau at work – the unique power of your being. Now that this part of you has been activated, it will always be with you."

Finally, some detail.

"You can grow it and diminish it at your will, but you can become dangerous and uncontrolled if you are led by your emotions without your intellect. So, keep those in check."

Uncle Morty's finger slid along the amulet. When he stopped, something clicked. A thousand tiny needles retracted out of my skin and I felt the engine of that Bau thing humming at the center of me.

"Whoa."

"Yeah. Whoa is right," echoed mom. "Could you please put the car down? Gently – and quickly as well."

Mom white knuckled the grab handle. We were about a foot higher than we were supposed to be.

Cool.

But we were on a seldom-used but still-public road. I calmed myself and willed the car down as gently I could manage. We landed with a thud.

"Well, at least this thing has great shocks," Uncle Morty chuckled. "You alright, Gil? Can you handle it?"

"Yeah. I think I got this."

I understood what Morty said about my Bau expanding and contracting. Knowing this thing was attached to me, or a part of me, helped me keep it in check. It was like breathing. If I didn't think too much about it, my Bau just was. If I needed to sprint, I got the feeling it could work overtime.

After a few seconds, Morty must have felt it was safe to continue. He put the SUV in drive and passed under the head gate. An electric shiver crackled through me. We must have gone through some kind of invisible force field, because as soon as we crossed under the GRIZZLY CREEK RANCH sign, things definitely got different, as if blinders came off my eyes. The main hall down at the compound buzzed with blue electrical energy that jumped off the structure in arching waves, like those plasma balls you get as prizes at an arcade. Every once in a while, one of them would shoot out our way or to another point along the property line, illuminating a membrane-like dome that divided this alien land from the human one without.

Down the drive, to our right, a massive black tunnel appeared and yawned open into the ground. The cave wasn't visible a moment before. And to top it all off, a small gold and black flying ship raced up from the compound to meet us. The pilot slowed abruptly and a brace of gold and black wings, almost like the pointy ears of cat, retracted from the fuselage where they had just been cutting through the air. They moved slowly back and rotated up 90 degrees to form a tail like a peacock. An embossed image of the sun was stamped on each wing, the ball of fire at the inner corners and lines of embossed sunlight radiating out to tips outlined in black.

Real sunlight caught the wings and they flashed brilliantly. The flying ship hovered and then descended vertically to the ground. Its domed roof opened, just like an F-14 fighter jet. Inside, a slender figure in a white flight suit stood up. The figure took off its gold helmet, revealing long curly locks of blonde hair which the owner shook out vigorously.

My heart skipped a beat and a sort of happy feeling flooded me. I felt lighter than air. Morty stopped the car, but movement caught the corner of my eye. My backpack had started to float next to me. I had to put my hand on it and push it back down, but it stayed there. I laughed quietly. I had to get used to this alien stuff.

"Oh stars, Morty. You're kidding me?" Mom exclaimed from the front seat as she opened the door and jumped out. The car hadn't even stopped yet. Her hair whipped in the wind from the ship's engines, which were still powering down.

Morty and I followed, leaving the doors hanging open too.

"Three days, Helen. It's been incredible."

That's when dad disappeared.

"No wonder you've been trying to reach me. I'm sorry I didn't call back. I didn't even have the nerve to ring you before last night to tell you what was happening with ... with ...." Even now she couldn't say his name. "I'm sorry."

"What's going on mom?" I interrupted mercifully as the girl in white made her way to us.

"We think the Aten has been activated." The girl's words were matter-of-fact, her voice clear and confident, if somewhat clipped. She carried her gold helmet in the crook of her arm, an image of the sun stamped there too.

She was beautiful. My age. And an alien.

The trifecta.

I wondered if she would be offended if she knew I was whistling at her in my brain.

The girl gave my mom a hug, and she eyed me curiously as they greeted each other, her long dark lashes hooding her large eyes only slightly. It made her alluring and mysterious all at once. Mom let her go and the girl's intelligent blue eyes fell purposely on me then.

She seemed so sure of herself. I liked it.

Plus, she was gorgeous.

Striking really. She was anointed with the kind of beauty that made guys stammer and forget themselves publicly. Me, well, it was stunned silence.

She had to be about 16, I thought. Her makeup, if she wore any at all, was simple. Maybe mascara darkening her eyes? Maybe lip gloss highlighting her mischievous tight-lipped grin. She walked toward me with graceful yet athletic ease. She seemed strong, fierce and self-assured, like she practiced kung fu and ran marathons before breakfast. I didn't think anything could stand in her way. In fact, I got the feeling she could hurt me, but I'd die happy.

My eyes fell unrestrained down the rest of her. She wasn't curvy. Hard work seemed to have hardened and blurred those lines, and she was shorter than me too, I realized, the kind of height where her head might rest perfectly in the crook of my neck.

Was I sweating? Why was I thinking like this?

I was pretty sure mom was stifling a laugh.

I broke my gaze only long enough to confirm it.

All these thoughts raced through my head in seconds.

She walked up.

"Hi, Gil." She knew my name. She seemed friendly and at ease but my insides felt like hot wax. "It's probably strange to meet someone who knows you, but you don't know them – I imagine," she added with a friendly hunch of her shoulders.

"Uh ... yeah." My eyes narrowed in confusion. What did she mean?

I tried to recover a semblance of coolness.

She laughed. "You have no clue what I'm talking about, do you?"

"No," I admitted, swallowing.

She laughed again. "There's not so many of us anymore, so – of course – I knew about you. And until yesterday, you couldn't know about me."

I still had no clue what she was talking about.

"Anyway, welcome to the ranch. I'm Alexandra."

I knew that name. Mom said it.

"Gil," I stammered in reply, extending my hand. "But you know that already."

Alexandra stepped toward me and reached out her hand, a kind of amusement filling her eyes, and I shook it. Her palm was a surprise; it was rough and calloused with hard work, not soft and girly like I thought it'd be. She pulled me toward her in an impromptu embrace, like we were the north and south poles of a magnet that couldn't resist the attraction. I think she shocked herself by doing it, because her body stiffened slightly against mine when we touched and she pulled away.

Then things got weird.

Electricity popped between us. Not the normal 'romance novel' kind of thrilling tumble of heart rate and breath acceleration and hormones and pheromones and all those things that send little signals to dizzily churn up your insides, but actual blue sparks of electricity. Well, admittedly, some of the crazy tumbling too, but in 3D. I know it sounds weird, but that's how it was.

Mom actually laughed out loud, but Morty harrumphed and turned away. The blue sparks danced between us and fell to the ground to extinguish themselves like the hot ash of a furious sparkler on the Fourth of July.

Our eyes caught briefly as we pulled apart, me smiling at whatever that was, but her – no. Her eyes flashed with surprise, then shock. She had to have felt the energy between us, seen it really, but she swallowed hard like she was pushing something down, and a kind of hardness glazed her eyes.

Did I cross some sort of alien line or something?

I hoped not.

But then she seemed to consciously flip a switch and was back to normal-faced Alexandra, but me, I couldn't think straight. Darn it, she even smelled good. I remembered how her gold hair brushed my cheek and her scent lingered on me, something sweet and earthy I couldn't place.

My mouth must have been hanging open.

Mom closed my jaw with two fingers.

Darn it, yep, public embarrassment kind of beauty.

A smile bloomed on Alexandra's face at my mother's public shaming of me. I wished it lasted longer, but as it was, it was fleeting. Her lips closed tight when she realized her mistake. Her unrestrained grin had revealed the slight gap between her front teeth, one she was good at hiding. Maybe for some, it would mar her beauty, but I thought it gave her charm her otherwise perfect face would lack. One thing I realized, Alexandra was self-conscious about it.

Morty pulled me out of my trance.

"Gil, she is my daughter." Morty wagged his finger between us. I had to blink to realize I was being spoken to. It was the kind of thing a father might say before mentioning he owned a shotgun.

Morty's daughter? I had time to think.

How did I not know he had a daughter?

This daughter!

His eyes lightened up though and he relaxed.

"She and you have a lot in common besides your age, and, well, the rest is obvious." He cleared his throat uncomfortably and tipped his head. Alexandra looked down. "So, yes, we'll have to pair you two together later in the arena. Test out those amazing Bau abilities of yours."

Alexandra scowled, which was a surprisingly ugly thing for her to do to her pretty face.

Only I caught it.

Mom and Morty pulled themselves to the side, leaving Alexandra and I to stare at each other. She wrung her hands together, her right hand pulling at her left hand's middle finger, twisting and tugging, like she wanted to pull it off, a marked change from her earlier display of self-assurance. She studied me a moment more and then moved over to join our parents, not speaking.

I followed.

"The Aten, Morty? You think the power surge was from the Aten of all things? After all this time who activated it? We don't even have a clear picture of what it's capable of."

"I think you know the answer to that question already."

Her eyes drifted away.

"The fact Joe went missing when this started makes me think he finally found it. And if it is what we think it is, it makes sense it powered the ship."

I thought mom would collapse right there. If he was right, it meant dad and Elaine could still be alive.

"So dad was on some super-secret alien artifact hunting expedition?" I tried my best to insert myself in the conversation.

Alexandra snorted. One look from Morty silenced her.

"It's not exactly like that."

Mom looked near-faint.

"Don't worry. Elaine was with him and she's one of our strongest. You know Joe? He's probably so overtaken with his discovery, he's forgotten to check in – or he's too far out of range and can't. He's using the old modified technology. We'll hear from him soon. I'm sure he's fine."

"You sent a team down, didn't you?"

"Yes, I've got a ship heading down as we speak."

"Good – and speaking of ships, Gil should meet Neter."

"Leave that to me," Alexandra said. "The next flight's hybrid only."

Chapter 5-I meet Neter

I never thought entering a dark, deep fathomless pit would be on my top-10 list. But I had to say, I was looking forward to this.

We hadn't even unpacked yet, and I was being sent on my first spaceship ride. No wait. Alexandra called this a planetary vehicle. It seemed spaceship enough for me though. We were taking it to see Neter, the real ship that brought my mom here to Earth from their home planet, Oases. Mom waved at me rather encouragingly for someone who didn't like to fly. Talk about throwing me right in.

"Come on newbie. This is going to be fun." Alexandra put on her gold pilot's helmet from the cockpit above me.

It was amazing to think she'd only been flying this vehicle for three days. Apparently, a lot of Neter's ancillary functions, including these ships, hadn't worked so well – or even at all – since the crash. Then three days ago, they woke up when Neter tapped into a power surge centered squarely in Palenque, Mexico – the city where my father had gone missing.

When people started putting two and two together this morning, that's when words like "Aten" started getting thrown around. Dad had always been fascinated by it. Pictures of it even adorned our home, but I wasn't sure why everyone was so up in arms about a hieroglyphic representation of the sun.

I started up the ladder that folded out of the ship's cockpit, only to stop and rub away the tension in my neck. So much had happened, and I was still in the same clothes from our overnight flight. My shirt and jeans hung loose on my frame. My t-shirt stretched low to the point where my collar bone stuck out. I yanked it up, but it fell again, lower this time, if that was possible.

I felt someone's eyes on me. Alexandra's baby blues studied me from the cockpit.

"What?"

She bit her lip. "Nothing." She squeezed them closed. "Come on." She patted the seat beside her. "We don't have a ton of time."

She took a quick breath and sat down.

A calm voice echoed out from the ship's interior, but I couldn't see her anymore. "First Neter, then they want you in the arena to train with Ryan. He's the ship's language expert, but he's got a real knack for training us halflings."

"Cool," I said and started to climb. At the top, I peered in. I was living every sci-fi fan's dream. The interior of the ship was clean-lined and curved, similar to the upholstery and styling of a boat. The seats were a kind of golden tan plastic leather lined in black and inside were two rows of bench seats in the snug cockpit for four flyers. But I was riding shotgun. Awesome.

Alexandra sat inside, her eyes locked on something straight ahead.

"Lost in thought about something?"

"What? Oh, no." Her eyes drifted to mine, then snapped back straight ahead like there was glue there. "Just anxious to get going. Come on." She patted the seat again.

Well, I guessed if I was getting in an extraterrestrial planetary vehicle with a girl who had only been flying for a few days, it would have to be with this one. Good grief, she was gorgeous. I hopped in the cockpit with my best jumping-over-the-door of a convertible move and slid into the seat beside her.

Man, I thought I was coming off cool.

"Really, hotshot." She rolled her eyes.

Guess not.

But I caught her smiling as she turned away.

"Okay. Buckle up. We don't want to kill you on your first day here."

That was encouraging.

She nodded at me like I should know what to do, but all I saw was the seamless bench around me. There wasn't even a place in the material where a hidden compartment might hold a belt.

Alexandra laughed.

"You think this is funny?"

"Yes. It is funny."

"Okay then, Ms. Know-it-All. What do I do?" I was happy to play along.

"Like this." She quieted herself, sat back into her seat, and closed her eyes. Then the seat bubbled and grew and molded around her, the material becoming translucent as it shifted.

It was truly mind-boggling to witness.

"Am I ever going to get used to all this alien stuff?" I poked my finger into the gelatinous material surrounding her torso. It was like flexible jelly, opaque golden yellow in color. My finger slid through it easily down to her collarbone, but she jumped at the familiarity of my touch.

I held her eyes.

"Not sure," she answered. Her breath caught and she bit her lip and her eyes followed my finger as I slipped it back out.

In the tight space, our faces were inches apart. I wondered if there would be more sparks. You could cut the chemistry between us with a knife, but the proximity seemed to make her nervous too, so naturally, I grinned. Really, I couldn't help it. I had taken an unofficial class as a sophomore called Flirting 101. I got far more use out of it than Latin. Alexandra pinked up instantly and fidgeted in her seat and her eyes went straight ahead again and stayed there.

Morty had clearly locked this one up too long for a smile in close quarters to drive her so crazy. I let my eyes rest on her briefly, hoping she'd find the courage to look back, but she didn't.

I relented. "Okay, let me give this a try."

I sat back and closed my eyes. Nothing happened. I peaked at Alexandra with one eye. She eyed me again, seeing if I'd figure it out on my own. Nothing doing though.

She wrinkled her nose at me. "Even hybrids can communicate with their minds. It's easier with the ship than with another Oasen. Use your Bau and feel outside of yourself for something intelligent. If you find my mind, it will be warm, but you want the ship, not a person, so feel for the intelligence that's cold. When you connect with it, ask it to buckle you in. Ask it nicely." There was a subtle curve to her lip. There was that personality of hers again.

"So, you mean we have telepathic abilities too?

Alexandra nodded and let herself grin.

"Cool. Well, let's give this one more try."

I mimicked Alexandra's earlier movements. I quieted my mind, sat back, and closed my eyes. I tried to find my Bau buzzing at the center of me and imagined it reaching out like I had for my alarm clock. It seemed a natural thing to do. There was something warm and curious. No. That's Alexandra. Better leave that alone – for now. Oh, there. There was the cold thing. Fiercely intelligent too.

The seat folded itself around me. My head tingled with the connection.

"Good job."

It felt weird, like I was sitting in my Aunt Vera's peaches and cream jelly mold – except this time, I was the peaches. My arms and legs were free to move, and even though my body was securely fastened, it could freely move too within the gooey jell.

"It's called Melio. It saved our parents in the crash. A band of this material runs under our seat to an exit portal on the outside of the ship. If there's an impact, the Melio absorbs the shock, dissipates it away from the body and is ejected from the ship – keeping you safe in your seat and hopefully unharmed. It's pretty effective stuff."

She seemed to enjoy lecturing me.

"Ready?" She arched her eyebrows. There was something mischievous about the way she said it, which worried me. She acted too much like her father before the supersonic drive to the ranch in the Hummer.

"As I'll ever be." I tapped the Melio that covered my chest. It jiggled slightly.

Yep. I'm in a human jelly mold.

The ship fired up.

I guess I expected a kind of quiet energy-efficient Prius type feeling, but it was nothing like that. It was like we were sitting on an over-stressed engine at the beginning of a street race. The gas was all the way to the floor, but someone had their foot on the brake too. I held my breath.

It was Alexandra's turn to do the grinning.

We shot up so high and so fast, gravity thrust me into my seat with the pressure. I reached for a grab bar, but found nothing. I thought my body might find a way to slip out the exit portal Alexandra told me about, though plainly she wasn't worried. Her exquisite lips were full-on plastered back toward her ears, smiling through the slit in her helmet – her teeth forgotten for once. But, for me, the tingle in my head became a headache with the force.

"I've been waiting for this my entire life!" she yelled as we catapulted straight up through the air and away from the Big House.

We arched up and up until I saw the blue hazy canopy of the dome that covered the property hovering above us. I thought we'd crash into it, but we stopped and hung in the air. My body stayed put until we dropped down again. Finally free from my seat, I experienced the shock of weightlessness. It was briefly freeing, then terrifying. I might have even given her a tight-lipped smile, but I kept my mouth shut in case I decided to throw up.

I wondered if this thing had barf bags hidden somewhere?

I was pretty sure we were going to die then, because we were rocketing down towards the earth – backwards. Backs to the ground, faces to the sky, we fell like a bullet. At the last second, Alexandra manipulated the ship's sleek controls and we roared forward in the right direction.

Yeah, I was pretty sure I was going to need one of those bags.

My head finally came un-plastered from the seat and all the G-forces. "Tell me, honestly. Was I screaming?"

She grinned at me. "Something like that."

My head spun. "You have to take it easier on me. I've only been an alien since yesterday."

This made her laugh out loud. She crossed her arms and took her hands off the controls.

"Please put your hands back on the controls." I stared straight ahead.

"Don't worry. It can fly itself." She reached for the slim black handles anyway. They folded around her hands becoming almost an extension of them and slowed the ship. Thankfully, my stomach evened out with her flying. She followed the farm road back toward the head gate where I spotted the giant black cave when I first arrived.

"What do humans think of all this when they come here?" I managed, gulping.

"They can't see any of the energy signatures. They get a little tingle like we do when they drive in, but they tend to keep it to themselves. Their brains can't interpret the wavelength. "

"Right." We hovered in the air outside of the cave's yawning entrance. "So, what do they make of this?"

"Oh, they won't go anywhere near it. Neter managed to get her cloaking ability functioning after the crash. So as far as our visitors are concerned, that is one big manure pit. No one gets why it's so close to the road, but the ship's lodged down there and it's good cover. It even smells horrible."

The ship hovered, rocking lightly side to side in the air.

"Ready?"

"As I'll ever be," I repeated myself. I gulped in advance this time.

We dove into the tunnel, but Alexandra slowed down so we didn't crash into the walls. The heat from the crashing ship must have melted rock and packed the dirt tight. The walls were uniform and smooth. The ship had been down here a long time too. Someone had installed lighting at intervals and there was evidence of vehicle activity on the long cave's floor.

My head still throbbed though, to the point where I it felt like someone was trying to beat his way out from inside. Connecting with the little ship must have messed with my brain.

We slowed down as we approached the ship. Neter wasn't your traditional flying saucer. She was a giant bullet, except her lines were cleaner. She was made for cutting through space; that much was certain. There were no embossed images to create friction on her unnaturally smooth hull, only the impossibly smooth transition between the two different colored metals, black and gold, that made her up. She might even have had wings like the planetary vehicle we rode on, but they had either been sheared off on impact or were retracted. I wasn't sure which.

Beautiful as it was lit by manmade lighting, the ship was also sad. It was dreadfully wedged in the earth at an angle at the end of the tunnel. She still worked on some level though. A hatch opened as we approached, and Alexandra flew into the holding bay. It closed behind us.

I put my hand to my temple. It pulsed and I felt slightly sick. This headache was turning into a full-blown migraine.

Coming to a stop, our ship's dome rose up and the Melio melted away. Alexandra vaulted over me and slid down the rungs of the ladder, but I took things a little more gingerly considering the riot now going on in my head.

I followed her out of the holding bay through a door that slid open so fast my eyes couldn't follow its movement. My head spun by now, so when we stepped into the hall, I stopped and put my head against a panel of lights to steady myself. A light flashed in my brain as if a switch flipped. I pulled away and put my hand on Alexandra to keep myself from falling.

"Hey! Watch it!" She jerked back and rubbed her shoulder like I stung her.

"Sorry. I think the ride was a little too much for me."

"Yeah, well next time, keep your hands to yourself, okay?"

I shrugged my shoulders at her venomous response and followed a fuming Alexandra up a gray-beige hallway.

What did I do?

Something like carpet lined the floors, and everything shone with modern clean lines. Another door slid open soundlessly. We entered an elevator. The door closed and we shot up and then, not kidding, left. I leaned against the wall.

The door opened into a wide room with a giant viewing window in the front, more than half obscured with dark earth. We were standing on the bridge. Alexandra was calm now, but she kept her distance, eyeing me warily from across the room. She walked to what must be the Captain's chair, resting her hands on top.

She went on talking like nothing just happened. "If you had come in here a few days ago, all these crew seats would have been frames with long empty holes that exited under the ship's belly. Most of the Melio that made them up was ejected during the crash, and Neter couldn't regenerate it until the power surge. All the holes are filled now. Too bad you didn't get to see that."

Her demeanor had changed since the incident in the hallway.

"I have pictures, Alexandra," stated a pleasant female voice ringing with what must be a strong Oasen accent. "On the account of its historical significance."

"Of course you do, Neter. Gil, meet Neter. Neter, meet Gil, Helen's son. He turned yesterday." She barely acknowledged me with her eyes.

An image flashed on all the screens of an Oasen woman with black-almost-purple hair and true-to-life purple eyes. She had a long neck and slender shoulders and her skin was pale as alabaster. "It is with great privilege, I make your acquaintance," the ship said. "I have come to have quite a fondness for you hybrid children."

Alexandra scowled a little. She didn't seem to like the idea I could be one of Neter's favorites too.

"It's nice to meet you Neter."

Neter, the purple-eyed woman, spoke from the panels that surrounded the deck and followed me as I walked. "The pleasure is mine as well."

She was graceful as she moved on screen, as I imagine she was when she's in the air. Now I knew why Alexandra liked her. She wasn't just a ship. She was a consciousness.

I walked over to the console to the right of Alexandra's captain's chair. She and I were like magnets again, except this time I repelled her. As I moved, she moved away.

But then my vision tilted and I swayed to steady myself, mumbling "My head doesn't feel right," as if Alexandra cared. I put my hand on the console and blacked out. But instead of passing out, I literally felt pulled into my own head, a singular speck falling into a black abyss, landing with a thud in a tunnel of shadows. Somehow I still sensed my body, but my mind was absent from it. A sea of moving darkness, filled with little lights like far-away stars raced past me.

Alexandra must have noticed something was wrong, because I felt her tentatively put her hand on my arm, even though I was still trapped elsewhere. And that must have taken some doing; she had shown a clear aversion to my touch.

When she did, something happened. A light filled my head like a nuclear explosion, and there, with her hand on my arm, was Alexandra. She wobbled and spun around in a circle taking in the maddening darkness.

"What is this?" she screamed. I realized she had to raise her voice because the black was so loud it drowned out our voices.

"I don't know! You're the one who's been an alien the longest! You tell me!"

"Neter!" Alexandra called out in desperation.

The loud sea of darkness raced toward us and abruptly slowed down. When it stopped, the girl with the purple eyes stood in front of us. "Yes, Alexandra," the girl asked calmly. Lights and gray color still raced past us, but it was quieter and less chaotic.

"What is going on here, Neter? How are you standing in front of me?"

"You have accessed my neural network through an electron connection. You are in a veritable matrix of my data circuitry. The bodies you see are a subconscious rendering of yourselves on a subatomic level. You are standing in my memory matrix. I was opening this matrix to access the photos of the bridge seats. Would you like me to access them still?"

Neter seemed unfazed by us joining her inside her circuitry.

Alexandra stood their dumbly.

"Uh, sure," I answered for her.

A wall of images, stacked in a deck like playing cards, presented themselves. The deck shuffled itself so fast I couldn't see until Neter stopped and pulled one out. It showed the seats on the bridge following the crash. Most were chair-like frames, enough to keep a person from slipping out the exit portal themselves, but below the frames, I saw empty, gaping holes. The crash must have been intense. They were lucky to be alive.

"Thanks, Neter," I said after studying the 3D images.

"You're welcome." She shuffled the images back into the deck. Then I did something I didn't know was possible but came naturally to me. I slowed Neter down and watched each image in her memory storage banks as she organized them.

I saw the history of their journey to Earth in seconds. There was mom and Morty and some other people I hadn't met. I saw them leaving the curved space docks of Oases, hovering above their huge purple planet. I saw them hurtling through space past a highway of asteroids. I saw them laughing and living life aboard ship. Then I saw where the crew were when it happened. I saw images of an earth ship coming at them – was that Apollo 13? I saw the calculations Neter made to steer them safely to...

"Hey, wait." I pulled that memory back out. There was something wrong. Alexandra furrowed her brows. Had she noticed too? The gray color surrounding us shifted darker again and sped up. It got louder too. Neter tried to wrestle control from me, but I wouldn't let her. Something wasn't right.

"Alexandra, can you get that? She's trying to keep it from me."

"Yeah, I think so." Apparently, this came naturally to her too, though I guessed most things did.

We worked together to keep Neter from filing away the memory card. She tried to seize it, wanted to hide it, thought about erasing it – even against her protocols – but they won out.

Alexandra concentrated beside me. There it was. Behind the data calculation was the shadow of another memory, attached to this one but nearly imperceptible.

"What is that, Neter?"

"I do not know," her voice slowed down. "I ... I cannot access it."

I didn't understand how I knew what to do, but it felt like part of my brain that had been dormant woke up. I inserted a calculation into her code and separated the gray memory card from its twin, placing them alongside each other. Neter became still. She was free.

"This is a trajectory. Isn't it?" I asked, my advanced physics class, useful for once. The memory showed calculations and an accompanying diagram. The girl with the purple hair approached. She seemed unencumbered now that the data had been separated.

"Yes. It is. But, it's more than that. It's an override command. It goes beyond my neural processing directly to my mechanical relays. They are linked, but separate as well. This appears to be ... no. It cannot be."

"What is it Neter?"

"It's a destruct code with a government signature."

"What does that mean?" Alexandra's voice turned slow and deliberate.

"It means the crash ... was not an accident."

Alexandra spun around. "What? Someone made you crash?"

"Yes, dear. The crew was never meant to survive its trip to Earth. My destruction was programmed before we even left dock in Oases."

The color drained from Alexandra's face. "How can that be? Why didn't you crash?"

The ship stared blankly ahead. I sensed her calculations behind the human facade, searching through data, mining for answers. She found nothing. "I am not sure, but I appear to have made a last-second adjustment that thwarted the crash." She searched again. This time, she hit on something. "It appears I was given back control just in time – from whom I do not know."

I must have shifted my weight in the physical world then, because my hand slipped off the console and we were back in true human form standing on the bridge.

Alexandra's hand still rested on my arm. She was conscious but still lost in thought. When her eyes found mine, it was like she came out of a waking dream. Her hand fell. "Gil." Her eyes were feverish. "You can't tell anyone about this. And neither can you, Neter."

"Why would we hide something like this?"

"Can you imagine what it would do to them right now? Your dad is missing. The Aten, which I know you know practically nothing about – well, I think your dad found it and activated it. That's why Neter is even working as well as she is now. This would all be too much for them right now. That's all." She tried to make it seem unimportant.

I huffed and Alexandra knew instantly I was unconvinced. "I get where you're going, but I don't buy it. This is a big deal. We need to tell them."

"You don't even understand how the Aten plays into all this." A well of kinetic energy sat just below the surface of her eyes, moving in response to her frustration. It made me nervous, but she threw her hands on her hips like that was all there was to it.

"So tell me then." It was remarkable I even had to ask.

"Fine. The Aten is part of the legend of the missing starship Barque's crew. To Egyptologists, it's just another pretty depiction of the mythological sun disk, but your dad recognized it for what it was – a technology so powerful, in the wrong hands, it could cause serious problems." She checked her watch. "Like your mom said, we don't know exactly what it is, but we think it might be self-aware. And it's missing – like your father."

She reached down for her backpack, throwing over one shoulder.

"Most of the old tomb paintings associate it with Ra. Fortunately, he must have been a good guy if he had control of it. Anyway, it went missing when the Barque crew did, so if your dad found it, and if it's what powered Neter, he may have opened Pandora's Box on the mystery of that missing starship. And then we go and discover our own ship's crash wasn't an accident. Think about it. It's bad."

She turned toward the elevator. "And remember, everyone on Oases thought that crew never made it to Earth or died tragically or something awful like that. That's why our parents came here – to find out what happened to them." Alexandra rocked back and forth on her heels. "Maybe someone sabotaged their ship too, but they figured that out and were hiding or something? And if someone back on Oases meant for our parents to disappear too ..." she added thinking out loud. "We just need to figure things out before we tell them."

At least I understood her. "You really think we should keep it from them?"

"I do, Gil." She reached out and touched me tentatively, a hint of blue sparking at the touch of her fingertip. She sucked in a breath and pulled back.

That got me.

"Okay. But when things settle down, we tell them."

"Okay. Good." She checked her watch again, the pink of her embarrassment slowly draining from her face. "Oh good gods! How long have we been talking?"

She ran to the elevator – a little faster than what I'd consider normal.

"Ryan's pretty chill, but dad isn't. He wanted you at the arena 15 minutes ago. Hurry." She backed into the elevator, waiting for me. "Later Neter. Please keep this under wraps too."

Neter bowed in solemn promise from her panel.

Then I remembered how intimidating her father was and ran for the elevator too. Just not as fast as Alexandra.

Chapter 6-She chooses the nunnery

One foot after the other, I told myself, coming down the steep rise. Thankfully, there were enough scrawny trees clinging to the hillside to offer enough handholds so I didn't Jack and Jill it down and break something. It was pretty steep and I was already exhausted from training yesterday, so that was a real possibility. After days of training, my muscles ached – muscles I didn't know I had – cliché maybe, but true.

I wiped the sweat from my brow and stopped to gaze down at the valley. The whole basin spread out before me, all the Oasens below like little ants. I spied Alexandra and her Oasen friend Amisi easily from my vantage point. Amisi was practically a child by Oasen standards. Only 500 years old. They said she practically grew up on the starship, but she was a genius, so it made her special. Her dark hair was cut in choppy layers like a 90s pop star, but her makeup was definitely 80s. She was a weird girl, but I liked her.

The two of them were straddling the trunk of a large tree that had toppled over near the Tack – right where I was headed. A couple of miniature-looking chainsaws lay nearby like the two of them were taking a break from dismantling the thing. One thing was for sure, no one was ever idle-handed at the ranch.

At least now I had some motivation to get down this hill.

I made my way down, careful to use my stealth training from yesterday. Maybe I could sneak up on them? I wondered what Alexandra would think of this trick. Would it be a smile today or a thrashing? I rubbed my arm, remembering how she bent it behind me and pushed my face into the ground after I caught her with a page-worn copy of Romeo and Juliet. Oh well, I'd add the results to my research. She had become something of a project for me.

I focused on my Bau. The stealth feelings flooded me: lightness, quiet, solitude. I started down the harsh terrain again, but this time, I felt light as air. Still, it was slow going. This wasn't the power you used when you wanted to get somewhere fast, but I still made it down to their tree without getting caught.

I started to make my way around to reveal myself, so I was still hidden by thick fir branches when Amisi spoke up, her black hair bobbing cheerfully, her words stopping me in my tracks. "Even I can see how weird you're acting around him. It's like you've gone all bi-polar."

Alexandra cocked her head. Her eyes wandered in my direction refusing to make eye contact with Amisi, but she didn't see me. "I have no clue what you're talking about."

"Oh, sure you do." She shoved Alexandra playfully but with enough Oasen strength to jog her. Her balance was impeccable though; Alexandra barely rocked.

Amisi frowned. "You weren't worried one bit about a guy your age coming here until those blue sparks, and now you're totally freaking out over him and NOT in a good way."

Blue sparks huh? I peeked through the fir branches and caught site of Alexandra's face. She scowled at Amisi.

"Those didn't mean a thing."

"Didn't mean anything? You've got to be kidding me. That, Alexandra, meant something. It's like a law or something."

Alexandra huffed and looked down, but Amisi kept talking, ignoring her friend's discomfort. "I heard Helen teasing your dad about it. I don't think they thought it was nothing either."

Alexandra rolled her eyes. It was definitely a habit with her.

"Roll your eyes all you want but his being here is messing with you – big time." She reached over and slapped Alexandra on the leg looking for a response. She didn't flinch. "You want to like him but you're so worried about sticking to your little plan, you can't see straight. I'm telling you, Alexandra, you're managing well enough for now but there's all these little cracks forming in your armor. You're a few more blue sparks away from losing it."

The golden-haired girl rubbed her forehead like she had a headache. "You know how I feel about that stuff. It freaked me out. Come on. It's me we're talking about."

Amisi nodded her head at this like she understood, but wouldn't take no for an answer. "Yeah, I know it's you we're talking about, but you actually like him. That's the problem. Admit it. That's why you're acting all Jekyll and Hyde. He's totally messing with your plans. And I'm telling you, it's only going to get worse if you can't figure out how to deal with it. So, like I said, admit it."

The words were feisty coming from Amisi.

"Okay." Alexandra twisted uncomfortably. "I admit ... I like him."

Amisi laughed and clasped her hands to her mouth, and my heart fell out of my chest. She was talking about me, right? I'm the blue sparks guy!

"As a friend."

Amisi's face fell, and Alexandra laughed at her friend for falling for it.

Wind. Out of sails.

"The sparks do complicate things," Alexandra admitted.

"So you don't deny they meant something?"

"They may mean something. I'm not sure what. But it changes nothing."

What did that mean? This alien stuff was all over my head.

"Ugh. You are so boring. We should pack you up for the nunner –"

A branch snapped under my foot.

Darn it! I wasn't in stealth mode anymore.

They noticed me then and I rounded the tree like nothing in particular was going on. Alexandra's face registered horror, then a mask of calm drifted down obscuring the other emotion.

"Oh, hi Gil!" Amisi sounded cheery. "What are you up to?"

I nodded toward the pack on my back as if I was walking by and not eavesdropping on private conversations. "Ryan sent me down to the Tack to pick up some rope. He's got it in his head to take me up to the ridge."

Alexandra went on like nothing happened. "That will be fun, but you better watch out up there. I remember that lesson. Ryan's pretty tough."

"Yeah, I'm sure. The toughest language expert on the planet!" I called back but kept walking. Now I was going to be late.

"Don't say I didn't warn you! There's a reason he trains us – language guy or no."

"Oh, I know! I'm kidding. He tried to kill me yesterday with a giant boulder. I barely tossed the thing away with my mind."

"Your Bau," Alexandra corrected.

"Yeah." I started jogging.

"Bye Sparky!" Amisi giggled.

Alexandra shushed Amisi, who tried to muffle her over-the-top giggles into Alexandra's shoulder.

Alexandra caught my eye. Something glinted there uneasily.

I smiled at her, and for once, unbidden, she smiled back.

■■■■

I made it back to the feed barn just in time.

"Get your gear ready!" Ryan called down. He wore his brown kick-about sandals and a white V-neck as usual, but even as casual as he seemed, hidden beneath it all was a soldier's lean body, the result of a life of regiment and hard work. He seemed to hide that part of himself well though, as if it was just a part of who he was and not something he needed to show off.

"Ben phoned," he went on. "He'll have everything set up within the hour. When I get that call, we need to go."

"Alright!" I yelled back up. "No problem. I got the rope!"

Ryan was perched on top of a 20-foot-high stack of hay bales, tossing the heavy feed down off his perch like he was flinging bags of cotton balls. These weren't the small rectangular bales either – not the kind you find at mom-and-pop farms – these were the industrial-sized ones.

I swallowed and watched him grab another and send it down with a roar. Dust and hay needles flew at me, but I barely registered them. A week ago those would have hurt, but my body had changed since I turned. My skin had hardened. Even the gash on my arm from the earthquake was a slim silver line now.

Ryan clapped his hands together to get the grit off. Standing precariously on the edge of the bales, he grabbed at another and tossed. A normal man would have fallen over with the weight of it, if he could lift it to begin with, but I had no reason to worry about Ryan falling to his death. He hadn't climbed up there. He flew. I imagine he could fly back down again, no problem. That was something to witness, but since I basically lived on a dude ranch for super heroes, I learned a lot fast.

"Hey, Ry. What exactly do I need this thing for?" I held up the bracelet mom had snapped on my wrist that first day. It was in my pack, along with a few bottles of water and a rope, one so old and brittle it would probably break with the slightest amount of weight,.

He peaked over the top of the bales. He seemed small that far up. "That's called an Amulet of Bes. She was the goddess of newborn babies, so the name stuck because we use it on young hybrids. We called it a controller on Oases, but Bes Amulet sounded better – plus we had to modify it for hybrids, so it's not exactly the same thing it used to be."

Two hands pushed me forward from behind and I jumped up.

"Whoa!" I hadn't just jumped. I floated awkwardly off the ground, arms flailing, defying gravity, and came down hard. Ryan turned away with a grin on the bales above. This was a first for me. Flying.

Alexandra stood with her hands on her mouth trying not to crack up.

So, she was the culprit.

"See." She regained her composure. "Ryan taught me to use stealth mode too."

I withered at the implication, but she let it slide. She took the amulet from my hand and tipped her head. "I used to think of this as my own personal Hybrid pacifier." She pouted at me in an attempt to be mean, but instead those full lips of hers just hypnotized me. She didn't notice. "It's pretty standard training gear for newbies. I wore one too – when I was five." She stifled a laugh.

Ryan called down. "It has different settings so you learn varying levels of control in more and more rigorous environments until you can balance your emotions and abilities. That's the goal. Your abilities are there and full power already – like any other hybrid your age. That's not the problem. The problem is what you'll do with them under stress."

"Why didn't I use this in the arena the other day?"

"The arena's pre-programmed to monitor and control Bau extremes, but you'll need this up on the ridge." She handed it back, careful not to touch my hand. "There's no external controller up there."

A cell phone rang above me. Ryan answered, hung up, and jumped down with a boom. Ben must be ready. When I looked back, Alexandra was already gone.

■■■■■

"Gil. Gil, man. Wake up."

Ryan shook my arm.

I couldn't wake up. The girl had me in her grips again.

She was as I left her, standing unmoving in her prison orb of moving colors, crowned by the strange light. I thought her raven hair a prettier crown, her emerald eyes better jewels, but her arms still reached for me in desperation.

"Can you hear me?" she said into my head.

I could, but I couldn't answer either. My tongue was lead.

"Please, Gil," she tried. "Come quickly or all will be lost. The man and the girl, they need you too."

The colors swirling around her shifted and obscured her, but revealed something else. There, huddled against the side of her prison, was my dad and the grad student missing with him, Elaine – the arms of light reaching out to touch them too.

Ryan's voice called again.

"I have to go," I tried to say out loud, but I couldn't give voice to my thoughts. I never could.

"Please," she begged again as if she knew I was going.

Sorrow rushed over me. This girl was ancient, alone, and very much alive.

"It's okay," I tried to say again to her. "I'll see you again soon."

Even unconscious, I knew. I would be back.

"Gil. Gil! No kidding, man. Wake up."

My eyes blinked open halfway trying to remember where I was. Oh, yeah. The afternoon came flooding back. We took Ryan's jeep up through the clover meadow to the higher elevations where the conifer forest began. Beyond that was national forest. He seemed so go-easy, but Ryan was a tough teacher. He ripped up a 40-foot conifer out the bare ground, roots and all hanging with dirt and earth worms, and hurled it at my head – all the while laughing. I rubbed my shoulder. He was merciless. And strong.

The frayed old rope was another story. Ryan secured it between two fir trees about 20 feet off the ground. Yeah. He meant for it to break to "encourage" me to fly. Brilliant idea, I thought, remembering. I wasn't sure you could call what I did flying, but he hadn't managed to kill me either. Score one for Gil.

Eventually we came back to the Bunkhouse for some actual instruction. Ugh. What did he say before I nodded off? I tried to remember but my head hurt. A branch from the tree had thwacked me on the head. I couldn't remember the lesson at all. I yawned. I probably had brain damage. No wait. It had something to do with electricity. Something about the importance of negative fields – or was it positive fields?

Admittedly, I wasn't sure.

I still wasn't awake.

Eyes, open already, I thought. I didn't want Ryan to hurl any furniture at me. That could hurt.

My eyes were sealed shut though.

He shook me again and yelled something rather unpleasant.

My eyes peeked open once more, unenthusiastically. My body and one arm were hanging off the side of the couch, my entire field of vision taken up with the room's massive rug – a bright blue, orange and cream-colored carpet stamped in a huge diamond pattern.

Satisfied I was waking up, he walked away.

My face was smashed into a long rectangular pillow with cowboys on horseback stitched into the linen fabric riding ram rod across. The impression of a horse head was firmly set into my cheek. I rolled over. The loft where I normally slept was above me, along with a set of sun-bleached elk horns hanging high on the wall's oil-smoothed hewn logs. They moved me in with Ryan my first day here. My bed was much more comfortable than this couch.

"He drools."

I did not just hear Alexandra say that.

My body was suddenly awake. I sat up and found her laughing at me. I touched the deep lines embedded on my face from the pillow. Her feet hung over the arm of one of the two deep leather chairs that faced the burnt orange couch I was drooling on – apparently.

"What?" I mumbled, still disoriented.

"You drool, I said." She got up casually and held a tissue to the corner of my mouth like she going to wipe the wet spot away, but instead, she screwed up her face and let it drop in the air. "Here. You do it." She leaned in and whispered as it fell. "Have you told anyone about Neter?"

"No," I whispered, happy to be this close.

"Good. Well, don't." She was breathless. "I found out hacking a computer matrix with your Bau is nearly impossible. Only three Oasens in history have ever done it and we're only hybrids."

Great. Another secret.

The outside door opened and Ben and Kos, the huge Oasen twins, burst into the room then, oblivious to our presence there. Ben was up on the mountain with us earlier and witnessed Ryan's crazy lumber jack show.

Alexandra stood up.

"You should have seen how Gil took that tree." Ben laughed loudly.

The two of them were like lumberjacks themselves in their matching red and black plaid flannel shirts. They were tall and wide like trees too, with thick beards that hadn't seen a razor in a while. Ben was obnoxious and noisy – as usual. Everything the twins did was big though and today was no exception. As he walked, he acted out what Ryan did to me on the ridge.

"First Ryan threw the tree at him." Ben stumbled like he got slammed in the shoulder by the huge tree Ryan threw at me, but then he righted himself and brushed it off. "It was hilarious. But Gil wasn't having it. He picked that tree up and hurled it right back." Ben snarled his face up, bent over and grabbed a massive imaginary object right around its wide middle and hurled it theatrically at the wall, spinning himself in a dizzying circle. He was as great a showman as Morty.

"Ha! Ha! I mean, really, Kos, I'm not even sure Alexandra could have done –" Ben caught himself then, noticing her standing there with her hands on her hips, but it was too late. Her brows lowered, and she pressed her lips firmly together. I got the feeling Alexandra was the one about to throw something.

"I mean, er – never mind." Ben took off for the bunk wing with Kos following on his heels. They moved fast. Alexandra fast.

"No newbie hybrid can best me, Ben!" She yelled after him, but he was gone already. Oasens were quick when they wanted to be. "Especially this one." She flung her hand in my direction.

Ryan came over and put his hand on her shoulder. "Chill out Alexandra."

He could get away with that kind of thing with her. I couldn't. She freaked out every time I touched her.

"They're just excited to have something new to talk about. And besides," he grinned as she sat back down. "You'll have plenty of time to take this one to task. Morty wants you in the arena together soon for a training sim."

Great.

"You better believe I will," she said. There was still bravado there but her words were quieter, less sure. "Hot stuff here can't handle me."

"Hot stuff, huh?" I grinned at her. I couldn't help myself.

The color drained from her face. "Whatever. Just wait and see."

She got up and fled the room.

"No dice then," I said.

Ryan laughed.

"She likes me though. You know it and I know it."

"You might be right about that, but there's more to that girl than you can handle."

"I get that." I leaned back with my arms bent behind my head. "She sure has a lot to prove for a powerful, beautiful and rich alien heiress." I stretched the sleep away and got up. "You want something to drink?" I walked over to our small kitchen. It was always well stocked.

I glimpsed Ryan sitting on his chair in the living room and took a coke out of our fridge. But he grabbed the door before I had a chance to close it, just a second later, and rummaged through its contents too. The speed thing was disconcerting to say the least. I had to shake my head while Ryan settled on a box of questionable Chinese takeout and was back in his chair in a second.

I walked back to the living room at the human pace I was used to and popped the top. It fizzed and the liquid spilled down my fingers. I flung it off into the carpet. Ryan frowned at me but didn't say anything. Instead, he went to work with some jagged chopsticks.

He still hadn't answered my question. "So? What's her deal? Something's not right with her."

"Yeah, well, imagine being abandoned by your mom at birth." His mouth was full. He stopped chewing. Noodles hung from his mouth. "I wasn't supposed to say that," he mumbled through the mush.

There was silence for a moment while we both considered what to say next. I could kick myself. Hybrids have two parents. One human and one Oasen. Why had I never thought to ask about her mom? I set my drink down on the coffee table and leaned back.

"That explains a lot actually."

"Mmm." Ryan agreed. "Alexandra's like a little sister to me." It seemed an important preface. "But not having a mom has really affected her. She's always trying to prove she's worth something, because she doesn't think she is. We kind of give her some slack around here for it. Morty didn't tell Alexandra's mom the truth of what he was until right after she was born. She didn't take it too well. Alexandra's mom was beautiful and ridiculously smart for a human, yes. Progressive, no."

He shook his head.

"I don't quite get how a super genius with a specialty in theoretical astrophysics is able to ignore something as spectacular as extraterrestrial life, but to each his own."

"Where is she now? Does Alexandra have any contact with her?"

"No, not at all. But Morty keeps tabs on her. She's overseas, 574 feet below the Franco-Swiss border near Geneva, Switzerland, working at the Large Hadron Collider – blissfully ignoring her encounter with an alien and her alien daughter." He frowned.

The mystery only deepened.

"Huh."

Ryan nodded in simple acknowledgment.

"Well, that certainly put things in perspective."

"I thought it might."

Chapter 7-The orphan in the barn

I walked around the corner but stopped short. The voices coming from the room were too low and soft for normal conversation. The two sat staring at his computer, rapt in their discussion.

"You really think the Aten caused the power surge?" Mom leaned over Morty who sat behind a grand mahogany desk in the middle of his dark wood-paneled library. They were looking at something on the monitor. A small morning fire burned needlessly in the fireplace. The day was already warming.

"I think it's likely, Helen, it is what we think it is." He raised his eyebrows and shook his head. "No matter how many times you ask me for another explanation. He must have found it this time." There was excitement in his voice, but he tried to mask it. "The power surge was in the southern hemisphere near their last known location. Look." He pointed at the screen and she leaned closer.

They were talking about the power surge Neter tapped into to repair herself.

"I hope he's okay somehow." There was nothing convincing about the way she said it. Dad and Elaine had been missing for nearly two weeks now. "And now apparently one of the other dig students has taken off to only god knows where too, took his things and everything. It looks suspicious with them being missing, but it doesn't make sense either if Joe found the Aten."

"That is something. But it has to be a coincidence. How else do you explain the surge?"

"True." She seemed to file that thought away and paced behind the desk in a tight circle, staying close to keep her voice low. "The team you sent, they did find traces of them but little else. I thought we'd at least pick up a Bau signature on Elaine, but it's like she tried to hide her trail. It's the only thing that gives me hope, Morty. It's as if they're hiding."

For once, I understood her. Ryan went over this in my crash-course in Oasen history. The Bau of an Oasen can be identified and dated like human DNA. Bau signatures are much more resilient than physical DNA, even though Oasen's have that too, so people in mom's profession, biology-based genealogists, rely on old, even ancient Bau signatures to create a picture of history.

"I can't believe he found it, Morty." She seemed resigned to the fact that's what he did. "Do you know how mad I was at him for wasting his time on this? Not in a million years did I think that temple could be the match. It's not even in Egypt." She finally stilled herself and pointed at the screen.

I tried to lean around the corner, but the computer faced away from me. I hid again.

"The blue print fragment he found at Het Benben last year, the one at the unfinished temple of Aten at Khut-Aten, there was a sketch of a temple on it with traces of Ra's actual DNA – almost like he drew it in ink mixed with his own blood. We knew it was important, but we could never match it to anything in Egypt. We spent weeks searching through thermal images of the dessert combing for undiscovered temple sites. We found nothing – well, no matches, that is."

She inhaled deeply through her nose, remembering it with agitation. "So we widened the search area." Her voice lilted up like the action had been the most reasonable thing to do in the world, but her words were hinged with sadness. "Joe even ran it on the world-wide database and got an unlikely match here." She pointed at the screen again. "At the temple in Palenque."

She paused, remembering things far away.

"I thought he was crazy." She pointed yet again. "That temple is nearly 1,000 years younger than Het Benben and nowhere near the center of ancient Oasen-Earth civilization. But he insisted it was there."

Her eyes wandered remembering my dad's words. "He told me only 10 percent of Palenque had been excavated and there were older structures there, hidden by the jungle, that may predate the exposed temple site. He was convinced an earlier version of the temple might lie hidden there. He told me he was going to find it Morty. He told me it was there. I was so mad at him Morty. I wouldn't even say goodbye."

Her eyes fell.

"I failed him in so many ways." Tears formed in her eyes. "The humans are right. Pride does go before a fall. I failed him. I was so convinced he was wrong. But I ... I should have been there with him."

I shifted my weight at the door. The rubber of my shoes caught the floor with a screech. Mom looked up, hastily wiping the tears from her eyes. She turned away embarrassed. Morty got up and walked to the door. Finding me there, he put his hand on my shoulder. "Alexandra's down with the horses, Gil. Why don't you go look for her there?" And shut the door.

■■■■■

Even before I got to the barn, I knew something wasn't right. Kos leaned against the barn door, crouched low to the ground, his knees bent up under him. I couldn't see his face because his head hung low and rested in his hands. It wasn't good whatever it was. He didn't so much as move as I walked by on my way into the open stable doors. I didn't think it wise to bother him though, so I didn't.

Ben and a man I didn't know were walking out of the stables as I went in, heads bent. The man carried a large leather satchel and wore small round glasses. Ben rested his hand on his shoulder and patted him twice there as they walked by. The man winced. Ben started to say something, but thought the better of it and went on out with the unknown man.

That's when I heard it.

Someone was crying in the barn.

It was a muffled kind of cry, like whoever it was, was trying desperately to hide their tears, but that kind of pained scream of a cry, muffled in whatever material they found to wail into, couldn't be drowned out. I stopped short and listened as the anguished sole reached a fever pitch and slowly fell into sobs that wracked the poor person like great dying pants until there was only silence.

I don't know how long I stood there. Should I go in? Everyone else seemed to have fled the barn. Probably for good reason. I started to leave too, but couldn't. I went down the aisle to find whoever it was who'd been crying.

Running my hand along the wooden stalls, I walked the length of the barn. It was my first time in the stables where the horses used to run the cattle were kept. I had been in horse barns before for birthday parties and a lesson or two when I was little, but this was nothing like I'd experienced. Those stables were low narrow alleys housing horse after horse after horse. This barn had a wide center aisle with open rafters that were crisscrossed with tresses as much for show as to support the tall roof.

Looking into each stall as I went, I thought these horses' pedigrees must far surpass their job titles. Their manes shone like show horses and their straps and saddles were all freshly oiled. Each horse's ample stall was filled with sweet-smelling hay and closed off by a wood and wrought-iron gate, the metal making a giant squared-in X across the warm wood grain. The place was beautiful.

But what I found in the next stall was not.

Alexandra lay hunched over a small wet body that wriggled with life, but another large one lay unmoving under a white sheet nearby that revealed what lay below perfectly well.

A mare had given birth. Recently.

The foal was so new it hadn't stood up.

But something had gone wrong. The door hung open on the scene, but there was nothing left that could escape.

Alexandra's face was red and wet with so many tears. I stood there unmoving, shocked. She wiped quickly at her face like she could cover up what was there.

"Hey! Don't do that." I grabbed her hands together and knelt down in front of her. Maybe I was rough, but I seemed to shock her into reality. "You don't have to do that. I'm here now."

She stilled herself, and her eyes transitioned from strong to pained in four seconds, her eyes and face seemingly collapsing in on themselves the way a face does when it tries but can't stop the tears that hide just below the surface. Great lolling drops rolled slowly down her still-pretty face. Even pained as it was, tears sometimes do more to reveal inner beauty on an outer surface than anything else can. This was a soul that truly loved. And lost.

Looking into my eyes, she let go, and collapsed into my arms, her body wracked again by tears and heaving sobs, until she was too spent to cry anymore. She pulled back and wiped at her running nose with the back of her hand, absentmindedly wiping it in the fresh hay we sat on – hay that smelled sweet and earthy just like her. She pulled at her eyes with her hands trying to erase the tears there again, though this time not because she tried to hide them, but because she was finally done.

"She was mine," Alexandra said quietly. The mare's body lay below the white sheet she cried into. Her wet tears still marked the spot near the horse's neck where she buried her head and wept.

"Dakota." She sniffed toward the dead horse, her nose still runny from crying. "It was only her first foal."

The baby, who glistened solidly black, was still very much alive and rocked back and forth on the floor trying to find its legs. Alexandra got up and closed the stall door.

"I'm so sorry, Alexandra."

She sat back down and gently touched the little animal. She sniffed again. "I wish I called the vet sooner. It might have helped?" Her eyebrows rose, her restless spirit quiet for once, wanting answers she could never have.

"Maybe, but we can't change what happened. You can only re-member her and go on." My thoughts drifted away to my dad. "I'm just sorry this happened to you." Too, I thought.

I took her hand in mine and she actually let me, sighing. I felt something electric, and probably blue, dance quietly between our hands but it was hidden between them. She looked up knowingly but didn't pull away.

We sat there in silence holding hands.

Alexandra finally smiled. "She was practically a foal when I got her." She let go of my hand finally, hesitantly, and stroked Dakota's newborn. "I wanted to call her Bamby because she hopped around the corral like a baby deer. You know, they do that out there in the clover fields." She nodded toward the ridge. "Dad wouldn't let me though. 'That's no name for a horse,'" she mimicked him. "But I'm glad I didn't. It isn't a name for a horse."

"Dakota is a perfectly fine name for a horse though."

"Yes, it was," she said, but didn't cry.

Just then, the little foal who at my arrival first rested, then wriggled, then moved around more and more as we talked, then finally rocked, found its feet herself and stood on toothpick legs.

Alexandra clasped her hands to her mouth, joy there at least for this small creature.

"Wow, she's standing."

"He," she corrected, gently petting him. "Coda. My dad will probably tell me that sounds like a bear, but that's his name. No take backs."

"Well. Coda is a perfectly fine name for a horse too."

"Yes. Yes, it is."

We were interrupted by approaching footsteps.

The veterinarian's little eyes, hidden behind small round glasses, peered down on us. He carried an over-sized bottle filled with thick white cream. His eyes were gentle and he seemed to relax seeing Alexandra calm. He shook his head though still, back and forth, like he wanted to say 'I'm sorry' out loud. "I've got good news," he said instead as he swung open the gate. "I made some calls and there's a nurse mare up at Davis Creek."

He bent down and put the nipple to the foal's mouth. It took Coda a minute to figure things out, but when he did, he went at it with gusto and made a huge mess.

"She lost her foal a day ago and from what I heard, she's been a mess without her. So, they've offered to take this little one on." The man laughed as the little foal shoved hard into the bottle like he couldn't get enough. "Until he's weaned. It will be good for both of them."

"Yes," Alexandra said, both happiness and sadness playing across her face. "A baby needs a mother."

Chapter 8-Whose idea *was* it to seal us in this giant bubble anyway?

W e spent the rest of that day riding up into the foothills on two horses from the barn. We were quiet, only talking when it felt necessary. It was peaceful and easy and everything I wanted. The wind blew her hair in my face once and we laughed. Then we stopped, got our feet wet in the branch and dried out for hours in the afternoon sun. She even borrowed my jacket when it got cold and we had to come back, leading the tired horses to the barn on foot.

Saying goodnight that night, the moon was high, but it was still dark enough to see the flash of blue that caught between us when I pulled her to me. It was bold of me, I know, but I couldn't help myself. I should have noticed then how she pulled away but relented and let me hold her. I should have noticed, but it felt like the stars were aligning. It felt normal and natural and perfect and easy and everything it should be, but I was too blind to see the truth.

When I saw her the next morning, Alexandra looked up at me like she couldn't help herself. I saw the same expression light her eyes from the night before. When her guard was down, it was always the same: pain and hope in equal doses. Both strange and beautiful. Then her expression changed. Her eyes lost their luster and she looked away.

And that was it. After that, she avoided me. And when we were together, her eyes were hard and glazed with more of the pain than the hope I'd seen before.

I couldn't understand it and I didn't understand her. The only thing I knew was she made me want to put my fist through a wall. I tried to tell myself I must be crazy, that I'd only known her a few weeks and she was just some girl, but I knew I was wrong. There was something different about Alexandra, about us.

But as much as she wanted to avoid me, today Alexandra couldn't.

Morty was forcing us back together under the training dome – like it or not. And I could say this unequivocally, Alexandra did not.

Today Alexandra's eyes were like storms.

"Hey. Hey!" She yelled at me.

This was the first time she'd addressed me in days. And I didn't think her tone nice.

"Snap out of it, will you? I've never met someone with their head stuck so far up in the clouds."

How very ladylike. It was clear she was raised by a man. Alien at that.

She stomped her foot and a spring of water shot out of the ground – but at least she was talking to me.

"Frustrated much, Alexandra?" I reached my hand in the direction of the water, making a patting motion with my hand and willed the earth to cover the spring. It disappeared, leaving a wet place in the pasture. Alexandra frowned. I was getting even better at using my Bau abilities and that wasn't helping. She was too competitive to appreciate the advances I had made.

She mumbled to herself and stalked in a wide circle through the grass. Her head was down and her fingers drilled against her lips. Amisi had gotten it right that day sitting on the fallen tree. It was only a matter of time. Alexandra had finally cracked.

She caught me watching, so I smiled pleasantly. She scowled in response. I wasn't surprised. She was especially agitated today.

"What is wrong with you?" I asked.

"What is wrong with me?" She stopped pacing and threw her hands on her hips. "What is wrong with me?" The pitch of her voice rose higher still, if that was possible.

Oh great, here we go again.

"Don't you get it, Gil-bert?"

"Get what?" I turned away, ignoring her.

She didn't like that.

She stalked up to me and lowered her voice so only I heard. If steam could really come out of ears, it would have hers. "I don't want to be here. I don't want to train with you. I can't stand that dad thinks we're going to be such a great team." More little geysers sprung up around her. "As far as I'm concerned, you and I are like two sides of a coin. I'm heads and your tails, and we're stuck together in the middle. We are sooo headed in opposite directions, yet no one can or even wants to tear us apart."

Her looks were striking like daggers, but that tongue of hers was worse, made for lashing its victims into stunned silence. Her words stung. "You're crazy, Alexandra. You know that right? Seriously, what is wrong with you?"

I felt my face go hot, as much from anger as hurt.

She started to look away, but then she shook her head, pursed her lips and held my gaze. Inexplicably, I couldn't take my eyes off them. Anger made them full. I wanted to run screaming from her, yet grab her and kiss her at same time. It was so confusing. She had torn me in two.

"How can you ..." My voice trailed off and I frowned.

I took another step toward her, wondering. She took a quick breath and I stopped short. My mind raced, replaying the past few weeks.

Gods, I'm an idiot.

I thought back to when we first met, how those blue sparks surprised her and how she pulled away. How she wouldn't touch me after that until Dakota, until she let down her guard and let me in. But I remembered too how Amisi talked about her plans and how I got in the way of them. How she was Dr. Jekyll and Mr. Hyde. And how her eyes had hardened like a shell designed to keep me out.

She didn't hate me. She might even like me. But she wouldn't let me in either. Talk about confused. If anyone was conflicted, it was her.

Alexandra stood watching me with her brows knitted together.

Maybe I was being juvenile, but it made me angry rather than sorry for her. I leaned toward her just enough to make her catch her breath and pull back. That was exactly the response I hoped for. "With a mouth like that," I pushed towards her with my body, not letting her expand the distance between us, "you'll never get kissed." I said those last words quietly, watching her beautiful mouth as I pulled away. It fell open. I walked away and kicked dust with my feet, stealing a glance back at her. Her cheeks were hot.

That got her. Finally.

With impeccable timing, Morty's voice boomed across the arena from his place on the metal spectator stand someone set up outside the practice dome. "Let the simulation begin!"

"Yeah, let's get this over with," I mumbled.

Morty took a simple remote from the pocket of his pleated khaki slacks. With one click, the world around me changed. He might as well have clicked play on a movie, because the whole arena blacked out and we plunged under water.

This was new.

Simulation or not, I panicked and opened my mouth to scream. Water rushed in and I choked. My mouth closed with fear. I hadn't taken a breath before the plunge and everything in my body screamed for me to open my mouth and breath.

I willed myself to hang on as my body shook and I sought purchase below my feet. If I could just kick off something maybe I could get to the surface in time. But I floated helplessly in an endless sea of blue. Black seas dropped below my feet and increasingly lighter seas rose up high above me. Too high.

That's when I heard her. In my head no less.

"Hey Sherlock. I mean ... Gil. Yeah, you. Over here." This was another first. Alexandra spoke into my head.

I swam in a half-circle and found her staring in my face, inches away. She kicked in place in front of me. She wasn't drowning and she wasn't afraid. She grabbed my shoulders and spoke in my head again, "Open your mouth. Open your mouth. Breath," she yelled.

I kept it tight shut. What? Is she kidding me?

She even tried to grab at my mouth and yank it open. I thought she had finally gone mad and wanted me out of her life permanently. I clamped it shut. She'll never take me out this way, I thought illogically. My oxygen level was at a serious deficit.

Alexandra tried to grab me, so I attempted to swim away, failing miserably. I was lightheaded. She had me.

"I am going to kill whoever programmed this," she said into my head, but then her eyes glinted madly. "You were saying?" And with that, she put her lips to mine. No doubt, I opened my mouth in response, oxygen deprived as I was. This girl was like a 10, not a 9 out of 10, a true 10. You don't swim away from those lips.

She pulled away laughing, bubbles exploding from her mouth. She clearly didn't mean it to be a real kiss, but try telling my brain that.

Instead of drowning, water flowed uneasily into my lungs and captured the oxygen I needed. I nearly gagged with each pull of water, but still I sucked in breath after breath until my head cleared and I stopped hyperventilating.

"Hey wait," I yelled at her in my head as she swam for the surface. The thought came out murky, but she must have heard me. She stopped until I caught up. Then she swam circles around me as we raced for the surface.

Man, she was fast. Even in water.

When she broke the surface, she twisted gracefully through the air and splashed back down, racing this time into the depths. We dove deeper and deeper, but then the water changed. There was a red tint to it, and it roiled liked a pot left on the heat too long.

"Oh, great gas giants!" Alexandra yelled in my head. "Lava! From the sea bed!"

I'd almost forgotten this was a training sim, designed to test how well we worked together and made up for each other's deficits.

Alexandra hesitated, thinking about trying to swim away, but even as fast as she was, I knew she'd never make it. The raging water was that close. So, I grabbed her by the waist and pulled her to me. She put her head against my chest like she was on autopilot and we tucked into each other, those maddening blue sparks crackling unrestrained between us despite her best intentions. I felt her heart beating wildly against my chest too, which made me terrified and happy all at once.

But I had a plan.

At the last second, I felt the tugging in my gut I needed. My Bau heated up just like the magma. I put my hand out as the red hot stuff rushed up at us from the depths. Spreading my fingers wide, I pushed out from the center of me, down through my arm and into my hand. Lava shot out around us. I felt the pressure and heat of the molten rock as it rushed around and about us, but it couldn't touch us. We were like oil and it was like water.

Alexandra raised her head up from my shoulder when she realized we were still alive. Seeing my hand outstretched and the lava obeying me, she let go quickly and grabbed my neck like a lifeguard rescuing a drowning swimmer. And kicked. Hard.

We shot up toward the surface, my hand still outstretched until we broke the water. Red liquid death blew up and out of the sea turning to hard projectile rock which threatened us now from above as gravity took over.

"Really?" My hand stretched out above us to form a shield. The rocks bounced off harmlessly.

Alexandra still held me fast. We weren't dropping back down.

"Queen of the Air!" she yelled and we flew up and away from the death storm below. As soon as we were clear, she let go and I dropped for a second, before I realized I could do this too. Just clearly not as well. Alexandra turned cork screws through the air. I tried to follow, mimicking her movements like a jerky reflection.

"Come on Gil," she scolded, though her voice was as light as the air she cut through. "You can do it too."

So, she was speaking to me again. And with something like encouragement. I guess conflicted girls give reprieves after you save them from a lobster boil.

"Well, if I can do this, then you can handle those." Grabbing her hand, I pulled her back toward the death storm below. We stopped above the spewing projectiles.

I still held her hand.

"You know I hate Earth powers, Gil."

"I know, but try it." I let go. There weren't any blue sparks, but she was holding her breath. "My Bau feels lighter in the air, as if I have to match the weight of the heavens. But controlling the Earth is different. My Bau feels heavy."

"Hmm," Alexandra looked down on the red churning death. She dropped a little focusing on her Earth powers, but stayed above it. Eyeing a target in the distance, she made a flicking motion with her hand. The rock changed course. She reached her hand toward a huge boulder that sailed up and, concentrating, flung it out over the sea. It bounced across the water like we were skipping rocks on a pond. Crazy girl that she was, Alexandra dove down into the fray like superwoman breaking the sound barrier, her hands in front pushing all obstacles out of her path. She rushed up toward me and laughed.

"Okay. That was cool. So, now, do electricity."

"Got it!" Ryan yelled from the bleachers, outside the simulation.

Whoa! That was disorienting.

No longer floating in the air, our feet were firmly on the ground of a barren wasteland. It made for an unsettling adjustment. I caught myself and tried to balance before I fell on my backside. Alexandra wobbled too. This felt familiar, like entering Neter's memory matrix.

My eyes had to adjust. The sky overhead was dark with night now and the air was still and hushed, but the hum of electrical energy filled the plain and distant thunder rumbled its approach.

"Got any pointers," Alexandra whispered. "This could get ugly."

"Um," I mumbled, thinking back to when I blew up the transformers and brought down that lightning storm on my school. I had been a mess. My head felt like it was about to explode. "Truthfully, the last time I did anything with electricity, I blew up a lot of stuff and started an earthquake."

She stiffened and turned her back to me like I had the plague. Looking at the sky, her rebuke was swift. "I thought Ryan and you went over this the other day?"

My legs felt suddenly numb. Well, that was short lasting.

"Really, Alexandra, did you expect me to learn everything about electricity in one lesson? Haven't you been doing this for years?"

Lightning crashed nearby. We both turned circles.

She bit her lip. "You know, you're not as amazing as everyone thinks you are. I'm so incredibly glad they threw me in here with you."

Well, that wasn't exactly an answer.

I leaned in, crossing well over the boundary of personal space. "You've been doing this since you were five, Alexandra. You should be the one giving pointers."

Hurt raced across her face, but smoothed over like surf erasing footsteps on a beach. Her eyes hardened once again. Thunder rumbled as it had outside my school and lightning struck too close. My hair stood on end. We both jumped back. Lightning hit yet again and Alexandra took off running as if distance could save her from the bolts.

I'm such a jerk, I had time to think.

"Wait Alexandra!"

But she was already gone.

I ran after her but she would always be faster than me. She could run like the wind.

She finally stopped, her eyes going straight to the sky. I pulled to a halt 15 feet away and followed her eyes to see what captivated her, but couldn't. The storm made everything gray. I would have to do better than that.

My vision shifted as my Bau took over my sense of sight. Energy coursed through the sky and air and across the ground like someone inserted a galvanoscope across my field of vision. I sucked in a breath at what I saw, but she couldn't. She didn't know what was happening. Maybe she sensed it, but she couldn't see or she would have run.

The cloud above her was dark and little bursts of light were emanating within it. Small channels of ionized air travelled down from the cloud toward the earth, splitting into branches like a tree. The tops of the branches reached out and touched Alexandra's beautiful hair.

Oh no!

Ryan's lesson came flooding back and I realized immediately what was happening. I had only milliseconds at that point. I moved so fast, it was nearly impossible, and threw myself over her. I tried to create the negatively charged bubble around us Ryan taught me about, but I didn't have time to finish it. It would only take macro seconds at this point. The electric current had established the channel. The bridge between the cloud and the earth was complete and the flood gates opened. The positive electrons still kicking about on us were neutralized instantly in the heat of the lightning strike. The unfinished bubble around us left only my left hand exposed and I cried out in pain.

All the sudden, the lights came on and we were standing in the pasture with the blue dome above us. Morty and Mom ran over with Ryan and Amisi following quickly behind.

"Are you alright?" mom asked.

"Isn't there some kind of failsafe on this thing?"

My hand throbbed like it had its own heartbeat.

"It won't kill us, but it will hurt us," Alexandra said as she stood and pulled me up. "Thanks, Gil."

Morty put his arm around his daughter.

"Do you remember the last time I tried this, dad?" Alexandra rubbed at a place on her arm marked with a long, pink scar, nearly faded to nothing. I hadn't noticed it before. "I spent three hours in Neter's med bay with electrical burns."

"Alexandra got hurt pretty badly in a training sim last year – this same one I think," mom divulged.

Now I understood.

Alexandra's eyes caught mine. She hastily wiped at them. She had a reputation to protect.

"I'll be right back." Mom touched my arm, and ran towards the stands.

Stepping toward Alexandra, I hesitated, but took her arm anyway. She flinched at my touch but let me. "I'm sorry. I didn't know." I hesitated again, but I couldn't stop myself. I traced the pink scar with the tip of my finger so lightly only we saw and felt the hint of blue electricity that sparked there, fading away instantly. "Why didn't you tell me?"

I saw Amisi take Ryan's arm and tug him away. Morty followed.

"Not sure." Her face flushed and she pulled away.

I leaned in toward her anyway, but didn't touch her again. "Look. I'm not sure what's going on with you, but I know me being here is seriously messing you up."

She gritted her teeth.

"I don't mean to make you uncomfortable."

Still, she didn't speak.

Still, I tried. "Honestly, I don't know why this is so hard?" I pointed between us. "I'm not sure you even know what you want. Maybe that's what's making this so difficult." I let the words sit for a minute. "You are one of the most complicated girls I've ever met, Alexandra, and I know practically nothing about you." Her eyes drifted down. "But I still really like you," I said quickly. Her eyes popped back up to mine.

We were standing so close. I didn't even remember moving toward her.

"Truthfully, I'm not even sure what 'this' is." I pointed between the two of us again. "But, I think we should at least try and be friends. Those ridiculous blue sparks that no one will tell me about, whatever they are, are at least trying to tell you that. I can't figure out why you won't listen."

Something in her face broke. She opened her mouth to speak. And mom ran up.

"Remember the basement?" she butted in – completely unaware.

My eyes blazed at her and she went silent realizing what she had interrupted.

Alexandra pulled away though, the spell broken, walking silently and slowly to her dad.

"Sorry," she mouthed. "But this will help." She grimaced and took my hand, moving a compact device over the blooming red skin there. The light it emitted brought cooling relief.

"That's pretty cool, isn't it?" Ryan tried.

"You know what else is cool, guys?" Amisi watched us carefully. She was an astute observer. "You can control lightning as well, not just hide from it. Did Ryan teach you that?"

Amisi didn't wait for an answer. Instead, she arched her wrist in a familiar Spidey style and shot a little bolt at his backside.

"Oww!" he yelled out. Ryan swatted at his butt, which actually smoked, and ran away. He shot a bolt back but missed. The crowd that had flooded the arena parted to avoid the beams and mom and Morty only looked amused, like they were used to this.

Alexandra finally relaxed. "Now that could come in handy."

Chapter 9-Don't call long distance

As soon as Alexandra figured out how to control electricity, I pretty much walked around covering my back everywhere I went. First she avoided me. Now this. She was practically as weird as Simon. Just clearly more pretty. At least my little speech seemed to have done some good. She was back to acting like the Alexandra who shook my hand that first day – just with a little extra something. She was Jekyll and Hyde or bipolar. I wasn't sure which.

I ducked behind an ancient pine tree as I made my way to the Big House. Sure enough, a shower of bark exploded off the back of the tree. Alexandra laughed and dive bombed me from the air. I ran zig zagging across the lawn. Looking back, I saw small charred circles of grass flying up at my ankles as she took machine gun aim from above.

Oh no she didn't.

I launched myself skyward and grabbed her by the ankles. I think I shocked her, because she yelled "Oh!" and fell. We landed with a thud on the steps of the Big House.

We were laying there twisted and panting as ash floated down from above. "Did you fry a bird or something?" I asked her as I spit the black stuff from my mouth. She raised her shoulders as if to say, 'I don't know,' and burst out laughing. Joining her, my body shook so hard, I could barely breathe, until really I couldn't and had to stop.

We lay there panting and staring at each other in silence, all the amusement suddenly fell away to something unexpected. Time slowed down.

Literally.

The rush of bodies around us came to a near halt. The people that once hurried in to breakfast only inched by us now as if moving in quicksand, but we stayed in normal time.

My eyes lit up in fascination as I watched the ash float down on us in leisurely slow motion. Alexandra's fingers tilted skyward to catch the slow-falling flakes. The air was heavy and charged. Even with the people moving slowly by, it felt like we were the only ones here.

Something in her eyes struck me. Suddenly bold, I reached toward her face and wiped away the black stuff that kept falling unhurriedly on us. Blue sparks danced off my fingers as lazily as the falling gray flakes. She took a quick breath at my touch and inclined her face into my hand, unable to stop herself. There was a war behind her eyes, but it was one she couldn't win in this hidden moment.

She was so still.

She didn't stop me.

I knew exactly what I wanted, but she didn't – still. Her eyes were troubled. My fingers lingered on her face, tentative because of what I knew she felt. Still, I found a stray curl that escaped her ponytail to tuck behind her ear. I kept my eyes locked on hers. She held her breath, but she didn't push me away.

I took her in with my eyes, and she held mine too. Her lashes were long and dark, her eyes piercing like an x-ray. Her mischievous grin softened. She trembled beneath my hand and her cheeks suddenly flushed with color, and her eyes fell, like it had all been too much for her, and she needed to get away.

"You almost got him that time, Alexandra." Ryan interrupted walking up with Amisi. Time sped up again.

In way too much of a hurry, if you ask me.

"Yeah, but he's too fast for you," Amisi added.

That couldn't possibly be true, I thought. She was the fast one. I was just prepared for her attack. That's all.

Alexandra, suddenly self-aware, huffed and got up, but it was hard for her to untangle herself from me. Ryan stifled a laugh.

"No, he's not," was her curt answer once she was free. "You'll see. I'll get him one day." Her eyes narrowed. She grabbed me by the elbow and roughly pushed me into the building, leaving Ryan and Amisi outside.

"Why did you do that?"

"Do what?" I asked innocently.

"Slow down time, you ... you. Ugh. I can't believe you."

"I didn't mean to. It just sort of happened."

"And just when it was getting better." She turned away and left me to stare at the back of her head. She couldn't take her eyes off me just then either. I was pleased and furious at the same time. What a weird dichotomy.

Though at least, for once, I was having fun.

I leaned in and whispered against her neck and got the response I wanted. The fine hair there raised up as my breath hit the skin under her long pony tail. "You didn't pull away just then either."

She shivered visibly, but kept her back to me, staying silent. But I wasn't angry. I finally resigned myself to the beautiful mystery that was Alexandra.

Amisi and Ryan walked up again.

"He's not faster than me," she turned to Ryan as if we'd been standing with them the whole time. "He got a jump on me. That's all." It was true. Alexandra was crazy fast.

She rubbed absentmindedly at a black smudge on her cheek. Ryan shook his head at us, and together, we all found a seat at the large dining table for a late brunch. Alexandra sat down on my right, even mad as she was at me. Maybe she was still going to try and behave herself.

Bacon and eggs wafted through the air and my stomach grumbled. I checked my watch. It was 11:30 a.m. The bell rang late today. Someone passed a huge bowl of eggs my way and I lost my train of thought, taking a heaping portion. Alexandra seemed to disapprove – if not for the huge helping, the time manipulating thing. I wasn't sure which.

Breakfast was the meal where the whole ranch came together. Mom sat near the head of the long table, spreading a liberal amount of strawberry preserves on a buttered scone, content for once, when Morty came up and whispered something. Her eyes perked up and for the first time in weeks, she smiled.

Hitting a fork against her glass, she drew everyone's attention. "Morty has news." Her voice rang out and the air crackled with energy. It was coming from mom. "The repairs to the communications array were successful. Soon we'll contact home."

Oh no, I thought. No. No. No. No. No!

"I thought it was damaged beyond repair," Alexandra said as we turned toward each other, practically knocking our heads together.

She made a face.

"That's what Neter said," she whispered.

"How is it possible?" A voice from the table called. "I saw the damage 40 years ago."

"We still don't have full communications," Morty admitted. "But we reconfigured the distress beacon."

Alexandra kicked me under the table.

"They'll send a ship!" She leaned in. "They're supposed to be dead. ET better not phone home."

"They'll come, but not for a rescue," I answered. "We have to tell them about Neter."

"I know. Suddenly, I'm not so hungry." She held her stomach and pushed back her chair, walking to Morty slightly too fast.

"Dad." She tried to interrupt him, but he shushed her. I motioned to try again, but she didn't get the chance.

"Morty!" A muffled cry carried through the room from outside. "Morty!"

The front door flew open, hitting hard against the wall. It slammed shut just as fast. Kos ran into the room, sweat pouring off his head. He must have run fast – maybe faster than I realized possible. I'd never seen an Oasen break a sweat – even while hurling medium-sized trees. And that's got to count for something.

"You didn't," he panted. "You didn't ... huh ...You didn't initiate ... the final contact sequence ... for Oases?"

"No?" Morty's brows furrowed.

"Oh, good." Kos collapsed to the floor, unconscious.

Morty ran to his side. "Someone get me some water."

I thrust my untouched glass into Morty's hand. He poured until Kos woke, choking and spitting, but the water somehow revived him.

"We can't contact them." He choked on the words too. They were practically a sob. "There's something wrong. Something's really wrong."

"What is it Kos?"

He stuttered, exhausted. "The Belisk satellite. Before she went missing ... Elaine uploaded a signature, a Bau signature. I only ran it a few minutes ago." His eyes found mom's. "It doesn't match the Bau profiles of us or the Barque crew, but it's from the time period after the other ship disappeared.

Kos went silent then, as did everyone else. Morty put his hand to his mouth.

A woman took the hand of her hybrid child. Another sat down.

Why were they reacting like this?

Alexandra didn't know either. She searched the sea of silent faces around us for answers.

"Morty," mom stammered. "Could it be?"

"I ... I don't know."

"But Morty!"

"I know!"

"Our clearance!" she screeched.

"I know!"

"We had to go through so many hoops."

Tears filled her eyes.

"I know!"

Mom shook. "Oh my stars. Oh, oh my stars..."

"What? What's going on? Mom?"

I needed to know.

Morty fell into his chair, his hand over his mouth for once, silent. Mom dropped to her knees on the floor.

"The unspoken," Amisi uttered and collapsed into her chair, like the wind was knocked out of her.

Only Ryan still stood. He was strong. His eyes searched me out. "Another ship," he said but even his voice was weak. "There must have been another ship from Oases that arrived here between us and the Barque, which means someone back on Oases already knew the Barque crew was here and safe before we came. It's happened before in history, but never in modern times." His voice broke then, and he sat down stony silent.

"What happened?"

"You know, your classic government cover up," Amisi finished. "We wondered for so long. Why would the Barque starship never contact Oases? Maybe that one was obvious," she admitted. "Why give up a life of riches and worship by calling home and admitting you've been playing god to an evolving alien race? But then, there's this: Why thrive here for 3,000 years like the kings and queens they were and then vanish without a trace? Why give it all up?"

"We have asked many questions," Morty interjected. "Why were so many of their Bau patterns obliterated in those final days? Why can we find so little Oasen technology in the ruins? I guess the answer was one we've avoided these many years."

"What dad?" Even Alexandra didn't understand where this was going.

"Someone killed them all dear." He was blunt. "Somehow someone on Oases learned what was happening here. They must have sent a ship to cover it up. I guess it was too much of an embarrassment." He scoffed. "How clever of them to turn what were once real Egyptian gods, so to speak," and he laughed, "into your fine creatures of myth, legend and lore. Choose a name at your pleasure." He waved his hand through the air, disgusted. "But I don't understand. Why do it? Two atrocities if you ask me. Why not try them for what they did? Let the ethics counsel handle it."

"So, someone in the government was afraid we'd discover what they did?" mom said. "That must be why we had such trouble getting clearance to come here. It must be."

"They never intended for you to do even that," I voiced quietly.

Heads turned my way. Even Alexandra reached out for my hand then.

"What did you say?"

"We found something. They never meant for you make it here."

Alexandra squeezed my hand and looked to her dad. A slight heat radiated between them.

"Dad, we made an electron connection with Neter. Me and Gil."

The murmurs started then.

"I know," like she couldn't believe it herself. "And we found something. Something bad. Someone sabotaged the ship. You were all supposed to die. The crash, it wasn't an accident."

Then there was silence, but it was the calm before the supernova.

Then it exploded.

Morty exploded out of his chair. His was the voice of the soldier he used to be woken after 40 years of silence. "Contact the others. This changes everything."

He hesitated another moment. This time his voice was quiet. "And I'm afraid we aren't going home."

"This is home," Amisi uttered under her breath. "But this is home."

Chapter 10-The Earth will bleed

The air was stale and dry. As I walked little eddies of dust sprang up around my feet like mini tornados. I had been in a place like this before with dad. A tomb somewhere in Egypt; one of the ones that had been cracked open after sitting quietly for millennia. Those were always so dark like the dead things they held. But this place had a steady, pale light from above that illuminated my path and kept me from feeling trapped.

I stopped and put my hand on a relief of a winged dragon above the doorway where I stood, then passed over the threshold and made my way down an inclined path until the space became so tight and the ceiling so low, I had to crawl. A sense of dread invaded my body like reaching fingers and my heart beat faster, but something pulled me forward and I couldn't stop.

The darkness ahead grew brighter, so I willed myself forward stopping where the tunnel exited a wall into a finished room like nothing I'd seen in an Egyptian tomb. A grate lay on the floor where it had been cut from the wall.

Footfalls sounded ahead.

A man holding a blue knife ran toward a shimmering girl who hovered unmoving in the air, a circle of light above her head. I didn't know what I was seeing. The man leapt and energy blasted from the light, burning him to dust.

Adrenaline surged through my veins. I started to back out of the tunnel, but the light above the girl seemed to take on more form, and I stopped. I couldn't take my eyes off her. Just as suddenly, a throbbing hum filled the room and rock fell. I braced myself, wondering if my tunnel would collapse. A whoosh of air rushed over me, and I felt suction as the air moved over my body and up the incline I passed through. Dust filled the cavern. The lights dimmed, but my passageway held fast – though I wasn't sticking around to see how long it would hold. I dropped onto the ground and made my way toward the girl, hiding my approach with the metal boxes stacked across the room.

The sun-like thing turned her in a dizzying circle, but stopped in front of yet another person as I got closer. He quaked while the orb seemed to weigh his fate. Then a hand of light reached out from the glowing sphere and touched the girl's cheek, willing her to face the boy I spotted. A low thrum echoed and the unmoving girl abruptly reached for him.

Her voice trembled off the walls warning him of his fate. Then she became still; every muscle in her body cold again. The orb pulsed and I watched in horror as multi-colored liquid filled the space around her until it covered her head. The substance oozed, a mix of clear gel and bright reds and some other colors I didn't know.

The room shuddered, the vibration barely perceptible, and the boy tripped backwards in fear. His face reflected off the metal storage box to his right. Staring back from the surface, I saw my own fear-stricken eyes reflected on the metal. Then the room around me aged like it was on fast forward.

My twin stood there staring at the girl, but I ran for the hidden tunnel.

■■■■

"I have to stop dreaming about that girl!" I sat bolt upright on the couch at the Big House.

"What are you talking about?" came a groggy voice from Alexandra. She twisted from lying awkwardly on her leather armchair and stretched. Apparently, we had fallen asleep here earlier.

"What time is it?" I yawned.

"5:30. Sun's up."

Sure enough, light crept in the windows. She stretched and her slender back arched as her muscles unwound from their cramped sleep. "I don't think I can go back to sleep now, even if I wanted to." She held her head like she was nursing a headache.

"Yeah, me neither. Wanna' go see Neter?"

"Sounds good." She stood and the light peeking through the window lit her blonde hair. She was angelic. I rubbed my eyes and the vision disappeared.

We walked up the farm road, stirring up dust.

"So, who are you dreaming about? Some crush from back home?" Alexandra had to force the words out and unsubtly crossed her arms over her chest.

I almost laughed. I hadn't thought about any other girls since I met her.

"No. No girls back home."

She relaxed her arms with my admission.

"But it is weird. I keep dreaming about a girl, but I don't know who she is."

"Hmm? Now that's interesting. What's your imagination come up with Gil Scott?"

"Ha. No. It's not like that. This particular girl happens to be trapped in a weird time-warp thing that keeps her from aging while the rest of the world goes on fast forward. I keep getting stuck in my dreams watching her while the rest of the world ages and falls apart around her, but she stays young."

"That is weird."

"You don't know the half of it. Before the light monster freezes her for all eternity, it unfreezes her long enough for her to reach out to me and rail on about how the Earth's gonna bleed. It's freaky is what it is."

We were walking down the tunnel road now.

She rubbed her head like her headache was getting to her. "Gil, did you say 'light monster?'"

"Yep."

"So, what exactly did your monster look like?"

"Just your basic light monster, really, a ball of light with long arms of light that come out of it." I showed her, flinging my hands like they were floppy noodles. "But on the end," I balled and un-balled my fists, "and this is the weird part ... it has these things like hands, but not hands. I can't explain it. They're weird."

Alexandra stopped. "You've got to be kidding me, Gil. Have you ever seen a picture of the Aten?"

I cocked my head at her. "Sure. A few times. It's just some drawing of the sun?"

She shook her head and threw her hands on her hips – classic Alexandra. "Don't you think the real Aten might have a little more dimension to it? Think about it. A ball of light with arms, holding ankhs – you know that symbol that represents life – like a cross with a hoop on top, right?"

I stood there dumbly. She was perfectly describing what I saw in my dream. "So, you think I'm dreaming about the real Aten? And there's a girl trapped under it? And my dad and Elaine are th –" I stopped myself, suddenly dumb – both the stupid and silent kind.

"Gil! Your dad and Elaine are in the dreams with her, standing under the Aten? Come on!"

"They were definitely in one of the dreams. Wait – so you think they're there, trapped? With the real Aten? And I dreamed about it? You're crazy."

"I've been called worse." She crossed her arms. "But I'm serious. Tell me all about the dreams."

"Nightmares," I corrected.

I recovered myself enough to explain. "I started dreaming about her right before dad went missing. They were pretty tame at first, but they kept getting more and more bizarre. More and more realistic too. Totally unnerving – for me even." I tried to smooth over that last part.

I cracked my knuckles and told her everything – how the girl was hiding from someone in the bunker, but they find her and almost kill her. How the Aten emerges from the necklace and saves her but locks her in the time warp. How dad and Elaine are inexplicably trapped there too. How she talks to me and begs me for help, but I can never speak to her.

Could it be real?

I'm an alien, was my answer. Was that supposed to be real?

"She was able to talk to you telepathically in your dreams. She could be one of us! I almost can't believe it. She's got to be real though. And she's out there somewhere with your dad and Elaine. And they're alive, Gil! They're both alive! Think about it! They're trapped like her!"

My dad. Alive? I felt a thrill of hope as we approached Neter.

"You've got to ask her where they are next time."

"Yeah. Yeah, maybe." My voice faltered. For some reason I didn't think I could. "See, the thing is, I'm always watching her in those dreams. Like I'm an outside observer. I can't even speak. It's like I'm seeing a shadow. I don't know. I could try."

The cave floor widened out, and Neter opened the hatch.

"In the meantime, let's see if we can find anything else in Neter's data matrixes. Maybe there's another clue?"

We went straight back to the same console that had let us in last time, though we put our hand on it separately this time and concentrated. I slid into my brain in a second, Alexandra right behind me.

Standing in the tunnel of loud rushing blackness, Alexandra called out to Neter. The purple-eyed ship approached and the data matrix calmed itself.

"Neter, we told the crew everything and we figure we should explore some more in your memory matrix. Can you help us? Maybe we can figure out who put that destruct code in?"

"I will do my best, Alexandra," Neter answered, bringing up the memory matrix and its ghost pairing. We manipulated the data, hoping for more hidden memory pathways while Neter brought her more precise calculations into play. We worked together mining through layer upon layer of hidden coding for hours until Neter hit on a hidden file. I inserted the code again and a crew photo displayed itself.

"Captain Ezz?" Alexandra's voice broke.

"It appears so," Neter answered. "I am sorry it was he who was responsible."

Alexandra's eyes were wide. "He was one of a few Oasens who didn't survive the crash. His melio exit port was blocked. He died on impact."

"It is sad news, indeed. But, there is something else. A hidden communiqué. I've found traces of several deleted messages between Ezz and Oases, but this one wasn't protected as well, probably because it was his last."

"Okay. Play it."

A video feed ran. Alexandra gasped. "That's Amun Ezz is talking to. He's the leader of the Oasen people! Oh my stars. Gil – he's like the president – well, more like the Supreme High Commander of Oases. What the heck is going on?"

Captain Ezz spoke then, though it was fuzzy. "We are on trajectory with the Earth ship. It will make fast work of Neter." The picture blurred then righted itself.

"Good Ezz. Your penance is almost done. Rest easy. Your wife and child are safe, now." The old Oasen leader's voice cracked with static, but Ezz's eyes filled with tears of relief.

"To think, all the trouble I've gone to to get back my own creation! But if I cannot have the Aten again, then no one will. That two-faced Ra, he hid it from me. Me!" Amun prattled on like he was talking to himself.

So, this was about the Aten. It didn't surprise me.

"Sir," Ezz was suddenly bold. "Why all this for, for the Aten?" He said the word like he was unsure what it was.

Amun chuckled and coughed violently. His eyes twinkled with delight, but they reflected how cold and hard a man he was as well. He was old too, even for an Oasen. "If Ra didn't hide it, there would be no need for this!" He spat as he talked. "But if I can't have it, then no one can. No one can have my precious Aten. Certainly not the lot of you."

"It can't be that important."

Amun looked up at the camera like someone stung him.

"Not that important. My life's work, eh? Have I never told you, Ezz?" He seemed mystified he hadn't. "The Aten is an ancient thing, very ancient indeed. Like me," and he laughed. "Stolen long ago and lost. Lost for so many generations. And then found, on little Earth of all places. A technology so powerful, I could harness it for conquest or creation or reanimation, and it's gone, gone because of that defiant Ra and his trickery."

The picture faded here a bit. But Amun wasn't done.

His voice continued to rise in pitch and fury – in stark contrast to the poor picture quality. "Cowards all of them. Leaving or hiding where my mercenaries couldn't find them. Erasing their footsteps so I could not trace them. They hid it from me! Me, a monster, Osiris says." Amun looked menacingly into the camera that recorded him. "Well, he took that to his grave with him, now didn't he?"

Amun fiddled with his ancient fingers.

"I came so close. I almost had it back, but they all pay dearly now for their treachery and they will pay the final cost soon. That girl may lie hidden and protected in the knot, but the knot cannot stay tied forever. Ha! Ha! It unravels even now, and when it does, the Aten will absorb all of the Earth into itself to find its key. Without its' key, the Earth dies anyway. She'll die too. Ra will finally be defeated. And no one will be the wiser for my actions."

"Morty was wrong," I whispered while the video played on. "It was a cover up, but it had nothing to do with the god's thing."

"Shh," Alexandra hushed me and tapped her ear.

"It has everything to do with the Aten."

She narrowed her eyes at me as Amum rambled on about Aten.

My mind spun in circles, half listening and half thinking. The Aten was so ridiculously powerful that Amun wanted it all to himself. I guess the Barque crew knew better than to turn it over to him, but who wouldn't listening to that crazy old Oasen?

Static crackled across the screen and it went blank. I hadn't paid attention to the end.

"The communication abruptly cuts off here," Neter stated matter-of-fact.

"Replay it," Alexandra commanded.

It did and when it was done again, Alexandra spoke. "We're in a lot of trouble. Did you hear what it said the Aten would do?"

"Yeah, the world getting destroyed doesn't sound so hot. What did it say? The Aten is going to absorb the Earth to find its key – whatever that means. "

"It's pretty wonderful. Five minutes ago, we barely knew what the Aten was. It was mystical and powerful and it fixed our ship and now we figure out what it is, and apparently it's going to wipe out the Earth."

"Yeah, the Earth will bleed..." My voice trailed off. I didn't feel so good.

I stood up inside the matrix, from where I had just been sitting, and jumped back out to the physical world.

Alexandra was right behind me.

"But not if I can help it," I said as her eyes opened to consciousness.

"What do you mean?"

I gathered up my things. We needed to get back to our parents and tell them what was going on – and fast.

"Amun said there's a key that can stop the Aten from destroying the Earth. If we find that key, we can save everyone." I stopped and leaned back slightly, puffing up my chest. "We can save the Earth, Alexandra."

She laughed, which wasn't exactly what I expected. I felt fairly Indiana Jones just then.

"So, you're basically saying your idea is to try and locate the Aten – and its key? A key, in fact, that belongs to an object so well hidden that no one's been able to locate it for thousands of years. One the apparently deceptive supreme leader of our people searched for using a starship full of mad-skilled mercenaries but still couldn't find? Yeah. Okay." She thought about it for a minute. "Good idea Gil. I say we dig Neter out instead and take our chances back on Oases."

"I second that idea," added Neter.

I rolled my eyes. Even Neter was a smart aleck.

"You're forgetting one thing – my dad. No one's found the Aten in thousands of years, except my dad – and Elaine – if my dreams are true. So, all we have to do now is find him. Then we find the Aten."

"Don't forget about the key. We have to find that too. I wish we knew how much longer we had before 'the whole Earth gets annihilated' thing? That would make me feel a whole lot better about this whole thing."

"Yeah, that is a problem. Amun said it was going to go down soon, but our parents have been on Earth a long time. Everything's fine still."

"Yeah, I guess you're right."

Neter interrupted us then.

"Alexandra? Gil?"

"Yes, Neter?"

"Please brace yourselves," she said, ever the polite ship.

And then, of course, all hell broke loose.

Chapter 11-"The end is coming!"

The ground shook for what seemed like forever. After it was over, I got a pretty severe scolding from mom and Morty before Alexandra and Neter convinced them it wasn't me. Good thing too, because after we watched CNN on Neter's interface panel to see what was really happening, we realized even I couldn't do that much damage. There were quakes all over the place: California (of course), Utah and even northern Georgia in the southern United States.

But it was worse than that.

It was planet wide.

Mexico City got hit by at 7.1, while Honshu, Japan and Northern Chile all reported activity around 6.2's on the Richter scale. Not to mention the quakes in the North Indian Ocean, Spain, Canada, Indonesia, the Tonga Islands and portions of the MidAtlantic Ridge.

It was that bad.

I don't think Alexandra and I even heard our parent's ship come rushing down the tunnel, or felt the wind off their other-worldly speed as they hurried off the elevator to grab us and hold us, so thankful we were safe, then yell at us for causing the quake. We were sitting there almost catatonic-like on Neter's bridge when they dashed in, trying to cope with what we learned and what had happened. Trying to work all the disparate puzzle pieces into something solvable.

Neter interrupted the brief reunion. "You should see this," she said simply and her interface panels lit up with news feeds from across the world, the reporters and anchors speaking in a jumbled mix of languages and with varying levels of worry.

Morty's phone buzzed in his pocket by now repeatedly, but he ignored it. "That one." He pointed at CNN. The other feeds switched off.

The pretty anchor went on speaking. "Seismic activity occurs every day on the planet, but never concurrently worldwide. So, experts are trying to understand how all this activity occurred at the exact same time, to the second, across the planet's hot spots. Jim?"

"Let's not panic." The expert sat up more straight. "Statistically speaking, the probability exists for concurrent seismic activity."

Another expert, rather frumpy in a gray wrinkled suit, interrupted. He was sweating. "You've got a rosy picture of the world, now don't you, Jim? Always did. Listen, I don't know how to say this, but I'll be blunt." He looked directly at the camera. "You should all kiss your mothers and take the day off to do something special." The camera hastily cut away from the emotional guest.

Wow.

The anchor gathered worry lines as the story progressed. She cut to a reporter on the streets of San Francisco. People were standing on the corners with signs shouting, "The end is coming!" This scene was repeated in several more cities in the States and across the world.

Another reporter showed a mob of people at an Arkansas Walmart hoarding supplies for the "coming apocalypse." Yet another showed the beginnings of a new island off devastated Tonga. It seemed a little overkill to me to be going nuts over a few earthquakes, but then again, I knew the end of the world was coming, so I had to give them some credit.

Try explaining that to your parents.

"That's enough, Neter," Morty rubbed at his mouth.

"Morty." Mom's face was pale. "The last time this kind of planet-wide seismic activity was recorded predated the Ta-hil Era, didn't it?" Her eyes drifted far away through time. "It was called Ratajagaha, I think. I learned about it when I was a little girl." She wouldn't even look up at him until she finished her sentence, but when she did, I knew why. There was terror there.

"What was called Ratajagaha?" I tried out the strange word using the same inflection she had.

"A planet." She spoke quietly. "It doesn't exist anymore."

"That's it then." Alexandra spoke up. "You were right, I guess."

"Right about what?" This time Morty asked the question.

"Umm. We're sort of in big trouble. Ratajagaha kind of trouble, if you know what I mean?"

"Do explain."

We gave it our best, tripping over our words, having Neter replay snippets of the video we uncovered on the interface. She took quite a beating in the quake, and a failed memory chip played havoc with the loop, but they saw most of it. Then, all there was to do was explain about the girl in my dreams – the very real girl in my dreams – and all the pieces finally came together. It all came down to the Aten: It had been found. It had been activated, and the clock had been set. We were on a countdown to planetary destruction – without the intervention of a missing key.

"I concur," Neter spoke up, as if she was in a war room providing statistical analysis of the coming battle. The room went dark and slightly smoky and the purple-eyed ship brought up a 3D outlined diagram of the planet. Its blue color was veined with red.

This was a seismic map.

The little fingers of red branched out from their source at Palenque – one finger in particular making its way all the way to an obscure fault line directly below the ranch. It was far worse than the media let on. The planet was bloody with crimson.

"Look at that." Alexandra's finger traced the line from the Mexican city where my dad was lost to the one we stood on now. "Looks like we were targeted."

Morty's arm swept through the air beside me, and I jumped at the sudden movement. It must have been some kind of signal, because the lights went back on and the smoke was gone. Morty got on his phone right away, throwing out quick commands to whoever was on the receiving end, and then rushed us back to their planetary vehicle, not even stopping to say goodbye to Neter.

The little ship's engine whirled with power. Alexandra and I were thrust into our seats on the back bench – the Melio doing what it could to absorb the shock of Morty's supersonic driving. He only slowed long enough to safely clear a group of Oasens who were walking out of the tunnel with shovels, rakes and several wheelbarrows.

"You were trapped down there for hours. We had to clear a cave-in before we could even get to you and the magnetic forces were playing havoc with our Bau powers. We had to do it Earthy-style."

Had we been down there that long?

He took off again.

We buzzed right past the Big House at a breakneck clip and landed instead at the Meeting Hall. He didn't utter another word as he exited the ship. Morty had never been more serious. We rushed out with him, straight into the building, joining a stream of Oasens who apparently had already been notified of the gathering. Ben stood outside the door like an armed body guard, his twin missing for once from the other post.

The outside of the building was as rustic as the rest of the compound's large cabins, so I was surprised when I walked through the door. Inside was a mix of modern industrial – all concrete floors and exposed ductwork– far too modern and sophisticated to fit in well with the cowboy theme I'd seen so far.

"This building is secure," Alexandra whispered, like she was revealing a secret. "We only use it in emergencies. I've never actually been in here."

We were ushered into a meeting room that reminded me of a college lecture hall – one of the half-moon ones that angle down with stadium seating towards the professor's desk. A smartboard hung behind a podium at the front. The news played on it, but it kept shorting out. This building was damaged too.

As we walked down the aisle, Ryan motioned with a thumb's up to Morty from the desk that faced the others at the bottom of the room. Morty pointed for us to sit on the first row, but never stopped to join us. He only stopped when he got to the podium. A few more Oasens walked in and Ben repeated Ryan's gesture from the top aisle, closing the door securely behind him.

"We good?"

"Yes. Secure video conferencing at go, sir," Ryan said. "All account-ed for."

Morty faced the room. Many people were still dirty from helping clear the cave in.

"Okay, let's get right to it."

An image of the globe appeared on the smart board behind him. Palenque, Mexico – the city where my dad and Elaine had gone missing – was bloody with crimson. Telling red streaks of seismic activity streaked from it to other points on the globe, one in particu-lar seeming to target our ranch. Somewhere in South America, deep in Palenque, the Barque crew had hidden the Aten to keep it from Amun, their conniving old ruler. It was the source of the quakes. That much was obvious now. And soon it would be the source of our deaths if we didn't find it and its key.

The video we watched with Amun and Ezz had explained as much. When Alexandra played the exchange for a second time, I caught the end. Amun had explained that the energy the Aten used to create the frozen girl's time warp – the time knot he had called it – would only last so long. Only a new key – or the planet' life – could sustain the Aten when its energy was spent. And apparently the Aten wasn't okay powering down peacefully either. Self-preservation was at the heart of its programming.

What had the gods been thinking? Had something happened to them before they could set things right? Whatever happened, it was thousands of years too late.

Morty began simply enough. "Today, we Oasens must take responsibility for the fate of this world."

I wondered if their hearts felt as heavy as mine hearing those words. But they had no clue, yet. No clue.

And what Morty would say next would change all our lives.

■■■■■

Neter ran through dad's credit cards and phone records leading up to the Palenque expedition, trying to create a trail we could follow. We wanted to know if we missed any other clues that led him to the Aten in Palenque. The search team certainly hadn't had any luck. Something was missing and we aimed to find it.

With a list of concrete to go on, I packed a bag for the trip. Alexandra sat on my bed in the loft with hers already done. It felt strange to be together like this. And oddly normal.

We were making plans when mom walked up with Morty.

"What are you two doing?"

"I'm finishing packing. I'll be ready in two seconds."

I grabbed a couple of white undershirts from my drawer and my still-dirty jeans and threw them in. I nodded toward Alexandra who sat on the end of my bed like this was our usual thing. "Alex is already ready to go."

I loved that nickname.

I kept packing while mom watched me. Her eyes were like laser beams, but she was dead silent. This was one of those moments I needed to stop what I was doing and find out what I was doing wrong.

"Mom, everything okay?"

She sighed. "Gilbert, you and Alexandra are teenagers. You're staying here. This is for Morty and me to handle." Since the two of them were the ranking crew members after Ezz's death, her statement held more weight than just the parental kind.

"Ryan and Amisi are staying here with you. You can hold down the fort and access Neter's memory matrixes again. Keep dreaming of the girl and help us that way, okay?" Mom ruffled my hair, but the way she said it felt so condescending, like she meant to give me a glass of warm milk and put me straight to bed.

It wasn't fair.

"But dad!" Alexandra exclaimed. "Gil and I are the ones who figured all this out! How can you leave us here?"

"Sweetheart." Morty sat down on the bed beside her. "You and Gil have done so much already, we can't expect you to come with us into whatever unknown dangers may be out there. It is here you can be most useful. Almost everything you've learned so far, you learned from Neter. And besides, Gil only started training. He's an unknown out there."

"What about his dreams?" Alexandra reminded him and absent-mindedly put her hand on my knee. I stared down at it and she quickly pulled away realizing. She was quick to recover herself. "Don't forget she speaks to him in his dreams. What if there is more to it than that? How can you abandon us here?"

"Now you're just being dramatic." Morty took his hand off Alexandra's shoulder and stood. "Helen and I are leaving for Palenque today and that's all there is to it."

Wait. What? I was confused.

"Wait. Palenque? I thought you were going to Cairo to check out that meeting dad had?" Our background search had revealed a meeting dad had gone to that not even mom knew had taken place.

"Yes, we thought that was promising, but it doesn't appear to be more than a conference of the minds on a lost Persian army that was killed in a sand storm 2,500 years ago."

"I don't get it. What happened?"

"He was at a dig site in the Sahara. Joe's old colleague discovered a mass grave there. He thinks it's the missing army from Thebes that went to Attack the Oasis of Siwa and destroy the Oracle at the Temple of Amun." Morty rambled, his professorness taking over. "The priest there refused to legitimize Herodotus Cabyses claim to

Egypt, so he sent his army. But, Gil, that was back in 525 B.C. The timeframe's way off. It can't be that."

I let that sink in, my stomach sinking with it, but didn't say anything.

"We can't waste time chasing flimsy leads, when we can use our own expertise in Palenque. We are much older and more experienced than those who went before us, Gilbert. Please trust me in this. We will find them."

She tried to comfort, but it didn't work.

"Gil, Alexandra, I know this is hard for you both, but we can't justify bringing you with us to Palenque. You're too young, and while you may both be half Oasen, you are still our children and it's our job to protect you."

"Mom, the planet's about to implode. I think you could use the help."

"Well, we don't plan on letting that happen. Stay with Ryan and Amisi where you will be safe. Help them in whatever way they ask."

And with that, the conversation was over.

Mom kissed my head and walked down the steps with Morty toward the ship Alexandra had flown to meet us in that first day.

I zipped my bag quickly, and we grabbed our things, chasing them with youthful hope and desperation, but they donned their gold helmets and climbed into the cockpit without us anyway.

Chapter 12-We Follow a hunch

"You heard them right?" Alexandra was saying. "We have to stay with Ryan and Amisi, where we will be safe."

"Yeah, I heard them." I kicked the dirt as I watched mom and Morty take off. I blocked the dust from getting in my eyes. This was crazy leaving us behind.

Ryan and Amisi walked up.

"Ryan, you're a linguist, right?" Alexandra said. "So you understand the nuances of language?" She cocked her head.

"Yep. I do. C'est vrai. Eso es verdad. Zhè shì zhēn de. That's true."

Amisi knocked into him with her elbow. "Show off."

Alexandra shook her head at him, but ignored it. "So, would you please help me understand something Gil's mom said to us before they left?"

Ryan nodded.

"She said we have to stay with you and Amisi so we'll be safe. She, however, failed to specify a location."

Ryan raised his eyebrows at this, and a crooked grin appeared, though he tried to hide it.

Oh good grief, Alexandra. That's what you were trying to tell me!

"So maybe we can do a little detective work from somewhere more useful than the middle of nowhere!" Her words grew louder and louder until she huffed and threw her hands on her hips and a geyser exploded nearby. Ryan grinned.

"I mean it's crazy staying here! I can't believe they expect you two to sit still while they go off to save the world either! You may be young Oasens, but this is way bigger than two people! I can't believe Helen and Morty!" She was fuming mad. She didn't even call him dad.

Ryan's eyes darkened and Amisi's cheeks pinked up. We were getting somewhere. I jumped right in to help. "Here's the deal guys, mom and Morty think they have all this figured out, but they don't. They're following my dad blindly to Palenque where what, they will all of the sudden be able to find a trace of them when the other team couldn't? I get it. They are trying to be strong for you all because they are your leaders, but they have nothing solid to go on and they're refusing to check any other possibilities, no matter how flimsy. They aren't sending anyone to pursue them. That's foolishness considering the end of the world is at stake!"

"You mean the professor in Cairo your dad visited?" Amisi asked.

"Yes, exactly. I know it's a long shot, but I have a hunch we're supposed to follow in his footsteps."

"Palenque was a long shot too – for your dad."

"I don't know, guys." Ryan shielded his eyes from the sun. It was hotter than normal today, especially for Montana in the summer.

"Morty is right. You two are you pretty young and only half bloods ..."

I grinned. Ryan loved Harry Potter.

He caught my smirk.

"Ryan, come on. You're one of the smartest guys I know. You'll come at this from a differently than our parents because you've lived here so long. Your perspective's wasted staying here. But we have to do this together. Half-blood or not."

"She called him by name!" Alexandra blurted out. "In Gil's dreams, the girl in the knot's always reaching for him. It's like she knows the answer lies with him. How can we stay home when that girl's telling us Gil is the guy! It's foolishness!" She threw her hands up in the air exasperated.

Ryan put his hand up to stop us from saying another word and pulled Amisi to the side. They had a hurried conversation and came right back.

"Honestly guys, we weren't planning on staying here another five minutes. We just weren't planning on taking you with us." Ryan's brow furrowed. "But, we can't help but agree with Alexandra about the girl in Gil's dreams."

I jabbed her in the ribs. Good job Alex.

Ryan went on. "It's kind of a big deal she won't let up about him. So, I guess you're going with us then." Ryan let his youthful smile back out from where he had it hidden and walked away, leaving us standing with our mouths open.

"What are you waiting for? Come on." He took off up the hill to where he parked his red Wrangler, ahem, Sahara edition – he never failed to mention the Sahara part. It was a pretty important distinguisher for a veritable relative of the Egyptian gods.

Alexandra beamed her beautiful smile at me, gap teeth and all, and her blue eyes actually sparkled, a hint of kinetic energy frosting them like ice. I grinned back at her ridiculously.

"Road trip!" I yelled and I grabbed my bag.

We ran, but fly girl jumped into the air doing corkscrews, bag and all, and cut through the air. She descended into the back of the open-top jeep, not even bothering to land and get in the normal way.

"Where are we going?" I flipped over the side into the back.

"You'll see." Ryan hit the gas pedal and we bolted up the farm road to the tunnel. At the mouth of the cave, I got the surprise of my life. Neter's beautiful black and gold hull peeked out, pulled by long braided metal cables attached to military-grade haulers. Ben stood waving his arms to direct the teams. I wondered if Neter was inside her data matrixes doing back flips right now. She was free.

"What!"

"How did you get her out?"

"We must thank the cataclysmic earthquake for that. It was centered so close, she was knocked nearly free right after it was over. She only needed a little extra help." Ryan waved at Ben who directed people to unhook the cables.

Amisi clapped her hands. "I hope no one minds. We're borrowing a space ship."

Neter's hatch was open by now too and several planetary vehicles were being prepped. Teams of Oasens in groups of four, dressed in plain clothes and gold helmets, climbed into the little ships. We weren't the only ones leaving.

"This was part of your parent's plan," Ryan mentioned. "Though they didn't anticipate Neter joining this fray." He waved his hand in the direction of the ship. "She's kind of big to be hopping all over the planet, but she can stay invisible, so as long as we park out of the way, we should be fine."

"Alright," I was nearly speechless. We stopped and watched as the other teams got settled in their ships and flew off on their own missions. Ben was one of the last to board, but he stopped and gave Ryan a high-five before joining Kos in the front seat and taking off. We waited for his dust to settle and then drove right into Neter's holding bay in the jeep. The hatch door closed behind us.

We locked the jeep down and made our way to the bridge using the sideways moving elevator. Ryan, the ranking crew member aboard, took the captain's chair and we found seats ourselves. Neter strapped us in the Melio, and the engine started up. I waited for the race car experience, but this time I got the Prius one. This alien stuff was confusing. The engine purred quietly.

"I wasn't expecting that."

"Me neither," Alexandra voiced.

"It's a lot different when you're travelling through outer space, I'll give you that. But, we'd draw too much attention if we went racing around the planet throwing out flares miles long. Her engine's basically set on 'fuel economy' right now." Ryan laughed and Amisi cackled too, her short bob dancing as her little body quaked.

But he was back to business soon.

"Neter, the coordinates are set. Initiate vertical ascent."

"Aye, captain," she answered joyfully.

We rose in the air, gracefully turning in a half circle and shot out over California and the ocean in an upward arch nearly 23-1/2 miles high. We avoided commercial air traffic this way and got a nice view of the curvature of the Earth as we crested the arch.

Ryan released his Melio belt and walked across the bridge to Amisi. He said something quietly to her and she joined him over at the window of the bridge. He put his arm around her shoulders and pulled her to him. They put their heads together and stared out the window long and hard.

I couldn't tell you what they were thinking, but I can only imagine they never thought they'd see this peaceful view of the Earth. Their arrival here had been nothing like this. I watched the whole thing through Neter's eyes; the crew had been terrified, falling, barely surviving the entry angle. The hull had blazed with heat, and they had felt the barely controlled free fall of their ship. They had seen death and just avoided it.

The two of us were quiet watching them. Ryan and Amisi eventually walked back to their seats, the Melio covering them in its protective layers. Neter calculated the entry and we plunged back down toward Cairo.

Ryan made a quick call to Egypt on the way down and arranged for us to meet Tamer Bashandi at his dig site. Tamer was my dad's friend and a Professor of Egyptology at the American University in Cairo. I knew him from when I was little when I first came with dad to see the pyramids. He was a kind man who told me exciting stories that made the past feel alive. I wondered how much he knew of my own heritage.

"Thanks, Tamer," Ryan said. "We'll see you then."

Ryan swiveled his chair. "We're going to drive out to his dig site. It's a big operation, and they are still unearthing bones and weapons from the missing soldiers, so it's there or nowhere."

"Sounds cool."

Amisi nodded. "Ryan's just excited he gets to drive his jeep through a desert."

"It is a Sahara edition. It's only fitting."

■■■■■

Neter put down in a location near enough to Tamer's dig site for us to get there easily in the jeep, but far enough away to avoid traffic coming near the ship.

The sand was rough and hot, but we finally made it. The dig site bustled with activity – a constant ding of chisels and men shouting back and forth in Arabic. Tents covered the areas the crews were working on to lessen their heat exposure. Otherwise they would faint from heat exhaustion or dehydration from the beating sun. It felt good to be back.

We walked up, much to the curious gaze of the workers. The jeep was flashy, admittedly. I spotted Tamer and pointed him out to Ryan who walked over confidently.

Tamer's wrinkled cream-colored suit and white collared dress shirt seemed out of place in the desert sun. It made me hot looking at him but layers in this climate were cooling. He was as I remembered him: a round man with sparse hair and too-large, creased hands. What hair remained to him, this time, clung together in gray wet slicks thanks to the pounding sun.

"Alsalam alaykum," Ryan extended his hand. Tamer countered with a long handshake and a hearty smile.

"Welcome. Welcome," Tamer answered in English. "I was so sorry to hear of what happened to Joe." He kissed me on one cheek and shook my hand, his eyes boring into me. "And welcome to you, young ladies." He eyed small little Amisi, but bowed in greeting to her and Alexandra anyway. Amisi curtsied back, but Alexandra nodded her head in her sometimes masculine way. She was raised by Morty after all.

"Come. Would you please join me for some tea?" offered Tamer who turned on his heals not waiting for a reply. We followed behind him toward a large modern trailer, the only one of its kind on the site. Catching up, he pointed out the various archeological activities at hand as we walked toward it. His men were pulling out jewels, bronze weapons and bones, "lots of bones," he told us.

When we finally finished the trek to the trailer, I was dripping. My shirt stuck to my skin – a physical reminder of the heat of the

Egyptian sun. And it hadn't been that far of a walk. Tamar opened the door and a flood a cool relief washed over us. Thank the heavens, this place was air conditioned.

"Here, sit," motioned Tamar, pointing to a snug table. "I will make the tea." We obeyed and he busied himself over a little plug-in electric eye, filling a bright blue enameled tea pot with tepid water from an industrial container of the stuff.

He made no attempt to hurry.

"Oh my goodness," Alexandra whispered to me. "Come on already."

"I know." I was losing my mind.

Ryan and Amisi weren't faring much better either. Ryan's knee bounced rapidly and Amisi kept squeezing her hands together over and over. As old as they were, you'd think they'd be more patient. But it wasn't the case. We all waited anxiously.

Tamer finally finished making his intensely aromatic hot tea and carried it over. Without the air conditioning, no one would have wanted it anyway, but thankfully that wasn't the case. Egyptian tea was wonderful.

Tamar sat down at last and studied Ryan with the kind of customary disconcerting intense stare Egyptians are famous for. But, Ryan, ever the understanding Oasen, politely stared back until Tamer broke the silence. "What brings you here, to my corner of this great world, in the midst of such trouble?" Tamer was acutely aware my dad was missing on the other side of the planet. He was an intelligent man. Dad was nowhere near this dusty corner.

"It is a long story, but we believe Joe and his graduate student are lost in an unexplored area of Palenque. He was on the verge of a discovery, we think, that was inspired by something here. It's a stretch, but we have to explore every avenue to find him."

Finding him now meant only recovering his body to Tamer. But he understood. "Lost in some crevice, I take it? That is why I work here. Sand fills everything up and must be removed. There is no falling into crevices with sand."

Tamer finished his tangent and went on.

"But, ah, yes. Joe. He was very taken with my army of 50,000 warriors whose bones now fill this desert." We caught a glimpse of someone holding up a dusty skull. "But, he was more fascinated with the Oracle at the Temple of Amun who this army's leader was bent on destroying. Truly, I tell you, Joe did not remain here long, but went with Noor to the Siwa Oasis. Obviously, our project here is linked greatly to the temple where the Oracle resided."

"Did he say anything about that temple?"

Tamer thought for a minute and laughed a hearty belly laugh. "Joe is ever the dreamer. He lends too much truth to old stories, but who can blame someone with so pure a heart? I cannot for one. Oh, how he made me laugh this time though!" Tamer pounded the table so hard it shook. "He said the Oracle must have drew on his heka, his magic, to bring down death on so great an army!"

There was a long moment of silence. We sat thinking on this, sipping our tea politely.

"I think that's a start, at least."

He only nodded, but it was obvious the meeting was over. We all stood.

"Thank you, Tamer." I shook his hand.

"Yes, the tea was lovely."

"And you have given us hope, however thin it may seem."

Tamer nodded at this. He thought our venture a wild one. "One can only hope." He led us out the door, but stopped short. "Wait. You'll need credentials to access the Siwa Oasis site. I can help there at least."

He went back and rummaged through a drawer and pulled out four plastic badges on long black lanyards. He quickly scribbled his signature on the papers within and handed them over.

I nodded in thanks. Silence pervaded at last.

After we had those in hand, we made the sweaty trek back to the jeep and drove back to Neter – air conditioning blasting.

Chapter 13-Breaking and entering

The Temple of Amun in the Oasis of Siwa was a beautiful old stone structure carved into a flat hilltop in the mostly abandoned village of Aghurmi. It was built during the 26th dynasty and flourished well into the Roman and Greek periods, but now large cracks and fissures can be seen on the sides of its foundation. The mud-and-brick citadel suffered a near-catastrophe in 1926 when three days of heavy rain dissolved much of it. Lying abandoned, but for recent tourism, the 800-year-old citadel stands against time, willing something else to try and destroy it.

The temple today is known as the Temple of the Oracle because of the mystical priestly seer who resided there and was supposedly able to foretell the future. He apparently used his magic to destroy that army of 50,000 with a terrible sandstorm too. The Oracle was also responsible for declaring Alexander the Great the "son of Amun" when he entered the country and saved the Egyptians from its Persian rulers in 332 B.C. When this priest greeted him with the words, "my son," Alexander's army and followers could not see the priest as he spoke and thought the words came directly from the mouth of god himself. Talk about an introduction. From then on, Alexander was revered like a modern-day Pharaoh.

Apparently dad was pretty fascinated with the Oracle after talking to Tamer too. He thought someone back then was sporting some other-worldly powers and killed that massive army when they attempted to march on the temple.

We were doing as much research on the Oracle as possible on the short hop over there. My eyes barely focused. We had been going non-stop since 5:30 a.m. this morning. Surely, I could catch a few winks before we got there. I closed my eyes and drifted off to sleep.

The black-haired girl was there of course, but this time she wasn't trapped. She was outside playing hide and seek with a boy. It was nice to see her alive and moving and having fun. The boy stalked her happily from the shadows.

When he finally caught her, he held her, inhaling the scent of her oiled hair. I smelled it too, like jasmine, brightened by the heat of the day. Then the boy produced the gold locket I knew so well and put it around her slender neck. She touched it tenderly, then touched his face.

The scene abruptly cut away.

It was the dead of night and the girl was running. She was older now. Behind her, the young man panted and ran hard, looking back over his shoulder. Their pursuers were lean and muscular men, reaching with their hands and making the earth rise and fall in front of the doomed couple.

The girl cried out to her suitor.

"It is the only way," he mouthed to her.

They kept running.

"No!" she pleaded, the words a whisper on the wind.

"I'm sorry, my love, but I must protect you."

He stopped running then and faced the assassins. He called out, "Ra commands the sun!" And light so dazzling it blinded came rushing from the heavens and filled the sky. The men stopped and covered their eyes. The girl fell and covered hers too, but Ra stared into the light, his eyes gleaming with kinetic energy, those eyes of his still seeing but totally white like they were blind.

The men withered on the ground like the light burned their flesh, but the girl stilled herself as Ra approached and knelt beside her. He placed his hands on her eyes, and when he removed them, she stared up at him, both their eyes now white and startling to look at.

Tears filled them as they knelt and held each other. "There's no time now, Isis. We must do this now. It is the only way. The Oracle said so. You know we must obey."

"No, Ra. We must not. You know what this fate may bring. You risk us in doing this. I cannot lose you forever to the Aten. The boy may not be able to finish it. She said so. And if he fails, I lose you forever."

"I will lose you forever now," he looked back toward the men, "if I do not." And with that, Ra grabbed her hair and the nape of her neck and kissed her. It was a kiss of desperation. A last kiss.

He pulled back and their white eyes cried. He took the locket from where it lay across her neck and opened it. Something like the sun rose from it and swelled and catapulted into the air above Ra until it was wider than his broad shoulders. The orb was as powerful and bright and as alive as the white-eyed people it now hovered over. It waited as if it already knew what they would ask of it.

Ra took one single breath, and did: "Aten, accept this gift of man and tie the knot of Isis." With that, the orb-like Aten reached out and held Ra in its arms of light. He glowed white hot like he was burning, but not, until his energy dispersed in a human shape and was absorbed by the Aten.

The Aten still hovered above the girl, Isis, and a now-familiar voice sounded from it. Ra said, "You will go to the temple I prepared for you. There we must wait for fate to be realized. It is as we all planned."

Then light burst from the Aten and turned the withering men to dust. Darkness returned and the orb collapsed itself back into her locket, which she closed. Sobbing wracked the poor girl.

Her tears flooded the locket, but it remained shut.

I woke up.

Isis, my black-haired girl, had a name.

Rain pounded hard against the window of the bridge. The sky was gray and dark and lightning flashed across the horizon. The others woke too, noticing the rain.

"Don't look at me. Not me this time."

Then I told them the dream.

They took it in stride as best one can when learning the sad fate of lovers. The girls had tears in their eyes, and Ryan kept glancing at Amisi like the two of them might relate. But Alexandra kept her eyes down.

Driving rain still battered the window, but the sky had somehow gotten darker.

"We are on approach," Neter spoke up.

"Better put the hardtop on. We're going to get wet otherwise." Ryan turned for the elevator and we followed him down to the bay.

Amisi and I helped with the top, but Alexandra busied herself with her tablet. She ran her hand across the tablet, changing the news stories she as fast as she read.

"It's like this everywhere. People are going crazy with this end-of-the-world stuff. I've never seen anything like it."

When I walked up behind her to see, I swore the hair on our arms reached out to touch each other because our skin didn't. She flushed and handed the tablet to me, walking away. I felt someone else behind me. Amisi and Ryan.

"Wow. It's getting bad out there." Ryan scanned the headlines.

"Uh, yeah, end-of-the-world. We better hurry."

I brushed Alexandra on my way back to the jeep and handed her the tablet.

With the top finally secure, Ryan and Amisi held the seats down so Alexandra and I could climb in the back. We left Neter in a hurry and raced over to the Temple through the pounding rain and hail before we entered the village gate.

The place was too quiet – the kind of quiet where the town's only residents were like the silent ghosts of people long dead. We knew the village was mostly abandoned, but there was a tourist hotel nearby so we expected to at least see some life. I finally caught sight of a guard peeking out of the minaret of the mosque that stood over the gate. Thank the stars. Seeing a living person took the edge off the spirit-world feeling of the place – somewhat, at any rate.

We drove through the eerily quiet city until we approached the temple in the northwest corner. A huge rock bounded down the cliff and nearly hit the jeep. If there truly were ghosts here, they were angry ones.

"Whoa!" Ryan yelled and swerved.

We all swung sideways against the door or each other. Alexandra bumped into me hard.

"Ow." I grabbed my arm. She grinned sideways at me but a shadow outside had my attention.

An Egyptian guard ran down the slope toward our jeep. "Closed," he said in English noticing us. "Closed now." He stopped at our jeep and put his hands on the window frame after Ryan rolled it down. Water poured into the car, soaking him.

Amisi held up the credentials Tamer had given us, but he shook his head and said "closed" with finality. He held up a large iron key that must fit a padlock and a sturdy gate somewhere. The man slapped the frame hard, and ran off to somewhere safer and drier.

It was getting late, which didn't help. The sun started to fall behind the horizon. It was now or never. Putting aside the security guard's warning, Ryan tried to park the jeep out of the way of the cliff face.

No one thought to bring rain slickers when we left Montana, so we all sludged up the slope to the Temple in sopping wet shorts and t-shirts. The worst part was my drenched sneakers, which slurped at the liquid filling them with each step. Alexandra's hair hung in wet ringlets that were plastered to her face, but her beauty still shone through, especially framed by the twilight. How she could still be that gorgeous drenched amazed me. Her blue eyes sparkled at the exertion and the corner of her mouth began to lift, noticing me staring, but she tried to hide it.

I didn't have long to dwell on it.

As we rounded the corner, we were met by a horrible grinding sound. A huge boulder bounded down the narrow ravine we just entered like a ball bouncing back and forth off the walls like an angry pinball machine. As it hit the cliff walls, huge pieces of rock cracked off and let rush a shower of dust and projectiles that flew at us with biting force. The freight train of its descent deafened me and my hands went instinctively to my face for some small measure of protection. That did little good. Debris bit and tore at my skin and blinded by my hands, I could only listen as the rock thundered down to crush us. All my other senses had gone numb.

Then silence.

The sudden quiet unnerved me more than the roar of falling rock. The choking dust was gone too. How?

My eyes cracked open.

Ryan held Amisi to himself. The little mousy thing was tucked into him as far as she could go. A hint of a smile lifted the corner of his determined mouth. His arm was outstretched. And power radiated through his eyes. A bright blue shield of protection punched out from his hand. Its appearance was like cold rushing water but it felt like fast-moving fire. The muscle in his forearm rippled and the intensity of his eyes made you want to avert your own. My usually mirthful friend hadn't been this severe since he threw that tree at me.

His gaze held. The shield held. Late-falling rocks bumped harmlessly off the domed surface that protected us. The iron gate lay outside the hazy blue protection, a mangled mess below the boulder that fell and crushed it. It had wedged itself firmly in the narrow opening, blocking our path.

Ryan held the force field as the shower continued to fall. "Watch out," he said casually. "This rain is doing the same thing to the Temple it did back in '26."

1926. Wow. Ryan was alive back then, I had time to think. Weird, but I nodded my head at him anyway, grateful for his quick reflexes.

He finally let Amisi go when the rocks stopped falling and touched her cheek. She stopped shaking. She was so fragile compared to the other Oasens I knew. It was nice she had Ryan.

With no one else around to see, and besides, now wasn't the time to be shy what with the world ending around us, the four of us rose into the air. I felt a small burst of power leave my hands and give me lift. Dust swirled below me as the energy of my Bau hit the ground and power encompassed my body. I felt gravity melt off me as I climbed higher and higher into the air, but not all of it. Some clinged to me, allowing me to climb and dip and curve through the air as I pleased. It was pretty amazing, but I still swallowed my heart every time I looked below too long, so I kept my eyes straight ahead while we flew low over the blocked temple gate and landslide into the temple.

We glided over two longs halls and down into the sanctuary which lay along the main axis of the temple site. We landed lightly and Ryan got out a device that glowed with Oasen colors. He scanned along the ground and walls hoping for a sign of dad or Elaine.

I walked around trying to get a feel for the place too. A depiction of King Amasis, who reigned during the building of the temple, framed the right of the entrance. His head and body were chiseled away, but his name was still inscribed there.

Poor guy. Erased by time.

In the relief, he offered wine to eight deities, one of which was the scum-bag Amun. To the left of the entrance, the relief was similarly repeated, this time with a depiction of the governor of Siwa whose only still-visible feature was a feather that stuck in what was left of his hair. The rest of him was gone too, ground away by crushing sand, or raiders and vandals, but he again offered wine to eight deities.

Here was King Amasis. He was the last great Egyptian pharaoh and possibly a descendant of a hybrid like me. Sutekh-irdes, the feathered man, on the other hand, was definitely a human – the chief of the desert dwellers he was called, if my bedtime stories served me.

Hmm. Something about it bothered me.

"Hey guys, can you come check this out?"

They joined me in front of the reliefs.

"This guy's probably some kind of hybrid and this one is definitely a human. I'm not sure what it is, but something strikes me as odd about this pairing."

I walked the wall. Beside the last deity on the chief's side, was an odd blank space. It seemed out of place there all alone, so I checked it. I considered how crazy this felt, but sucked in a breath when my finger found a deep groove under the smooth-seeming mortar. There was something there. Or more fittingly – there was something once here – a doorway that was now sealed off.

A rock crashed again nearby and the rain beat down on us even harder. The evening was more than cool now because of the pounding rain and shrinking sun too. I caught sight of Amisi. She shuddered through her entire small frame and her big gray eyes darted around to find its source. It was far enough away not to do us damage, but she quickly left off what she was doing and went to stand with Ryan.

"Look here." Alexandra called out on the King's side above the din of the pounding rain. A smear of red glistened on the wall. "Here." She pointed to Amun's vase. "Ancient paint wouldn't smear like this? What is it?"

The normally bone-dry temple was being saturated. Ryan brought his tool over and scanned the substance. "It's blood." He tapped something on his screen. Another window opened. He looked floored. "Elaine's blood!"

"Hey! Over here!" I called out from the other relief. "It's over here too." I pointed to the goddess Tefnut's wine vase. Ryan ran his scanner again. I thought he would drop his device, but he quickly scrolled through his programs again. "This one's Joe's."

Amisi got out a knife.

"What are you doing?" Ryan asked as Amisi slit open the tip of her finger. He was green. I watched the blood pool there. This was an interesting reversal.

"Your turn." She handed me the knife. I nearly fainted.

Alexandra stepped in front of me. "Boys." She wiped the blade clean on her wet jeans and punctured her finger quickly. She winced, but she stood her ground.

The girls walked over to their respective kin. "I hope this will work with a half-blood." Alexandra laughed nervously. "I'm only half human."

"On three." Amisi stood next to Amun's vase.

"On three." Alexandra stood next to Tefnut, the goddess of moistures, depiction.

"One. Two. Three." They said it together, offering the blood off their fingers to the vases as Joe and Elaine had done.

Nothing happened.

Well darn it. I guess I need to fly back to town and get a full-on human's blood. Oh great! Now I am turning into a vampire. I knew this would happen.

We stood together in disappointment. Maybe nothing happened when dad and Elaine did it too? But then, the hidden doorway beside the last deity on the governor's side rumbled, and non-human colors emanated from the edges of the sealed entrance.

"Yes!" Alexandra fist pumped.

Light shone out and consumed the stone filling the space until it was gone. A black gaping rectangular now stood in its place. I stepped in and held myself by the door jamb looking down. Don't worry. I didn't disappear into another dimension or anything, but I did get a sense of vertigo, because the doorway was the entrance to a long dark shaft that dropped down into oblivion.

"After you ladies," I suggested, offering my hand to anyone who would take it.

"Not this time." Alexandra pushed me into the hole. I dropped down, down, down, but slowed myself so I didn't break anything before I splashed into water at the bottom of the pit. Rain came in from somewhere above filling the shaft quickly.

I yelled up. "It's okay down here, but it's full of water. We should be fine though." I remembered my lesson in the mini dome. We could breathe under water.

"How deep is it?" Alexandra called down.

I took a quick peak, swimming down, holding my breath the old-fashioned way. "I'd say about 12 feet."

Pretty deep.

"Move to the side."

I did and just in time too, because Alexandra did a graceful slow motion dive into the water beside me. She spit water in my face as she came up and laughed.

"Your turn guys," we called up, but there was only silence.

Alexandra flew up to see what was happening.

"The wall's filling back in. Come on!" I heard her try to yell to them, but it was useless. They didn't answer.

She descended slowly this time, hovering down. "I watched their mouths moving, but I couldn't hear a thing. They're trapped on the other side. There was nothing I could do."

"Interesting perspective. I'd say we're the ones who are trapped."

I was glad for once I wasn't claustrophobic.

There was only one direction we could go now.

Down.

"Come on. I think you know what we have to do."

Alexandra shook her head and disappeared below the water first.

It was uncomfortable doing it again, but I let the water fill my lungs until I could breathe and swam through the murky water until I caught site of Alexandra's feet kicking below. The light that flooded down from far above us faded this far down until we were left in uncomfortable shadows. Yet muck and dirt still swirled visibly around her limbs as she propelled herself down to the bottom where another doorway fed a flooded hall.

It was our only way out though, so we swam in. Alexandra's feet kicked right in front of my face, stirring the water even more. The hall became pitch black, but then a new light glowed, lighting the passageway enough so that it became a murky cocoon of water. The light emanated from Alexandra's wrist.

Cool trick.

We swam to the end of the hall where a cave in blocked another door.

Maybe this wasn't here when dad came? He was here? Right? That was his blood upstairs on that relief. We were on the right path. The thought was thrilling.

"Stand back," I willed the words in my mind to Alexandra. It felt warm and comfortable as I connected.

"What?" Her voice was clear in my head. She pointed to her ears. "You sound like a bad cell signal."

"Stand back!" This time, when I motioned for her to move, she did – whether from the telepathy or the hand signals, I'm not sure which.

I felt my Bau grow heavy and I moved the rocks forward slowly one at a time. Water poured out of the hall, but then I got overconfident and the rocks filling the door shot out like cannons into whatever the next room held. The pressure of the built-up water rocketed us out of the shaft into a wide-open cavern, dispersing so quickly, we rode the white water until we found ourselves catapulting down a muddy tunnel-like river that twisted and turned through an underground cave. I breathed normally again, but the air was cold and dank from disuse.

"Ahh!" Alexandra screamed as she hooked and took a different tunnel. She disappeared into the honeycombed rock. I didn't have time to think before I slip-slided into another myself. The shaft I twisted down was slick with water and mud. I whipped around turns at ever-increasing speeds until I was completely covered in mud. I tried to wipe my eyes free, because I would catch glimpses of Alexandra through the latticework of rock when I wasn't blinded by the muck. Specks of light from her still-glowing hands kept peeking through.

"Alexandra!" I called out to her telepathically.

"Gil!" she screamed right back into my head. Her mind nearly burned me this time.

The light got brighter through the latticework and my tunnel hooked right. Shooting out into yet a bigger cavern still deeper in the earth, Alexandra careened into me from the shaft to my right. We grabbed each other and held tight.

The force of our collision whipped us around in a circle though, so now we turned in sickening twists as we plummeted down into yet another opening – but this time together. We slid in those nausea-inducing circles until the shaft ended abruptly and the earth fell away. We screamed as we let go of each other and dropped into a cavern lake filled with fluorescent fish, most of them huge.

The water was colder than the air and my body shook so hard from the temperature change, the water rippled. Alexandra came up gasping and we swam for each other. When she got close enough, she spun left to right, right to left, taking it all in. Then the light faded from her hands until the only light left was from the massive scary fish moving slowly beneath us.

The lack of light helped though, because it was then we noticed an odd-shaped square of light glowing at the bottom of the lake. Alexandra hunched her shoulders and dove into the water toward it. But she shot back up just as quickly coughing violently. "I can't breathe the water! Salt. It's filled with salt!"

I stuck my head in and tried it myself. I nearly gagged, but I could stand the burning – unlike Alexandra. "It's not super comfortable or anything, but I can. I'll swim down and check."

Just then rock fell from somewhere up above. A big slow-moving fish startled below us and whipped out of the way suddenly, knocking into Alexandra. She was flung like a rag doll and floated limply in the water ten feet away.

"Alexandra!"

She didn't respond.

I swam over, and just in time too, because something above gave way with a groan and crack and rock careened into the lake from above us. Alexandra came to and I pulled her to my side, throwing my hand out to form a shield above us like Ryan. I was surprised by the weight of the rocks. They bore down on me, slowing crushing against my powers. I was too new at all this and I was already exhausted. The rocks pushed against me and my face read like a book. The strain was nearly too much.

Alexandra tried to raise her arm to help, but it was dead weight.

Her eyes fluttered. "You have to let me go." She spoke quietly into my head.

She knew I was in trouble.

"This is too important. The answers are down there." Her face was slack and unnatural. "We're on the right path. You know it now. We can save the Earth. You can save it still, Gil," she corrected. Her mental voice went quieter with that realization.

What was wrong with her to talk like this?

"There. Down there." She tried to nod her head in the direction of the square of light below our feet, but it just rolled. Her eyes brimmed with tears, and she tried to pull away from me. But I held her tightly.

"Are you kidding me? I'm not letting you go!" I yelled out loud. "Good ancient false gods, you are fatalistic!" Adrenaline surged through me and I pushed out through my hand. She made me angry. There was no way I was losing her. Not for billions of lives. It was hers alone I wanted to protect. I couldn't lose her. The rock above us rose slightly at this burst of heated energy.

Her eyes fluttered as I held her in the cold water, my body somehow finally still. She reached her hand for my face. Wounded as she was, she acted without her usual restraint. "You never give up do you?"

"Not when you're involved." She said nothing, but she heard me. Her eyes fluttered again and half closed.

I was desperate. My Bau was fatiguing. My eyes searched everywhere and nowhere all at once. I had to save her. There had to be a way. I had to jog her slightly to wake her. This was so unlike her. She was practically limp. I wasn't even sure she was still conscious anymore. Her eyes hung open glassy this time.

Oh, God, please let her not be dead.

All around me, falling rock, choking water, giant fish. All of it was capable of killing us. None of it could help.

Unless.

I wasn't so good at the telepathy thing. I talked to ships, mumbled to Alexandra. Could I catch the mind of a simple fish?

I tried it.

I focused my attention on a massive whale of a creature far down below and waited. It shot up through the water, its mouth open in a gaping hole.

Ah! Maybe this wasn't such a good idea!

The fish's massive body was translucent. Its guts and veins bulged purple, red and black under its scales as it approached. But it also glowed phosphorescent too, allowing me to see it in all its horrible glory. It turned its eye on me at the last second and swallowed the two of us whole. Water poured out of its mouth like a waterfall as it arced above the lake. Then it closed its mouth tight as we dove, so we had the privilege of air along with a great view of the other titan fish swimming around its clear body as we rocketed back down to the bottom of the lake.

The fish was fast moving and avoided the falling rocks by swimming zigzag through the water, sending an already hurt Alexandra tumbling around its massive slimy sandpaper tongue. The air wouldn't last forever and I willed it to swim quickly for the square of light below. I didn't know what would happen when we got there, but I felt sure it was our only hope.

The fish stopped in front of the light and I tried my best to thank it. I think it was confused at first we wouldn't be a permanent meal, but its mind was simple and it accepted without much fuss. It swam in front of the doorway of light and let me take it in a moment before expelling us. I was pretty sure there was something behind the blue light. The material was similar to the stuff that made up the mini dome we practiced in, so I was confident for the first time in 20 minutes.

It was something at least.

Alexandra was semi-conscious now and looked around in wonder realizing where she was at. A slow smile spread across her face as she planted a hesitant hand into the fish's spongy tongue and accepted my help. "Hold your breath, Alex." I gently took her in my arms. She pinched her nose lazily and took a deep breath. Her face was slightly spacey. Our fish friend opened its mouth and we burst across the barrier into a dry room filled with air.

Chapter 14–The Oracle at the Temple of Amun

Alexandra, semi-conscious and now fueled by adrenaline, looked around at the room we had fallen into. It was an underground temple of sorts. The thick dust that coated everything gave away its age but there were modern boot prints here too, still visible on the floor. And one of the prints was larger than the other. One a man's. The other a woman.

Dad and Elaine.

There was a wooden plank table off-center in the room and an alcove featuring a too-tall stone statue of a middle-aged woman sitting on a throne with one outstretched hand. She was completely made of chiseled gray marble, so beautiful Michelangelo himself could do no better. No paint adorned her, but it didn't matter. That would have only distracted from her perfection. In her extended palm-open hand, she held a ring embellished with green emeralds sized only for a woman's finger. Her stance was an invitation.

But I was wary.

"I wish Ryan was here." Alexandra limped over and traced her finger along an inscription on the dais the statue rested on. She had giant purple and black raging bruises on the back of her legs and arms. They grew worse by the minute, the color spreading like two shades of paint being stirred together. I tried to put it out of my mind and made my way over to see what she found.

"It's Arabic." I ran my fingers across the rough edged stone, piecing together some of the words. "I think its Egyptian Arabic, though. It's older."

"Seek Truth." I mouthed the words slowly. "Umm, this is 'ring' and I think here it says 'bearer' or 'wearer.' I'm not sure."

Alexandra faltered and I rested my hand on her back. She leaned back into me, worrying me even more.

"I think you know what I have to do."

The extended hand was an invitation.

I nodded my head in agreement. I didn't want to let her do it, but I stepped back.

I hope this will work.

Alexandra approached the statue's hand. She reached out and her hand hung there in the air. "I'm going to borrow this for a minute. Please no Indiana Jones and the Last Crusade stuff today, okay? I don't think I can take anymore."

The statue stared blankly ahead. "Yeah, okay."

Alexandra took the ring from her hand without a problem. Sighing in relief, she put it on her right index finger and slowly slipped it down, but became instantly rigid and trance-like with her hand outstretched just like the statue, turning to face me, just as it did.

It was creepy, but then it got worse.

The stone lady stood up to mimic Alexandra. When the statue moved, Alexandra did as well, like they were tied together. The statue moved her mouth and a deep woman's voice emanated from both her and Alexandra's lips in echoing stereo.

"I am the Oracle of Amun and I wake for a second time in two millennia in so many weeks. What fate do you seek, child? Approach."

Huh, the oracle was a girl.

I didn't know who was calling me, but walked closer and chose to kneel below the stone ladies' living hard eyes. "Gilbert Scott, uh," I stammered, "my lady, from California."

She touched my head. Alexandra made the same motion in the air, but remained standing where she was.

Creepy.

The Oracle spoke slowly, deliberately. "Ah." A shiver coursed through the rock she was made of when she touched me. "You are finally come Gilbert Alastair Scott. The fates named you long ago. Your destiny lies in the Knot of Isis."

My heart raced hearing her words.

The statue stopped talking then, but Alexandra stepped forward. The strange voice that came from her mouth was different now, deep, unnaturally slow and monotone, but with a scary undertone. She looked into my soul and spoke. "You possess your blood, Isis. You possess your power, Isis. You possess your magic, Isis. The amulet is a protection for this Great One, created to drive off anyone who would harm her."

Alexandra became still.

The Book of the Dead. She was quoting from the Book of the Dead.

The statue spoke with no emotion, Alexandra again copying and voicing her words. "The girl Isis lies hidden in the knot, but even now the knot unravels and the Earth dies with her. The blood she possesses drains from her. Her power dies next and her heka. Her magic."

The Oracle held her hands out and a round hazy ball formed there. The haze swirled into focus and I could see Isis as she was today, hidden in the knot – the thing I thought of as her time warp. Her head bled from its crown and dripped into her open eyes, but she could not blink to clear them. It was a disturbing picture, adding to the fact that tentacles reached out from the Aten and held my dad and Elaine there as well. They had come too close to it and paid the price. They too were frozen.

The vision evaporated. "The Aten takes these as payment for its sacrifice. But when she loses all her gifts, then the Earth will be called into the Aten as ultimate resolution. Without the key it calls to itself, the Aten will choose its own life. It will not die to protect the girl, and it will consume its host planet to save itself. It has happened before."

She stood still as a statue.

Scary.

"But," she intoned, "there is one who was fated from time to save the Earth. But fate and choice may destroy one and save another. There is a choice, Gil Scott. A choice that must be made."

I couldn't believe I was talking to the ancient Oracle. "You spoke to Isis and Ra long ago. You told them about me?"

"Yes. You have eyes to see Gil Scott. They wait for you in the belly of Palenque. But first you must find the library of Egypt's rescuer. It hides but for those who seek truth. There you will find the path."

And with that, she walked backwards into the alcove. Then time reversed itself. The ring slipped back onto the Oracle's open hand from Alexandra's finger. We fell into the fish's mouth through the electric barrier and shot backwards to the surface. I held back the rocks. Then, I helped a just-hurt Alexandra. We swam in circles round each other and away. We fell up into the twisting veins of the cavern where we hugged each other tightly and spun in circles back up to the surface, back through the burst rock wall that closed itself and sealed us in the water-filled hall, backwards into the black shaft where Alexandra went up and down, then swan dived gracefully up to the open doorway, followed by me flailing my way up to the door too where I looked down and leaned back. I walked a step backwards and witnessed the door seal itself shut.

I said the words, "ladies you After." Ryan and Amisi laughed. Alexandra fist pumped, said "Yes," and then fainted with blood flowing out her finger and the knife clacking to the ground. Time started forward again.

"Oh no!" Ryan exclaimed. "She fainted."

I raced to Alexandra and checked the back of her legs and arms, much to Amisi's confused disapproval. The bruises from the glowing fish were gone. Alexandra got up and proceeded to check her own arms and legs, much to Amisi and Ryan's continued bewilderment.

"It didn't work." Amisi's shoulders drooped, but Alexandra and I jumped up and hugged each other tightly, blue sparks flaring.

"We did it. I can't believe we did it! And I'm okay now." She showed me the back of her legs. "No more bruises." She ignored the sparks.

Ryan and Amisi stood staring.

"We did nothing."

"No. We absolutely did do something. We just visited the Oracle and we have an idea of where to go next." I grabbed Alexandra by the arm, yanking her up into the air. "We'll explain on the way back to Neter."

And off we flew.

■■■■■

Their bewilderment grew exponentially as we made it back to the ship to consult with one another, but they believed us. After all, Alexandra hadn't tried to blast me with mini lightning bolts in quite a while.

Ryan held two fingers against his forehead. "It's not like you even disappeared and came back. You were there with us the whole time! I can't wrap my head around it."

"I think that's the point," Amisi said. "She wouldn't be an oracle without being mystical. She even spoke in riddles, for goodness' sake."

Ryan raised his eyebrows at that.

Alexandra was quiet.

"Woo whoo," Ryan made ghost noises. He could be so sarcastic. "So, the grr-eat lady of the lake said we needed to find 'the library of Egypt's rescuer?' Okay then. Let's do that."

"Already on it." Amisi typed into Google. The screen populated itself and she scrolled. "Umm, I'm getting results like Egyptian National Library. Oh, and here's one about a bunch of rare books being burned after a protest. Sad."

"Seems to be a habit around this place." Ryan took a bite of an apple squirting juice all over my arm. "First the Great Library of Alexandria was torched and now that place. Egypt's got a book-torching problem."

He went on chewing.

We all stared daggers at him.

"What?" He spit little apple bits at me as he talked. Crossing his arms over his chest, he leaned back.

"You're a genius, Ryan. The Great Library of Alexandria! That's got to be it. Alexander the Great commissioned it after he rescued Egypt from the Persians. He was the guy who the Oracle called the Son of Amun. It all fits."

"Sometimes you can be annoying, Gil, you know that?" Ryan threw the apple core at me. It exploded in a billion little bits off my arm. Neter frowned and disappeared from the monitors. Ryan was picking up my bad habits. "You make it hard sometimes to forget you're the son of an Egyptologist."

"What can I say? I paid attention. Those were my bedtime stories."

"Right. Well, anyway." Ryan leaned forward and rubbed his eyes. "I already did think of that, but Alexander didn't build it. His friend Ptolemy did, after he died. See." He lifted his iPad.

"You're right." Amisi peered at the screen like she needed glasses, but I'd seen her shoot an apple off a tree from 50 feet. She grabbed it from him and typed a new query. She read through her results while Ryan got up for another apple, picking up most of the one he had thrown on the floor.

"Here," she pointed and joined him on the couch where he'd gone back to relax. We were in the ship's lounge. "But without Alexander's vision, the library would never have been built. Maybe smarty pants over there is right."

I waved. I was on the ground at Alexandra's feet by the coffee table. "It's the kind of answer my dad would have come up with." I put my head down on it. My brain was slowing down with fatigue. "Okay, so where is the library?" My voice was muffled by my arm. "I hope it's nearby."

"I'm guessing in Alexandria, on the coast." Ryan tossed his second apple core and this time it landed in the trash. Neter reappeared. "The Great Library of Alexandria," he intoned sarcastically.

Amisi ignored him. "There's one problem, guys." Her face fell. "I'm pretty sure I know what the Oracle meant about the library being hidden. There's no ruin. Nothing. It's not on any map. No one even knows where it's at."

"What are you talking about? It's probably a seriously cool tourist attraction."

"No. Don't you remember, Ryan? It burned down so many times, it just sort of went away." She motioned in the air like a bird flying off. "Then there was a tsunami." She went back to scrolling and pointed at her screen. "And part of the city slid into the Mediterranean. Yep. It's all here. Modern Alexandria was built so quickly, they built on top of ruins. So no one knows where it is. The library is buried somewhere under Alexandria." She threw her hands up in frustration. "They can't even find the tomb of Alexander the Great!"

"Well that isn't good." Ryan looked at me like I might magically know something.

"Hey, no! I'm only 17, remember? You were supposed to leave me at home."

We all laughed, but didn't know what to do next.

"I say we head for Alexandria and," Alexandra finally spoke. She yawned so big just then my Aunt Vera would have said she'd catch flies in her mouth if she didn't shut it. "And, get some sleep. We'll figure the rest out in the morning."

We all agreed. It was late.

My head felt like it was filled with cotton balls by now.

Ryan gave Neter the coordinates for a secluded place to land near Alexandria and he and Amisi left for their bunk rooms, Ryan slipping his arm around Amisi's waist as the door shut. But I stuck around to wait for Alexandra. She was still packing up, so I leaned down to tie my shoes. She put her tablet in her bag last, zipped it up, and walked away without saying goodbye.

Wow. Cold.

Now wasn't a good time for her to return to her whole bi-polar thing.

"Hey. Hey! Wait up, Alexandra!" I ran over and grabbed her arm again before she could leave.

She flinched.

I let go, a sudden flood of cold reaching through me.

"What's the matter?" My hands dropped to my sides. I wasn't sure what to do with them. My touch bothered her – again. "I thought we were beyond all that now?"

"Beyond all what?" Alexandra turned away. She wouldn't even make eye contact. But she knew what I was talking about.

The icy chill reached deeper.

My voice was raw as I turned her shoulders so she had to face me. "I think you know what I mean? After everything that's happened between us, this is how you act?"

She spun away out of my grasp so she didn't have to face me, but I wouldn't let her. I took her hand in mine and pulled her around. I wasn't letting go this time. I held it firm.

Her eyes found mine, unwillingly. A single tear hung in the corner of one eye. She was tyring to hide it. "You couldn't understand," she gulped but didn't try to pull away. "I'm trying to be your friend, Gil. Isn't that enough?"

How could I answer that?

No! I wanted to scream.

Instead, I swallowed, tried to talk, but nothing came out. Squeezing her hand, I took the other. They fit perfectly in mine. Like they belonged there. We stood face to face. I had locked her hands down and her eyes; I held them prisoner with my own.

"I don't understand," I finally found my voice. I shook my head at her. "I don't want to be just friends and neither do you." This was blunt. "We never have. Not since the moment I met you. Why are you so at war with yourself? You're killing me."

Huge tears filled her eyes then and rolled down her face. There was no stopping them. She tried to speak but only air came out. She had lost her voice and pulled at my hands to release her. But I pulled back. And this time, everything that had been building inside me. Everything that had been building inside her. All the desire and fight and confusion spilled over and I pulled her into me. No hesitation.

Our lips found each other's with desperation. For once, I wasn't alone. We collided like a billion protons smashing together, all the energy of the universe released in their explosion. Our hands, finally free, came up reaching, pulling, tugging at each other as if we might finally be able to fill them. They had been empty too long.

I felt her heart pounding against my chest, and her breath catch in small gasps, but who needed oxygen when they had this? My heart pounded along with hers, and a racing happy fever spread through my arms and legs and chest and everywhere. Blue sparks danced madly between us.

She tasted of salt, then honey.

This was like a fever breaking.

She made a little noise, like desperation.

And the spell broke.

"No. No, Gil!" she practically screamed. "I can't."

She pushed me away. The separation felt like my soul being ripped from my body. I watched as little blue sparks of electricity fell away from between us to the ground to extinguish themselves. She choked back a cry and covered her mouth.

But her eyes were hers again. Fear there.

"Oh, stars! Never again. Please. This," her voice broke with unadulterated sadness. "This can never happen."

Crying because she couldn't control herself for once, she ran away, leaving me alone, speechless and confused.

My hands empty of hers yet again.

■■■■

I lay down on the bed with exhaustion so complete nothing could keep me from sleep. I couldn't keep my eyes open if I wanted to. What had just happened?

This time when I slept, though, I dreamt of nothing. It was the best rest I'd had in weeks.

■■■■

When I woke, I wandered groggily into the lounge where Alexandra, my Alexandra, I thought possessively, lay on the couch with a pillow over her head.

Something wasn't right.

I kneeled down next to her on the ground, but I didn't touch her. "What's wrong?"

"The dreams." Her eyes were wary, still she spoke. "I didn't think they would be so bad."

"What are you talking about?"

"I dreamed your crazy dreams last night. Every time I woke up and went back to sleep, another dream."

"Did you try to talk to her?" I got up to sit in the arm chair so she had more space.

"Yeah, a few times." She tried to sound casual. "But she ignored me and only talked to you. Didn't you hear her?"

"No. I wasn't in the dreams. I only slept last night."

Ryan walked in then with a backpack slung across his shoulders and shook her. "Get up lazy!"

"No way." She threw her pillow at him. "I dreamed Gil's crazy dreams last night." She refused to raise her head.

The next thing we knew, she snored. There was nothing pretty about that. I had to laugh or else I would cry. We left her alone to sleep it off, and grabbed a quick breakfast without her. Amisi joined us and we sat talking, discussing the huge storm systems that rocked the planet yesterday, when Alexandra shot up with a start.

"Okay! Alright! That was weird."

She rubbed her eyes hard.

"What are dreaming about now?"

"Ugh." She hung her head. "I was at a library, but this preachy old librarian wouldn't let me past the front desk without my library card.

She told me I could come as the guest of someone with one and showed it to me. But I'd never seen anything like it. Then she dropped her glasses, and when she bent to pick them up, there was a tattoo of the Oracle on her neck and another of the Oasen star Juniper. And inscribed on the wall, right where she had blocked my view standing, were the words Bibliotheca Alexandrina. She stood up and winked at me and the whole library became old and she became young. Then I woke up!"

"What did the card look like?" Amisi's voice was clipped.

Alexandra squinted at her. "It was a little square card, clear, kind of thick, with a silver star burst on the top right corner. The star moved when it caught the light."

"Did you see her name on the card?" Her voice was cautious.

Alexandra thought for a minute. "I think it may have been Sasha? Something like that?"

"Was it Seshat?" Ran was fidgeting now.

"It could be? Why?"

"Because that was the name of the historian on the Barque crew. And she wasn't an Oasen. She was a Nyad."

Ryan got up, walking fast for the door.

"What's a Nyad?"

He stopped in the doorway. "It's a species from another planet in our solar system, Neuriiata. Oasens and Nyads sort of grew up together."

Ryan bolted up. "Do you have it still then?"

"Yea. I think so."

"Okay, go get it. Hurry."

"Nyads are shape shifters." Amisi had turned to us. "They live even longer than Oasens because when they shift, they rebuild their DNA each time. They can basically live forever if they aren't hurt or maimed. And they can manipulate people's minds. You know, make them think they are somewhere when they aren't. Manipulate emotions. That kind of thing. And maybe, just maybe, they can dream walk? Who knew?"

Now my curiosity was peaked.

Amisi kept looking at the door. "What's taking him so long?" She got up and walked out.

"Those two are acting weird." That was ironic considering what was going on between the two of us. But before we had time to discuss it, they rushed back. Amisi must have met him in the hall.

"Was it like this?" Ryan held something.

Alexandra grabbed the card. "Where'd you get that?"

"It was my library card on Oases. I brought all my stuff with me."

Amisi pulled another one from her pocket. "I know it's weird, right? But I keep it close because it makes me feel nearer to home. I was the ship's historian after all."

"So, we need to find that library then." I shook my head and the others nodded their heads in assent. Alexandra grabbed a bagel, and we made our way out to the jeep to search for a needle in a haystack. Wait. Scratch that. We made our way out to track down an ancient library hidden in a metropolis. Fun times. But at least the weather was nice today.

Chapter 15-Hidden in plain sight

The Bibliotheca Alexandrina rises like a sun dial from the Mediterranean Sea. Sitting on the edge of the ocean, its huge round, tilted glass roof ascends at an angle from a pool of water, only protected from flooding at its lowest point by a curved dam that holds back the tide. This dam wraps around it, allowing the water to curve gracefully around the building. Inside, 11 levels cascade down through the building leaving room to hold eight million books. It was the Great Library of Alexandria reborn.

We stood in the lobby staring up at each floor, open to the one below. Honeyed hardwood floors warmed the space and huge soaring pillars of Aswan granite held up the slanted roof. Carved text from more than 120 languages graced the granite walls and light poured in from above. It was a sight to behold. While some people sat quietly reading, others, like us, stood jaw dropped taking in the splendor of it.

"Now what do we do?" Alexandra brought us back to reality.

We had come to the reincarnated Library of Alexandria on a hunch. If we couldn't find the old one, perhaps the new one had what we needed. We must have looked confused though, because a young man with a pot-marked face and a crisp uniform soon approached.

"May I help you?"

"Yes, um." Ryan read his map. "We're looking for the museum of antiquities, I think." He turned the map all different directions trying to orient himself.

"Ah, yes." The young man had a heavy accent. He leaned over Ryan's arm, stopping his wild movements, and pointed. "You will find it here."

"Good, thanks."

The young man walked away, job done.

Ryan talked to himself again. "Now, if only Seshat would give us one more hint."

The young man abruptly stopped. He approached again. "Excuse me sir. Maybe I can be of more assistance to you." He reached out and put his hand on Ryan's forearm. Ryan flinched and his face flushed. "Ah yes. Yes I can. I realize now what you truly desire. Would you please come with me?"

Ryan didn't say a word, but followed like the young man had him on a tractor beam. We went with it too, following on his heals to a nearby bank of elevators. Potmark called the lift, softly rocking on his feet, avoiding eye contact with us while we waited, then followed him on. The doors were almost closed when someone forced a hand in and they bounced back.

Our guide took a step back as the intruder pressed in. He wore heavy black glasses and a muted striped turban. His skin was olive and he had an air of aristocracy and overconfidence that made me dislike him at once. Without a word, he leaned against the wall imperiously, his heavy robes rustling as they settled. He was surprisingly young with the start of a clean-lined beard and his face was all perfect angles, but he was hidden under too many layers of stuff to really tell.

Our guide eyed the turban-wearing man and shook his head like he was ridding himself of some memory. There was a hostile energy radiating off the young man but the guide, ever the professional, collected himself, and asked him a single question, extending his hand: "Do you have your library card?"

"Of course," he said with a voice like gravel being raked, and pushed his glasses over his dark eyes and searched his pocket. "Here it is. Now let's carry on." He didn't smile.

Our guide tisked and handed it back. "No sir, I am afraid you do not have the correct clearance for our restricted level. Here you are." He handed back his card and pressed the door open button. "I'm sure you understand. You must have the correct clearance for this level. And you do not." Our guide gestured with his hand to show him off.

The young man blinked twice and backed out. The doors closed soundlessly on him.

"Now, then. Cards please?"

It was now or never. Amisi and Ryan produced their Oasen library cards, handing them over. I held my breath.

"Thank you. That will do." The attendant pressed a sequence of buttons and the elevator lurched. He gave the cards back and then morphed into a beautiful, and I mean, BEAUTIFUL, young woman. The boy's dark hair grew into a long mass of black ringlets that framed a pink perfect porcelain face. Full lips, dark mysterious eyes and graceful proportions all fit the happy-seeming Nyad who now stood before us in her simple linen shift, tied with a gold belt.

"Seshat, is that really you. You're alive?" Amisi boldly hugged the girl, who squeezed her right back. "We thought you had all left or worse."

"Yes, little one, it is me. Alive even, yes." She patted Amisi's arm. "You have come to the house of an old, old lady though. I have been hiding here for millennia all by myself, guarding our knowledge or what was left of it. Just bits and pieces. It's mostly old human relics I hide away now." Seshat had a distracted quality. "Thank goodness for this new library. I was getting quite bored."

She stopped. "How did you find me anyway? I've been alone here forever, and then I get two visits within weeks. Did that Oracle send you to me too?"

My mouth practically hit the floor.

"My father," I stammered. "My dad was here? Joe? And the other Oasen, Elaine? Were they here?" I talked way too fast.

Seshat mimicked my anxious face as I spoke, but settled back into her placid expression. She crossed her hands delicately in front of her. "Yes, dear. They were here, asking about the temple that sweet, but hot-head Ra built to hide his love. Is that the one?" Her head tilted to the side, questioning.

"Yes." I fell against the wall of the elevator. My dad was here. We were on the right path. She knew about the temple too. "But we have to track down my dad," I blurted out. "We have to find that temple too."

"I'm glad they found it. But if that's the case, why the hurry?"

"Because the Aten trapped them after they found it. The girl in the knot told me as much. But we have no clue where they are either!"

Seshat's face went slack, but I went on explaining.

"It has him and Elaine trapped, right alongside Isis, in the knot. The thing is, the knot is unraveling and it's unraveling fast, and we're trying to save the Earth, so we need to know where Ra hid her, so we can try and get her out and save the world before the Aten destroys it!" I took a breath. "That's basically it." It was the best book jacket explanation I could give in 15 seconds. I wondered if it was okay for me to collapse again now.

"Oh dear." Seshat pinched her nose. "Something's gone awry. I didn't realize the time had come already. I guess it was fated to happen and one cannot stop the fractals of time. That over-bearing Oracle knows a thing or two about that. Humph."

Seshat's serene guise masked whatever else she may have thought.

The elevator came to a jerking stop, interrupting her. "Ah, here we are." We had descended deep into the earth. "I've had a lot of time on my hands," offered Seshat as we stepped out and looked around. "Alexandria is built antiquity upon antiquity. A veritable cake of time and culture with the sweet icing of new on top." She pointed up to where the new Bibliotecha Alexandria sat somewhere above us. "I couldn't let all of this go to waste though, now could I?"

A city lay before us, an underground labyrinth. Seshat had been excavating and preserving the old city for years. The door opened on another world. We stepped out onto the dusty, old and cobbled streets of ancient Alexandria. Everything here was preserved.

"Look." She waved her hands in the air. The old streets and buildings suddenly became new. Horses clopped through the streets and women sold wares on the corner. A funeral procession marched down the street holding a gilded coffin. People wept and others laughed. The vision ended.

Seshat could manipulate our minds. Wow. It had felt so real; it had even smelled like it must have back then, a mix of spice and heat and animal dung and sweat and even dirt. But even with all that, it had been intoxicating and beautiful.

"I miss the past. It was a quieter time in history. The people were so much simpler. It was good for us to live so humbly."

My mind spun. I couldn't quite pair pretending to be gods with a humble existence, but there would be time for questions later. "That was cool," I said instead, taking in the old buildings studding the lane. Somewhere light lit the streets like the sun.

"How did you stay hidden from Amun's troops though?"

She had that coy look of hers ready. "It is easy for a shape shifter like myself to stay hidden. I have many tricks at my disposal." Her fingers thrummed the air like she was playing a harp. "They never had a chance." She laughed as she danced down the street. It sounded like bells ringing, but she cleared her throat quickly and was quiet again.

"What happened to everyone else?"

Her eyes became dark and stormy. "It was chaos boy." Her curt answer was startling after all her gaiety. "We were unorganized when they came. Some were able to flee. Others died. Still others may have hid. I do not know. Only Ra knew what was coming. The Oracle probably. She sees things in her dimension we cannot." Her eyes drifted away to something unseen.

"And he was the keeper of the Aten, in the locket," I fished.

"Yes, he was. He was the match. But the Aten is a fickle thing. It is hungrier for knowledge than even me!" At that, she laughed again. "But, yes. Ra was the last keeper of the Aten. It found him, you know? As soon as we came, it called to him. He understood it in a way I could not." This didn't please her. "But then again, his profile was such a near match for the thing. They were so compatible, they connected almost seamlessly. Just about, that is."

"What do you mean?"

"The Aten is a curious thing. It is rooted in biology, but nonetheless, it is a mechanical thing. Artificial intelligence you might call it. A computer. It calculates coldly, ruthlessly when necessary. Other times, it acts with kindness."

Seshat abruptly stopped and crossed her hands, like she was a tour guide ready to explain the next attraction. We were in front of a Temple of Isis. "However, I digress," she said. "From what Ra explained to me, the Aten is linked to Oasens and humans on a biologic level. It was probably sourced from your own ancient joining."

Joining?

"It always seeks its key. Even a near match keeps it in peace."

"The key," I blurted out, remembering. Do you know about the key? I nearly forgot."

"Yes. The Aten knows there is a new key. A much better key. It can sense it. It calls to it, but it is hidden in the belly of Palenque where it cannot be found as yet. Is it not?"

"The key is in Palenque?" I was confused.

"You will see. But I am forbidden to say more. You will make your choice when the time comes."

"Why all these riddles?" Alexandra stomped. She was the kind of girl who made things happen. She didn't stand around waiting for things to fall into place. She put them in their place.

"Riddles upon riddles. Antiquities upon antiquities. So many hidden things, but hidden for good reasons," answered Seshat in her sing-song way. "Choices are made from choices. I cannot choose for you. If I do, I change the pattern. And the pattern must be fulfilled. It is known."

Seshat had been underground a little too long.

"Enough standing about." She clapped her hands, snapping me out of my inner dialogue and walked into Isis' temple. We followed her through its massive stone columns where she walked up to the dais.

"Should I bow down or something?" I asked under my breath. I wasn't impressed that the crew had decided to play gods to lowly evolving humans.

"Don't be impertinent, child!" Seshat slapped me hard across the back of my head. It stung. I held my head in shock.

Okay – so she heard me.

"Why would you say such a thing in a school for heaven's sake?"

"This is a temple," I spit out as I turned toward the arching ceiling atop us. "A magnificent, narcissistic place of self-worship."

"Humph. We will have to right this view immediately. An unfortunate turn of history, making them into deities. But, alas, as the Oasens always say, 'History without perspective can be quite flawed.' A poor translation 'god' and 'goddess'; more like 'being of great power, strength and knowledge.' Isis much preferred 'teacher' though and I do not blame her. We are all mortal here." Seshat shimmered a second and rebuilt her DNA. Her words must have reminded her that her mortality was a different thing.

"History without perspective," Amisi repeated, beaming with this new knowledge.

"But again. Let us get to it. Here. Approach, boy. I have kept this safe for many, many generations at Ra's command. He knew you would come just as I did. I have been waiting so long here for you. And you are finally come."

We approached the dais where a beautifully carved black and brass sphinx sat immobile. I remembered how the stone Oracle took on life before my eyes. Was this thing going to wake up too? I swallowed readying myself.

"Here. Please help." Seshat climbed on top of the sphinx' back like she was riding a horse. She put her weight behind the creature's head and pushed forward. Not knowing exactly what to do, Ryan and the rest of us tried our best to maneuver ourselves around it and pushed.

It creaked and groaned and then gave way with a little pop of pressure.

"The seam was well hidden. I concealed this in the bay and became a shroud of coral around its neck when they came. Not a chance. Not a chance." She was impressed by her own cleverness. "Thank you dear sphinx. You have long protected Egypt's secrets. Even now the great sphinx hides a great mystery. Humans may try, but they will always fail in the revelation of such things."

She shimmered again, reached in, and pulled out a scroll. "He left this here for you, Gil." Seshat took up the ancient scroll and carefully handed it over. "2,300 years before your birth, he knew you would hold this one day."

I swallowed but my mouth was dry and I nearly choked. I took the crumbling parchment from Seshat, showing it the respect its tender age required, and walked over to an old deeply-grooved stone table to roll it out. The corner was missing. My friends crowded around me. What mystery would we find this time?

On the paper was a note, quickly scribed:

Make the right choice, Gil Scott – for the sake of all love. Fate has offered you choices and you must choose wisely or all will be lost. But

I do, I put my faith in you to fulfill the promise. I do. I truly do.You must go to the eye of Ramses which chance or luck has chosen to save from its own watery grave. There you will find the path to the Torey where your journey is nearly at end. Gil – please make the right choice.

- Your brother Ra

"That's heavy." Ryan put his hand on my shoulder.

"Another mystery."

"Fate," Amisi added. "We have come this far. We will find the eye of Ramses."

"You certainly will. But it is the Torey I would worry most about." Seshat shivered, but this time out of concern.

"What is the Torey?" Amisi was ever curious.

"No what, but who," she corrected. "Who is the Torey? Someone who knows things. Just ask the Oracle. Even she fears her."

Seshat swept her hand across the dusty table. Its dull surface took on a polished shine as she manipulated our minds to see the past again. "But first come. There is a little time yet. We must follow the funeral procession. I simply must show you the grave of the Great Alexander before you leave. The poor humans will never find it down here."

Chapter 16-The tourist trap

We sat in a little corner eatery outside the library sipping a roast so dark someone might as well have hooked me up to a caffeine IV.

"I needed that."

"You needed that. I needed that." Alexandra took a big gulp. She was still groggy.

"Yeah, you did." I playfully shoved her; it was worth a try, but I immediately regretted it. She pushed me back so hard, I nearly fell out of my seat. Apparently that kind of thing was off limits now.

There were curious glances our way from the other patrons.

"What?" My face went red.

Alexandra didn't give it a second thought though. She was good at burying her feelings. I was well aware of that by now.

"Well, that was interesting," Ryan uttered through a mouthful of traditional Egyptian Ful. "Of course," he went on, "I'm talking about Seshat and not whatever that was." He waved his hand in our direction.

I smirked at him, but Alexandra remained detached.

He scooped another large bite into his mouth with a piece of hearty flat bread. Through his munching, he tried to give his opinion on the matter but it was unintelligible.

"What?" Even Amisi didn't understand him.

He swallowed. "I said we've got a decent clue. We have to find the eye of Ramses that was saved from a watery grave. Any ideas?" He pinched his forehead. "Aren't there like a million ancient statues of Ramses?"

I reached over Ryan's plate, grabbed a piece of his flat bread and stuffed it in my mouth, silencing myself. I had nothing either.

"Is it one of the statues they found in the sea?" Amisi pointed. "They destroyed a ton of artifacts rebuilding the breakwater in the bay before some French archeologist went scuba diving and discovered a treasure trove of ancient stuff out there." We had read about it in the brochure. The Antiquities Museum was filled with items that had been salvaged from the Mediterranean. Amisi flipped through the pages of a guide book she had picked up in the gift shop.

"There's nothing really here."

"It was a good thought anyway."

We became quiet again. A few of us pulled out our smart phones to get to Google. It was our answer to everything lately. But not Alexandra. She sat back and crossed her arms, staring straight ahead.

"What?"

"Nothing. Thought I saw someone."

I raised my eyebrows at her, but she wouldn't talk. She narrowed her eyes at me and then pretended to push a pair of glasses up her nose, making a horrified look of rejected confusion.

"Oh him. From the elevator?"

She nodded.

"Was it?"

"Not sure."

A noisy tour bus interrupted our exchange as it ambled by and stopped on our corner. There were advertisements plastered on its side. I read out loud. It gave me something to do. "One way flights to Aswan only $1,100 Egyptian pounds. See Abu Simbel at Lake Nassar,"

"That's pretty cheap. Only $160 US."

"Yeah, but look. Is that who I think it is?" Below the advertisement was a picture of three colossal statues of Ramses II sitting on thrones built into the side of a mountain, a gorgeous lake mirrored below it. A fourth lay broken off and fallen to the ground. The picture was taken at night and the electric lights at the base of each statue cast them in rich golden tones. Long shadows illuminated the details of each huge figure which sat enthroned in a recess carved into a hill, the open door of the temple entrance below a small figure of Ra with what must be the Aten crowning his head.

"Pretty," Amisi voiced. "How'd you know it was Ramses though?"

"It says it right there but it's written pretty small." I got up and walked over to the bus which idled in front of us. A few passengers were ambling on still. I followed the words with my finger as the bus pulled away. It was written in English. "Saved for all time. See the world's most magnificent temple, the sun temple of Ramses II and Nefertari. Hmm?"

"I got something." Alexandra held up her phone. "There's a Web site." She pointed to the bus which by now made its way down the street. "In 1964, they relocated those temples when they flooded the Nile Valley after building the Aswan High Dam. It says right here they cut the temples into 20-ton blocks and reassembled the entire thing 65 meters up and 200 meters back from the water in an artificial hill. That way the inside could be reconstructed too."

"So, are you saying those temples would have been underwater if they hadn't moved them?"

"That's exactly what I'm saying. Who knew fate and tour buses worked together?"

"I think the world is way more connected than I ever thought possible. Choices. Choices. Choices." I mimicked Seshat. "Thank goodness for Ryan's never-ending appetite. If he didn't choose this place, we would never have seen that."

I hit him on the back.

"What?" Ryan coughed through a mouthful of food. "Oh, yeah. No problem buddy," and he went back to his lunch.

■■■■■

We made it there by late afternoon. Thankfully, Neter didn't have any trouble finding a place to land. The temples of Ramses and Nefertari lay in a remote location 143 miles south of Aswan in Nubia, southern Egypt. She put down near an abandoned field of fig trees that hadn't been tended in some time. The few figs the trees still produced hung dry and dead on the branches.

The sky was painted with a pink-purple haze as we drove out of the ship in the jeep. We had the top down. The weather was oddly calm after so much chaos, disconcerting even, but we welcomed the wind in our face anyway. As we drove, I realized the air felt kind of heavy though, like energy had been bottled up and threatened to break forth in unexpected fury. Suddenly, I felt the need to hurry.

We arrived at the site, and I realized we had a huge problem. The two temples were crawling with tourists.

Okay, this was going to get interesting.

I shielded my eyes as we got out of the jeep. The sun beat down on the massive rolling dunes around us so that its blinding light refracted off the trillions of tiny grains like a giant mirror. Alone one grain of sand could do no harm; together they could blind you or grind your bones to dust where you'd join them in the dunes. It was a lesson any traveler to these sands should never fail to learn.

I took this all in as we bought our passes and walked up to the impressive sight with the other tourists. A strong desert wind blew, reminding me just where we were.

Egypt.

The wind was heavy with dust and sand and kicked up in great billowing clouds. I held my breath so I didn't fill my lungs with it, but it wasn't the dusty wind that suffocated as much as it was its weighty heat. Sweat poured off us as we approached. I tasted salt in the air and salt on my lips, which only served to remind me of Alexandra.

I shook off the thought. The statues loomed above me. Four thrones held the intimidating 65-1/2 foot tall statues of Ramses, though one had toppled. The figures sat bolt straight in their thrones. Staring straight ahead, the massive identical pharaohs rested their hands on their knees in a position of calm power.

Two each of the great statues sat to either side of the temple entrance. Above the doorway another recess held a carving of a now-familiar person.

"Hey, there's Ra with the Aten sitting on his head." Alexandra pointed at the central figure.

"His head looks kind of like an alien." Ryan laughed. The Aten weighed so heavy on the carving's head, it squished Ra's face into the familiar shape of Roswell, New Mexico's favorite green man. But Ra, not minding, stood straight and proud with his arms hanging to his side. Below his hands, stood the figures of two Jackals at the end of a long neck like a snake. They were like two tall staffs, standing at attention below each hand.

"There are a couple of statues of Ramses out here, some inside, and a bunch of other depictions. Got a hunch which eye we're after?"

"Maybe it's the one whose body and head fell off." I patted the head of the fallen figure of Ramses which lay at my feet. His crowned head lay splintered on the ground in front of his throne.

"He's cracked straight through the eyeballs." Alexandra peaked under the break which sat nearly entombed in sand. She felt under the eyes. "There's no secret levers or anything. Probably not this one."

We kept walking.

"Look. Their eyes are blanked out like my dream." I pointed up at one of the still-intact statues of Ramses. "I don't think that's a mistake. Maybe Ra gave him the white vision."

"These statues stare right into the sun too."

A tour guide walked a group up beside us. A few heavy-set men in Birkenstocks were with her. They talked loudly. Their wives wore heavy perfume and fanned themselves with gusto. It was hot out.

Welcome fellow Americans.

The polite young Egyptian woman guiding them motioned to the entrance of the temple. She continued talking to her group in perfectly accented English. "This solar phenomenon occurs twice a year, on October 22 and February 20, having moved a day forward due to the temple's relocation and the accrued drift of the Tropic of Cancer during the past 3,280 years. It is quite a sight to behold."

"What exactly happens," someone interrupted; flashing a picture as he talked, while chewing gum.

Wow. Talent.

She smiled sweetly. "The rays of the sun penetrate the sanctuary and illuminate the four statues who sit on their thrones against the back wall of the inner temple – all except the statue of Ptah, a god of the underworld. He always remains in darkness, of course. You will have to come again and see this great marvel when next it occurs."

That wouldn't be for another four months.

The tourists blocked the entrance to the temple.

"Excuse me, excuse me," Ryan called out loudly in mock imitation of the rude tourists. He shot a smile at the pretty young tour guide. She tipped her head and pushed her group out of the way.

"I've got to see this." He walked through the temple door into a long hallway guarded by eight statues of Osiris. We followed him in. The four Osiris pillars on each side of us made the walk an intimidating one. Their haunting eyes followed us the 200 feet walk to the back wall where Ptah, Amun, Ramses II and Ra sat waiting for the sun.

"Peace be to him," Ryan and Amisi mumbled under their breath with respect to Osiris.

Alexandra and I copied them and kept going. Several people were running out as we went in. Standing at the back of the temple, a young woman with black glossy hair in curly ringlets stood alone facing the statue of Ramses. Her long slender neck and pink perfect flesh was all too familiar.

"Ah, wonderful, you are here." Seshat turned and hugged each one of us like old friends. "Fate or wisdom or maybe some of both has brought you here. And I am glad to do my part. Fate has its hands upon me as well."

"Seshat, this is a surprise." Amisi hugged her back.

"Yes, well. That overbearing Oracle demanded my presence here long ago. You need to see here what cannot be seen now. And only I have that ability."

"You mean the sun? The next solar phenomenon is not until October. That's why you're here – to make it happen today."

"Yes, child. Ra hid the path well. His trust was great in those who lie along the line. If I'd chosen a wrong path these last 2,300 years, I would not be here for you today." She shimmered in the air. "I will bring you the sun, but you must do the rest. Are you ready or do you need time?"

"I don't know what you mean."

"You will boy."

And with that, Seshat, in dramatic fashion, threw her hands in the air. Her hair whipped out and energy poured forth from her hands in visible yet transparent waves that rippled the air. The energy pulsed out. I heard the tourists outside scream and run too as it reached those in its path.

"No one likes snakes." Seshat's vibrant giggles were in stark contrast to the screams of fear she just created. "Those especially clumsy Americans just found themselves a pit of vipers. They are all running away now."

With her hands in the air still, she boldly walked out toward the great statues of Ramses standing guard outside. "Come along, won't you. You won't do much good back here."

With that, we followed her. As we walked, Seshat morphed into a man wearing a green jacket fringed with gold tassels, a red and white sash, khaki pants, heavy boots and a beret. She held a walkie-talkie and talked into the device as she walked through the hall of Osiris. We emerged into daylight with her.

"I've just received word," came a deep authoritative voice from the once-lovely Seshat, speaking in flawless Arabic. She/he called out to the other temple employees who were helping calm the fleeing tourists. "We need to clear this area immediately. They are sending a team over to make sure the temples are clear of snakes before we can reopen. Heads are going to roll over this."

She/he shook his head in frustration at someone's lack of dependability in managing the local snake problem. "This temple is clear," she/he added. "I personally checked myself. You should leave as well though. If someone dies here, even one of us, we may never hear the end of it."

"All clear over here," came a voice on the walkie from the Small Temple, known as the temple of Hathor and Nefertari. It was built into the other artificial hill at the site.

"Good," Seshat responded. "You and the workers must leave now too. The boss said."

"Yes, sir," came the reply. Small figures went running for the buses parked at the temples' massive parking lot. Tourists, guides and workers all climbed into their buses and vehicles. The last bus waited, as one worker searched for Seshat, but he gave up and boarded the bus to leave. We waited for them to drive off.

Finally, they were gone.

The silence was profound.

"Now this will be fun," Seshat said.

I turned around to find her back in her preferred female form.

My preference as well.

Chapter 17—We come eye to eye with Ramses

"**Y**ou must do your part now, Gil Scott," Seshat said and changed.

Amisi, Ryan, Alexandra and I stepped back quickly and averted our eyes as light so bright it blinded arched to the sky from where Seshat had been standing. Seshat guided herself skyward in the form of a small sun until her light path fell on the temple. Alexandra watched the light enter the temple. The rest of us held our gaze aloft.

Look!" she cried out.

Behind us four great statues of Ramses gazed down at us from their thrones. Seshat had transformed into the sun, veiled our eyes to the present, and opened them to the past, restoring the temple to its original beauty.

"Watch their eyes," Alexandra called out. Sure enough, as Seshat moved into position, the beams of her sun cast light into the great Ramses' eyes. For a brief moment, as the light passed over them, they glowed. I followed the photovoltaic stream from each that bounced off past my shoulder to four gleaming black and gold stelae that had appeared behind us. The light bounded off these pillars, inscribed with a thousand gold hieroglyphics, and back toward the temple. But then the streams evaporated. Seshat had moved too far away. As she changed her position to allow her light path to fall into the temple proper, the strange phenomena ended. The light she cast would soon illuminate three of the statues sitting at its innermost chamber. I needed to get moving. Didn't I?

"What was that?" Alexandra asked.

"I don't know."

"It seemed important!" She gave me her know-it-all look. It was perplexing how she could be so familiar and so distant at the same time.

"What I am supposed to do about it?"

"I don't know, Gil but she said you had to do your part."

Seshat wasn't enough, I realized then. She brought the light into the temple on her own, but she needed help with the statues of Ramses. They played a role here too.

"We need more light," Ryan called out to the sky thinking the same thing. Seshat tried to glow brighter, but it was too much for her. She could only do so much to reveal the past and become the sun. It had to be costing her so much energy even to do this.

"Do it, Gil!" Alexandra shouted at me, finding the words.

I stood there dumbly, then ran backwards, turning in a half circle, thinking. I thought back to my friend Ra in the dream. I was like Ra. The Oracle had implied that, hadn't she? I might as well give it a try.

I mimicked him. "Gil commands the sun!" I called out. I felt an invigorating pull, like strings were anchored in my belly and yanking at the real sun, the one 93 million miles away.

Then something really strange happened; I felt time pull forward 8-1/2 minutes and then back to the present. The light from the sun, light that would normally take that long to travel to the Earth, arrived instantaneously. But I knew the truth. I had somehow manipulated time, space and light. My head was about to explode, but instead an explosion of light illuminated the eyes of the four great Ramses.

Their eyes glowed white hot as my own eyes did now. I knew it because my friends had collapsed to the ground covering their own in pain, but I saw through it like the haze in my dream. I ran over to Alexandra first and covered her eyes as Ra had done to Isis. She stood seeing through white eyes too. I did the same for Amisi and Ryan.

"Whoa." Alexandra's eyes adjusted to the light and took everything in.

"I know, but do you feel that?" Amisi asked in awe. A sort of energy buzzed in the air. Then Ramses' eyes shot out streams of photovoltaic energy toward the four stelae pillars behind us again. The pillars returned the beams, but this time met their target: the Aten above Ra's head. This time, the beams were much stronger.

"Would you look at that?" Ryan's voice betrayed his awe. The Aten was no longer a block of rock carved into the hillside but a huge diamond. The air heated up around us as the blinding sunlight was concentrated, amplified and directed toward the beautifully cut stone. The rock sizzled and boiled, then melted. Oh stars, I didn't realize; could you melt diamond?

Watching through white eyes, the two staff-like jackal heads below Ra's arms rumbled and moved down and out from the wall like two raised bridges lowering into position. They were now black as obsidian and the jackal's eyes glowed green like emeralds. When they finally stopped, they hung out over the doorway of the temple. The diamond Aten melted and slowly trickled down the sides of Ra's body into the staffs. The diamond flowed through them like water exiting a pipe into a deep pit that appeared below the door. This pit was the mouth of a long, shallow trench that made its way down into the depths of the temple. The diamond pooled below the door and flowed out of sight toward the four statues at the back, three of which Seshat now illuminated from the sky.

We ran toward the temple entrance avoiding the sizzling heat from the stelae streams and the dripping hot diamond that only slowly trickled from the recess above the door now. We each took turns hopping around. The stuff was hot. Going last, Ryan called out as the tiniest hint of liquid brushed his arm. It left raw flesh.

He swallowed, thankful it hadn't been worse and we ran, skirting the narrow and long black pool that fell away at a slight decline toward the end-most sanctuary. We barely kept up with the flowing liquid as it rushed in mass toward the four statues. We reached the end, Oasens and liquid diamond, together.

Another stelae, now gleaming black, gold and perfect, rested at the feet of the four statues. We had seen it earlier today, but then it was but a stone relic falling in pieces at the feet of these ancient men. It stood proud and tall now. The liquid pooled at its base where the trench ended and rested there.

Alexandra extended her hand toward the pool like she was on autopilot. The viscous diamond defied gravity at her command and traveled up the gold hieroglyphs carved into its sides. Seshat's light continued to illuminate three of the four figures, casting Ramses in the brightest glow. The hieroglyphs grew and took on a dimensional quality as the substance reached them and filled in.

As the last hieroglyph glowed bright with diamond, a burst of energy shot out toward Ramses. His eyes, once nearly scratched away by millennia of sand storms and the heavy encroaching sand that had filled this temple when it was rediscovered, now took on a brooding powerful glare and filled up with light from the stelae. The photovoltaic stream that shot from the stelae to his eyes held constant, but nothing else happened. Ramses sat like the colossal statues outside, with his hands resting on his knees, still and upright.

"What do I do now?" It felt like time was speeding to an end. This couldn't last forever.

Alexandra still stood with her hand extended toward the pillar. "You must go to the eye of Ramses." She pointed with her free hand. "Like the scroll said."

Her words scared me. I had the same inclination as her, but I couldn't imagine how getting beamed in the eye with direct sunlight would be a good thing.

"My eyes? Are they still white?" Maybe that offered me a measure of protection?

"Yes. Now go."

I ran.

I sat down on Ramses lap and positioned my eyes to catch the photo-stream. But nothing happened. I didn't lose any eyeballs either, so that was good.

"It's not working. What do I do now?"

I glanced right and left. It was faint, but I noticed the light stream also fell into the eyes of the three other statues.

"Oh gods. Hurry! You have to sit too. There's light in their eyes." I patted the knee of Amun on my right.

"I got dibs on Ra." Ryan ran for his statue. Alexandra hesitated to drop her hand, but went for Amun next to me anyway. The diamond stayed in the hieroglyphs. Amisi sat on death's lap, the underworlds favorite friend, Ptah. The light stream hit our eyes. We all became still. Energy flowed in and the world went dark.

This was familiar.

We were inside a computer matrix, but this one wasn't Neter. This place was ancient, even if dust couldn't exist and coat everything, I knew. Yet, erything still hummed. Ryan stood at my right, struggling with the disorientation of first entering a matrix. Alexandra stood on my left, but Amisi sat on the ground already fallen. The loud throb of black moving energy coursed past us.

"Whoa!" Ryan called out but righted himself.

"I know," I said quickly. "Hello. Excuse me?" I yelled out. "I think someone left a message for me here."

I waited. Alexandra even took my arm. Amisi stood up. It all happened so quickly. The black movement amassed itself and slowed to gray. A man stood in front of us. It was the very image of Ptah.

How fitting.

"Now this is interesting," said Ptah or the computer or whoever this was. "I'm not sure that I should still exist."

"I'm not sure that you do exist," I answered in all honesty. "This is all way above my head."

Ptah nodded in acceptance. "Do you now come, Gilbert Scott?"

"I do come." I felt something outside breaking. The link was weakening. "But you must hurry Ptah. The connection is failing."

"Yes," Ptah sighed at his short reanimation. "Here is the map." Something flashed, and an image was seared into my brain. We all jerked as the image torched us. "Make your way to the Torey," Ptahs's voice faded. "She is the gatekeeper."

We were brought back to the present. Light still shone on the three statues thanks to Seshat, but the world she made for our eyes flickered. She was tiring. I got a bad feeling and yelled out her name.

I took off running as the temple fell into ruin again, leaping into the sky as I burst from the door.

Seshat fell limply in her female form from high up in the sky. I caught her as my three friends erupted from the temple. Gently lowering her to the ground, I brushed wet ringlets away from her face. I tried to wake her but she didn't move.

"Oh no! Oh no!" Amisi cried and knelt over the limp body. "No, no, no."

Alexandra fell to her knees and grabbed the lifeless girls' shoulders. She shook them. "Seshat, no! You fight. Do not give up. Please," she begged.

Still nothing. The sun burned a little brighter momentarily and I felt a presence.

"Hello boy," the Oracle stated flatly. She pointed down. "This one's time is not yet spent. Nefertari!"

Behind us, stone ground against stone and a lone figure stepped out from the feet of one of the large statues of Ramses. The statue walked forward fluidly as she shrank down to our size. The stone woman turned her eyes on me and I flinched. She seemed to bare my soul for all to see, but then she focused on Seshat. She reached out with her cold hand and lay it across Seshat's heart. Seshat moved her arm and shimmered.

Then Nefertari stood, still unnaturally silent in her movements, and went back to her alcove, but she took one final spine-tingling glance at me. The others, tears streaming from their eyes, helped Seshat up, but I could only watch as Nefertari grew taller and returned to guard Ramses. She turned still as the stone she was made from, but her eyes felt curious still.

"Many things are hidden, boy." The Oracle nodded at Nefertari, then back at me. "Many things. And truth is never discovered with idle hands."

Then she was gone.

Chapter 18-The wolf's grotto

I stood in Neter's memory matrix handing over the coordinates Ptah had given me. Neter made a copy for her own matrixes and winked at me. I popped back out to reality.

"There. She's got 'em," I collapsed into my chair on the bridge. "What a day."

"You're telling me." Seshat, sat wrapped in a long silver shawl set with blue flecks that sparkled as much as her personality. She wore white fitting slacks and a silk blue top that brought out the color in her wrap. "And I thought Die Another Day was just a movie?"

We all laughed at that.

Melio surrounded me and I felt Neter lift off into the sky. The map was complicated, but apparently she understood. We were on our way.

"Where are we heading purple eyes?" asked Ryan.

"The Grotto of Anubis." She spoke from her interface panel. "In the city of the Wolf."

Seshat shivered, but she wasn't rebuilding her DNA. She sat up straight, at once, paying attention. A map of the area appeared on the consoles in front of us. A marker indicating our intended destination blinked on the city of Asyut, 234 miles south of Cairo.

I was curious. She knew something.

"Why's it called the City of the Wolf, Sesh?"

She sat back deeper into her seat, unsettled. "Because of the Jackal gods they honored there. The Greeks renamed it Lycopolis in their honor, in fact."

"You mean lychans – like werewolves? You're not going to tell me those are real too, are you?"

"No ... not exactly." She didn't convince. "Maybe you remember Anubis from your dad's work, or perhaps even Wepwawet?" Her voice was soft. "The wolf gods, as you might recall them?" She shifted around.

I knew who Anubis was, the jackal-headed god of ancient Egypt. The one with the great pecks and half-human body. "I think everyone knows Anubis – or at least knows what he looks like. Though I'm not sure about Wepwawet?"

"He was like Anubis, but just a boy. Yet unlike dear Anubis – you'll remember him as the guide of the underworld – Wepwawet was a scout. He cleared routes so armies could attack. He was strong and brave. They always depicted him as a white or gray-furred wolf. He stands proudly at the prow of his solar boat in the reliefs. His name meant 'opener of the ways.'"

Seshat sure knew a lot about the wolf men.

"Yes, they are certainly an interesting part of the myth of our ancient Egyptians."

We all nodded our heads at this, but she didn't say more, so we settled in for the ride to Asyut. Considering what we just went through, I expected things to get far more interesting heading to the home turf of the lychans.

The trip was short. Before we knew it, Neter touched down. We got our packs together quickly, even exhausted as we were. We had no time to lose. We drove out of the hatch in the jeep toward the wolf's lair. Seshat, though, waved goodbye to us from the ship's hatch. She had had enough for one day and decided to stay with Neter.

Ryan drove the jeep toward the blinking red dot, following his GPS as we made our way through the city. It was a mix of modern and ancient buildings cobbled together with areas of lush greenery. Palm trees dotted the landscape and canals brought water from the River Nile into and around the sprawling city, its waters feeding the valleys and crops. It almost felt cooler here surrounded by so much water, but it was probably just the wind as we drove.

We skirted the main canal on Al Ibrahimeya, and took a left onto the bridge road that crossed the Nile into El-Nasereya. From there, we found a ferry captain and bargained with him for a ride to Banana Island, at the end of Sharia Salah Salem. We waited for a few more tourists to finish negotiating with the captain too, but before long everyone took their seats.

We sat on multi-colored pillows and had to talk over the other passengers speaking in a jumbled mix of Arabic, English and other languages. Ryan fiddled with his tablet and leaned in. "The map says the entrance to the Grotto is on the island." He pointed down, but a nosey young tourist in a red ball cap tried to peak too. Ryan tucked the tablet back in his pack. Several others perked up hearing him talk of the Grotto too. I overheard their excited discussions.

"Good one," I mouthed. Ryan was too loud for his own good. There would be more than a few of them asking how to get there this afternoon.

"Anyway, it's nothing. I'll show you later," he quipped, yawning indifferently, and leaned back. His way of tuning out any inquiries was a surprisingly real sounding snore. Amisi relaxed alongside him, and I turned toward the river while the last family tried to squeeze in.

I was right about the wind in the jeep. My shirt stuck to me now. It was hot, even this late in the afternoon. The gray river sloshed at our boat, while the heat licked at my skin. I welcomed the breeze the moving boat would bring.

When the last family found seats in our overcrowded boat, the captain wasted no time. He cut on the engine and moved out into the current. I had to cover my ears, the darn thing was so loud. As he pushed the throttle up, the engine strained and groaned and got even louder. It did the job though. We picked up speed, moving surprisingly fast for a boat as overfilled as this one.

Alexandra's golden curls danced in the wind.

"Alexandra?" I needed to talk to her. It wasn't right to leave things how we had on the ship that night. I figured now was as good a time as any.

She didn't agree.

She pointed to her ears like she couldn't hear, and leaned back with her eyes closed. I couldn't either with that engine going. But I wasn't giving up.

"Alexandra?" This time I tried telepathically. "Alexandra?"

Nothing. Her eyes stayed tight shut.

"Faker." Defeated, I settled back and let the cool breeze coming off the water roll over me.

We bounced down the river across small white caps and the wake from the river's other occupants, jostling for position amongst the other open-air ferries and felucca sailboats that clogged the waterway. The ferries were like cabbies in New York City fighting for the best position, but the feluccas were majestic, leaning into the wind with long open white sails, the Rolls-Royces and limos of the Nile. Not to be outdone, our own little boat was decorated in green and red flags that caught and slapped the wind as best they could. It was a nice touch, but they didn't compare.

We raced on past lush green vegetation on both sides where the foliage drank deeply from the Nile's waters, turning them their beautiful shades, until the trip completed, we pulled into a dark little inlet. The boat's engine finally died.

"Wow!" Alexandra pretended to wake up. She stuck her fingers in her ears, jiggling them. "I couldn't hear a thing with all that noise. I barely slept."

That she even attempted to pull that over on me was insulting. I rolled my eyes. There was disdain in my voice. "Sure. Me neither."

She wasn't sleeping and we both knew it. Lucky for her, the man at the helm yelled, interrupting, and gestured at us using a creative mishmash of language and hand signals. I caught a few English words, but the rest was Arabic with a hint of barbarized French. I wasn't sure he knew he was yelling; I was pretty sure he had hearing damage from his boat's engine. The passengers disembarked anyway as most of us got the point of his commentary. It was time to get off.

The captain walked us around a bend to a little manned hut sitting hidden amongst some tall foliage and a long fence that blocked our view of the fields. The ancient woman stationed there seemed sweet at first, but turned out to be the grandma equivalent of the Egyptian mafia. She shook us down for still more money before we could even step foot on the plantation. Ryan tried to argue, but she wouldn't budge. I couldn't help smiling at the triumphant toothless grin she gave me as we went through the tall reed gate onto the banana fields while she counted all our money.

Turned out, it was worth it.

The banana plantation was, admittedly, cool. Walking through the gate was like entering another world. There was row after row after row of trees heavy with fruit. They were perfectly spaced yet so close together that their tops touched and formed a canopy of green over our heads. Light still managed to peak through, making the small vortex's of dust our feet kicked up turn into mini-tornados. The dry shade of the ground matched the tree's trunks, which were brown too and peeling. The trees stood in stark contrast to their own waxy dark leaves and pale green bananas, bunched close together and growing toward the sky.

We walked around pretending to enjoy the scenery while Ryan checked the location of the pinging dot. He oriented himself away from the river line and looked toward a distant hilltop, pointing, but Amisi pulled down his hand.

"That guy's following us."

It was red hat from the boat. Realizing we caught him, he did a remarkably poor job of trying to gaze past us. His eyes squinted hard and he thrust his hand into the leather satchel he carried across his chest. Pulling out a slim cell phone, he put it to his ear. He glanced to his right, then back at us, dropped his head, and spoke into the phone, throwing his hands around as he answered the caller. He took one more noticeably frustrated glimpse in our direction and ducked into the hut they used to hang up the harvested bananas.

People are weird.

Ryan laughed, probably thinking the same thing, and pointed to a tall hill far in the distance. We took off running, finally free from the nosey tourist. Eventually we slowed, checking again for any signs of him. But he was long gone, apparently having given up touring the grotto with us.

We dropped into the drainage ditch that skirted the farm. A few cows and donkeys were grazing here, so nearly the only obstacle left was watching where you stepped. We shimmied up the other side through a rise of high-growing wheat-like grass, and with one last bit of effort, jumped the tall fence that stood guard there when no one was looking.

An untamed forest lay beyond.

We ran at first, Oasen fast, but had to slow down, hampered by several unexpected villages that had us walking as fast as "humanly" possible instead. These villages' remote inhabitants walked like shadows amongst the foliage, making it nearly impossible to avoid surprising them. Their rough dwellings dotted the landscape here and there. Even though the quiet villagers sometimes watched us curiously, they didn't want anything to do with us either. Only one ancient crone chittered angrily at us to get away from her village. The children that ran in circles around her feet laughed at her for calling us cursed, and left to follow at our heals – much to her chagrin – until they got so bored or tired they gave up. It was frustratingly slow going. It was already late when we started too.

At last, the sun dipped, light faded, and night fell. The day grew black and inky. The moon hid, and the lights of Asyut become a nearly faded memory, making everything darker than I thought possible. Finally we ran, but Amisi tripped over her feet, marred by shadows, and Ryan had to catch her. She was lucky she didn't break her ankle.

"I can't believe I got myself into this," she stopped and slapped a mosquito from her arm harder than she needed to. "I'm basically a librarian, and here I am hiking through the jungles of Egypt into gods know what?"

"You're doing fine." Ryan patted her back. "You may be a librarian but you're also an Oasen. You can take out any bad guys with your lightning bolt." He blasted a tree branch off with his wrist to prove the point. He was right; Amisi did have rather amazing Spidey-like abilities.

Amisi giggled. "Yes, or I suppose I can start a fire for us if need be. It's already getting cold." She wrapped her arms around herself. "This weather cannot make up its mind."

She was right. The air took on a surprising chill.

"Wasn't it blazing hot five minutes ago?" Alexandra added, not even breathing hard from all the running.

"Pretty much." Amisi stopped and dug in her backpack, shaking out the waterproof windbreaker she picked up after getting soaked at Siwa Oasis. We all had the new gear stuffed in our packs.

I couldn't agree with her more, but for different reasons. I felt electricity in the air. A storm was coming. I knelt down and found mine in my pack.

"Yeah, feels better." Alexandra zipped up her red jacket.

Ryan stayed still. "You guys are lame."

He still wore only his white undershirt.

"Whatever man," I zipped up my blue one. "Just wait." I put my hand up, anticipating. "Three, two, one ..."

The sky opened up and I laughed as Ryan went to his knees to get out his jacket. Water dripped off his chin, it came down so hard. His white t-shirt went translucent.

"Where did that come from?" Amisi tried to help Ryan pull it over his head – little good that it did at that point.

Alexandra cinched her hood tight. "More end-of-planet stuff."

"And it's gonna' get worse." My Bau was sending off warning signals I couldn't ignore. The wind picked up too. A banana leaf blew by and hit me in the face. "I think we need to find shelter." The tingling sensation running up my spine was hard to ignore. I took off running, ducking another wide leaf as it blew past. Rain pelted me like a belt. The storm came in fast, with too much fury.

"Hey! Over here! Shelter!" There was an ancient sycamore tree nearby, its massive trunk bent over toward the ground in a bowled out curve. The tree was odd but beautiful. Most of all, it provided us with protection.

The others came running and just in time. The wind switched gears and much bigger debris joined the banana leaves flying through the air. A branch broke off and the storm blew it at us with biting force. Lightning cracked, and Ryan reached out with his Bau to form a protective shield around where we sheltered.

"When you get tired, let me know. This storm's not going anywhere for a while."

"Figured as much. My Bau's never felt like that before."

Another branch blew by, a limb really, this one bigger and with more speed. It bounced harmlessly off the blue shield. Nearby trees bent to the ground as the storm intensified, but our ancient tree stood its ground with the help of our force field. Yet another tree succumbed nearby, rending through its wide middle with an awful cracking sound. Its leaves and branches thwacked the ground staccato. More projectiles sped through the air. Brush fell all around us, but still, we were safe.

"Hurricane anyone? Lovely weather we're having tonight."

Alexandra made a face. "This weather," she emphasized, "is starting to tick me off." She brushed sticky wet hair from her face and pulled her feet up from the sucking mud we stood in. Water flooded in despite Ryan's shield. The ground here sloped gently toward a culvert that quickly became a raging creek alongside us.

"You would pick the only shelter around us in a mile and it turns out to be a flood zone," Alexandra added. "But hold on. Thankfully, this, I can take care of."

She concentrated and the water that pooled at our feet collected and swung wide around the tree, making a new trench down to the creek. I helped too, forcing the ground below our feet to soak up the water that remained. It took seconds.

"Might as well settle in." I sat down on dry ground. "This storm's gonna' be a while."

"It's cold too." Amisi snuggled into Ryan.

He stared back at her. The look lasted a moment too long. Amisi cringed at Alexandra and me. But there were no secrets anymore. We knew full well what was going on with them. And they knew full well the weirdness going on between us. Needless to say, it was awkward. Ryan grimaced at us foot-in-mouth style and pulled just slightly away from Amisi.

"It's okay." I waved it away with a flick of hand. "Figured."

Alexandra was quiet, whether in silent forgiveness or blatant apathy – I wasn't sure.

I wish I knew which one. She sat across from me in the curve of the tree trunk. She scooted farther into the bend to put more space between us. Her body language spoke loudly. I rolled into a ball on the ground, twisting the silver ring on my finger as my mind wondered to a thousand different things. Still, I didn't sleep. When I finally came back to reality, I caught Alexandra watching me as I had her. She noticed me returning her gaze, and her eyes drifted away. Maybe she was sad too?

When the storm finally abated, Amisi released the shield and popped her head out. It had been her turn to hold it.

"Check it out!" she called.

I stuck out my head. Gray clouds were moving through a dark sky faster than I thought possible.

"Whoa."

"You got that right."

Somewhere that pretty anchor sat at her news desk with sweat beading her forehead trying to explain this new weather phenomenon. The others joined us, shaking their heads at the danger and beauty in the sky. "Things are getting worse, I presume. Good thing, we're almost there." The tablet Ryan held showed the pinging dot marking our destination. It practically jumped, we were so close.

"Well, at least there's that." I shrugged off the last few hours. "Meet you there." I took off running across a low gravel field and up the short rise to the base of the hill. I needed to put some space between Alexandra and me, so I raced slip sliding across the still-wet earth, jumping downed trees in my in my race to the hill. It took only seconds.

"No. Come back." The voice was soft. It was Alexandra's. It came telepathically but was muffled. "The sky." This time I heard her clearly, but it was tentative. She hadn't left our shelter. Her blonde hair reflected the moonlight in the distance.

Was she talking to me again?

I took off, this time running just as fast straight back to her. When I stopped, I followed her gaze up to the fast-moving heavens.

She blushed. "It's pretty incredible." She tried to sound casual but I realized immediately she hadn't meant for me to hear. That she had wanted to share this with me, but hadn't intended to. She used the telepathy by mistake. She pointed and stepped away.

Above me, the night sky was clear, blue-black. The fast-moving winds had pushed the smog away. The air was clean. Across the river, the city of Asyut lay blanketed in darkness. The power grid down. The night sky was darker without all the light pollution. Even the moon hid now.

"There!"

Something danced across the sky – a lazy, extraordinary kind of light. The Aurora Borealis, in all its glory, painted the night sky in dreamlike fantastic colors – right over Egypt. It made the dark night curiously bright. Its light touched Alexandra's hair again making it shine like it had a moment ago.

"We're too far south?" Ryan wondered.

I sniffed the air. How I identified it, I don't know. "There was a solar storm too. Still's happening. I think that's why we can see it this far south." I put my hands up toward the sky and painted, letting the necessary energy flow out of me. Alexandra sucked in a breath at how I turned the sky into my own canvas. I grinned. The lights followed my command. Green and blue smears of light stroked the sky.

She stood so close. I couldn't help myself. "Here, you try." I stepped behind her so quickly she didn't have a choice. I held her palm to palm and laced my fingers with hers. The touch sent electric shocks up my arm. Hers too, I guessed by the way she shivered. She could deny me all she wanted, but the chemistry between us couldn't be.

My heart ended up in my throat at my boldness, especially after how she had ignored me under the tree, but I swallowed it back down again quickly. Alexandra's breath caught, and she leaned back into me, breathing a sigh of contentment. This was her pattern. When she got this close, she couldn't help herself. Maybe the stars were aligned tonight too, and that meant something. Maybe in the war for her heart, I would win a few battles. Whatever it was, I took it.

The heat between us grew brighter and the light intensified at our touch. She looked back at me and I smiled down on her. She pulled away like she remembered she couldn't allow this kind of thing, but I held her still and put her hand up to the sky instead. She gave in and I helped her brush stroke the heavens, sending energy up into the sky so that it followed the pattern she made with her hand. She laughed impulsively, as much from fun as from the shock of our sudden closeness.

I felt alone with her even though Ryan and Amisi stood right by. "Beautiful as this is Alexandra," I whispered, our heads inclined to the heavens together, "It cannot rival your beauty."

She turned her face to mine suddenly.

"Oh gods," she said under her breath and her hands dropped and she pulled away.

I said too much. The familiar blue sparks drifted down.

Amisi turned away.

"Come on you two." Ryan threw his pack over his shoulder and grinned, but he hadn't seen how her face changed.

Alexandra pulled Amisi away from us then, the two running ahead. They put their heads together. Amisi drew her arm around her friend finally understanding. Instead of a grin, my face wore a mask of disappointment, and Ryan realized too what went on. I followed at his heels the last hundred feet to the rock outcropping at the hill, silent and slow this time. Joining the girls, we climbed Oasen-quick up to the top. A mass of volcanic rock capped the hill's peak.

The light blinked on the map. We were here.

"There's nothing here to indicate any kind of grotto entrance." Alexandra was back to business. She pounded on the rock. "None of this makes sense. It never does."

For practical Alexandra, that was the worst part of this trip.

"Yeah, you're right. So I guess that means it's time for Gil to do his Mr. 'The One' thing."

Ryan knocked me in the shoulder and waited.

"Listen, I am way more suited to playing video games and reading comics than this."

"Nope. Right now you've got to put on your 'The One' hat and make something happen. I'm soaked, wet and cold, and my feet are killing me. So do something already."

"Yeah, about that ..." I turned in a circle. I was about to be very sarcastic, but something caught my eye instead. I couldn't believe I didn't notice it before, but the view from these heights solidified it. The curved shape of the tree. The water nearby. It made total sense. I took off running down the mountain, leaving my friends there alone and confused.

"Um, what are you doing?" Alexandra yelled, jumping down the steep rocky hill like a mountain goat, right after me. "We're here already. Hey, Gil, wait up. Come on. Stop."

"We just got here!" Amisi complained but the chorus of voices couldn't slow or stop me.

"It's the sycamore tree." I yelled back, but ran faster still down the hill away from them. "It's a boat! It's Wepwawet's solar boat. He's the opener of ways. Get it! His boat's gonna' take us to the grotto." The others ran faster, still bewildered, but silent now. You could almost make out the boat's shape in the tree.

When I reached the sycamore again, I nearly collapsed from exertion. The others made it too and stopped to catch their breath. Ryan and Amisi sat on the ground. Alexandra leaned back against the tree. We had come down fast, and we were already spent from using our Bau during the storm. We all stood panting, out of breath for once.

I held up my finger in the air and tried to speak. I hunched over my knees trying hard to catch my breath. "Okay." I stammered, talking to myself. "Okay, Wepwawet. We're here ... at least I think. What do we do now?"

"Funny you should ask." The tree behind Alexandra moved like it was alive and she jumped. "Well, hello darling," came a smooth voice. Strong camouflaged arms emerged from the sycamore and wrapped around her waist in a tight but playful embrace. The thing squeezed Alexandra around the middle, leaving her muddy.

Amisi scooted away on her butt and I jumped back too, in shock from the sudden movement.

Whoever or whatever it was that held Alexandra blended perfectly into the tree. Its face was gnarled and brown, gray and lichen green, with bits of spiky broken off branches, just like the sycamore, speckled throughout. He finally released her waist and she took a timid step away, but she didn't get far because the thing now held her firmly by the hand.

"Fancy meeting you here, dear?" It said with a hint of pleasure. It caressed her hand with its long thumb.

Horror mixed with amusement crossed her face. I don't think I'll ever see its likes again. Everyone took another step back, but for Alexandra, as it stepped out from its hiding place to relative exposure. The thing's head became more obvious, standing out against Alexandra's normal flesh tones. It might be a disconcerting sight, but "it" was only a man.

"I didn't mean to scare you, darling." He let her go finally with a squeeze of the hand. She stepped away slowly. His eyes, handsome ones I now realized, sparkled at Alexandra. He was playing with her.

He took a cloth from his pocket and wiped his face. "There now. See. Just makeup."

I had a hunch who this was.

"Are you Wepwawet?" I had a short fuse after the sky painting letdown, and I wasn't in the mood for games.

He was amused by my discomfort. "Yes, I am." He took a flowery bow. "Though I'm thinking of changing my name should I finally get to leave this place. It's not much of a modern name, is it? Wep, I guess. Call me Wep then. But, alas, Gil Scott, I'm glad you noticed me here. Though it could have been sooner, if you ask me. You left me in the rain all night while you took shelter without me." He shook himself like a wet dog trying to free itself of the rain. "Anyway, that was the rule Ra set down. The One must find the boat himself." He patted the tree and leaned back, blending in slightly again, but for the smear across his face.

Alexandra stood watching all this with a great deal of amusement, game to play along. "So you hung out here for 2,000 years all dressed up in that makeup." She boldly dug into the thick goop on his arm.

"Not exactly, sweet one." The newcomer laughed at her boldness. He was charming, even covered in mud. "The barge only works on nights when there is a solar storm. And those are rare these days, as you might have guessed. Ra used to call down the storms so I could take her out, but it's been a while."

"Indeed." I scratched my chin, unconsciously mimicking Wep's archaic speech and mannerisms. Ryan shook his head at my weird copycat behavior.

A smile cracked across Wep's face. He missed nothing. "Well, I'll say, we better get going before we lose the tide." He pointed up at the solar storm that still filled the sky with color. "Alakazam and all that!" He waved his arms. Nothing happened. We stood there staring at him. "I'm kidding. You didn't think that's how this worked, did you?"

We just stared.

"Well then, to the other side then people!" Wep led us around the trunk to where the sycamore leaned over to the ground. He reached up into its curve, then the earth shook and part of the wood of the sycamore broke free.

So that's how it worked.

The tree stayed put, but the boat, hidden in its bending arc, pulled away. "You might want to step back," Wep warned as the vibrations grew.

The ground moved under Ryan's feet. Dirt and grass tore.

All the vibrations owed to the fact that the solar boat was partly underground. It slid slowly out of the earth along the curve of the sycamore. Wep stood there with his hands on his hips, watching his boat break free, his smile not hidden by all the goop. Finally liberated, the old ship slowly rolled onto its side, right into an upright position and landed with a little splash in the wide creek that had formed in the culvert during the storm. At the bow and stern, long decorative wooden pillars grew out of the curves, up and up in the air, until they were tall and imposing. They resembled stalks of papyrus and gave the boat the appearance of an elongated U from the side.

"Just a little worse for wear." Wep walked around inspecting his ship. He got wet slapping around in the shallow creek. Mud came off his legs. "This will do, but I don't care much for the dirt." He knocked at its side and great clouds of the stuff broke free. He shooed the particles away from his face.

"That's funny considering." Alexandra stood there with one hand on her hips, the other pointing to Wepwawet's dirty face, her quiet resolve and confidence back on display. Wep reached up, touched his muddied skin and snarled, remembering.

He literally snarled.

Alexandra made a face. She had to reign in her laughter.

"You're right. You're right." Wep's tone was pleasant and his eyes laughed too. He glanced up at the solar storm, quickly gauging it. "One minute. I'll be right back."

He sloshed through the water, jumping into a deeper part of branch. Amisi and Ryan hunched their shoulders at Wep's mini bath and went to explore the boat. Alexandra stood watching him too, catching me with an amused expression. Maybe she thought he was weird, too? She turned her attention back to Wep though, who scrubbed at his skin and clothes in the churning brook.

His shirt came off. She arched an eyebrow.

I looked away.

A few minutes later, Wep walked up soaking wet, but mostly clean. Now that he was free of the mud mask, I realized he had course black hair and contrasting bright blue eyes that went perfectly with his maple syrup skin. His shirt hung loose and unbuttoned on him like he hadn't had time to finish it up, or he just wanted to show off. And why not? He was ripped. His skin was brown and the muscle in his forearms even rippled through the clinging fabric of his shirt as he moved. He looked about 18. A boy, just as Seshat said. Though he must be older – much older.

Alexandra stared.

Wep shook his head and water flew out of his hair, like a dog shaking after a bath. But from the look on Alexandra's face, I'd say she thought him more like a male model in a shampoo commercial.

Great.

He was competition.

She flushed. I ground my teeth. I couldn't believe it.

"Come on," Wep sang out and boldly put his arm around her shoulders, getting her wet and breaking her gaze from mine simultaneously. He looked back at me like he knew exactly what he was doing. She started to pull away, but catching me watching, thought the better of it and walked on with him.

Wep led her to the ship, stopped, reached up and catapulted himself over the edge of the boat. It wasn't much of a jump considering its low sides, but he did it impressively. It reminded me too much of my own attempt to come off cool for that first ride in the planetary vehicle.

Wep reached out his hands to help Alexandra aboard. "My lady." He winked and pulled her in.

"Tough luck, kid," Ryan mouthed from the ship.

"You're kidding me, right?" I mouthed right back. He only hunched his shoulders and put out his hand to help me in. I brushed him off and hopped over myself.

Alexandra was already at the front of the boat with Wep, so I left them alone and went to check out the rest of the ship alone. It was made of brown wooden planks that matched the tones of the sycamore it had been hiding in for a millennium. I couldn't imagine how this solar boat fit so perfectly in the tree. Of course, a lot of impossible things had been happening lately, so why not this?

The boat was long and shallow, probably only two feet deep, like a long canoe, only bigger. The narrow prow and sterns both curved up to the sky in front and back. It was striking, even covered in dirt.

"Now for some heka," Wepwawet winked. A console rose up that was clearly not the stuff of old-plank construction. This was Oasen technology. He manipulated the controls, the ship lurched with sudden power, and we moved down the newly-formed waterway that flowed toward the hill. "Hold on," he called out. "And please sit." We did, but Wep stayed standing, letting the chilly air hit his wet skin. It made me feel cold, but he didn't mind, even as the boat picked up speed.

I leaned over the side and realized that while we started out in the water, we were now riding on a tide of solar light. We rapidly approached the mountain's base too. We weren't slowing. I reached for something to hold onto, fearing we'd crash into it, when a river of green light shot down from the sky and we rose into the air on this new tide. Wep reached out to steady Alexandra, but she gritted her teeth at the help. He let Ms. Independent go and focused his attention forward instead.

Darn it, he was perceptive too.

Wep stood casually with one foot resting on the side of the hull as the boat climbed up the side of the mountain toward its summit. "A quick word of warning," he called out. "What I am about to do is perfectly normal – consider it an ancient seat belt."

He keyed in a new sequence and a golden net appeared from the top of the papyrus bow. It shot out over the boat, and settled over us like a sheet being tossed over a sleeping child, fanning all the way to the stern scroll. Another part of this gossamer material rose up and caught the wind with one great sail like the feluccas on the river earlier.

"The boat's too shallow," Wep yelled over the wind. "We might fall out without the golden canopy."

Wep called for more blue light from the Aura Borealis. It met the other already under the ship to form a deeper sea blue haze. This new mixture was like rocket fuel. We shot skyward over the summit of the hill, pushed suddenly down into our seats. Then the boat flipped perpendicular to the ground and hung there. Alexandra, of course, grinned.

"Hold on!" Wep shouted. "This is it!" The net pushed us down. Then the ship fell toward the earth – our aim the summit below us.

Right before we hit the ground, the volcanic rock opened up like a mouth and swallowed our ship. The stern and bow and the great sail that caught the solar storm plastered back as well fell down a long vertical shaft lit only by solar light.

"Oh man!" Ryan called out. "This is way too Willy Wonka for me."

Amisi turned green in agreement but Alexandra laughed. This was very much her kind of thing.

"What's Willy Wonka?" Wep asked.

"I'll explain later," Ryan gripped the seat in front of him as we continued to accelerate. Finally, the ship slowed and we dropped into a huge underground lake, sending up an enormous splash of water.

The cavern was ethereal, bright with light – even so far underground and the walls were made of blue and white marble, the two colors swirling together in patterns that dipped and turned with the rock itself. That rock arched up and down forming a natural cathedral ceiling – like the place was some great lost Renaissance church plunged far under the ground. The water itself was as blue and clear as the Caribbean and nearly the same color as the vein running through the white marble. The water here had been higher once too and fast moving. It had hollowed out the rock, forming all the alcoves and cut-throughs and passageways that led into still more caves. It was fantastic.

"Welcome to the halls of the Grotto of Anubis," Wepwawet gestured. "Welcome to my home."

Chapter 19-The Torey speaks

The solar barge drifted through the low cave tunnel I had spotted into the next marble hall. Light from the solar storm danced around the cavern like it was trapped here. Maybe it had been for generations? It illuminated the swirling marble whose color mimicked the aqua waters beneath it so perfectly. Its brilliance made the room feel alive and otherworldly. Even I could tell how abnormally beautiful this place was.

"The water's high tonight," Wep commented as his boat just cleared the tunnel ceiling we drifted into. I nodded at him and reached up to touch the rock. It was smooth and cold. My hand slid across the hard stone until we exited into another cavern, this one even grander in proportion than the last.

A long white pier cut through the water. Pristine lake water sloshed against its moorings and, on the shore, a grand marble villa was carved from the cavern wall. It was strange but oddly perfect. The turrets and balconies and the rise and slopes of the roof lines were somehow both a natural expression of the rock and the finished plan of a master architect.

Wep steered the boat toward the pier. Even with the current that ran through the cavern lake, he was able to pull the boat alongside it without so much as touching the dock. He simply had to reach out and pull the boat in to tie it up. He was an expert boatman.

Our ancient brown barge stood in stark contrast to the rest of the cavern's occupants. Three other vessels were anchored here. These were newer, cleaner, perfectly white, and adorned with colorful pillows piled high on the decks, just like the feluccas above us on the River Nile. When our old boat was secured, we climbed out and walked the long pier to the shore. The Eye of Horus was carved above the villa's great doors – the symbol of the ancient cult of Anubis.

"Mother? Mother?" Wep called out. He ran up to his house and walked in the front door leaving us alone on the beach. Alexandra raised her eyebrows at me, but followed Wep toward the house. I decided to take a walk down the sandy beach instead. I'd had enough of Wep's antics for a while.

"I'm taking a walk," I said. But no one cared, which bothered me ever more. I kicked a rock as hard as I could and walked down the blue and white flecked beach toward the place where the cave wall ended in a curve into the water. I needed a few minutes alone to think.

Turned out, I wasn't alone.

Stretched out at the end of the bank was a huge dog that looked like a Doberman, but was far too big for that. The creature was black as night and its coat was sleek and shined like someone rubbed oil into. It had the tall pointed ears of a Dobby, but the color was strangely gold inside. This matched the dog's only adornment – a heavy gold ribbon knotted at its throat.

It was a marvelous specimen, but I slowed, worried about its posture. Its ears twitched, listening, and it sat up, alert, as I approached, its long black neck straining up at me. Its fur was slightly raised too and bands of muscle rippled beneath its skin. I tried to slow my walk, but feared stopping or turning would startle it to action anyway.

I walked on, drawn to the massive creature like a weak moth to the flame that would burn it. I put out my hand for it to smell me. I was too close now to do anything else, but it snubbed me and turned away instead.

Wep and the others ran up from behind. He looked back and forth between me and the dog who glanced up at Wep noncommittally and stretched – all its previous intensity melting away in the slow movement. The animal reached forward with his paws, craned its neck in a low bow and lengthened out its back legs. Its toes spread out languidly the way dogs do, but then I got the shock of my life. Delicate women's fingers grew out in their place. Its front legs morphed into mocha-brown arms, the back legs became long graceful legs, and the dog's black coat became the coal-black oiled hair of a beautiful woman. She stood up from her crouching position and extended her hands toward the ceiling to complete the stretch.

"Ahh. That feels good." Her voice was deep and sultry. It had an almost silky meets sandpaper quality to it and her words were heavy. You felt the weight of them settle into you and not let go as she spoke.

I looked her over. I couldn't help it. She wore a long black dress and the same heavy gold ribbon tied around her neck that had been there when she was the dog. Hooped gold earrings graced her earlobes and thick bands of gold circled around her toned arms. Her skin was even darker than Wep's and her hair was lustrous and deepest black. Her green eyes were done in the ancient Egyptian style, but in shimmering gold rather than black kohl. Her eyes were like deep wells. You could lose yourself in them.

Her power was strong.

"Mom, was that really necessary?"

Wep's mom?

I felt suddenly sick at my unguarded thoughts about her.

Her mouth arched up. The turn of her lip was rather devious and as much for me as it was for him. "Well, they should know what they are getting into, now shouldn't they, dear?" She stroked me under the chin with one of her long fingers. This time her big smile revealed white teeth that had only recently been sharp ice-white canines.

Yikes. She was scary when she wanted to.

"Hello young ones," she cooed. "I am Anput, wife of Anubis and mother of young Wepwawet, here." She tilted her hand toward him and he tensed.

I stood there staring back and forth between Anput and Wep. His hand rested protectively on Alexandra's lower back – and she let him. I caught her eyes. They jerked away.

I wanted to hit him across the face.

She's mine, I thought possessively.

How dare he touch her?

I shifted my eyes to Wep. "Does that make you a dog too?" I said without thinking.

Amisi pouted in disapproval and I immediately regretted my comment.

"Jackal, boy," Anput sneered at me. I jumped back. Her white teeth flashed, reminding me of her earlier fangs. The ones she showed me now were unnaturally sharp for human teeth. Almost imperceptible. "We are jackals, and are not so much unlike yourself, except instead of a human father and an Oasen mother, we are the progeny of a Nyad and an Oasen."

Anput was protective of her pup to say the least.

Wep smirked.

"Sorry Anput." I raised my eyebrows and stammered. "I meant no offense ... to you."

Anput bowed her head just slightly in response. She seemed to get my inference, making a face at her son. He wasn't having it though. Wep howled at Alexandra. There was instant laughter. I gritted my teeth even more. This guy was smooth.

Anput put her hand on my shoulder. "Come, Gil Scott. We will waste no more time with these trivial things or other things will end badly." There was a finality to her voice that unnerved me. She turned on her heels, propelling me forward with amazing strength. I tripped over my own feet as we walked back toward the marble villa and entered through the now-open heavy oak doors. We went down a long hall, out into an interior courtyard, and back into the villa, but this part was set deep into the cave wall. It was dark here, quiet and damp.

"Are you taking me to meet the Torey?"

"You have met her, Gil Scott," she replied. "I am the Torey." She kept walking, silent now. The thought was unsettling. My palms sweated and I became even more unnerved. A woman who has two names is most certainly trouble.

We entered a dark room with a small dais like the one in the Oracle's chamber. On it was a chair. Anput let me go and sat down. She untied the gold ribbon from her neck, though so slowly the action became uncomfortable. Her eyes bored into me. "What do you get when you birth a child of an all-powerful Oasen with that of a shape-shifting Nyad?"

She waited for me, but I hunched my shoulders. I'd never heard much about her.

Anput huffed and answered herself. "Something quite spectacular, I can assure you. And, I child, I am even more unique than you can imagine. Anubis gets all the credit, big strong man that he is, but even he cannot match me. I can bend the rules of the physical world like you, and while I can only shift my shape into that of the jackal, I can become something else quite entirely."

There it was again. She was otherworldly. And scary.

Anput paused, reveling in the moment.

She stood and extended her foot which turned black as coal, deepening the color of her already brown skin. Barefoot, the color started in her toes and spread upward. "When I put one foot into the world of the Oasen." The jewelry on her arm jangled at her movement. "And when I put my mind into the world of the Nyad." She reached up and touched her forehead. Her head shimmered. "Then I am the Torey. Something ... else ... more ... entirely." Her voice changed.

If I thought I was scared before, I misjudged myself. This was terrifying. Her transformation happened in front of us. Her body remained human, but her head morphed into the black jackal. She became the very image of the half-jackal gods of ancient Egypt, standing before us on her dais looking down on us with intelligent yet animal eyes. Her pointy ears were golden inside and black without, and gold and black human hair in great dreadlocks hung in mass down her back. She reached up and tied part of it back. When she moved, her curves moved with her. No man could miss them. They were unavoidable, locked up the way they were beneath her tight black dress. She remained silent, letting us take her all in. Even the girls couldn't turn away.

Wep leaned with one foot bent against a wall watching it play out. He hesitated after her change, but finally walked toward her holding a heavy Wesekh collar he took from the alcove beside him. The wide collar was made from tubes of golden beads arranged in six rows alternating with files of small black ones. The collar matched her dark dress and the thick gold bands that she wore on her arms – one on each upper arm and one on each wrist. She was intimidating and dangerously beautiful too.

I wasn't sure what to do, and I hadn't quite recovered enough to speak, so I did an awkward little bow instead and waited. The Torey's long mouth widened into a friendly doggy grin, but it made her sharp canines all the more obvious.

She liked the vibe she put off.

I was still sweating but I thought I might be able to speak, so I tried. "Seshat said the Oracle was afraid of you." My voice was quiet, but it was enough to break the silence. "She said you knew too much." I spoke louder this time. This fact now worried me.

A dark human laugh emerged from the jackal's mouth. It was deeper than her normal voice, more powerful, more worrisome. Her x-ray gaze pierced me. My mind tingled. Something felt wrong. "No one likes competition. Now, do they Gil?" Her eyes went slowly, knowingly between me and her son, and my stomach sank. She knew. And this wasn't some kind of special maternal instinct. She knew. And I knew she knew – without a doubt. I gulped and shook my head, peaking at Wep. How did she know that? Wep acknowledged my fears with one look.

His mother was in my head. I could feel her.

"Gil Scott, you are right to be worried." The Torey's voice dripped like honey laced with cyanide. "When I am in this state, I have the ability to read the minds of those closest to me." There was a shuffling noise behind me and my friends jerked; she had invaded their minds too. They had felt her reach out and touch them.

I swallowed hard and tried to lock all my secrets away, but she smiled all the more. I was laid bare, my mind naked before her.

I grabbed my skull. "Get out of my head!" It didn't hurt, but my mind was the only place no one else could go – until now.

"Oh, don't worry. I'm not much of a tattletale," she said unenthusiastically and laughed.

I felt like running, but she took her attention off me briefly, moving to the rest of the room. I breathed for a second. It was a gift.

"So many secrets." She looked at Alexandra.

There were tears in her eyes.

But Anput, or the Torey rather, was back in my head and I couldn't focus. I felt her inside me like she was a worm crawling through, tunneling out a new home. "It's not unlike your ability to enter the data matrixes of computers," she explained. "I, however, am able to enter the biology of your mind."

"This is too much," I cringed, begging, but there was no hope for a reprieve. The Torey was inside my head, and she wasn't leaving anytime soon.

"You can't imagine the half of it." Wep crossed his arms and leaned back against the wall again. "Imagine growing up with her."

The Torey turned her jackal head on her son, "We'll talk later."

Wep flinched. Then she turned her attention on Alexandra, which left me sick to my stomach. Wep seemed sick too. I felt for the guy then.

"As for the Oracle, she doesn't like me knowing her secrets and she has many." She laughed again. "But, as for how I am to help you Gil Scott, I must open the link you share with Isis."

Yes. That's right. My brain stuttered. I was here for a reason.

The Torey was a friend. She was to help me.

"That's right," she acknowledged me. "I am here to help. I know this is not easy." She stepped toward me and put her hand on my forearm, sending a chill up my arm. "Yes, you share a link with that lovely trapped girl. You haven't been able to talk to her though yet, have a conversation?"

"No, no matter how hard I try."

"Well, that is why Ra sent you here." She patted my arm with her human hand. Her touch was cold, unnerving. "I will open the gate, but first, you must sleep. Wep!" she called and took me by the elbow, steering me from the room. Everything was sudden with her. Everything happened quickly.

"Yes, mother." Wep ran out a side door.

The Torey led me back through the halls to the open air courtyard, navigating the maze with expertise. The others followed. Light trickled in from the opening. Normally, this would be welcome after leaving the dark recesses of the villa, but this light only served to remind me how exposed I was in the Torey's presence. We stopped at a lounge chair that was set up with ample cushions. I didn't notice it before. She motioned for me to lie down as Wep walked up holding a drink.

She took it from Wep's hands, offering it to me. "Don't worry. It's fairly decent. It's made of honey, valerian tincture, apple cider vinegar and hot milk, oh, and a little something else." She laughed again and Wep made a horrible face behind her.

"Wep, dear, I may not be able to see you, but I know exactly what you're thinking."

"Yes, mother."

No wonder he wanted to get out of here and see the world.

"Good idea. Not a bad one at all, considering." The Torey looked toward Alexandra.

"Did I miss something?" she asked.

"Probably." I held my nose, but didn't answer. I wanted this over with. I downed it and gagged. My stomach went warm and my head felt strange. I faltered. Wep grabbed me by the shoulders. My head slumped and rolled, and my body went halfway numb.

"Whoa..."

Wep leaned me back and I was gone.

The room was dim in the half light. Poor Isis hung motionless in her swirling bath of moving colors, but they seemed sad, slower and less vibrant than the last I was here.

I felt for her.

Blood had dripped from the crown of her head, running into her open eyes. The image was unnerving with her hands outstretched to me. But at least the blood had stopped flowing. It caked at the top of her head, but the red tears lay frozen on her face. If any girl had something to cry tears of blood about, it was this one.

"Yes. Plenty to cry about," Isis answered me in my mind.

She heard me. This had never happened.

"Trapped here for more than 2,300 years with the love of my life bound to the Aten and silent just feet above me, and only you to talk to when you came to me out of time and in your dreams. Thank you Gil Scott. Without your visits, I might have gone crazy."

What was she talking about?

"You've come to me," she answered. "These last 2,300 years. I've talked to you since you were a tiny baby. That was when I first entered the knot. In your dreams, you came to me out of time. You grew up listening to my voice, Gil. It is why you did not turn until you were so much older than the others. All your Bau energy has been concentrated on the link we shared since your birth – well, since before that really. But, your Bau is stronger than any I've ever encountered, even amongst the elders, even amongst the pure Oasens. You are young now, Gil Scott. We will discover what you are capable of as you grow." Her voice was resolute, familiar.

"Isis." Saying her name was such relief. "I'm glad I was here for you." I meant it, but my father was still trapped beside her. "But what about my dad and Elaine? How did they get here?"

"I do not know." Isis was suddenly unsure. "It was not in the plan. It was not foreseen. I don't know how they found me. But the Aten has taken them as well. They are alive, Gil. That is all the hope I can give you."

I swallowed. I might see my dad again.

I'm not sure how long The Torey can hold the link," I remembered. "I have to find you and free you from the Knot or the Earth and all of us will be destroyed. The Aten is on a countdown to planetary destruction, but I don't have the key to stop it. And, I don't know where to find you. Can you help me?"

"You have the key, Gil Scott. You just don't know it yet. Do not worry yourself on this point."

She cried out in pain then. "Ahh! Oww! My power is going, Gil. Ohh! It helps sustain the Knot. Oh ... I am as tied to it as it is to me."

My stomach sank. "I'm sorry, Isis. I want to help." I remembered at that moment that I could move in this dream state. I wondered this time? Would it work?

I walked toward her. Reaching in my pocket, I felt the soft embroidery of the hanky my Aunt Vera made for me. I wanted to at least try. I reached into the Knot of Isis and my hand passed through like I dipped it in water. It grew and found a vibrant rhythm that increased at my presence. I felt Isis calm. I dabbed at her eyes and wiped away some of the blood, doing my best to wipe the crusty stuff from her face and crown. There was some left, but she looked much better than before. She could at least see now. I put my hand on her shoulder and she sighed at the human touch.

"You used to pull at my fingers trying to get me to play with you when you were a toddler. When the link was strongest, like now." The room quivered. We were running out of time.

Isis realized it too. "Gil! I reside near the temple proper of Palenque, in a hidden burial chamber, far to the left of the main sanctuary. At noon, the sunlight touches the entrance to the chamber. But, that access point was closed by the Aten." Her words were desperate.

"But, Gil. In your dreams, you found another way to me, even after the first was closed." She hurried. "Do you remember the ventilation tunnel you climbed through? The one your dream twin found? The one where the Oasen soldier destroyed the entry grate and dismantled the alarm? You've been there Gil Scott?" She said my name like it was her only lifeline – and it was.

"I remember. It was long and narrow. Where is its entrance?"

"I'm sorry." She spoke hastily. "I do not know where the entrance is to that tunnel, but I know it's the only way left. Listen though and listen well. Ra was very serious with me once. He told me to remember it as if my life depended on it, and I now know what he meant. I've been thinking about it all these years. Ra said, 'When Orion falls, to Draco goes the spoils.' I know it is not much, but it is the answer. I know it as assuredly as I know you – and I know you well, Gil Scott."

The room seriously quavered then, but it was the connection breaking not another earthquake. "Again, Gil Scott: When Orion falls," she gulped, "to Draco goes the spoils."

I reached out and took her hand. "I will figure it out Isis. I'm coming for you. I promise."

Her voice faded but she yelled at me so I would hear. "Do not die on your way to me, Gil Scott, for the path has become violent. The Earth trembles in defiance at the Aten. It knows its plan and tries to fight back." I squeezed her hand again. I felt the comfort it sent her.

She kept repeating the words as the link broke. "When Orion falls, to Draco goes the spoils. When Orion falls, to Draco goes the spoils. Gil!" she screamed, "When Orion falls, to Draco goes the ..."

Her voice died. My eyes fluttered open. The hazy world came into sudden sharp focus. Eight human eyes stared intensely down at me, and one set of knowing jackal eyes.

I sat up suddenly, reached into my pocket and pulled out my Aunt's hanky.

Everyone gasped.

I watched with them as the sullied cloth fell noiselessly to the ground to stain the marble red.

Chapter 20-Riding with the dead

I sat there fuming as Wep's boat glided through the dark maze of underground rivers. The Torey had followed through on her promise to send her son with us and I wasn't happy about it. "It is his specialty," she had conferred through her wolfy mouth. She grinned as my mind withered in discomfort at the thought. "You can read all about it in the hieroglyphs. It is known." Yeah, yeah, he's the opener of ways and all that. I get it. She tipped her head in acknowledgement and sent us on our way.

There was no time to lose. That much was clear by her hasty dismissal of us and her wolf son. Wep stopped only long enough to pick up a single pack that sat waiting by his front door, and walked down the pier to one of the newer boats. The Torey took on her full female form once more at the dock and dutifully kissed her son goodbye. He was slightly more comfortable with her when she was only Anput the mother and not Torey, the mind worm.

A gentle current flowed through the grotto and we drifted along with it into another cave. The current carried us on until we had travelled far from the Halls of Anubis, carried faster and faster into smaller and yet smaller caverns until the ceilings became so low that the grandeur of the marble grotto faded to a distant memory. The marble transitioned to ordinary rock and the crisp odorless smell of the Grotto was replaced with damp earth. We'd left most of the solar light far behind too and it was dark except for the electric lights on the boat.

It was unnerving being this far underground too. You felt the crushing weight of the earth above you, but the feeling was somehow familiar. I had been on a ride like this once at Disney Land – except there were singing pirates. This, on the other hand, had no sound track playing to quiet my nerves. There was only thick darkness and cold and quiet. The air chilled my skin and the spray from the water didn't help the cold that settled in my bones either.

Wep and Alexandra stood together in shadows at the helm. He navigated the ship through the twisting tunnels with one knee bent and resting on the bench seat beside him. Alexandra stood alongside him with perfect Oasen balance even as the boat rocked. She was like a blonde Cleopatra regally poised at the ship's helm, an icon of beauty and authority with all the mounds of silken pillows piled high as her backdrop. Wep was her pharaoh. All she was missing were the servants with palm fronds and grapes.

I wrung my hands and held on as we picked up more speed. The small vessel Wep had chosen was admittedly perfect for navigating the narrow tunnels. He knew what he was doing, sure. The guy had at least a thousand years' experience, but I didn't think it beneath him to toss me out of the boat by taking a corner too tight either. If I'd learned nothing else about him over the last few hours, it was that he was extraordinarily competitive, and I was more than positive who the competition was over.

Cleopatra.

The thought worried me at the moment with him in charge.

The fact that I was only the first halfworlder Alexandra's age that she'd ever met was not lost on me in this moment either. Maybe I was just a novelty? And now that she'd met Wep, she had an opportunity to move onto something better; someone more interesting? I mean, why hang around with a 17-year-old hybrid when someone like Wep was interested. The guy was a smooth-talking, good-looking, ancient, victorious, solar barque driving, howling, shape-shifting, makeup artist of a wolf man. What's not to love? I growled mentally.

And Alexandra laughed. The honeyed sound of it carried even over the roar of the waters, and Amisi shrugged her shoulders at me watching me watching them. I wanted to die.

We pushed forward through the dark and shadows another 30 feet until another tunnel took shape on our right and Wep halted the boat, powering down with a slosh of water off the stern like beer foam sloshing off a tall glass. Rock framed the tunnel's entrance, but it wasn't natural in formation. The rock was carved to look like teeth. The stones arched around the tunnel opening forming a gruesome open mouth. A twisted nose and two frog-like eyes were chiseled into the façade and glowered down at us as we floated through. A blast of wind hit, making the mouth howl at us, even as it swallowed us whole as we entered. Wep kissed the ceiling for good measure. It was a superstitious gesture.

"That was eerie."

"Yeah, I hate this tunnel," Wep added. "But this is the way we're going."

We drifted slowly in. The engine was quiet, as if Wep turned it off. Only the current pulled us through. And it was dark again, but somehow worse. It didn't just consume light, it consumed you.

The boat floated silently another 10 feet and then the tunnel opened up. Light-filled braziers adorned the long watery hall. And there, along both sides of the walls, were catacombs, but these weren't ancient Egyptian. These were the catacombs of the Oasens. Beautifully carved Egyptian columns rose from the raised walkways on each side every 15 feet.

"I should have warned you. But I wasn't sure how. It's ... it's different," Wep gulped and let us look. Down each side of us were stacks of gold metal coffins with transparent glass viewing panels built into the sides. Each revealed a different person in various states of dress and various ages too. Some were children. Some were in their prime, and some were old and wrinkled with long life. And each was perfectly preserved.

Wep caught his breath. "Behold your brothers and sisters for we are in the burial vault of the pharaonic princes and princesses of Oases."

Wep let that sink in.

"These are children of those who came here on the Barque starship. They are the Earth children born to them during their 3,000-year reign. Most are interred here, but some chose to be buried the ancient way."

The silence was eerie as we glided past all the dead. That this place was here, that all these people were here and had lived, it was almost too much.

"Why is that tomb empty," I gulped, pointing to a lit but vacant sarcophagus, but for a gold and black mask upon the pillow.

"That is the empty tomb of Tutankhamun. He was the son of Akhenaten. Poor boy." He was buried in the ancient way, but he has a place here as well. A vial of his blood sits under that mask, preserved here for all eternity."

I shivered involuntarily. Alexandra snickered at me.

"Peace be to them," I said trying to find some dignity.

Her face grew serious and they all said the words with me. "Peace be to them."

Even Wep said them.

We floated through the graveyard for what felt like an eternity, finally emerging from the house of death through another cave tunnel. The same frog man guarded this side as well. The warm air of the burial vault mixed with an icy frost, until the brief mingling of temperatures gave way to only cold.

"We're almost there," Wep shivered.

Alexandra pulled her arms around herself. The tunnel system wasn't exactly warm so far under the ground, but it had never felt this icy. "It feels like winter."

"Yeah, it's super cold." Amisi took Alexandra's arm and the two girls huddled together. The boat slipped into another section of tunnel and we emerged from the semi-darkness into a cave section flooded with light. I had to close my eyes for the sudden brightness. High rock walls climbed up each side, but the earth had caved into the tunnel from above and briefly opened it to the sky. Wet cold snow fell onto our faces from the heavens above.

Wep caught a flake in his hand and watched it melt. "How is this happening?" The white stuff caught in his eyelashes too.

Vertigo hit me as we plunged yet again into the darkness of the underground river system.

"Wait!" Amisi called out. "We need to go back. We have to contact Neter. Maybe we can get a good signal out there?"

"A better one anyway," Wep threw the boat into reverse.

Amisi rifled in her backpack and found her tablet. "Let's try it."

She pinged the ship and Neter's face appeared on the tablet.

"Amisi," Neter stated curtly. "You're coordinates state you are near Minya. Please explain."

"Nice to see you too Neter." She rolled her eyes. "We left Asyut. We need to meet you in Minya."

"That is impossible," Neter stated flatly.

Alexandra leaned over Amisi's shoulder. "What are you talking about Neter? Do you have a bug in your software?"

"No, Alexandra, but you must not go to Minya. There has been an outbreak of violence there since the storm systems began."

"Storm systems?" I leaned in.

"It's snowing in Egypt," Alexandra chided.

"Yes, and much more than that." Just then, the screen jerked and Seshat appeared. Neter complained in the background.

"Wait your turn, Micro Bolts." Seshat looked off-camera at something. I caught Wep's eyes going wide.

He knows her!

Wep ducked out of the way to inspect something suddenly important on the ship. He listened still, but seeing Seshat had thrown him.

"Listen, I'm glad you're alive and all, but while you guys were off playing, the planet went haywire. It's snowing in Egypt and Greenland's in a heat wave. People are freaking out." She looked around quickly and turned back to the camera. "I'm freaking out." Her voice squeaked and she got too close to the screen. Her eyeballs filled the monitor. I almost saw nose hairs. "Look, I know it's crazy, but I think we should meet in Alexandria. The violence isn't as bad there, but it's getting rough otherwise. Definitely steer clear of Giza and Cairo. We can meet up at the library. The old one. It will be safe there."

"How are we supposed to get to the library fast enough on a boat through an underground river system?" Amisi asked.

The tablet screen split sideways, controlled from Neter's end, and a real-time satellite image of our location filled the screen. Neter zoomed down on us in sickening fast motion until an obscure image of the five appeared through the cracked earth.

"You still have Gil?" Seshat looked behind her like she heard something.

"Yes, of course."

"Well, get him to call down one of his solar storms and get that boat in the air. Hurry." The camera rocked and the screen went blank. They were gone – just like that.

"Good grief, I hope she's okay."

"She'll be fine," Wep said. "She always is." He walked back to the helm avoiding further inquiry. He backed the small craft up again into the center of the snowy tunnel and gauged the size of the opening. Crisp vegetation hung in frozen splendor from the opening above us, obscured only by the white haze of snow that still fell peacefully.

"Good thing this is my latest solar model." He grinned at Alexandra. Whatever had thrown him over Seshat was gone now. "I built her 100 years ago. And," he stared up at the opening above us again, "I do believe she's small enough to get out through that."

Wep idled the boat, and walked quickly around it opening a port at each corner. He walked back to the helm and backed the boat up some more. "Sit please," he called out. He checked to make sure we obeyed and then pressed a button. A shimmery clear veil flew out over us. This time it didn't press down, but formed a transparent dome above. We were sealed in like a submarine.

Wep raised a wind sail and motioned to me. "Your turn."

"Right." I wondered if I had to call out 'Gil commands the sun' again. It seemed a little overkill. This time I decided to do it modern style. I quietly reached up with my Bau and tugged at the sun. Time accelerated, reversed, and a solar wind flew down at us melting the snow as it went. The boat rose vertically as it caught the particles. A sail billowed out.

"I hope this thing has some sort of cloaking device, Wep, because we're about to draw a lot of attention otherwise."

"Oh yeah, thanks. It does. I forget we're not in Ancient Egypt anymore." He toggled a switch and an electric current shuddered through the boat.

"Here we go."

This time, we accelerated heavenward toward Alexandria.

Chapter 21—We have sandwiches at Seshat's Place

I never thought I'd see the great sphinx covered in snow, but I never thought someone would tell me I was an alien either. A lot could change in a few weeks.

As we flew over Giza, we swung low to check out the big cat. Ice crystals grew between his toes as he stretched upon the frozen sand. I caught something else gleaming in the light while we flew by, but we were going too fast to find out what it was. If it wasn't for the troops standing guard over him like so many frozen popsicles, children might be playing on him – or from the appearance of the nearby city – terrorists might be destroying him. It was a coin toss today.

It was like that in so many of the big cities we flew over on our way north to Alexandria. Different religious groups blamed each other for the chaos the world had fallen into, and the result was catastrophic. A Christian temple sat smoldering in Minya. A Muslim mosque burned with bright orange flames near Cairo, unquenched even by the heavy and wet falling snow.

There was chaos in the air too; the heavens as angry as the people milling beneath. From almost the moment we rose from the underground tunnel, the wind held the solar barque in a stomach-twisting embrace, like two lovers caught in a tragic quarrel. The wind, however, was not without its moments of tenderness. For the time being, we floated through calm skies. The reprieve was welcome. Everyone but Amisi took the chance to stand and stretch or lean out to see what was happening below.

"Look at that," Wep yelled out as the clouds parted. He hung precariously out over open air, holding on with an arm and a leg wrapped around the mast of his broken wind sail. He was like a sun-bronzed pirate of the air, the mast bent beneath him at an awkward angle after the last burst of turbulence we went through. It's only use now was that of unstable lookout.

The man was crazy. Or maybe some kind of heroic bad boy daredevil by the way Alexandra was always watched him?

Little currents of air ruffled his hair and his eyes flashed with the risk he took. "Have you ever seen anything like it?" he asked in that breathy way he had. I ignored his Titanic moment, though Alexandra couldn't by the way she watched him. She leaned back on her elbows against the opposite rail staring. I took her in with my eyes while she watched another, and then turned to check out what Wep was actually talking about. A line of cars stretched as far as the eye could see up the Desert Highway. The line ran from the fire-riddled and sprawling capital city of Cairo to the port city of Alexandria on the coast.

We weren't the only ones seeking refuge there tonight.

Alexandra walked over and stood beside me. Her eyes briefly rested on me, then fell toward the highway, taking in the snake of cars below. You could sense their fear and their hope as they travelled that road. It heaped responsibility on my head. Their hope wasn't at the end of that road though. It flew along with them above their heads. They just didn't know it. I wondered if Alexandra felt as burdened as I? We were responsible for the fate of this planet.

"There must be thousands of cars on the road."

She only nodded, lost in her own thoughts.

"I can hear them honking," Amisi squeaked from her seat. Her voice sounded small, because her head was wedged firmly between her legs. It was the best she could do without a paper bag to blow into. "Oh, I can hear them honking." This time, she put her fingers in her ears to tune them out and started rocking.

Ryan went to sit beside her.

Alexandra's eyes rested on Amisi now. "All this must be so terrifying for them." She caught my eyes and went silent again.

"I can't imagine what they're thinking. The fabric of our world is going crazy and they don't understand why."

It was hard for me to forget what was at the end of all this if we couldn't find a way into Isis' bunker in Palenque. Terrifying, yes. Most definitely. The potential for total annihilation does that to a person.

I turned Isis' words over and over again in my head as I had since she spoke them to me in the dream walk. When Orion falls, to Draco goes the spoils. When Orion falls, to Draco goes the spoils. When Orion falls, to Draco goes the spoils.

Ugh.

The wind picked up, tossing Alexandra's blonde curls into the air. The bluster was so strong, it made her blue eyes water from the sudden bite of it against her cheek. It blew again and this time so hard, she fell against the railing. I reached out to steady her.

Her back felt slender under my arm. I took my hand off before there was a chance for the blue sparks to come and embarrass and remind her.

One thing I knew: The wind was going to get violent again.

"Get down Wep," I commanded. He couldn't fly like us and to fall would mean death.

"Coming." He shimmied down the mast and jumped into the ship. He wasn't a fool. He knew it as well as I did; our lover was angry again. Another gust hit. This one was bitter cold and smelled of burned things.

Amisi groaned from her seat.

I risked one more peek over the side before returning to the helm. Night fell and the car's lights blinked on like dominos falling over in the darkness. It was a peaceful, almost normal sight in the midst of such chaos – but for their sheer volume. The stars were coming out too, becoming pin pricks in the night sky. "When Orion falls, to Draco goes the spoils," I said aloud. "What does it mean?"

A burst of light shot up behind us and exploded in the twilight sky like deadly fireworks sent too early. They broke the half-silence we had been enjoying. Someone was firing haphazardly into the air.

"That was close!" Ryan ran astern to check for damage. Even Amisi raised her head, but she coughed and had to drop down again. If the air choked with smoke before, it was worse now.

Wep rushed to inspect his boat for damage too, but he should have been more careful. A brutal gust of wind hit and tossed him to the boards. The ship reared up at the sheer force of it and came back down hard against the solar winds we still rode north. Wep had disengaged the solar veil so he could climb out on the mast, and that meant another gust could send us all flying.

As soon as it was safe, Alexandra ran to kneel beside Wep. "Are you okay?"

She reached out and stroked his forehead, brushing his hair from his eyes.

I couldn't watch.

He winced and rubbed his knee as he sat up but his eyes sparkled. "Yeah, I think I'll make it princess," he added and grinned. Her mouth arched up to match his expression involuntarily. I was going to be sick and not from the nausea-inducing winds.

Amisi's face was green.

Grimacing internally, I went to check on him too, but I didn't have to be nice about it. "What the heck were you thinking? It's crazy up here," I scolded. "Be careful." I thrust my hand out to yank him up and he accepted, but I pulled him so hard, I nearly launched him into the air and over the side of the boat. I grabbed at him with my other hand and managed to bring him back down again but too hard.

Ryan snickered under his breath, and Alexandra narrowed her eyes at me, but I didn't care. Like I said, Wep was a pretty perceptive guy. He knew exactly what he was doing to make me so angry. He was lucky I didn't let go.

Wep stood and dusted himself off and grinned smugly at me. His mouth revealed lines of sharp white teeth – and probably rabies. I wished I could smack that superior expression off his face. Anger knotted the muscle in my forearm. I clenched my fist so hard the tendons there went white with the strain. The way I reacted, my body would rather punch the expression off his smug face. I noticed Ryan's eyes go wide in alarm. Even Alexandra pulled back on Wep's arm noticing my change.

"Careful." Ryan grabbed me by the shoulder and leaned in close to whisper to me. "You don't know what you're capable of angry, Gil, and I personally don't want to experience it for the first time 1,200 feet above the Earth – even if I can fly. Now, calm down," he commanded.

"Okay," I shook him off, flexing my hand to release the tension. Wep would love it if I hit him, since it would probably fuel Alexandra's affection for him. I didn't want to give him the satisfaction. Instead, I pursed my lips, clenched my jaw, and walked back up to the helm.

Alexandra stared after me.

I swore her mouth hung open slightly. I narrowed my eyes back at her in contempt. If she wanted to hurt me, she was doing a great job. She saw and bit her bottom lip, revealing the gap in her teeth.

Darn it, I loved that gap.

I turned away.

Anger and love and jealousy do weird things to a person. I tried to slow my breathing. Someone would have to cuff me with a Bes Amulet if I didn't calm down. And that wouldn't exactly be great considering I had to keep up with the solar winds or we'd fall out of the sky.

I better be calm and ready, I thought, not having a tantrum over a reticent 16-year-old girl I kissed once and the ancient wolf man who had a thing for her.

Wep hastily relaunched the protective veil over us – and just in time. Something tugged at my Bau, sensing what was coming before it arrived. The solar winds I controlled pulled against me in protest. Then the Earth winds came and tried to rip them from my grasp. I bit my cheek so hard I tasted blood.

There wasn't much time for warning.

"Everybody, hold on!" Alexandra was out of it though, staring off into space. "I said hold on Alexandra!" My voice was seared with an odd mixture of anger and fear. She snapped out of it just in time.

The boat lurched and we dropped down toward the earth as the wind ripped the solar tide from beneath us. I watch the blue and green colored solar winds shoot out away from our ship. The Earth winds drove the stream so far from us that we flipped and twisted in an out of control descent toward the ground. Thank the stars for the veil that held us down or that would have been our end.

I held my breath and called the solar winds back. They flew in below us, and we landed hard on the tide as it rushed under. My neck was jolted with the force, but I willed us higher anyway – away from the ground.

"That was close," Ryan screamed. He held the arched pillar on the boat's stern. "We almost hit."

"I'm sorry!" I called out. "That came out of nowhere!" I made us climb as quickly as possible; still the Earth winds raced around us and threatened to chase us out of the sky. We had just gained altitude when we fell again.

"Oh!" Amisi yelled out, terrified and sick.

The boat swayed and dropped 30 feet. Thankfully it wasn't as bad as the last one. I was ready this time. The solar winds raced back to catch us, but Amisi's face turned an even more unnatural shade of green. I felt for her.

"Hold on Amisi," Ryan yelled over the cacophony of wind as he tried to make his way back to her. "We're going to make it."

He spoke into my head. "I think."

I swallowed and tried to focus.

"Thanks for the vote of confidence, Ryan," I returned mentally. "You could always fly there yourself."

"No thanks. Not in this."

We flew on toward the Library, dipping and swerving and falling and rising back up as we went. I was never more grateful for the rollercoaster rides Alexandra took me on in the planetary vehicles than now. It was preparation for this. The ship rocked and buckled and tried to throw us, but I held on. When we finally approached the city, Amisi, who I honestly thought had passed out, stood and pointed with uncontained glee. "There it is!" she shouted. "There ... it ... is!"

The library's slanted dome was right ahead. Snow had fallen across it and a slush of blue ice had formed on the dam of water surrounding it. It was breathtaking as usual. Unfortunately, that was all the beauty left this place. As we circled down, I realized the unrest had made its way here too. Even pristine, modern Alexandria wasn't immune from the panic seizing the world. There were bands of mobs roaming the streets. Fires burning. People screaming. And if it was like this here, what was going on back home? I hadn't even thought about the States since we arrived.

I felt a hand on my back. "I'll take it from here, friend."

"Okay, buddy." We stood sizing each other up, Wep a full head taller.

Then I walked to Alexandra and sat down. He frowned at my play.

"Seshat was supposed to add something unique to the design of this new library for me," he said. "Let's hope she came through, or we all might be dead in a moment."

"That's reassuring. Thanks Wep."

He grinned and grabbed the controls like he wouldn't let his own self think any more about it. The boat turned and arched sharply down at the reflection pool. We were picking up speed and about to hit the middle of the icy pool when a circle of Oasen light formed on the water and a crust of ice dislodged and drained down into a vortex of swirling water. Our boat plunged into the newly-revealed tunnel and the hole sealed itself above us. Lights switched on and we slid down a corkscrew of water into an underground lake. There, at the bottom, was another long dock with a metal elevator at its end, waiting for us.

"That was much more interesting than I imagined." Wep wiped the sweat off his forehead.

"What is it with you guys?" Amisi stormed at him – finally free of her seat. The usually demure Oasen had finally had enough. "Why is everything underground and why do you have to dive into all your secret little lairs?" She threw her hands on her hips, but Wep only grinned.

"Because it's fun." He shrugged his shoulders. Amisi huffed.

Wep sidled the boat up to the short dock and tied up. "Come my lady." He offered Amisi a hand, eliciting an angry smile. Wep had a way with women.

Amisi took it and stepped out of the boat. Her legs shook but you could tell she was glad to be on solid ground again. Ryan took over for Wep and led her down to the shore where she collapsed. Alexandra ignored us both and jumped out by herself. She'd had enough too – but for different reasons.

We ended up following her down the narrow dock together.

"So, we take the elevator?" I asked, making conversation.

"Oh, you're smart too," We countered. "Here, make yourself useful."

He took off the leather necklace that hung round his neck. A glass tear drop swayed from the ropey hide. He shoved it at my chest and grabbed my hand, raising it in the air like I was an incompetent child who couldn't manage alone. Some of the solar light dancing around the room rushed at it and the tear drop grew and swelled until it was the size of a small lantern. When it was finished, he pushed it at my chest and hurried for shore without me. I stood there watching him and wondered how everything with Alexandra had spiraled out of control so quickly. What did she see in that guy?

Still hanging back, Wep was almost to the elevator when a blur of movement came from the shadows right at him. The thing hit Wep so hard, he went flat to the ground and remained there with the creature hovering above his still form. Ryan and Amisi froze in place. Alexandra flinched but it didn't go for her either. I had time to wonder how something so massive could be so silent, but then saliva dropped from the creature's mouth onto Wep's slack face, and I couldn't think straight. Was he even breathing? All I saw was the wet goop mixing into the dirt Wep was pinned to.

"Mother planet!" Ryan yelled as soon as he took a breath and fell back. The creature's head followed Ryan's voice, steam emanating from its wet nostrils, but it stayed hunched over Wep's unmoving body, unwilling to abandon its prize.

Amisi tensed but she didn't run. "No one move." Her voice was forceful but her lips were as still as a ventriloquist's. "Don't move a muscle."

Ryan froze. We all froze. Wep lay unmoving too.

The creature had the body of a lion but the head of a falcon. Its neck rotated sideways like an owl's too, eyeing our last location curiously. It starred with its bright gold eyes, watching for more movement.

It twitched. It waited. The thing was terrifying.

Wep lay pinned under its massive weight.

He still wasn't moving.

"That ... is a hieracosphinx," Amisi risked. The creature heard her and watched for us, but we remained still. She stopped talking.

The thing turned back to Wep and made a terrible noise before pecking down at his skull with its beak-like head. Wep moved, finally awake and I wanted to be sick. I looked away, movement or not.

"Leave off, Aker," Wep shouted using the Egyptian name for gate-keeper. His voice was raspy like his vocal cords were adjusting to normal after being crushed. "It's me, Wep, you stupid bird. You're scaring everyone. Not to mention, you're about to crush me to death."

I turned back around.

That's when I noticed the creature wasn't having Wep for dinner, but was licking his face with a curiously long tongue like a loyal family pet. Of course, my family pets were never prone to leaving me momentarily unconscious, so you'll have to forgive the lapse in judgment.

Wep wiggled underneath him and pushed Aker off. The hieracosphinx obediently moved aside and sat down on its haunches. Its tongue lolled out of its beak-like mouth as if it was smiling. Wep took a minute to get to his knees and winced when he did.

"Been a while, huh, old friend?" Wep wheezed and stood in front of him, scratching at his ears which moved up and down opposite each other in response. The creature was still higher than Wep even sitting down. A large bone, picked completely clean, lay in the dirt nearby – the femur of a cow I suspected. Wep spotted it too and tossed it out over the lake like he was playing catch with his dog. The creature's responded instantaneously. It unfurled its huge wings and went airborne revealing feathers arranged like a rainbow kaleidoscope. They made his takeoff majestic, but then they blurred the air, he moved so fast, creating a rainbow effect over the cave lake. Aker caught the bone before it hit the water and returned gliding low over its surface until it came to rest in its earlier sitting position. It dropped the bone at Wep's feet. And waited.

"Everyone, this is Aker." He tossed the bone again.

Again, the creature launched and returned.

"He can be sweet when you get to know him."

"I'll take your word for it," Amisi pointed at the elevator button.

Wep nodded. "I'll be back soon, Aker!"

The bird heard and ignored the bone, which landed in the water. Ake returned to the shore and Wep petted his oversized head. "Remember these ones." He pointed to all of us though he hesitated when he came to me. "They are friends."

The cosphinx sniffed at us so he would remember, and then went to curl up in the shadows. Something thumped, there was a crunching noise, and I got a glimpse of the rest of that cow.

"Yes, nice to meet you too Aker," I added. Aker's eyes peeked out at us, catching the light. A strip of red meat hung garishly from his beak. "Definitely, remember me next time, okay?" I gulped.

Even Wep had to stifle a laugh at that.

When the elevator doors opened, we made our way down to Old Alexandria. But this time, the elevator doors opened on a world of darkness.

Wep seemed surprised to find it in this state, but he played it off.

"Seshat's not one to waste resources."

He grabbed the glowing solar lantern from my hands. This threw the shadows into some order but it was still dark.

"So, where to now?"

"This way. We're going to Seshat's place."

We followed him down the long-forgotten streets of Alexandria. Wep finally stopped at a tall white-washed house. "Yes. I think it's this one. It's been a while." He approached the door and knelt down. He felt along the door jam, finding a small hollow recess carved into the stone and pulled out a red-foiled candy.

"What is that?" Alexandra asked, uncomfortable.

"I think it's a Hershey's kiss." He put it in his pocket quickly and tried the door. Finding it unlocked, we stumbled into a long entrance hall. The place was very old inside from what I could tell with so little light, like we were about to get a candlelight tour of a restored castle.

Wep felt along the wall and then electric lights flooded the house. He tried another switch and the "sky lights" that lit the underground world came on too.

Wolf man shoved the light at my chest and walked deeper into the house. He walked down the main hall and took a series of corridors until we came to a small study. The house was only sparsely furnished in an old style and plain, which surprised me considering the vibrancy of Seshat's personality. Then Wep found a hidden panel in this room, and this time, a wedge of Oasen light appeared on the floor, and the ground opened to reveal a hidden staircase.

"This is the real house."

"Another subterranean dwelling," Amisi added. "How surprising."

We descended into a modern home adorned in deep reds and purples and sparsely scattered jewel-toned blues. This was more like it. A big sectional sat on a fuzzy white rug scattered with even more lounging pillows in those wine colors. A modern plasma TV hung on the wall above a false fireplace set in white stone. The room was huge and open. Adjoining the den was a sleek white kitchen, set off by black granite countertops that brightened the windowless room. A huge island set with six barstools hugged the space between the living room and kitchen. It was like Seshat knew we were coming. Wep went straight to the stainless steel fridge and pulled out an ice-cold Orange Fanta.

"Seshat has good taste. In cola too. Could you toss me one?"

Wep obliged and kept rummaging around the fridge mumbling "I'm starving" from its interior.

"Me too, man." Ryan ran up behind him and leaned in. Even I couldn't blame him for his appetite after today.

I sat down at the counter and sipped my drink, but it was too quiet.

"Seshat's not here." I dared to mention.

There was an audible sigh from around the already quiet room. Amisi came and sat down next to me with a root beer she had gotten from Ryan. Her forehead was crowded with worry lines. She popped the top and fizz trickled down the side. She wiped it on her already dirty sleeve and drank deeply.

We were all a mess.

"I hope she's okay." She almost drained the can. "Do you think something happened to her? That picture going dead like that; did something happen?"

We were all wondering it.

"Let's try and check in with her," Wep offered between bites. "We can do it from here. That was the next thing on my agenda but the fridge was calling. I can't go forever without eating."

Ryan put sandwiches and chips in front of Amisi and me and took a seat. "You too."

"Thanks buddy."

"No problem."

Wep plunked down on the sofa with his plate of food balanced on one thigh and found a huge remote by digging in the cushion beside him. The sound was off, but the picture was tuned to CNN. The frame was split into four squares. In one, the pretty anchor was back talking but more disheveled than last time. Another showed the Great Sphinx sitting outside in the furious blizzard. Yet another showed Greenland, the ever-frozen country, with patches of green peeking out of its melting snow. And the third was the empty podium in the press room of the White House.

The anchor put her finger to her ear and glanced away. The screen cut to a singular view of the White House Press Room. The President walked out. Wep hit another key and the picture went blank.

"Hey!"

"What? Do you want to know what that guy has to say or would you like to actually save the world?"

"Smart aleck."

"Save the world," Alexandra finished for me.

"Okay then. What's Neter's identification port?"

"One sec man." Ryan swallowed quickly and walked over to help. The picture shifted to a view of Neter's empty bridge.

"Neter?" Alexandra called out.

Neter's image filled the screen.

"Where's Seshat?"

Neter's purple eyes were bright and her black hair pristine as usual. I wondered if she would look disheveled had something gone wrong.

"With you, I assume?"

"What do you mean?"

"She left here three hours ago. She should be there by now," Neter said flatly.

"Oh my stars. Did she try to come here on foot ... through all that?"

"Yes, but she assured me she was well-equipped to handle the situation."

"Maybe not." Amisi bit her lip.

Neter didn't respond.

"Get the solar light back out Gil," Wep commanded. "We have to go back up there and find her." The lantern sat idle on the counter in front of me. Solar light still danced trapped within it.

"And how do you propose we do that?"

Wep stood, elongated himself to his full height of 6' 3". "Oh, don't worry, Gil. I've got a nose for these kinds of things."

Chapter 22–I walk the dog

I was enjoying this way more than I should, considering. I couldn't believe he let me do it, but for some reason I got the job. His feet padded along silently in front of me, his neck bent low to the ground. He wasn't kidding when he said he had a "nose" for this kind of thing, though he was being far more literal than I realized.

Wep was on all fours in his wolfy form at the end of the leash I carried. He had rummaged around one of Seshat's drawers and produced it. Its leather was as old as the hidden city, but oiled and well preserved, like someone lovingly cared for it each day of its long life. The deep-brown leather was marked by a thousand tiny hieroglyphs burned black into the hide. It was a story about a boy, he said. It was one I wanted to read if I lived through this.

Wep's wet nose glistened black and sent out little puffs of white steam as he snuffled along the ground searching for signs of Seshat. Around us, smoke choked the air and night draped around us like a black veil. We walked briskly toward the ocean where Neter left Seshat hours ago. I wondered if the smell made it hard for Wep? Or if the maze of streets made it harder to find the water?

A car alarm blared somewhere nearby.

Wep made his way down a side street through a broken fence. He sniffed the air and circled back. We turned a corner and the ocean peered at us from between two buildings. We were a few streets away. He found it.

Smart, Wep.

I almost reached out to rub him behind the ears, but stopped myself. His wolfy face became stern when he realized what I was about to do, but I saw laughter light his eyes too.

"At least you're living up to your name." I patted him on the head anyway. "You definitely saw that opening."

His tongue lolled out happily.

It was easier to like him when he was in doggy form.

As we got closer, a salty breeze came off the water even through the smoke. Fires had been set in abandoned cars and most of the storefronts here were vandalized. People were yelling and cursing from the windows high above us. A woman screamed. A glass crashed and shattered in the intersection behind us, the homemade bomb bursting into flames. We passed yet another smoldering car.

This didn't bother Wep at all.

Every once in a while he would stop and shake wet flakes off his back, sending a shower of ice our way. It made his thick fur bristle up on its ends like he was about to lunge at someone, but instead he'd turn his head to look at us with laughing eyes and a tongue hanging out of his mouth, panting with the heat his exertion even in the midst of this cold, frozen world.

A gun shot sounded nearby and I reached out my arm instinctively to shield Alexandra. This one was close. She glanced sideways at me as we pushed on through the dirty slush, and I removed my arm from across her chest. Her ever-intense eyes watered in the cold and made their blue shine brighter. Her golden ringlets hung down in frozen perfection, and her breath blew out in white clouds.

A group of young men rounded the corner cursing in Arabic. They hauled a huge television through the snow. A nearby store alarm was blaring and Wep whined at the noise, snapping at them as they passed. One nearly lost it on the slippery pavement, but the thief steadied himself and ran even faster to get away with his prize.

Wep continued to bark and snap at them even though they were far down the road and I realized I was holding Alexandra's hand. She noticed too and pulled away, the tiniest hint of a spark falling to the ground, its electric sizzle warming my hand just slightly from the cold. She bolted toward Amisi and Ryan who had pulled ahead. She made me sad and happy at the same time.

"She's beautiful, capable and fierce," I said out loud so the gray wolf would hear me. I stood watching her run away. "Everything I never knew I wanted."

Wep huffed back at me in agreement.

"No hard feelings Wep." It was funny talking to a dog. "But I'm not giving up without a fight."

The wolf held my gaze with his intelligent eyes, snorted at me, and put his nose back to the ground. But then he stopped. He dug his nose in again huffing in whatever scent he just caught, and whined and tugged at his leash.

"Hey guys. Wep's got something."

Alexandra came back, kneeling down to scratch between his ears. "What'd you find?"

He nuzzled into her hand.

Wep stole a glance my way.

Only I caught its meaning. He wasn't giving up either.

He sniffed at the ground once more and yowled, then bolted toward the seashore, stopping to nose the ground as he went.

"Whoa! Slow up there, Wep!"

But he dragged me toward the waterfront anyway where a looming stone fort sat guard on the edge of the Mediterranean.

Wep turned his doggy head back toward me, and it morphed into a human one. It happened just long enough for him to say, "Something's not right. It doesn't smell right," and his head changed again to the wolf. I was glad we were running so hard my brain didn't have time to process it, because Wep's human-headed dog body totally freaked me out.

"Hurry!" I yelled back. "Something's wrong."

The others sprinted to catch up, running slightly faster than humans are capable until we reached the stone archway that led into the fort. It was abandoned which was odd considering how much chaos was happening a hundred feet from here. The silence was unnerving, in fact. My Aunt Vera would have said it was so quiet you could hear crickets, but I thought it too cold for that anyway. Amisi shivered hard and wrapped her arms around herself, but not from the cold. Ryan's eyes narrowed cautiously and went to stand next to her. Even Alexandra took a step backward. Something wasn't right.

Wep morphed back into a man then – all the way this time – completing the transition on one knee. I saw a dark-eyed man scramble away from nearby shadows. If he saw Wep change, he wasn't interested in sticking around for more.

Wep stretched up toward the structure, pointing as he stood to his full height. "She's there." He pointed at the highest parapet. "She's keeping the rioters away with her powers."

Someone threw an exploding bottle off a side street, maybe the dark-eyed man again, but the fire hurler wouldn't approach any closer.

Wep stroked the stubble growing on his chin. "Do you not feel it? This place feels cursed. No true Egyptian would set foot here."

I felt it. And it was creeping me out worse than Wep's human wolf-head combo. I held my breath and tried to swallow back the fear that wound round my neck like a snake cinching tight. "Well, it's a good thing I'm not an Egyptian, then," I blustered.

"I'm not sure I am either," Wep returned. "So, I guess we both have to push through." He swallowed visibly.

"Whether she's cursed this place or not, Seshat's wigging me out with her voodoo vibes." Amisi's black hair bounced and her head swiveled, just waiting for something to jump out at her. Her silver eyeliner sparkled in the moonlight. "Let's get this over with."

The dread was like thick water that had to be plowed through, but we pushed through it together until we came out into a courtyard where the crushing pressure dissolved as we broke into the open grounds.

"Oh gods," Amisi said. "I hope that was it."

"That was rough," I admitted.

Wep shook his head in agreement and sniffed the air again with his human nose. He pointed to the same tower.

"There. I see her."

Seshat's small form sat motionless atop the structure. She was hard to see, sitting silent on the rooftop. I hoped she was okay. I wondered even more why she was up there.

Across the courtyard, we marched to her building. Wep didn't have the privilege of flight like we Oasens, so we climbed the stairs instead, practically falling out the door onto the roof. Even Oasens get tired after so little sleep.

Seshat sat there resplendent in her pixie-like beauty, her pale skin glowing in the moonlight. She sat cross-legged with her face to the sky, but turned toward our noise, confused by the interruption.

Our identities dawned on her like she was waking, but one person in particular peaked her interest. Her eyes went wide and Seshat ran straight for Wep. She hugged him so tight, I thought he might pull back so he could breathe, but instead he just buried his head in her neck and wept. Alexandra stood stiff watching their display of unchecked emotion. Finally they pulled away, holding each other at arm's length, tears streaming down their faces.

"Wep, darling," she choked. "I thought this day would never come. Your mother finally released you from that dungeon of hers?"

He kissed her cheek. "Yes. Here I am! I fulfilled the promise I made to Ra too. We were at your house. I found the chocolate," he prattled, pulling it out.

She held him to her again.

My stomach twisted. While this turn of events was squarely in my favor, what Wep was doing to Alexandra was cruel, even if he did spend a few thousand years underground with no one but his scary mom to hang out with. You didn't hit on the first girl you saw until you met up with your old girlfriend. It was harsh.

Wep noticed us staring. "Oh." He held Seshat's hand in his. Alexandra was examining this. Wep laughed out loud. "This is my grandmother, Seshat. On my dad's side. I haven't seen her in a long time. Like thousands of years, long time."

I nearly fainted.

Grandma! You have got to be kidding me!

Well that blows.

Alexandra kept her face a mask of stone, but I swore her eyes crinkled slightly with a well-hidden smile.

"I didn't expect that," I said out loud. Ryan nearly lost it at my lack of a filter, but Amisi smacked him on the leg so he would shut his mouth.

"What are you doing here of all places, Tetta?"

He called her the Arabic name for grandma. How cute.

"Tay-tuh," I said under my breath. "Isn't that sweet?"

Apparently it was, based on the looks being exchanged.

"Why are you here and not at the Library?"

Seshat shook her head like she was coming out of a trance. "I'm not sure. I was on my way there, but then, I don't remember anything at all ... until you fell out the door." Seshat looked up, then went still and touched her neck like something was wrong. "What's this?" She pulled out a necklace. "It's not mine."

On it was a familiar emerald ring, glowing softly.

Alexandra reached out reflexively and touched it. "I know this ring. It belongs to the Oracle." Her eyes went wide as she reached for it. "Here, would you let me?"

Seshat nodded yes and pulled back her hair. Alexandra unclasped it and slipped it off the chain onto her finger.

Alexandra became still as stone.

Nothing happened at first.

"She usually talks by now."

We all leaned in.

Instead of talking, Alexandra jumped without warning onto the ledge of the building. I tried to grab her, but she landed like a cat, stopped, and looked out over the water, without hurting herself – or falling over. Thank the stars.

The voice of the Oracle spoke from her lips. Her hair blew wild from a sudden breeze. Her voice was low and unnatural – again. "I am sorry for this interruption, but I have foreseen the destruction of my people." Her monotone voice was slow with sadness. Alexandra glanced back at the sea like it haunted her. "They do not have to die tonight."

Her eyes found mine and held.

"I have seen another path along the line should you so choose, Gilbert Scott. But first I must tell you ..." She said this as if it was a law and not gesture of good will, "... that you will suffer a great consequence to save them. Sacrifices must be made when salvation is attainable. It is known."

She let this sink in.

"However, Gil Scott, this consequence will not disturb the final pattern. But it will make your journey that much more difficult."

Perfect, I thought. "What is going to happen Oracle?"

"Tens of thousands will die here tonight without your intervention," she answered, forthright for once. She gazed out over the water. "It is good for you that you have found this high ground. You may have need of it yet." And with those words, she was gone from Alexandra who slumped in exhaustion and slipped the ring from her finger. She threaded it back onto the necklace and tried to give it back to Seshat.

She refused, waving it away with her hand. "You wear it. I want nothing to do with the Oracle."

Alexandra nodded and clasped it on her own neck instead.

"Death is everywhere tonight." Wep's voice reverberated off the stone walls of the fort. "Everywhere."

"I don't think we can let thousands of people die? Can we?"

"Even if it means things are about to get much harder for us." Ryan kicked a loose pebble across the roof.

"How much harder can things get?" I raised my shoulders, but they fell just as fast. They could get way worse. That was the answer.

The others nodded. They understood that too.

"The question is, what is about to happen?" Alexandra bit her lip. "The Oracle is notorious for withholding important details."

"Something she said bothered me, but I can't put my finger on it. She was talking about high ground and ... and ... I'm not sure. Someone said something to me once about that – about high ground."

My mind went blank, then realization dawned on me.

"Oh my goodness!" I jumped up to pace on the ledge. Everyone's eyes went to me. "Simon! Simon was the one."

I must have seemed crazy.

"My friend," I tried to explain, "from back home. He's always drawing these crazy disasters and the last time I saw him sketching one, he told me, if you don't find high ground during a tsunami, you're toast." I paused long enough for them to understand me. "I think Egypt's about to get slammed by a tsunami!" I finished by jumping back down.

I peered over the edge of the roof top. The sea still lapped calmly against the shore.

"How do we stop a tsunami?"

"Well, if you can stop the ..."

The ground vibrated under our feet.

"... earthquake, no tsunami," Amisi finished her thought as the quake picked up strength. "Too late for that."

There was a sharp jolt, then the earth began jostling us back and forth and wouldn't stop. Glass shattered nearby and stones tumbled down, stirring up centuries-old dust, maybe older. One of the crumbling parapets nearby succumbed to its age, its rock crumbling down in a shower of grit and stone. I hoped the rest of this fort could withstand it.

When it was over, I felt my Bau tugging me toward the water. "The quake was centered there." I pointed out to sea, north-east of our location. "I guess I have a built in Bau sensor for these kind of things. There's a fault line out there. A big one. This is not good."

My nails were down to nubs. I tasted blood as I chewed them.

There was a loud roar and I thought the tsunami was coming, but then I felt a blast of air.

"Neter!" Alexandra yelled. "She's programmed to protect us. The tsunami must be coming." Her hair whipped in her face from the force of Neter's engines, but the ship was still camouflaged, flying unseen above us.

I wondered what that Egyptian hiding in the streets below thought about all this now?

I heard, as much as felt, a port open beneath Neter's hull and identical cylinders fell towards us, glistening translucent enough for us to see them stack one on top of another until they reached roof to ship.

"Go," I yelled. "Get out of here now."

Alexandra hesitated. "What are you doing, Gil?"

My feet were planted.

She refused to budge further, aware now that I didn't intend to come with them.

"Go already," I shouted. "The Oracles said I had to choose to save them. It's all on me."

I was pretty sure I sounded angry. This weight of the world on your shoulders stuff was getting old.

"Go on, Alexandra" This time I tried to be soft. "Find me after it's over, will you?"

"But Gil!" She ran back and grabbed my hands, unchecked.

Neter's engines whined with the anticipation of flight.

"Go, Alexandra."

Still, she didn't move. She held my hand, the blue energy flowing locked between them. For once, Alexandra's fast feet were frozen.

"Wep! Come get her."

He ran and picked her up, against her will, throwing her over his shoulder like a sack of angry potatoes, and ran back to the ship, her legs and arms kicking and hitting as she went. Wind was kicking up off the water and blew hard now. Alexandra's eyes never left mine, even though her long curls struck her eyes as the wind whipped it at her face.

"You jerk," she spoke in my head, still angry I forced her to go. "But be careful."

"You too," I answered mentally.

"You better take care of her, Wep." I added out loud.

He nodded and ran under the cylinder. Ryan and Amisi had just gone up. The cylinders came back down.

She stared back at me unbidden. "Be careful Gil. Please."

And then they were gone as Neter swallowed them up.

Chapter 23-I hang ten in Egypt

I t all happened much faster than I wanted it to. The water pulled back from the shore. The ship flew out over the sea and I jumped off the roof. Luckily, I remembered I could fly after I panicked halfway down.

Oh, yeah. Alien super powers.

I landed with one hand and a knee on the ground and gazed out over the wet land that had amassed after the sea pulled back to gather its waters into one bone-crushing tsunami.

I never felt less capable than I did right now. Here I was alone – even though I asked to be. And I didn't know what to do to save them.

I looked back toward the city.

Or myself.

How could I let my friends stay though?

It was the only way to protect her– to let her go, which made me think back to all those pharaonic princes and princesses in the burial chamber. Some of those guys were my age. They should have lived much longer. What kind of heroics had they tried to pull that put them there? The thought was disconcerting for a person about to face a killer wave alone.

"What am I supposed to do?" I screamed up at the sky. "Save the world! I haven't even done that yet. Now save the Egyptians? Anything else while I'm at it? I'm only 17!"

Then I did something crazier than jumping off a building. I sat down defeated while a killer tsunami formed at sea. The wet sand crunched coldly beneath me, and I buried my head in my knees. I shifted my weight over the knobby sand. It was already freezing. I picked some up and turned it over in my fingers and heard the roaring waters begin heading my way.

Great.

Not in any hurry though, I surveyed the beach. Two men stood 100 feet out where the sea used to be.

So, they'll be the first.

The sand stayed frozen between my fingers, not even melting from the heat of my body. It must be artic cold out here. I shivered even though my Bau helped keep me somewhat warm. The wave would be here soon. The Oracle believed in me, but there was some consequence coming too. What was I about to do to save the day while simultaneously messing things up?

I squeezed my eyes shut and mentally flipped through all my favorite comic book characters. What would they do to stop a tsunami?

My eyes opened wide. And I ran.

And I mean, I really ran. Like super-Oasen super hero kind of fast straight toward the approaching death wave. I heard it before I saw it.

But then it loomed. I reached deep inside me until I found my Bau. It was warm inside me, but that's not what I needed right now. I melted away the heat until the cold within me was nearly unbearable.

The edge of the wave was five miles south of me. I'd start there and finish at the end, I thought. There wasn't enough time though. But there hadn't been enough time in the gym either when the walls were coming down.

This wouldn't be the first time I manipulated time.

The cold within me fought against what I wanted, but it didn't have a choice. It was going to obey me now or we were all going to die. Time slowed to a crawl as I ran faster south, freezing inside, until I caught the wave and rode it like the Silver Surfer north towards where it ended.

I ejected the subzero chill I housed within me until the waters turned to frozen rock beneath my feet. As I rode the wave north, I stopped the killer surf in its tracks. Exhaustion nearly collapsed me, but I wasn't finished yet. A sound like metal grinding distracted me and I saw a force of cold water escape the wave and head toward the shore while my attention was diverted. Thankfully it dispersed harmlessly across the empty sea bed.

I must have frozen a boat, I thought. I hoped I didn't hurt anyone. But I kept on pushing until I reached the end and collapsed on a sea of hard ice in exhaustion.

I wasn't sure how long I lay there before Alexandra found me. Her frozen curls tickled my nose as she leaned over me and my eyes peaked open at her. My whole body felt stiff.

"Gil!" She grabbed me without restraint. "I thought you were dead!"

"Oh. Ow!"

"Sorry."

"I feel dead." She attempted to pull me to standing. I wobbled on my feet.

"How did you do all this?"

She pointed as I leaned hard against her and saw what she meant.

"Oh ..."

"It's 47 miles long," she interrupted.

A giant mass of waves – stretching on seemingly forever – lay locked in their fury, entombed in ice.

I staggered and fell on the ground. Consciousness left me. Alexandra reached down and stood me up again, but there was no way I was going anywhere by myself. My legs refused to move. My eyes rolled back in my head.

"Hmm." In true Alexandra form, she squatted down and grabbed me by one leg and arm and maneuvered me onto her shoulders. "I can't believe I'm doing this," she said so I could hear.

Me neither, my semi-conscious brain protested. I dangled from her shoulders, but I didn't complain. My mouth wasn't working either.

She touched an earpiece before I passed out. "I got him."

I woke again, dropping in and out of consciousness. Alexandra was strong. I always knew that, but this was taking it to a new level. After miles of hauling me across the plain of frozen ice behind the tsunami, she finally slowed down.

"Five more." She took another step. "Four, more." Her voice faltered, but she pressed on despite her labored breathing and unsure footsteps, not once stopping to rest. By the time she made it back to the ship, she staggered and dropped to her knees. I felt like I was falling in slow motion, but then again nothing had felt normal since the tsunami. Time was still in flux for me.

On my way down, I glimpsed Neter sitting on a frozen span of ocean ice, hidden behind the frozen tsunami from the shore. There was a narrow river of slushy water breaking up the ice there. Water gushed through it like churning river rapids and dispersed back toward the shore.

Curious.

The others ran up.

I never hit the ground. Ryan caught me as she went to her knees.

"Where did you find him?" He helped ease me onto the ground and took off his coat to slip it under my head.

"He was at the end of it." She collapsed onto the ground, "where I thought he'd be." She rested her hand possessively on my shoulder. My eyes barely opened at her touch. Her breathing was labored. Finally able to stop after walking for so long with me as her burden, she could barely talk for breathing. Her white breath hit the frozen air over and over in little raspy gasps, but she managed a deep breath and tried again. "With one hand lying in the water and the rest of him lying on the edge of an ice shelf." Her face twisted as if the words made her sick and she nodded toward me. The others followed her eyes. Theirs' narrowed too and Amisi turned away.

"He was lucky he didn't fall in." She swallowed something back.

My eyes blinked open. Alexandra lay with her fingers locked together over her heart, staring at the wintery ceiling of the sky. It was strangely bright to be this late. My inner solar clock told me it was still the dead of night, but the snow refracting all the light floating around in the atmosphere made it look like a white-blue morning. It made everything feel wrong.

"Did you make any progress?" Alexandra asked.

"I think so." Wep had knelt down beside her, putting his hand on her forehead tenderly. She moved her head to shake it off.

My eyes fumbled open wider.

Wait. Something else registered.

"What did you say about my hand?" The numb cold had worn away; now it was throbbing. I tried to see through the haze my vision had become. I pulled it away from my body and gagged. It was badly swollen and looked like a rehydrated prune in both color and texture.

"Oh, no!" I tried to sit up. Hands pressed down on my chest to still me. That's why her eyes narrowed in disgust. "I'm going to lose my hand." I gagged again and rolled to my side.

Talk about your consequences. I really liked that hand.

"No, you're not, Gil." Alexandra pushed herself up. She got to her knees beside me. "No, you're not." She put her hand across my forehead like she was feeling for fever. "Let's get him to the med bay. Or maybe one of the portable devices is still working?"

Alexandra peered into my eyes. They flit back and forth. I tried to hold her gaze through the fog I felt and blinked. Her lips tilted up in a halfway smile, but I don't think she realized I was conscious.

"I think he's going to be okay."

My vision and hearing blurred to momentary unconsciousness and then righted itself again to reality. I watched Wep pull her to standing from the slit in my eyes. Snow caked her pants. She knocked it off in great chunks.

Ryan stood me up next. I tried to put my weight on my feet to help, but faltered. He threw me onto his shoulders easily though, and followed everyone back to the ship. Neter was covered in a blanket of white snow, blending easily into the environment. Wep stood at the hatch door and nodded at me as I was carried by. I saw him lift a huge metal winch in his hand and manually close it after I passed.

Odd.

I paid closer attention.

"I don't think he can climb the service ladder," Ryan whispered. "You'll have to haul it down."

Amisi nodded and disappeared into a maintenance hatch. Her arms reach up like she was climbing.

Weird too.

I passed out again.

My life was a blur.

But it was only a moment of unconsciousness, because we were walking out of the storage bay door then. It didn't slide open at our approach. It was already open wide. They carried me through and down the hall to a cabin right off the bay.

Why didn't they take me upstairs to medical or to my room at least? No one slept down here.

Ryan laid me down on some stranger's bed.

"What's going on?" My tongue was thick like it'd been shot up with Novocain.

Why did Wep have that winch? Why was the storage bay door stuck open? Was Amisi climbing a ladder? Why am I here? Why didn't they take me to the med bay?

"What's wrong?" I stammered more aware now. "Something's wrong here," I had time to say.

"Shh." Alexandra came into my line of sight with her finger to her lips. That's when I noticed it in her hand. A syringe full of syrupy orange liquid.

She injected me with it.

I lost consciousness yet again, but this time, it was more permanent.

When I woke up, hours had passed and every one of us was huddled under blankets sleeping together in the same room. It was as cold as a meat locker. Ryan was snoring millimeters from my ear. I bolted straight up, which scared everyone else awake.

My strength was back. My hand was tucked under the covers. I yanked it out to check. I turned it over and over again. Thank goodness. It was abnormally red, but I wasn't going to lose it. I guess someone fixed me.

"What's going on? And no sleeping serum this time." I gave Alexandra my best cold stare – which was pretty easy considering how freezing it was. "What's wrong with Neter?"

"Oh Gil," Amisi said with concern.

"We were just trying to help." Ryan propped himself on an elbow. That didn't sound good.

"What do you mean?"

Ryan shook his head trying to wake enough to talk. "We had Neter fly low over the tsunami so we could use our abilities to slow the wave from here. But that's when we ran into you." He yawned. "For all her capabilities, Neter couldn't stop in time and we crashed into whatever it was you were throwing out to freeze it."

That metal grating sound. That was Neter.

"She's frozen?" Somehow I asked calmly.

"Well, parts of her are. Some important ones. We had some trouble thawing her out too."

"So, that's the consequence then, not my hand." My skin still stung in reminder. "We don't have a ship?"

"That's the consequence. After Alexandra knocked you out and fixed your hand, she spent a few hours unfreezing part of Neter's operating system. We think, ahh," he yawned. "We think the housing protecting it must have been damaged the first time Neter crashed, so it wasn't protected as well. That's the part we're having trouble with – the part that basically runs the ship – heat, flight, doors, all that."

"I might have made things worse too." Her voice was quiet. "I used a laser to unfreeze it at first. I wasn't thinking. I messed something up."

"But then you used your Bau," Amisi said encouragingly. "That worked well."

Alexandra shrugged.

"We'll find out more in the morning. Now, everyone needs to go back to sleep." Commander Ryan was talking now. "None of us can keep going like this without getting a few hours. We'll talk in the morning. Hopefully, the world can wait."

We were silent in our obedience.

After a few minutes, a symphony of snoring began. I lay with my head on the pillow – no way would I sleep again.

I yawned.

"Hi Gil," Isis said in my dreams. Never mind, I thought.

I tried to talk to her.

"I can't hear you," she said. "The connection is weak. Are you okay?"

I nodded my head up and down. "Something's wrong though?" she inferred.

I nodded my head yes.

"Can you still make it here?"

I hunched my shoulders, but thought better of it and nodded yes.

"Good. Now, go back to sleep."

Amisi had to shake me awake, but I felt alive again. My hand felt even better this morning too, and I was hungry. We made our way up the service ladder to the lounge and food.

"Ryan got the food unit working almost first thing." Amisi giggled carrying me over a plate of hot scrambled eggs, bacon, sausage, buttered biscuits and a heaping dollop of strawberry preserves – and a coffee, for good measure.

That was a good thing.

I dug in while Amisi watched me eat. The others had been up for hours already.

"Alexandra's been rebooting all the systems connected to the hardware she damaged. It has to be done manually, but she thinks it will work. Anyway, Neter's acting like a schizophrenic because of it. Only some of her programs are working and she knows it. It's totally weird."

The interface panel blinked then and a confused-looking Neter appeared, poked around, and then phased back out.

"See what I mean? She keeps searching for her missing parts."

I wanted to laugh, but it was serious too. We needed the ship to get to Palenque.

"What exactly did I freeze?"

Amisi squirmed visibly. "Neter took a direct hit to her neurologic relays. Some of the mechanical relays were frozen too – especially those near the exterior of the ship, but Wep fixed those already."

She stabbed at a bit of eggs on my plate nervously and spoke through the food. "But the problem is mostly neurologic – the control center stuff. And after the issue with unfreezing her hardware, the rest of us are worried about making things worse. Alexandra's fixing the problem from within the matrix."

I pushed back from the table. "What am I doing here then?" I was the only other person who could access the matrix. "We need to get out of here as fast as we can." I grabbed one last bite, talking through my eggs. "And not because we've got to save the world still and all that. People are going to try and come out here soon so they can say they walked on a frozen tsunami."

"We're a sitting duck."

"Exactly."

Water was flowing through the ice river that had escaped when I got distracted when I hit Neter. When it settled down, it would create the perfect place to dock a boat for anyone who wanted to try – right next to our uncamouflaged ship.

"Thank goodness for that ice river." I wiped my mouth clean. "It's keeping a lot of people away – for now anyway."

Amisi's head tipped crooked. "It did a lot more than that. Gil. I'm not sure you understand everything that happened yesterday."

The look she gave me bored into me like Alexandra's laser had into the damaged hardware.

"I have never, and I mean never ever in my life seen even a full-blooded Oasen display the kind of energy, control and power you did out there yesterday. And, oh my stars Gil, you were manipulating time too. The kind of power you were throwing out would have frozen us solid right down to our atoms if you hadn't gotten distracted and stopped – even for that small moment. Forget Neter's protective housing. It wouldn't have mattered. That ice river, that moment of distraction, is the reason we're all still alive."

I wanted to throw up.

Amisi had a way about her though. "Anyways, so as you can imagine, I'm much obliged." She put on her best cowboy accent and tipped an imaginary hat at me. A smile lit her face. She was Montana through and through. Then she stabbed at my eggs with her fork again.

Chapter 24-Thawing out and heating up

After Alexandra and I finished rebooting Neter's system from the Matrix, Neter herself gave a throaty growl and she began to purr like a happy cat after a long nap. The tunnel we sat in had been calm and quiet for hours. None of the usual loud rushing black energy to give me a headache. And when her engine revved back up; I was never gladder for a migraine in my life.

Neter ran at us – energy coursing through her. The black crashing noise rising to a fever pitch around us. She stopped and stood motionless, looking sideways, distracted again.

Did it work?

My stack of processes began recoding. Neter stared at them, everything else tuned out, including us. The deck of cards shuffled itself, restacked, and flew away into the dark tunnel, lost in whatever lay at the end of the vortex.

She stopped. "Not bad for hybrids, but there were some errors. Probably some more over here."

I realized then I was holding my breath.

"We did it!" I jumped up and hugged Alexandra. I didn't even give my actions a second thought. "We got her working!" I shook her by the shoulders.

"Thank the stars!" She hugged me back and paused to look at me, letting me go quickly. But she had held my gaze one second too long.

I noticed. And she knew it too.

▪▪▪▪

Everyone was sitting in the lounge watching CNN. It was nice to have things back to normal again – well, relatively speaking. The world was still on a countdown to planetary destruction and all, but at least the TV was working. Everyone clapped when we walked in, drowning out the male anchor's voice. I took an overly-dramatic bow, nodded to Alexandra, and went to get a drink. The volume went back up on the TV. Everyone chatted pleasantly. Things were looking up. The heat was even working, but then CNN cut to an image of Alexandria's beach, so of course the room went silent.

"Oh my," Seshat said.

A helicopter videographer panned the area to show the world the ice wave in all its perilous beauty. I could just make out Neter's shape covered in snow and the blue ice I encased her in near the ice river. Nature had done a good job of disguising her from the world's eyes. Thankfully her real camouflage would be fully functional in 10 minutes. I checked my watch. The picture changed to show the shore crowded with Egyptians. They had come to see the thing that would have killed them. Some were even trying to get into small boats, but a few officials on shore were holding them back. It was time to get out of here.

Despite it all, the male anchor was calm. I wasn't sure how he was managing to stay so composed considering everything happening on the planet this week. Earthquakes, snow storms, heat waves and now ice waves. If it wasn't doomsday a few days ago, it clearly was now.

He spoke. "People are comparing it to the movie The Day After Tomorrow when sudden atmospheric thunderstorms flash froze anything caught outside in -150° F temperatures. Metrologic critics panned the science behind the film, but now, people are talking. Let's go to our guests, Jeff O'Keefe, with the National Weather Service, and Mindy Striker, with the National Oceanic and Atmospheric Administration. Mindy, I'll throw to you first." Oh, now I understood; that was the Showbiz Tonight guy reporting.

Wep muted it. "How long until we can take off?"

Neter appeared on the interface panel. "Approximately 2 hours, 25 minutes."

I sat up straight. "Wait a minute Neter; we fixed you. What's up?"

She crossed her arms on the screen. "There was some unrepaired damage to the relay mechanism which will require additional time to repair."

Wep's body became rigid and he stormed up with his palms to his eyelids.

Wep had been responsible for repairing relays – and he had missed one.

"Listen. What matters is getting out of here as soon as we can. I don't think we have two hours though. Those guys on the shore in the boats are going to come out here." The TV showed a group of Egyptians trying to put a boat into the water despite officials on the beach. The officers were tiring of the idiots, but still trying to hold them back. Neter's camouflage would keep them from seeing our ship, but it couldn't keep them from walking into her. Invisible or not – we were about to be exposed.

"This isn't good. Neter are you getting this? Those guys are going to head straight for us. How much time do we have?"

She ran the numbers. She had a calculation for everything. "Judging from their boat's projected speed, and calculating for the pay grade of the officials trying to stop them, I estimate the boaters will be here in under 53 minutes, plus or minus seven minutes."

My voice dropped to a whisper. "And we'll still be here."

■■■■■

We were an hour away from being discovered.

Let me tell you – if you've never been in a situation involving impossible odds and utter dread, I'll tell you how it goes. First, you stand there numb and unmoving like an idiot. You tell your mouth to open and command your arms to fly up in panic, but nothing happens. Nada. Got me? Then, suddenly, your brain trickles awake, like someone dripping water into the sink. You think, oh good, something's finally coming out – and then the pipe bursts ...

That's kind of what happened to us.

Dead silence. Still bodies – and then ...

"You have got to be kidding me!" Ryan jumped up yelling, discovering the use of his legs.

"What do we do?" Amisi's head dipped from face to face and her hair bobbed cutely as usual, oblivious to the change in the room's mood. "If they find us, we'll be swarmed and swamped, and who knows what else? Oh stars! They'll blame us for all of it!"

Alexandra vaulted up like a prize fighter about to get in the ring and, of course, began pacing. Wep and Seshat brought their heads together, bringing thousands of years of experience to bear – although in hurried, loud and somewhat angry conversation.

The entire room had exploded in a bomb of chaotic useless noise. There were no answers to be found in this melee. I couldn't take it anymore.

"Shut up!" I yelled. "Shut up. Shut up! Shut up!"

A bunch of heads turned my way disbelievingly.

"This isn't helping. Come on people. Think? What exactly do we have going for us?"

Ryan slapped at his mouth, and put his finger in the air like he had a bright idea. "The cloaking feature may buy us some time. If we luck out, no one will find us and we'll be able to take off after Neter finishes her repairs."

"What? And kill everyone within a hundred feet as we take off?" Alexandra said. "No way. Neter's too powerful. Besides, it will only take them minutes to bump into her."

Seshat shot Wep a quick look like she was about to get in trouble for what she was going to say. "I can stop them!" she blurted out.

Wep almost growled at her. "You'll cause a panic. I already told you."

She ignored him. "I can make them think the ice is collapsing, and the water is rising. No one will come near us then."

"Seshat," He tried to calm his voice. "Only the people on the beach will see the illusion. How would they explain what's going on to the TV viewers? All the news channels are broadcasting this live."

Her countenance fell.

Wep softened some. "She can't affect what people see on TV."

"People might panic and get hurt too. There's so many of them."

"Neter, we're running out of options here. Got any ideas?"

Neter was thoughtful – for a computer. "I have completed the initial physical repairs. They were more minor than I thought initially. The real issue is with how my neuro processes interact with the relays. That is where the real damage is."

Neter went unnaturally dead still thinking. Then she moved again.

"Let me explain. Imagine a bridge between two islands that is broken in half. I cannot cross the bridge to control the flight function. And I cannot repair it fast enough to get us out of here." Neter paused and looked away into space again. I sensed the calculations running behind those eyes of hers. She stopped and arched one eyebrow only slightly. Her purple eyes grew wide. "Wait. I have an idea. But it is risky – for you."

She was looking at me.

"I'm listening."

Neter paced on her screens, in mimic of Alexandra. She was on 10 interface panels at once. As she walked right, all 10 of her would briefly disappear off the monitor and then reappear on the one to her right.

"It is possible for you to bypass me and access the flight function I am disconnected from directly within the matrix. You will control that part of the neurologic function – the relay mechanism – for me. I will control the other flight functions and loop back the connection to you within the matrix. Basically, we will be creating a new bridge. Do you think you can do this?"

"Are you saying you want me to fly you, Neter?"

"Well, not technically. I'll be flying. But you will be ... driving. That's your island, so to speak."

Ryan's eyebrows went up.

I wasn't quite sure what the distinction was, but I went with it. I grinned inwardly and nodded yes. "Okay, let's do this. What do I have to lose?"

Only Alexandra made a face. But there was no time to waste. We took off down the hall towards the bridge. Neter followed switching from interface panel to interface panel down the hall like a set of falling dominos.

"I hope this works. What exactly does the relay mechanism do?"

"Flight power is distributed using the relays. Electromagnets move a pari-iron band at each intersection that allows heavy electrical currents to move or switch through each relay. The currents flowing through these are dangerous, large currents, because they give life to my flight capabilities. The level of power flowing through each switch will dictate how fast or slow, how hard, and what angle we fly. Do you understand?"

"I think so."

"For all intents and purposes, you're turning the steering wheel. Got it?"

"Got it."

"I think," I said quieter. Alexandra flashed me a look. She heard me. I stared back at her. She was running behind me. She wasn't an awkward jogger. Sometimes pretty girls run funny, but hers was clean and efficient. How was my mind in the clouds now? "Neter. Would this go better if Alexandra and I worked together?"

Neter calculated the odds. "It would be cognitively safer for you, but Alexandra would take on a portion of the risk."

I hadn't even asked what the risk was. There was no time. No other options.

"I'll do it." Without thinking either, she ran faster to catch up. "Gil needs every brain cell he's got left."

There was snickering behind me, but I kept running.

We made it to the bridge.

The situation was urgent, and we rushed along with it. Ryan, Amisi, Seshat and Wep fell into their seats around the bridge, while Alexandra and I settled down and made the electron connection at our console. I felt the Melio settling over my body as I dropped into my brain.

A virtual chair settled under me inside the matrix. Alexandra waved as she dropped into her own virtual command seat. A curved viewing screen appeared all around me like I was sitting in a semi-opaque grid-lined ball. This was new.

I settled into my seat, but wobbled when I looked down. The sensation of falling hit me. My seat was nearly transparent and there was nothing below me now but ground and that was far, far below. It was as if I was sitting at the heart of a transparent Neter. The frozen tsunami and ice river were just beyond the hazy shimmer of the guts of the ship surrounding me. I gulped hard and felt the seat below me with my hands so I would stop panicking. I saw Alexandra's moment of alarm too – until she realized she wasn't going to fall either.

"You have to see where you are going," Neter answered our unspoken question.

A crisscrossed grid spread around the surface of my spherical ball. Numbers designated latitude and longitude and a horizon line sat still for now. Alexandra sat in its twin to my right. It was like hanging in the ball turret of one of the B-17 bombers they flew in World War II. Under us, over us, beside us, all around us was an almost transparent, slightly opaque ball with views to every side of the ship. It was still snowing outside.

"Very much like a ball turret," I heard Neter say.

What? She can read my mind now?

Yes, and you mine, she answered. And Alexandra's.

Alexandra looked over at me then.

It was at that moment I realized I could hear her thoughts too. They went something like, Oh, no. Oh, no, Oh, NO! She was mortified and faced forward concentrating hard on not saying anything else.

I squeezed my eyes shut. If I wasn't obvious enough already without this weird telepathy thing, there was little I could do to mess things up any worse for her reading my mind. Alexandra tapped her eye balls trying to shut me out, but if she didn't know how serious I was about her before, she did now. My thoughts about her flowed unbidden.

Sorry, I thought. She dropped her head down lower.

Snow balls. Kittens. Kool aid. Alexandra's train of thought was hilarious.

Her lips cracked into a smile. She knew I heard her.

This is too weird, I thought.

Agreed, she voiced. Haircuts, oil slicks, peanut allergies, aspirin.

Monkeys, bananas, aliens, mom, I answered back.

We burst out laughing.

"That's enough of that, you two," Neter scolded out loud. "We must share this deeper mind connection if we are to drive this ship as one. You must open yourself up to it. As hard as that may be for you two," she admitted. She was privy to both our thoughts now.

"You, Alexandra, will control opening and shutting the relays. Gil, will push the power through and vary the amounts. Prepare yourself. We must hurry."

The space around Alexandra and I changed. My feet were now tucked into heel rests and there were simple controls around me too. I manipulated them and as I did, my seat swung around the ball in the direction I moved the controls. I went left, right, up, down, angle to angle of my choice. It was cool. I cocked my head toward Alexandra. "You know I love video games. And this is like the best one ever."

"I'm not so bad at them myself, Boy Wonder."

Neter interrupted. "Information download in five, four, three ..."

I stilled myself for whatever the information download entailed.

"Two, one." A waterfall of information cascaded through my brain and Alexandra's simultaneously. I was seeing everything in duplicate, thanks to our shared brain function, so the impact was doubled. The cascade of information wasn't like water flowing freely into my head, filling every empty nook and cranny. It was like concrete was being shoved into my brain and caked together in layers, then all that crushing weight smashed into a thin but still swollen layer. Then it happened all over again. And again. And again, until the caked layers were so heavy and painful I nearly lost consciousness.

When I felt like I couldn't take it anymore, I felt Neter pull back and found I was still breathing. My head ached and I twisted to look at Alexandra. She was staring down and panting. Both our minds were blank for once.

I shook my head. Alexandra mirrored me reflexively. She looked up and we locked eyes. There was fear there. Mine too, I realized. We were truly connected now – but separate. If before was weird, this was weirder. Whoa. I felt like a stained glass window. A whole and beautiful portrait, made of separate fused shards of cutting glass. I ached at the weird fragmentation of my mind.

"Are you ready?"

I couldn't be, not like this. I felt broken. Yet I felt whole.

I felt a tingle of acknowledgement from Neter. Then a flood of relief. She did something – something to solidify us. I still couldn't talk, but I didn't feel so oddly fragmented. I nodded. Alexandra as well. We were ready.

Now, Neter said.

We moved and worked as one. Neter had fused us, and she had trained us, in seconds. I felt Alexandra open the first relay – the one that controlled the thrusters.

Easy Gill, she reminded me. Not like the rocks at the bottom of that shaft. Remember?

I remembered. I remember.

The echo of our minds was uncanny.

I eased a minute amount of energy across the pari-iron bar and Neter went skyward at a slow clip.

Hold. Somehow Ryan's voice entered my head.

Alexandra closed the bar.

How is Ryan speaking to us?

How is he doing that? Alexandra echoed.

He's speaking from the bridge. You hear him as I do, Neter answered. He commands us.

Oh, Alexandra said.

Okay, I answered.

This is getting weird, I thought.

Mm, hmm, came her answer.

Ryan interrupted. We have to drop the snow cap off of Neter. We don't have time to melt it and we can't take a disc of snow on a flight through the sky in front of all those people. It'll fly off and then that anchor lady is going to go nuts."

He made sense. How would CNN explain floating flying snow?

Ryan commanded from the deck. Forward at a clip to the tsunami cap. We are going to break the top of it off and drop the snow with it to the water. It shouldn't be enough to cause a panic. Wait for my mark. We're avoiding the helicopters now.

This is going to be fun, I thought. Here we go.

Yes, fun.

When the helicopters were out of range, we crept forward and gently rammed Neter into the cap of the ice wave. Well, I wouldn't call it rammed, more of a bump.

45 degree back pitch, our joint mind called out. We manipulated the bands and energy fields to jostle the snow free of Neter's roof. 60 degrees and jostle. Hold. Back and down. 80 degrees. Hold.

The ship rose up quickly and we saw the effects through the lens of Neter's unequalled mind, not our human one. The snow spilled down the side of the frozen tsunami while the ice rent down through its middle with one great crack, but in truth, we watched it splinter into a billion brilliant patterns from its crest to its trough. And then it hung, holding on for dear life to some vestige of its once-solid state, and then it dropped dramatically vertically to the slushy water below. Gravity pulled it down to drown it in the frozen surf.

A wave of icy water rolled to the shore, which gave the boatmen pause, but it was too small to cause any real panic. The surf tumbled on toward the people on the beach, but there was little to it. We hovered out of range a few minutes more. Time was precious though and we took off for the safety of empty southern Egypt.

For once, our trip was uninteresting. Alexandra and I quietly flew the ship back to the field of dying figs where Neter set down to repair herself. When we landed, Alexandra and I sat still in our command chairs, exhausted and silent. Neter appeared and fussed over us like a mother does sick children, and in the end, it felt like Neter unplugged us from a wall socket. Magnitudes of power, complexities I didn't know existed, and a sense of infinite abilities drained from me, leaving me feeling like an empty shell. Just human. Or Oasen, or whatever. I wondered how Alexandra felt. I couldn't hear her or feel her any more. And that was weird, somehow.

Chapter 25-Laundry day

Quiet normality is unnerving after riding in a giant fish mouth, talking to living statues, and meeting wolfy people. I mean, I used to read comic books. Now I was in one. I used to play video games. I practically became one yesterday. But now – here I was – sitting on my bed realizing all my clothes were trashed and the only thing that needed doing was laundry. There's nothing more normal than that.

Not even a clean pair of boxers left.

I picked up a plaid pair and sniffed them – and dropped them quickly to the floor. I would need to find an industrial grabber to get those with later. I was pretty sure they were toxic. I collapsed on my mom's bunk and stared up at the room's bland ceiling. My hand tapped my chest in monotonous repetition warding off the inevitability of what needed to be done. I sat up quickly.

"Neter. I can't believe I'm saying this, but I need to do a load of laundry."

We were flying slowly over the North Atlantic Ocean now, finally heading down to Palenque. Neter had made enough repairs to fly independently, but she wasn't 100 percent. Still, we decided to gamble and leave for Palenque anyway even knowing she would have to continue repairs on the way. Conditions were decent enough for flying and who knew how they would change in another day? Anything seemed possible.

"Laundry is on each level, Section 2, Door Teth." Neter interrupted.

I nodded my head and scooped up the toxic underwear with my bare hands, tossing them into my open suitcase which rested in the corner of the room. I figured I could handle them after the whole tsunami incident, toxic sludge or no. I grabbed my suitcase awkwardly in my arms, still gaping open like it was a laundry basket, and headed down the hall.

I wished I had a headache. Then at least I would feel something. My head should be pounding from all the thoughts that chased each other around, but it wasn't. I felt numb. And why wouldn't I? Last night, walking to my room, I ran into Wep and Alexandra. She was leaning against the wall, and Wep was practically standing over her. She flinched, but I didn't stick around to see anything else. I swore things hadn't gotten that far with them. I swore there was still a chance for us.

I practically raced back to my room to put on the Bes amulet so I didn't destroy anything. The way she had looked at me in that moment catching them standing there, I couldn't shake it. Her eyes betrayed a million different emotions. I couldn't place them all. But Wep's eyes said plenty. He had won.

Back in my room, I noticed a scrolling mass of alerts on my phone. Now I added guilt to the mountain in my mind. My phone had finally connected with a satellite and downloaded all my voice mail messages. And there were lots of them. Mom had figured out we weren't at the ranch and her messages had become more and more frantic as the days and our silence progressed. The last ones had been more steeled. They hadn't found dad and Elaine either – or the Aten. The messages said as much.

It was hard hearing my mom so scared. I wanted to feel for her, but all my emotions had solidified into a tiny pinprick buried somewhere deep in my brain. Not even I knew where it was. I guessed my brain was protecting itself. Otherwise, maybe it would implode – especially after Neter pounded that concrete wall of information in there. All of it together was overwhelming. I hadn't forgotten about Isis either in all my jumble of thoughts. We still had to locate the ventilation shaft and all we had to go on was an obscure rhyme. Then, of course, there's the key that I have, but don't know I have. Right... now where did I put that? I should be worried. But, I was numb – just numb at this point. The fate of the world rested in my hands, but it was a simple girl that kept me prisoner in my head.

I wandered down the hall to the laundry room, letting another stray thought in to join the rest. Just how does Oasen laundry work? I stopped outside Door Teth to think, but I couldn't even have that quiet moment. If I wasn't on a ship with intelligent moving doors, then I would have had to knock it open with my knees myself. As it was, Neter kindly opened the door immediately at my approach.

The room was lined with 10 identical machines, all like modern front-loading washing machines. The front viewing window was transparent glass. Of course, if Oasens liked to parade their dead, why not their laundry? Argh. My head was a mess. I nearly apologized to myself for that comment.

I tried to open a machine, but nothing happened.

"It opens on top," Amisi stopped to pick up a sock she dropped in the doorway. Her room was on this level too. "Here." She dropped her laundry basket noisily and shoved me to the side. She pressed a tiny symbol on the upper left corner. A light shown around a central circle at the top, and then retracted like a backwards-moving whirlpool.

Looking at her while I did it, I dumped the entire contents of my suitcase into the top and grinned my best sinister grin. No sorting of colors today.

"Nice." She eyed me but pressed a sequence on the top of my machine anyway. "So, I guess you'll be washing these on cold?"

I raised my shoulders in ambivalent consent. Truly, I had no clue what I was doing. I had been a little off since Neter's mind meld anyway, so she let it go. Amisi eyed me, but went back to her own load. I, as in my unnaturally silent self, collapsed Indian style in front of the machine and watched as tiny white flakes like wet cold snow fell onto my clothes. Yep. This was definitely the cold cycle. The machine turned over like normal, and the effect was multiplied. It was Christmas in my washer. That, at least, was cool.

I woke with a start. My head slipped off the perch of my hand, leaving behind a trail of slime. Yuck. I had nodded off, but not long enough to let Isis slide into my head too. Thank goodness. Behind me, the washer had stopped. There were dry clothes through the glass. I tossed them unceremoniously back into my suitcase and headed to my room, looking down at the blue jeans I wore as I stepped out. Great, I forgot to wash these too.

■■■■■

I was popping open my third Dr. Pepper, and busy taking out my frustrations on the limp remains of a lime, when Alexandra walked into the lounge. She threw herself onto the couch. "This is taking forever," she said casually, lying prone on her stomach, stopping to perch her head on her hands.

I wanted to ignore her, but I couldn't. Instead I said, "I know," and turned back to the lime. I wanted every ounce of pulp it had. It was giving me something to do on this painfully long trip across the ocean. When I finally let the lime rest in peace and dunked it to the bottom of my glass, it bobbed before settling to the bottom. Alexandra still watched me from the couch.

"Remind me never to get on your bad side."

I laughed. I couldn't help it. "You've got a lot of nerve, Alexandra."

"It's not wh..." she started to say, but then the door swung open and I heard laughter.

Ryan and Amisi walked in holding hands, but they let them drop as soon as they noticed us there. "Hi, you two," Amisi's cheeks pinking. "Everything okay?"

I scowled. "Oh, you know, contemplating how we're going to find the ventilation shaft to Isis' chamber when no one else can and save the world, that sort of thing," I stated grumpily while bobbing my straw up and down in the cold liquid. "If only I could figure out what 'When Orion falls, to Draco goes the spoils' means to the salvation of this planet and one ancient trapped love-sick girl?"

I said love with too much emphasis. Amisi made a face at me, and I huffed at her – much to Ryan's disapproval. I left the bitter drink on the counter and went to fall into the arm chair near Alexandra's head. I was a mess.

"Neter messed you up."

"Maybe. Or maybe it's just a girl," I said quietly.

Alexandra wouldn't look at me, but she heard.

Then the door slid open and Wep and Seshat walked into the room. "Speak of the devil," I grumbled under my breath.

Wep grinned widely. He had a lot of teeth.

Wolf man went straight for the couch with Alexandra. Wep scooted her legs out of the way in a too-familiar way and my mental tirade went off. He's thousands of years older than her. How does she miss that little fact? It's worse than dating your grandfather. Way worse. Except your grandfather is nothing like Wep.

I wanted to scream.

Wep noticed me staring and whispered something to her. His mouth curved up, an edge of meanness to his lips. Her eyes flew up to mine unbidden as if he mentioned my name and she couldn't help but look. Her eyes narrowed as she listened. And she shook her head.

"No," I heard her say, and then Wep put his hand on her shoulder, but she moved it away and he let it fall.

He got up then, his face confused.

Yeah, well, welcome to my world buddy. She's Jekyll and Hyde.

Maybe this was her pattern.

And then she did something unexpected; she let her eyes reach mine again. This time, on purpose.

What in the black hole is going on?

Alexandra stood up and smoothed down her slacks. "Gil," she looked right at me. "You're an idiot and sometimes things aren't what they seem. Wep's a friend and nothing more, even if he wants it to be."

She looked right at Wep, and he dunked his head.

"And Gil's right – even if he currently seems to be losing his mind." She stared at me with intent.

Okay. Wait. What's going on?

"We're gonna' have to figure out the Orion rhyme if we are going to finish this." Her hands flew to her hips. She was taking charge. Alexandra was back. "So – let's split into groups and come back together in two hours – or sooner if anyone has an epiphany – and see what we come up with. There's too many people in here with too many ideas." She looked right at Wep. "And not the right ones."

Alexandra walked for the door but turned back. "Come on." She faced both Wep and I. "What are you waiting for?"

It's now or never.

I stood up. She smiled.

"Good. You've figured one thing out today. Can you figure out another?"

She walked out the door leaving me behind. The room was silent,

I shook my head. "Don't ask me. I gave up trying to figure her out a long time ago."

Wep shook his head like he understood.

I followed and felt the pin prick I had buried in my brain explode.

I could feel again.

Chapter 26-My Favorite jeans

Well, after nearly a year with a crashed hard drive, and this novel sitting on it, my documents were finally recovered this week.Sorry for the LONG wait, but I'm happy to begin posting the final chapters of HalfWorlder. And happy to have my novel back!

******

Alexandra sat with one leg tucked under her and the other hanging off her bunk, kicking it over and over again like the anxiety she felt might flee out her toes. All her earlier confidence was gone.

She sat like that the last 20 minutes, stopping only to mention if she read anything worthwhile in the giant tome she had open on her lap. She kept on kicking away, her toes painted a bright corvette red, surprisingly vibrant for a girl who disdained all but simple makeup around her eyes and the occasional touch of pale gloss on her mouth.

She had fallen into a pattern of reading for a few minutes, only to look up, think for a minute, and bite at one of her fingernails. Then it was back to the book. When she did it, she held her mouth open to reveal the little space between her front teeth, oblivious to my eyes on her.

I couldn't help staring. With her mouth closed, you'd never notice the little flaw. Her face captured you first with her wide blue eyes, hooded with perfect brows, so when her full lips smiled to reveal the hint of the gap, you only saw it for what it was, a beautiful imperfection.

She noticed me staring then. Her mouth pinched shut, and she closed the book on her lap. Tension made the muscles in her neck taught. She wouldn't make eye contact.

"I like it." I walked over to the cot to stand in front of her. She grimaced. I sunk to the floor on my knees to be close to her. "It makes you so unique."

"Dad wouldn't let me get my teeth fixed when I was little." Her eyes finally met mine. Her walls were down for once. "It reminded him too much of my mom to let me see an orthodontist." She smiled. "And by the time I was old enough to decide on my own, something held me back. It still bothers me. It's a constant reminder, but it's me too."

It was strange to hear her talking about her mom.

She never talked about her mom.

"She has it too," Alexandra tapped her front teeth twice with two fingers. "My mom."

I nodded.

"I get the feeling you look a lot like her."

I thought about Morty's brawny face and my mouth arched up in wry grin.

Alexandra caught my meaning and laughed. "Yeah, you're right. I do. I've seen pictures."

"Do you miss her?"

She bit at her fingers again unaware and answered me, a bit muffled with one finger still in her mouth. "I don't know if I can miss someone I've never met." She shifted her weight. "But I think I do."

I thought I understood that.

"You never talk about her. Why now?"

Her face pinked up. "Wep. I guess. I guess you can say he has mommy issues too. It's helped me to talk about it."

"So, that's what you've been doing together? Talking about your moms? It's not because you like him, you know, like that?" I tripped over my words trying to get them out. I felt weird admitting my insecurities.

"That was a huge part of it ..." Her eyes drifted down. "At first. But, honestly it's not all his fault. I let him think it might be more. In some small way, I thought if you got the idea I liked him, you'd give up and leave me alone."

I sat there dumbfounded. "But why would you ever want me to do that?"

Would this girl ever make sense?

"I never wanted to hurt you," she stammered, the words spilling out. "But you got in the way of everything. I had this whole plan worked out. I didn't have to have anyone like you in my life. I didn't need anybody. No one. I was okay being alone."

She was almost talking to herself now.

"No one, Gil. I could have done life all alone."

Of course she could.

"I made this vow to never let anyone in. Only Amisi knew about it and she chalked it up to the ramblings of a 16-year-old half-human mind, but she couldn't know how serious I was. And then, the blue sparks happened and I panicked."

"Wait. What are the sparks? Ryan said they were like visible hormones."

This made her blush. "No," she faltered. "They are rare. Ryan was just covering for me." She bit her bottom lip. "They're more like love personified." This was hard for her to say. "It makes them hard to ignore."

"Love, huh?" I said it playfully but took her hand in mine. She nodded and held tight. My heart nearly escaped my chest. She wasn't letting go. "But then you panicked, right?" I brought her back to her original train of thought.

"Yes." She took me in with her eyes. "You were the one thing in the world I never wanted to happen. I made that vow. And then, there you were, and you were funny and smart and caring and everything you should be – and I didn't get the chance to even try to deny those feelings because of those darn sparks. It was horrible."

"Thanks."

"No ... you don't understand." She turned my hand over in both hers. "I vowed to never fall for anyone, Gil. That way no one could ever hurt me. And I could never hurt them." She squeezed my hand. "Because of her."

The unspoken name hung in the air.

"Your mom?" I thought, but I didn't understand.

Alexandra nodded her head solemnly. "She didn't even give me a chance, Gil –" Her eyes teared up the same way they had in the horse barn when she lost Dakota, but these tears she pushed back down again. This pain was far rawer.

"Anyways," she sniffed. "I'm dealing with it."

She wasn't dealing with it.

"Alexandra. I am not like her – on so many levels. And I'm not going anywhere. There's no reason for you to worry about me leaving you. Ever." I may be 17, but I knew. She was mine.

She pulled her hand away and stood up quickly.

"No."

She said the word quietly.

"No!" This time she shouted it and her voice broke. She paced to the other side of the room like a small attempt to run away. But she couldn't. She hiccupped away her tears. "It's not you I'm worried about. It's me! What if I'm like her, Gil?" Her voice echoed through the small room, gaining volume. She threw her hands in the air and tapped hard on her teeth. "More than this!"

The words erupted from her.

"What if I let myself completely fall for you? Then what? What if I ever give myself to you?" She shook her head pacing. "I can't do that, Gil!" It was an all-caps kind of scream. "I can't ever, ever give myself completely to you," she sobbed. "Because if I'm like her, if I'm truly like her," she tapped her teeth yet again, "one day I will leave you too.

And then where will you be?" Her arms hung limply at her sides, spent. Her voice was small, raw. Her eyes were like dead things. "You'll be gutted, Gil. That's what you'll be just like me. I'm not someone you should love. I'm broken."

She collapsed back onto the bed near me. Her head hung low. She panted, out of breath. Her face dropped into her hands but there were no more tears. "I'm not a whole person, Gil. I haven't been since she left me. I've never really been."

Kneeling beside her on the bed, I put my hand on her back. I ran my hand along the slender rise and fall of her shoulders until she shivered involuntarily. She felt so small in my hands. She needed me more than she knew.

"Alexandra, you can't fear becoming something so much that you create a barrier to the one thing that will free you." I pulled her up and into my chest, and she didn't resist, couldn't. She clung to me as I spoke. "Sometimes the risk is worth it."

She pulled back and looked into my eyes. Startled realization there. We were locked together again, but this was more intimate than a kiss. This was blue sparks kind of love.

■■■■■

It was night. Again.

No one had any revelations – at least about the Orion/Draco mystery, so we drifted apart as soon as we came back together. It was better that way. Wep wasn't exactly thrilled to see us. We moved like magnets, but this time you could see and even feel the attraction. We left nothing to mystery.

Alexandra and I lay on our backs on the observation deck at Neter's crown, unable to sleep. Our heads close together, our bodies lying in opposite directions, we stared up at the inky black sky, the heavens punctuated by a smattering of bright stars that winked and flared their distant histories for just this moment. But, not to be forgotten, their light and life tumbled on past us to be shared with some distant, unknown people on another planet hanging in the sky somewhere far from us.

"Stars seem so permanent. But even they are not."

She lay still with her hands crossed over her chest. Her breathing was regular. If I didn't know better, I'd think she was sleeping. But she wasn't.

"I know. To think, Ra and Isis probably lay down and gazed on this same sky."

She sat up and pulled her knees to her chest, laying her head down on their tops to stare down at me. I pulled myself up to join her.

It felt strange being this close – that this was allowed.

We rested our heads on our knees just staring at each other.

I hadn't kissed her since the bridge so long ago.

A meteor flared brilliantly across the night sky. Its tail jutted out in brilliant technicolor.

And that's when I stopped time.

You almost had to hold your breath watching the tail of the meteor smear and halt there in the heavens. I reached up and pulled at the light, brightening it until Alexandra had to close her eyes for its brilliance. I breathed her in and drifted slowly toward her. Her breath caught at the blind realization of what I was about to do. Those seconds before our mouths touched were like a slow fire building to burning to torching. The anticipation was as brilliant as the moment our mouths finally crashed together.

This kiss was different than our last. It was as slow as the time that halted around us. There was no fever and no rushing, just feeling, just experiencing. It was amazing how much you felt when you weren't compelled to hurry. When you realized that real love could wait – that true love never need rush.

We had all the time in the world.

■■■■■

We woke up on the hard deck, the sky still above us, but this time it was blue. Daylight had come. Alexandra lay with her head fitted perfectly in the crook of my neck, as I knew it would when I met her. I smelled strawberries, but it was just her hair.

We stretched and sat up.

Time finally sped back up.

The stars were veiled behind blue skies. No storms today. For now, at least.

Alexandra gave me a lazy grin, but when she spoke, her tone was serious and she wasn't talking to me. This fit her perfectly well.

"Neter, what's our ETA?" she asked.

Today was the last day, the day we would finally land in Palenque.

Neter's voice sounded around us, but there were no interface panels on the observation deck. "We are on approach to the temple city. T-minus two hours, 24 minutes."

My eyes were blurry from hard sleep. "That's not much time." The weight of it pressed down on me again.

"No, it's not."

Alexandra stood and stretched. She wasn't the kind of girl to waste time. "Let's find the others and try and get a plan in place, whatever that might be." She pulled me up, but I feigned being too heavy and pulled her down on me.

"Gil, come on. Be serious." She patted me twice on the chest. "We've got to get moving."

"Theoretically, two and a half hours is more than enough time for this and that," I offered smiling, but she didn't bite. She frowned and shoved me in the chest, and I knew this would have to wait until after we saved the world.

"Oh, alright," I caved. We grabbed each other's hands and yanked r up. We ended up facing one another though, so I put my arms around her in one last attempt at a kiss. My hands were low on her waist and she willingly copied me, her thumbs finding their way into my back pockets.

"What's this?" Alexandra pulled out a crinkled piece of paper – one that had recently gone through an Oasen wash cycle.

She began unfolding it and I grabbed it playfully out of her hands. Then I remembered. "Oh, yeah. You know my friend Simon, right?" These were the jeans I wore the day I blew up the gym. He drew this." I crunched it and tossed the folded paper haphazardly in the air. We watched it float toward the ground. The black scratches of his drawing peeked out from inside. "He's always drawing weird stuff."

"You're just going to leave that there?"

"No, ma'am." I walked back to pick up the trash, but this time, I could see what Simon drew.

"Oh, great blazing supernovas. How in the ..." Mentally, I was back at my high school, sitting in the ambulance, heart racing. Simon sketched away, focused, other-minded. I remembered how he looked at me deliberately, calculatingly when he had walked away that day to go home.

"For the last day," he'd said, giving me a thumb's up.

Today was the last day.

But Simon knew that already. He knew it weeks ago.

The answer had been in my jean's pocket the entire time.

Chapter 27-Point of origin

The sideway moving elevator doors opened and the four came tumbling into the room together in record speed.

"What?" Ryan worried. He was slightly ahead of the others. "What's going on?"

"This!" I held Simon's drawing out, my hands practically shoving the wrinkled, crease-lined paper in their faces. "When Orion falls, to Draco goes the spoils."

The black charcoal scratches were like no sketch of Simon's I'd ever seen, this one all hard lines and dots and quickly scribed old hieroglyphs. When I saw it moments ago, it took my brain three seconds to interpret the symbols, and that's when I knew what I had in my hands.

"These are overlapping constellations. Orion." I pointed slowly and flipped the paper upside down. "And Draco." I ran my finger across the lines of the constellation. "I think Draco's inverted too. Here, show them, Neter."

"Yes, Gil." The room fell dark and the blue sky above us winked out, replaced with deepest black. The observation deck felt suddenly cool, like a damp mist had fallen. The mist swirled at the ceiling above us into a vortex of shadows that formed themselves into a 3-dimensional diagram of the universe, the stars in the constellations on Simon's paper brightening against the others that hung there with them. Lines radiated between one of the constellations. The figure of an archer, his bow drawn back tight, ready to let arrow fly, took shape. "This is the constellation Orion, named for Osiris long ago." The stars of his constellation turned from white to startling blue so they stood out against the others.

Another constellation took shape, these stars brightening to brilliant white. "And this is the constellation Draco, the dragon constellation." Shimmering lines connected the stars here again. This one wasn't as obvious. It was more like a serpent than a dragon. It snaked its way across the sky. "Draco never sets below the horizon. So, this constellation cannot be observed from the skies of Palenque."

Draco turned bright red against the white background stars which abruptly winked out, leaving Orion and Draco hanging alone above us. Then Draco grew, rotated 180°, and flipped transverse. Then the whole sky, both constellations, swiveled nearer to us for a better view. The image of Draco shrunk again and moved to overlap Orion. Both constellations had a trapezoid cluster of four stars that now fit almost perfectly atop the other. Orion's bow and the dragon's tail crossed each other as well and pointed in the same direction like two pathways leading to the same thing – I thought, maybe the same chamber? The chamber Isis was in.

"I felt pretty dumb when I saw that." Alexandra waved above her. "We should have figured it out ourselves. Egyptians have used constellations to map out pyramid shafts before."

"It makes sense Ra used the same format at the Palenque temple, but he was smart about it too. To use a constellation no South American would ever lay eyes on in ancient times. He hid Isis well."

"Yes, but where did you get that?" Amisi pointed at Simon's drawing.

"My friend Simon. My weird friend Simon," come to think of it. "He gave it to me the day I turned."

"The tsunami guy?" Ryan remembered. "Is he Hazel's son?"

"No, they are in San Diego."

"I don't think we're going to be able to explain this today." I shook the paper. "He must have some sort of second sight or something. He liked to draw disasters, that sort of thing. This," I said, "this is different, but he knew we would need it. He handed it to me when he left from school and told me it was for the last day."

"Today then," Wep added. "Today's the last day?"

"Yes," I answered. "It must be."

■■■■■

We stood on Neter's bridge, crossing a sea of green grass, finally free of the real churning sea of gray and blue, as we flew on toward the temple city. Below us, miles of wild jungle finally ended, juxtaposed against a manicured temple estate, a collage of buildings spread out over half a mile. Many structures still stood, taunting the jungle for not collapsing them, others hid high and crumbling on hilltops, shamed by the roots and vines and limbs that twisted their once-glory to ruin.

On the outskirts, waterfalls cascaded down smooth-worn boulders from great heights into pristine pools of aqua that continued their journey in rivers and smaller streams just as blue. On the main estate, sandy colored pathways meandered across wide expanses of bright green lawns, connecting commanding gray-stone stacked Mayan pyramids with steps so steep and high they were nearly vertical; with long imposing palace plazas crowning terraced earth; with crumbling low structures, towers and other buildings topped with cap-like roofs.

As we hovered above, Seshat briefly worked her magic so we could see the city in all its former splendor. Now we saw it as it was: new-cut stones, rough at the edges, made up the buildings. The wide expanse of grass remained, but tame black jaguars with chilling yellow eyes prowled across them amongst a colorfully dressed people. A group of three bound men, bodies painted entirely in brightest Azul blue, were being led up temple steps. One tripped and was pulled back up roughly by an unpainted man, a rough long knife hanging garishly from his hip. The image vanished and I shook my head to clear it.

This place once teamed with real life – and death.

"Are our parents down there?"

"Tracing their Bau signatures now." The view we had of outside vanished from the bridge window, replaced with a bird's eye view of the ground below overlaid with a map marked with each structure's name. Red Bau signatures swept back and forth like furious brush strokes across the map designating where the Oasens had trekked here and there at the temple site searching for my dad and Elaine and the Aten. The Bau signatures were concentrated on one temple structure in particular.

"They are focusing on that," Wep pointed out. Seshat nodded in agreement beside him. He ignored Alexandra.

"You're right. Neter, zoom in on this structure, here." I walked over and pointed to a spot on the map. "This temple must be the match dad found on that scrap in Het Benben."

"You are correct." Neter appeared on an interface panel on the side wall. The image on the large window screen zoomed in on the spot I indicated.

"That's strange." I fingered the location. "See what their Bau patterns are doing here." The Oasens on the ground had poured over this location many times, creating a red smear of paint in the shape of a bow and arrow.

Amisi was startled. "That's Orion's bow."

"That's what I thought. But if they found it, why haven't they located Isis yet?"

"Because," Alexandra realized, "that structure is too young. They aren't looking in the right place, but how clever of Ra." Her voice betrayed her approval. "He gave us a sign within a sign. See where the arrow's pointing?"

We all took a step toward the map. The arrow was fixated on a spot farther out in the jungle, where the vegetation still claimed many of Palenque's secrets.

"Oh, my," Amisi said in wonder. "They would have never realized it from the ground."

"What?"

"Not all of them stayed at that temple. They weren't all concentrated on that arrow. Several Bau patterns go out to the other temple structures. See here, where their Bau patterns stop, like someone or something is erasing them as they get closer to this point" Her finger ran upwards and landed on a seemingly random place on the map. "The point of origin."

"The point of origin?"

"Yes. Isis ... and the Aten."

A sort of haphazard spherical boundary marked the spot on the map where teams of Oasens had crossed into the territory of what must be the Aten. The Aten radiated some kind of energy from its location in a circle like a giant eraser destroying the Bau pattern of any individual that came too close. It left a line of Bau patterns flush against the outside edge, cut off, erased as they approached closer to the point of origin.

"It must be there," Alexandra inferred from the image, "near the Temple of the Jaguar."

She got up and grabbed her ever-present bag.

"Now we know. Let's go."

■■■■■

Neter dropped the cylindrical transfer shafts near the edge of the jungle, just beyond the Aten's circle where the jungle broke enough for them to fit down amongst the trees. The air was charged and the sky had turned a strange shade of red and blue and purple. It felt like the nanosecond before a lightning strike, but this energy held constant. It was scary.

With the skies the way they were, we didn't have time to waste. We hadn't even bothered to triangulate mom and Morty's current positions to call them. It would take too much time to explain everything in too small a window. Suddenly we felt like Cinderella one minute to midnight. The end was near.

We followed the path alongside a small brook, walking upstream. This part of the temple city hadn't been wrestled from the jungle. Creepers reached amongst the trees and small monkeys darted in and out of the branches hooting warnings at us. Birds made calls, and the ground buckled sometimes below our feet, rock peeking out from damp moss and tumbling roots and dirt in great jumbles. We were probably walking on top of an undiscovered ruin. There were too many rocks below our feet to be natural.

Ryan held his scanner. "This is it. We've reached the perimeter. The Bau patterns end here." He looked down at his watch. Neter appeared on a small rectangular screen there. "Could you triangulate the Aten's location using the three most distant Bau patterns along the perimeter – along with my location here."

"Of course, Ryan."

We were almost 200 meters south of the main temple group. The ruined structure of the Jaguar temple was falling down in front of us as it peeked out from the jungle. We only had a short hike and a flight of stone steps left to go to reach it. "The Aten appears to be centered approximately 36 meters due south west of you."

118 feet or so if memory served me.

"Can we just drill a hole?" Wep asked smugly. He still wasn't happy with me

"Smart, but I'm guessing not." I started up the path to the temple. The others followed.

We stood at the door of the Jaguar.

So this was Isis' temple?

It was falling down around us, an old ruin left to decay. There had been entrance pilasters with hieroglyphics along the doorway, but only fragments still survived. A stucco relief was on the rear wall of the temple too, depicting a king whose limbs ended in jaguar heads. Only part of the seat and a claw remained of it, though; the rest was worn away by time and ancient hands. Along the relief's side, we knew a staircase led down to a funeral chamber below.

"Neter," I spoke into my identical wrist watch. We all wore one now. "Can you get a thermal read on what's below this temple structure? See if you can align any open-air tunnels below to the star chart? There's a staircase in here that goes down to a funerary room. Maybe we can access the entry shaft there?"

Alexandra rolled her eyes at me.

"What?" Her ease amused me.

"I can almost hear Ra saying, 'too obvious,' right now."

She was probably right.

Neter answered. "There are un-accessed air shafts off the funerary room, but nothing matching the star chart."

"Told ya. Decoy tunnels."

Neter interrupted. "Yes. There are many tunnels off the funerary room leading to nowhere, but there are also shafts down there that match the star chart which weave in and around the decoy tunnels. The entry point to that tunnel group is 400 meters due south of here. I am downloading coordinates now."

Finally. We had coordinates.

There would be another hike though – this one requiring the machete Wep brought along, straight through untouched jungle. Until now, we had been following a path through the temple grounds, but no one had ventured where we were going. The vegetation outside the manicure grounds was chokingly thick. Wild animals probably roamed there.

Ryan shielded his eyes from the odd sun. It baked us in an abnormal light.

A hard wind blew and the air suddenly crackled.

"Ahhhhhh raaaaaaaaaaaaaa!"

Surprised, we covered our ears. The deafening sound of screaming filled the valley. The monkeys around us went crazy. Even with my ears covered, their shrieks were earsplitting. Seshat fell to her knees and the entire valley sounded with the cries of the howlers that had only just been playing in the trees. They were screaming – screaming in terrifying, mind-numbing pain, some wisely holding furry hands to human-like ears.

Twenty, maybe 30 of them spontaneously jumped out of nearby trees, though other groups were doing the same farther away. They ran uncontrolled along the ground and up and down the temple behind us all the while screaming. They were hysterical, cutting in and out of our feet. We couldn't hear the piercing noise that terrorized them, only their deafening wailing response.

The valley sounded with animals in anguish.

Then the ground shuddered.

Another quake.

Ryan was knocked to the earth, and one of the monkeys darted sideways to get out of his way and jumped onto Amisi. It yanked at her shirt over and over. Amisi's face registered fear, then shock and compassion. She took the little thing in her arms and hugged it. It calmed immediately and buried itself in the crook of her arm. She held it there and with her other free hand, flung out at the air like she was releasing something from the soul of her. A shockwave flew from her, a visible noise sounded too, and the monkeys stilled themselves and went silent.

Ryan's jaw dropped. "How ..."

"I ... I don't know. I didn't know I could do that."

Wep walked over. "You're young yet, Amisi. Wadjet could do that too." He patted her gently on her shoulder and helped her up from the ground.

"The goddess of protection?" Ryan asked.

"Yes."

Amisi shook, but set the howler monkey down. It scooted back to its mother who held it and stared at Amisi with confusion and something like gratefulness.

The sky was darkening now to a deep bruising purple and electricity buzzed almost visibly in the air. Drops of rain fell, gentle at first, but they became great stingers and then the sky fell open.

Since electricity and water weren't the best of friends, I figured we should get going. "Uh, guys," I stated the obvious; my skin and clothes were soaked. "I thing we better hurry."

Wep ran ahead, hacking at the thick growth with his machete. We rushed in close behind him, straight into the jungle, grateful at once for the protective canopy that covered us there.

Chapter 28-Dragon path

We pushed ahead as quickly as Wep could clear the path. And that was pretty fast. Wolf man was a beast on at least two levels. His shirt came off and sweat glistened off his hard muscles, but I didn't catch Alexandra staring.

We were lucky at least that whatever prowling animals usually haunted this place had holed up from the rain and bizarre weather and left us alone. I didn't blame them. The pounding rain even found its way through the thick jungle canopy. I would have holed up too if I could, but it was the heat mixed with the humidity that was worse. And the jungle itself was so thick, we barely saw a foot in front of us. So, when the machete found rock, Wep stopped short and hacked around it.

We were nearly at the coordinates anyway.

He took a step closer.

"Whoa!" Wep rocked forward uncontrollably and nearly fell. Ryan moved faster than sight and pulled him back. Either Wep lost his footing or the earth gave way. It was hard to tell in the matted vege-tation.

"Thanks! That was close."

"Is that a hole or something?" Amisi took a step back as if the earth might swallow her too.

"Not sure. The brush is so thick through here, but I felt like I might fall straight to hell." Wep had a way with words. This was a man who'd seen war. He wiped the sweat away from his brow and got down on his hands and knees to feel around. "I can't believe I almost lost it."

His hands moved along the damp earth, feeling cautiously. Sur-prised, he hacked again at the ground. The vines and tangles of vegetation were so thick, it was like standing on a rug woven from tendrils and creepers. They ran along the ground and through the trees and everywhere. He took one more whack at the vines on the ground and a heavy clump fell away, pulling down more and more as they fell.

And fall they did, down into a deep well of earth that was hidden there. Dust rose up as the vegetation continued to collapse into it as Wep ran hacking around the perimeter. But this wasn't a hole or even a pit. It was manmade and circular, at least 60 feet across and nearly as deep by the time Wep rounded its perimeter.

"Huh, that's pretty deep." I took a step back even though I could fly.

Wep stood taking in his work too. Cut rock lined the wall of earth that fell away into darkness below. A solitary structure rose from its depths toward the sky. A moment ago, Wep had been hacking at this very edifice when he nearly fell. It rose up only a foot inside the pit where we stood. It was so close, we could lean out and touch its edge. I thought it was a dead tree, condemned to be strangled and veiled by the jungle creepers and vines that ran along here, but it was more than that.

Wep leaned his long body over the pit and propped himself against it with one hand. Finding it sturdy, he took a whack at it with his machete. Another large swath of dead vines fell away like a mask being peeled back. Our tree was a stone tower.

There was a ledge rounding it at the height we stood at, so of course, Wep jumped onto it and hacked away at the vines there. It took more shape as he cut away the green from its middle and up its height. The tower had four flat sides that rose up from the earth like a giant stalagmite, growing narrower as it reached its pinnacle. A series of ledges rounded the tower at equal intervals from its base to its high point. Each of these ledges was punctuated with holes drilled deep into its sides. Water from the rain that had found its way into the jungle poured out these drains. And each of the four corners of the tower was ribbed from top to bottom, like thick icing outlining a cake. The smallest ledge, nearly at its apex, held some sort of figure aloft on top.

Wep decided to climb it and hacked once more, revealing the grotesque creature that crowned it. The thing was a great frog. The strange creature's mouth hung open and its tongue reached up like it would lick its own bulbous eyes. It sat on haunches like it was more dog than frog, and its overly large hands rested on its knees. The mouth was huge. Inside it was painted the same bright blue the men that climbed the temple had been, but it was stained with thick rusty brown crud around its cruel lips too.

"Oh. Oh no!" Seshat lunged, looking away. She had eyes for this. "This is a place of sacrifice, an unholy place." She shook her head.

"Those men, the blue painted ones," Alexandra remembered our shared vision, noticing the same blue color I had.

"Yes." She was haunted still. "No one would ever come to this place for fear of that." She pointed but wouldn't look. "And no Mayan would ever reveal such a dark place if ever they knew it was here."

I was afraid what the caked stuff on the frog's mouth was now.

Wep scaled back down the tower like he wanted to get away from it too. This was a place of pagan sacrifice. It was slicker now that his handholds had fallen away, but he made it. Ignoring what he found up top, Wep asked another question. "What's down there then?"

"I think we should find out. Amisi? Spidey time."

Amisi grinned and the two girls went to work on the dry foliage hanging around the ravine. They sent white hot lightning bolts flying that incinerated the old growth in a storm of flames. This briefly lit the inverted temple. I made out the frame of a doorway lined with a heavy stone slab far below. Whatever hall led from it, it skirted back toward the Jaguar temple and the Aten. Then the fire died and the pit fell into semi-darkness again.

"I think," Alexandra peered down, "we might have found the entrance."

"Here," Wep reached out to her. "Let me."

She hesitated, but Wep insisted. He was ever the gentleman, or he figured he still had a chance – especially standing there with his shirt off. She took his hand and stepped the short distance to the tower, lightly arriving on the ledge there. Wep helped Amisi too; we aliens are nothing if not chivalrous. But Ryan and I made the leap ourselves.

WHOOOOOOMMmmm. We were standing on the middle ledge when it happened, though Alexandra's hair whipped up before I even heard it. It was a noise like crashing thunder. It came from south of us. It was rushing our way.

Whatever it was brought with it an avalanche of sound that only got louder. Wep scurried up the tower for a better view amidst the paralyzing cacophony. He arched up and squinted, his eyes trying to see what was coming. He shook his head like he couldn't believe them and strained even farther forward. This time his head morphed into the wolf and I watched as Alexandra swallowed hard. Seeing that was unsettling. This time his doggy eyes went wide, and Wep leapt down, literally leapt all the way down, the distance to the bottom of the ravine like he couldn't get away fast enough.

That wasn't good.

"Hurry!" he shouted unhurt but obscured by the darkness below.

We half flew, half shimmied and slid down the tower, roped with dead massive twisting vines, as fast as our legs and arms could take us. The sound was growing unimaginably louder and my body vibrated with its approach.

When we hit bottom, Amisi held one of her lightning bolts in her hand, giving us a view of the sunken temple. Alongside the doorway we spied from above, just feet from the tower we slid down, was a blocked-off doorway scored with six sets of handprints set deep into the stone like it was once wet concrete, perfect for casting.

"There's no time!" Wep yelled above the growing cacophony and violent shaking. He still hadn't bothered to explain what was coming. Wep ran for the door and found a set of hands that matched his perfectly. Without hesitation, I ran for my matching set. We put our hands into them and the stone below grew red hot. Wep's too. It felt like the stone heated to magma just cooling in the air, not quite liquid, not yet hard stone.

The rest rushed over then too. We each of us sunk our hands into the impression that was made for us millennia ago and watched as each hand hold blazed hot and a grinding noise rumbled behind us to join the maddening noise approaching so close now. It was now – or never, by the sound of it. A huge thick panel of the tower from the middle ledge down, not the door surprisingly, slid forcefully into the earth as fast as Neter opens and closes her own. This was Oasen technology at work.

"This one must be another decoy," Alexandra found time to say. Her hair whipped up into the air violently from whatever was coming. Her already giant blue eyes somehow grew bigger. She took her hands off the rock and ran for the now-open tower, no longer interested in talking about decoys. Her handhold still glowed hot, but immediately faded.

Seshat stood frozen. I grabbed her arm and pulled her to the tower.

The wind seriously kicked up around us as we ran. Small micro bursts dropped into our cavern to lift up dirt and ash and dust and vines in maddening choking slapping swirls. The sky above somehow fell from midday light to darkness in seconds, the absence of light both solemn and treacherous in its coming. Everyone fell into the open tower and ran down the inclined path that dropped away from the door. I was last in and just in time to see a throng of jungle trees mown down above the ravine by a gray swirling mass of wind that hurled trees like toothpicks to shutter the ravine while gray darkness crushed down from above.

I ran covering my eyes.

A minute later there was a rumbling and I knew the tower was sealing shut behind us, but not before a sickening burst of debris and dust flew in and nearly suffocated us. We sat there coughing and retching, but there was air enough that death couldn't take us.

Just enough.

"Come on," I coughed and dragged myself forward slowly on hands and knees. It was all I could do. My body was scratched, bleeding and battered – even wet still from the earlier rain. The others followed behind in some kind of mimic of me, and we pulled ourselves down the incline until it opened up into a space that was fed air by some hidden shaft, this stuff clean and lifesaving. There was even light.

We sat against the walls, panting and coughing.

"I don't know what that was," Wep finally said. "But it wasn't like any cyclone I've ever seen."

Ryan leaned his head on the wall and pulled himself up, willing himself to keep moving. He was always so strong. We all tried to stand. We had to keep moving.

"I've been here before," I realized as I took in more of the room. "In my dreams."

"The Aten's only meters from here. We're that close, but which way?"

The room was a small hexagonal cathedral with six open doors going in different directions into semi-darkness. Maybe a few would take us into depths where we'd never find return. Maybe one would take us to a cave in, the tunnel of Osiris, and yet one more may be the path to the Aten, the only open path left.

"I tried to raise Neter." Ryan tapped at his watch, "but I can't get any signal so far down." His voice fell. "I hate to tell you this, but we never downloaded the diagram."

"No doubt." I was unfazed.

I walked over and brushed away the dirt at the top of one of the doors. A hieroglyph was emblazoned there. It was the Eye of Horus, the sign of the house of Wep. "Your house."

He walked up. "Also called the Wedjet Amisi, a symbol of protection."

I went to the door we came through and coughed. Dust still mingled the air here, but I cleaned off the dirt anyway to reveal another symbol. "What's this one Wep?" He knew them all.

"It's the djed column, the hieroglyph representing stability. Humph," he laughed. "Fitting."

I walked one door right and, brushing that one off, saw it.

"Draco. The path of our dragon."

We didn't need that diagram after all.

Chapter 29-The Aten

I t was as I remembered it – down to the little eddies of dust that swirled the air outside the door with the relief of the winged dragon. This time, though, I crossed the threshold with five friends. This time I would be here in person, not the personification of myself in some ethereal dream state, out of time and place, comforting a girl who had known me 2,300 years, but who I barely knew.

The air grew stale and hot as we made our way down the inclined path to the place where the space became so tight and the ceiling so low that we needed to drop to our bellies and crawl through. I poked my head out to tell everyone what was ahead when the vibrations began.

"Oh great." Ryan shook his head. "Something's happening – again."

"To say the least." I remembered the otherworldly cyclone we barely survived outside.

"The last day," Wep said with finality.

The last day, I thought. So, this was it.

The hall we were in had narrowed so much, there was barely room to stand one next to the other. If the walls caved in now, we were in trouble. I faced the narrow shaft we had to climb into. If it caved in while we were in there, this would be our grave.

Amisi steadied herself, and Alexandra's eyes grew large as the vibrations increased in magnitude and a throbbing waaam sound joined the pulsations. This wasn't an earthquake. What was it? But we all knew the answer. It was the Aten. It was the last day. And it was the start of the end of everything.

Wep stood there stoic and strong and not moving, but Seshat was terrified, her face gone sallow. This was completely out of her comfort zone. She was blind for once. We were headed into an unknown future, not a known past. I looked rapid fire around, and then did the only thing left to do. I dropped to my stomach into the shaft and shimmied toward Isis.

"It's holding up," I called head back. "But hurry. I'm not sure how much time we have at this point."

A slapping pounding noise started behind us then. It sounded liege something was following us down into our tunnel, which was all the more motivating. "Come on! This shaft drops out right into Isis' chamber. We are 20 feet away. We can do this."

"Just hurry."

Slap. Slap. Pound.

Something was coming.

Scared though I was, I began the uncomfortable journey forward. It was like crawling through an amplifier. The vibrations here were somehow worse. The humming settled in my bones and teeth to the point where they chattered. This thing was probably going to crumble down on top of us.

"Hurry up," Alexandra shouted from behind me. Her voice rose unsteadily into a near shout, but it was shaking, as much from fear as from the pulsing sensation that rocked through our bodies and the narrow shaft we slid through. Great clumps of dirt fell from the low ceiling too, mingling with tiny roots I had to spit from my mouth, and the air, once stale, now suffocated. I tried to move faster, but there were too many bodies, too little space, and too little time.

The vibrations were only getting worse, quickly too. Much worse. The already small shaft was shrinking around us as dirt came loose. Sweat poured off my body, mixing the soil to something like mud, but my mouth was strangely dry when I tried to swallow down my fear.

I didn't want to die when victory was so close.

I didn't want to be crushed and suffocated, buried under tons of earth with the roots of jungle plants pushed into my nose and mouth like the beginnings of a human flower pot. My heart tripped over itself as it tried to keep up with my imagination, but it wasn't doing a good job. I panted hard with adrenaline and untamed terror.

The pulsing was growing in magnitude every minute like the Aten was firing up pistons in a cosmic engine. Every time a new piston fired, the Aten's energy rose to a higher plateau, then leveled off, only to pulsate up again to the next frequency and hold there as another fired, before plateauing yet again. But this was energy like

I never knew existed – at least contained in a thing as small as the Aten. Maybe a dying star? A three-foot orb of conscious light bent on planetary destruction? No.

Well. Maybe.

Of one thing I was certain: The Aten was revving up and that couldn't be a good thing considering today was the last day and all, as Simon predicted.

"Hurry!" A voice cried out behind me. Fear panicked it. Other voices rose up behind me then, and I felt myself pushed and propelled urgently from behind as hands, maybe a face, got too close to my feet.

"Move it, Gil!" Alexandra shouted.

"I can't see," Seshat moaned. I didn't know if she was lamenting her second sight or if dirt was caking her eyes.

"Almost there," I called back coughing the swirling dust from deep in my lungs. I was hurrying as much for them as for me and as for the Aten. I felt its driving energy physically pulling me forward. The draw was powerful, magnetic, like we were two polar pieces who couldn't stay apart in such close proximity. Somehow I knew I had felt that pull, from the ranch in Montana, to the desert sands of Nubia, to the cold shore of Egypt.

It was calling me. The Aten was calling me. It would come to me if it could, but it was trapped here by the knot. Fixed to this place by its tie to Isis. Fixed and waiting for me to come to it.

I was almost there.

I sensed it in every part of my being. I held my breath as the break in the tunnel came into view. "There," I choked out. The others were crawling close behind me, urgently close, but in that moment I felt worlds apart from them. I didn't even notice the electrical box, or the grate that was broken out of the wall as I emerged, all I saw was Isis. Even my dad and Elaine were obscured. It was just Isis, with her black blunt cut hair and her jade green eyes, pleading in all their desperation, but somehow more alive than I remembered in my dreams.

Old blood crusted her brow like a crown. Here was flesh and blood and life – barely hanging on.

Here was the Aten in its final moments before it annihilated my planet.

I sensed it, the energy it was creating, energy that would blast out over and through our planet, to destroy and yet somehow capture it in all its essence, to pull it back into itself, taking with it all the life and love and hate and destruction and good and bad and beautiful and mundane.

Alexandra emerged beside me, coughing and choking. She stood up and sucked in a breath, but not because she needed air. This was awe. The Aten was overwhelming in first view. Its brilliant noise cascaded like crashing waves through the room. Alexandra's lips moved like there was something she wanted to say but I couldn't hear her.

The others spilled out of the tunnel in rapid succession behind us, emerging on hands and knees to breathable air only to stop short and watch the blazing ancient orb standing staunchly, unmoving, holding pleading Isis.

Then it spun slowly.

The last of us stood up unsteadily. The Aten took Isis with it on its slow path of rotation, but it picked up speed as the throbbing hum and vibrations increased in magnitude and complexity and power. It was strange and beautiful and terrifying all at once. The energy that flowed from it was so pure and brilliant my Bau felt instantly hot and full of life.

It pulled at me.

I took a step in its direction.

The Aten recognized our presence then, and woke up, like its consciousness had somehow been shaken alert. But somehow I also knew, it was too late. Just one step, and one second too late. It had already begun.

Isis was silent in the spinning mass.

In that nanosecond after its recognition of us, the room's electric lights brightened at the Aten's expenditure of sudden energy. It blasted out and I felt the Aten's pain and desperation and remorse as that circle of light radiated out powerfully from its center, pulsing into the room and through the walls out beyond. It was as if the Aten tried to reach out and pull it back in one final plea, but there hadn't been enough time.

It was too late.

We were too late.

One second too late.

I couldn't finish it. Just like Isis said.

I failed. She would lose Ra forever.

My eyes found Alexandra, this girl I just gained; I would lose her forever too. Not just my life. Her life. All our lives.

Alexandra's eyes found mine too, and I saw she knew it too.

The Aten sounded one last screech of desperation and spun so fast, it threw dad and Elaine away from it into a wall. They hit hard, but still stirred. They would have a moment of consciousness before their death.

Then there was a great rending sound, and the ceiling on the opposite side of the wall from us collapsed. Dirt and rock and people crashed through. Living ones. Mom and Morty and Ben and Kos and others. They righted themselves and covered their ears. The sound coming from the Aten was debilitating.

My mother stood up, taking everything in. She was shocked finding me and my father across the room. I thought she might collapse like the ceiling had above her, but she stood strong.

Alexandra called out, "Dad!" and they ran to each from opposite sides of the room, stopping near the spinning Aten that stood between them. Alexandra's hair whipped from its speed, and tears filled her eyes as they hugged each other tightly.

I didn't run to my mom, but I sent a message telepathically. "How did you get here?"

"Kos saw the glare from the transport shaft come down from Neter. We followed your path through the jungle." Her words spilled out quickly.

"I thought the tower door closed?"

"A tree." She spoke into my mind, "A tree from that cyclone jammed it at the top. We crawled through."

"You took another tunnel. The Aten must have jogged a weak spot in its shaft?"

"WAAAAAMMM!" The Aten accelerated even more and then sounded loudly, almost to remind us of its presence.

"I failed mom. I was too late. It's happening. And I'm sorry for everything."

Movement caught the corner of my eye. My dad was trying to get up. The noise must have jogged him awake. He tried to rise. Her eyes drifted to him. They hadn't left things well.

"Go to him."

She gave silent consent and ran.

Could I do anything? Anything at all to stop this?

I was frantic. Maybe we could get back to Neter in time? Leave the planet in time. My thoughts were frenzied, unrealistic.

Woom, woom, woom. The Aten powered down. The lights went out. There was only black darkness so thick it almost had texture. The Aten went silent, but it was still spinning. I felt air coursing from it.

This was the calm before the storm of final destruction.

In the blinding darkness, there was a rustling noise behind me. It came from the shaft we just crawled through. It was the sliding thud of yet another person making their way into the room from the tunnels that fed it. Maybe one of mom's crew found the Draco tunnel? But then the lights flickered and revealed the intruder.

"Oh my gods, Khonsu, you dirty little animal." Wep recognized whoever it was. He walked boldly up to this new person. "How did you get here?"

My brain tried to place him. This guy was familiar. I squinted. No, was it? I pictured him wearing a turban and heavy glasses or maybe a red ball cap? The Arab! The tourist! This person – he had been following us.

"Nice to see you too, Wep. But where are you manners?" Khonsu wagged his finger at wolf man. "Do you often prostrate yourself so lowly in the presence of royalty?" The boy's eyes gleamed with madness. "For I am Khonsu, son of Amun, our great leader, and Mut. I am the god of the moon, the god of time, the companion of Thoth, the lover of games, and the winner of this one, I might add."

He gave a flourishing bow.

"You've got to be kidding me." Wep spit. "This, all of this, is your fault! You and your conspiring murderous father's fault! Come here you little ..."

I couldn't hear what else Wep said as he stalked towards him, but that was probably best.

"There are no winners here," Wep yelled at Khonsu as he approached. "You're getting a front row seat to your own destruction – along with us!"

"That's what you think!" Khonsu taunted back. "But enough of your prattling. It's getting quite old, and so are you." Khonsu was suddenly behind Wep, moving in a blur. He grabbed his neck and pulled back hard. Wep dropped unmoving to the ground. He lay glassy eyed on cold stone. A sound like I've never heard escaped Alexandra's lips and she fell to the earth in instant grief. I couldn't believe it. How could this happen?

I wanted to be sick.

Wep now lay crumpled in his wolfy form on the ground at Khonsu's feet. Wep had turned in death. He didn't even have a chance to protect himself.

The Aten still spun, oblivious to the death around it. The noise it made was subtle now, but its vibrations still hung heavy in the room. Restrained as it was at this point, it was still reminder enough of what was to come – at any moment.

The grin on Khonsu's face was maddening, standing there over Wep's body. He held a weapon of blue light in his hands. It was familiar. It was the same blue light that had blazed in the hands of the would-be assassin who tried to kill Isis when she first hung silent in the knot. Khonsu brought the weapon up to his face. I had a bitter taste in my mouth. Yes. He was definitely the tourist from the boat. The Arab from the library. I imagined him following us the entire time, peering out at us from the tents in the desert of bones, gazing at us from the watch tower at Siwa, maybe even sneaking onto Neter on the ice shelf.

"He wasn't right, you know?" Khonsu's voice had the same slithering quality of a snake. He kicked the limp body of the wolf that lay at his feet.

Seshat wailed.

"I will be well and gone before this thing takes the Earth." He gestured at the Aten and spit down on Wep in further insult. His eyes, even from this distance, were sure and defiant. "But first, I wanted to look one more time on you." He took a step in my direction. "The one Ra meant to save himself and Isis. Tisk. Tisk. You're a complete failure, you know that? You couldn't save Isis or Ra or your own self or your mother or father or even your beautiful girlfriend." Khonsu's eyes fell on each person throughout the room as he spoke their names. They stopped on Alexandra though and he drank her in. My blood boiled with fury.

But his was raw fever and zeal.

"Ra ... you who would defeat my father and steal his great possession?" Khonsu went on and gestured wildly toward the spinning orb. "No! I think not!" He seemed mad. He ran at it, but stopped short and screamed at it maniacally, spittle flying from his mouth. "Ra, who will watch his plans fall short from the heart of his precious Aten. Ra, who will watch his lover die today." Sweat poured from his face. His tone was harsh, mocking. Every time he spoke, he stacked on more fury and hate. "And Ra, who will remain trapped in the Aten for whatever eternity he is allowed to ponder this day, to never forget how he failed her, to never forget who killed her."

Khonsu laughed his sweet revenge.

He was a rampaging, rabid dog. "Do you hear that Ra? It draws her power even now. We defeat you today! My father and I. We defeat you today! Today, I take everything from you! Just like you did to me!" He screamed the words. Spit flew again from his mouth.

The Aten abruptly stopped. The room went from half-darkness to blinding light. Khonsu laughed viciously, because in that moment, a human sort of cry escaped from the Aten. It was Ra moaning. Ra screaming. And Isis screamed from inside the Aten too, and we watched as she broke free from the long grasp of time and fell to the base of her prison – the weird light bath falling to the floor too but her shell remaining. She could move again, but her movement was writhing.

I ran to Isis' prison and put my hand on the surface. The Aten's tentacle arms were still holding her there, but loosely. Khonsu was closer to me now too. He circled the room behind me in Alexandra's direction. Maybe I could try and take him out before the Aten finished it?

He eyed me strangely.

The surface of the knot felt like jelly, but it was impenetrable, unlike my dream. Isis, noticing me then, clamored up from where she writhed in pain at its base. She put her hands up to match mine.

"I'm so sorry," I mouthed.

A tear formed in her eye and slowly fell, but she was silent. She grabbed at her stomach and hunched down again, incapable of continuing.

Her prison was breaking. She was breaking.

Khonsu was nearly to Alexandra. "Move away," I told her in my mind. She backed up, but her legs seemed hung with lead. He edged closer still.

Ra moaned from the Aten. Isis heard him above her too. She reached to him and screamed with suffering – but not for the pain she felt. This was the cry of deep agony only the loss of love can bring. Not a cry for her own death – but a cry for her separation from him, from Ra, from her love – for the realization of what was happening – for the realization of the utter pointlessness of it all. This was the cry of true hell – to be separated eternally from love.

Khonsu reveled in their maddening last moments, shoulders quaking from laughter and his excitement. "You have all of eternity to remember this Ra." Khonsu faced the orb. He had edged his way close to Alexandra. "That is, until the day I find the Aten again and pull you out from that thing and end you." His voice grew slightly louder and dripped like burning acid. Ra would have to remember his threat too if he survived as Khonsu believed he would.

Then Khonsu turned his attention on me then.

His eyes flashed oddly as they had moments ago. He walked slowly, menacingly in my direction. What did he want now? We were about to die in seconds anyway. But the seconds clicked by thickly like we were in a time dilation. Everything was set on slow motion, yet everything felt like it was rushing forward with great momentum too. I guessed I did this. I could try to slow down time all I wanted, but it was only a stop-gap measure. The spell would be broken eventually.

The Aten grew in size and even brightness then. Khonsu was in my line of sight too, but I ignored him. So, this was it. The world was going to end now – slow motion or not. I wouldn't let Khonsu have the pleasure of being the last thing I saw though. I fell into

Alexandra's big blue eyes. I wanted only to hold her. I felt the last seconds spinning down, but I couldn't get to her before the end. I knew that, so I decided to spend my final seconds lost in her eyes.

I settled into them unaware of the other coming danger.

"I love you," I spoke into her mind.

"I love you back." It would be the first and last time we'd say it. We held each other. I wish I could say it was in each other's arms, but our eyes would have to do. I felt warm, but the spell broke suddenly. Alexandra's eyes went wide with sudden fear and realization, and I watched as if outside my body. She ran for me. Running faster than the time we had left. It was then I noticed Khonsu was running at me too. He held the bright blue weapon in his gloved hand.

It was strange watching Khonsu and Alexandra racing for me in that oddly fast slow motion, almost running together, the one trying to beat the other to me first.

Khonsu only had seconds himself. The end was here.

He threw something, I thought at me, but it sailed past me in the direction he was running, like a silver coin flipping through the air. A sea-blue portal opened up in the room as it touched the ground just two feet past me. Another world stared back through the soupy haze of gelatinous material that made it up. So he would find refuge after all.

He ran past me, aiming his body at the portal, and brought the weapon up in trained precision as he sailed by. It pointed at my heart.

He fired and my mind screamed.

But it didn't find its mark.

Alexandra was faster than the bullet. She was faster than Khonsu.

The heart it found was not my own.

The heart it found belonged to her.

She rocketed by me with unquenched momentum, our bodies briefly touching. She jerked at the impact and her blood mingled with flaring blue sparks as they splattered and stung my dirty white shirt. I choked back sobs watching the blue sparks dance with the blood, declaring for everyone what we meant to one another.

"Nooo, Alexandra!" I screamed and tried to catch her, but she was moving so fast, her momentum carried her straight through Khonsu's portal into the other world.

He hadn't slowed down either and rocketed through it after her. I tried to rush in, but he put his hand up to touch the portal's other side and the thing became clear and hard as glass. I watched, unable to get to her, as Khonsu leaned over her bleeding lifeless form. He looked up once more, and then the portal and Alexandra were gone.

Morty dropped to his knees screaming.

I realized two things in those next seconds.

One, I realized I was still alive. The Aten had somehow stopped. And two, even though that was true, without Alexandra, I was dead inside anyway. Only my body wouldn't let me believe that. Everything within me burned. I felt engulfed in fire. Maybe this was the end?

"Gil!" my dad cried out. His eyes were wide, staring at me. "Gil, look."

I looked down at myself. A raging blue fire consumed me, but didn't consume me.

I knew what this was.

This was the tangible reality of the love we shared. This was her sacrifice and my pain. This was our hopes and our fears. This was everything we weren't and were and could have been, all of it growing and colliding and pouring into the Aten – the Aten, which had gone completely, totally still. The Aten, which should have destroyed our planet by now.

Isis faced me in her knot, hands firm against the membrane that held her back. Her face registered wonder and fear, but she was still. The pain had gone.

Dad held his arm like it was broken. Mom stood in stony silence, her eyes wild with kinetic energy like she might still try and do something to save us all. I looked at Morty, still screaming for his daughter. I looked again at the Aten, the so-still Aten and wondered. My body raged in pain. The blue sparks of Alexandra's sacrifice, the blue sparks of my love for her, the blue heat of our story, everything that was our love – it captured the Aten, held it still, and gave it resolution.

I understood then.

It was a principle as old as time itself. The Oracle had told me once, and now it was emblazoned on my heart. When there is no longer hope, when man fears his end, when salvation is at stake, only sacrifice can bring redemption. 'It is known,' the Oracle would have said. I knew it as surely now as I knew the world would see tomorrow.

I felt the pain pull away from me, and the sparks multiplied and spun silently round and round the Aten until there was only a whirling sea of deepest blue. The Aten, the knot, Isis, all of it was hidden under the royal color. It burst out from its center to pulse into the room and through the walls out beyond; then they flooded and folded back in on themselves and were gone.

Isis stood whole and alive beneath the silent orb, staring quizzically around. Her knot was gone. Blinding light flared and Ra appeared in his human form, light and energy and heat forming into bone and living flesh. They stood facing, staring, not touching. Their anticipation felt like a solid thing. They finally took each other in their arms, and blue sparks danced maddeningly between them too.

All was silent and still.

I walked away quickly trying to escape this place and fell, collapsing alone to the dusty earth to heave and cry until there was nothing left.

I had gained the world and lost her.

She had given me the world and my life.

But she was gone.

I was alone now. Totally alone.

My skin prickled. There was something above me.

Not totally alone.

The Aten reached down its arm-like rays and embraced me. I was its key.

It was finished.

Chapter 30-Emergency surgery

Wep was still alive.

He had morphed into a man some few minutes after the Aten went silent. After the blue light had bounced out and back, he changed. I thought it signaled he was finally dead from the wound Khonsu had inflicted, but Seshat had screamed, "He's alive" and brought most of us running but for a few.

Dad and mom were still holding Morty who had finally stopped screaming and become still like death itself. He numbly stared into the distance. Maybe he was reliving his life with her in his mind? Cradling her as a baby? Watching her take her first steps? Or maybe his mind was peacefully, finally numb? Whatever it was, he wasn't well.

He just lost everything.

Ryan and Amisi knew enough to leave me alone and stood off to the side, as did Ra and Isis, taking a cue from them.

I was angry.

They stood there as silent outsiders, not knowing exactly what to do. Not knowing exactly what to say. They had planned for everything but the aftermath. The life and the death they would cause.

We let them stand there and went about our own business. They had waited this long; they could wait a little longer. I wiped the snot and tears away from my nose and my dirty face and got down on my knees next to Wep. Seshat moved behind him and gently held his head.

His eyes cracked open just slightly. "Did we do it?" There was something wrong with his voice.

My words were cryptic. "No. She did it. Alexandra did. She saved us all."

Wep swallowed hard. I closed my eyes and tears squeezed out unabashedly. I wiped them away hard and sniffed again. His eyes moved to where they fell and something in his face changed.

He knew. I saw the moment his eyes registered it.

"She's gone, Wep." I choked out the words. "Khonsu killed her. Show him Seshat."

And she did.

I got caught up in the vision too. I watched Alexandra run along with Khonsu like they were in a race for the same finish line. I caught the way her mouth curved up wryly the second before she took the bullet for me, in the second she knew she had won. I marveled at her. I saw how her body and head had jerked back as she was hit. I saw her sail through the portal and become lost to me, sealed away on the other side, leaving me nothing to bury in the watery halls of the catacombs. I saw Khonsu kneel beside her and check the pulse at her neck as blood pooled around her chest, a sort of dark purple through the haze of the blue portal. I saw the blue sparks and blood spatter and how it had saved us all. I watched as our love and her death stopped the Aten from destroying the Earth. How Alexandra saved everyone and lost her own life in seconds.

We emerged from the vision, each of us trying to breathe. Wep was filled with grief and sadness and new understanding, but he didn't speak. He didn't need to. It was strange, but we drew odd comfort from our shared pain and loss.

After, he tried to move, but grabbed at his throat in pain and made a horrible gurgling sound. Seshat's eyes narrowed in anger. "He broke your neck." Her hand flew to his shoulders to still him. "Don't move, Wep. Even you could become paralyzed."

He grunted. "I don't feel right. My hands are tingling."

"Excuse me ... I'm sorry" Isis walked up. "Perhaps, I can help?"

Wep narrowed his eyes but didn't move. "Isis." His voice sounded like gravel. He said it like he was speaking to an old friend, but one he wasn't happy to see.

Ra came up too.

"Ra?" Wep's eyes moved to find him, but his body remained still.

"Yes, it's us. We're alive."

"Some of us aren't," Wep said bitterly.

Ra buoyed up at his rebuke, but Isis stood timidly. Wep couldn't move but he was an intimidating presence even then. Isis shoulders narrowed in guilt.

They hovered above us. I almost forgot they all knew each other, were friends even. Wep and Seshat had played an integral role in their plan – one they sacrificed their lives for in some ways. They had known Isis would be tied in the knot. They planned everything thousands of years ago, together. It was difficult for me to realize how involved they had been for so long.

Wep stared daggers at them from the ground. Even sweet Seshat sat unmoving and angry. Tension strung tight through the air and threatened to break. Ryan and Amisi walked up. Even mom, dad and Morty appeared to notice, catatonic though he was, but Ben and Kos had gone back into the tunnels to see if it was safe to leave. They weren't here to watch the scene unfold.

"I thought you said none of us would get hurt?" Wep's voice was weak, but coming from a prone man, it was an oddly hostile accusation. "And it was the girl," his voice choked. "The girl who died ... Alexandra. She ... she died."

"I'm ... I'm so sorry," Ra's voice faltered. "Not one of us was supposed to die. The Oracle said so. She said none of this group would lose their life – as crazy as the whole plan seemed. She said it was the only way. The way to save the most lives here on Earth. I don't understand it Wep. I don't." Ra paced and gestured with his hands. "That's why we did it! That's why we all went along with it in the first place. The other paths, they were easier, but they led to so much death. You know that. If Amun had gotten a hold of the Aten, you knew the consequences. You helped decide the path. This wasn't just for us," he gestured to Isis. "It was for this world – and for other worlds. To protect them from what he would have become had he taken control of the Aten. Amun – that man – he is a destroyer."

Wep grunted. He was in pain, but he acknowledged him.

"She did say that," Isis voiced. She watched me carefully. "But she also said Gil may not be able to finish it." Her lashes hooded her eyes sadly, remembering. This had been a particularly hard idea for her to bear all those years trapped in the knot, and her worst fears were almost realized just minutes ago. "We tried to ignore it, Ra, but she implied that if Gil failed, there was another path, an obscure path, one that had a serious consequence. We ignored that, Ra. It was easy to do."

He hung his head. He did remember.

Ryan's eyes were red and swollen. "Khonsu must have done something, got in the way somehow and thrown off the time table. That's why we didn't get Gil here in time."

I appreciated his sentiment – that I hadn't failed Alexandra, and the world, alone.

"The fractals of time aren't always as clear as the Oracle would have us believe," Seshat cut in.

"That may be true, Seshat, but I think the Oracle already knew something had gone wrong by the time I got to her in the cave. I thought she was being cryptic, but she said there was one who was fated from time to save the Earth. But fate and choice may destroy one and save another. She was talking about Alexandra, about the other path." I raised my eyes to Isis and put my hands in my pockets. I felt numb. "The Oracle knew. She knew that a choice would have to be made to finish it, and she knew what Alexandra might choose."

Isis touched my arm. It was a familiar touch. This was a person who knew me, who watched me grow up, who talked to me every night, a person I kept sane through her 2,300-year willing imprisonment. "I'm so sorry, Gil. I saw what happened." She swallowed. "I know the sacrifice she made." Her eyes filled with tears.

I didn't have any more tears to cry.

She took my hand and held it, and my friends surrounded me as Wep looked on alone from the ground. "I'll never forget her Isis. Never."

"None of us will." Wep was hoarse. "Not one of us."

The Aten glowed brightly above me at that moment and somehow I knew it was asking a question. Ra acknowledged it as if he spoke its language – one I didn't yet know. He touched the soft spot on Isis' neck where the locket rested. This startled her, but she knew what was needed. She silently removed it from her neck and placed it on mine. The Aten seemed to exhale above me and collapsed itself back into the little trinket. The Aten was home. I was its new keeper.

▪▪▪▪▪

Ben's feet dangled from the ceiling above. He didn't even wait to drop down to give us the news.

"It's tight in places, but it is holding up." His voice was slightly muffled, but he was trying to project. "We can make it out, but," he dropped gracefully down this time. Elaine shimmied down behind him. "I'm worried about the aftershocks. We need to get out of here soon."

"And no one's using the Dragon tunnel anytime soon," Koss added, emerging in near synchronization with his twin from the other tunnel – the one we came through. He was almost completely covered in fine dust. "This one's toast," he coughed. A literal cloud of brown swirled from his mouth.

This would be welcome news provided we could all crawl. But that wasn't the case. All eyes wandered in Wep's direction. Tender-hearted Seshat cried. Wep was critically hurt.

"Has it been that long, Seshat," Isis leaned down over her old friend. "Have you forgotten so quickly my gifting?"

"Wait." Ryan stepped in. "In the histories, Isis was a protector, not a healer."

"Yes, well that's Isis my mother, not Isis me."

My dad got up and stumbled over to Isis, imploringly, excitedly, like he was a five year old about to open a present.

"Do you mean?" He couldn't finish his sentence.

"Yes. I am a hybrid like your son. Isis was my mother, but a lowly country farmer fathered me."

Ra took her hand protectively.

"Fascinating," was his only response.

"Now, try to be still." Isis motioned for Ryan, Kos and Ben to come over. "You will have to hold him down."

"No ... No!" Wep said.

"I'm sorry. It's the only way."

The men came over and took their places around him at Isis' direction. Ryan held his head and Ben and Kos got his shoulders. Ra was last. He sat on his thighs. Even Morty came over and held his feet without being asked.

"I wish I had something for the pain," Isis worried. "This isn't the way it's usually done. I usually medicate patients before surgery."

"This is surgery?"

An aura of golden light appeared under one of her hands and she held it flat like she was a human MRI machine, running it across Wep's neck. Her eyes were calculating, thoughtful.

"Yes, this is surgery. His neck is fractured in two places. Part of his spine is shattered and impinging his spinal cord here." She showed us pointing and Wep whimpered and flushed. She scanned again and the light changed to deeper amber. "There's bleeding here too," she stated quickly. "Oh my stars, he's hemorrhaging!"

Wep's eyes rolled back suddenly as if the news was all he needed to let go and make his way to God.

"No Wep!" Seshat shouted. "Oh no, oh no, oh no!" She fell into Amisi's arms. This was her grandchild after all. Her own son's son.

"I can stop it!" Isis shouted, and she brought her hands up expertly. All the men holding his body became tense. The light from her hands shifted red tinged with black, like she was a human cautery. "Hold him!" she shouted as Wep tried to arch his back. His nerves were still firing. That was good news. Pain here now was good. It meant he was still alive.

Wep screamed and came to.

"He's lost a lot of blood." Isis' voice was unsteady. "But I have to finish it." She bit her bottom lip and motioned like she was conducting an orchestra above Wep's neck. Instead, she was sewing together bone and sinew. Moving shattered pieces of his vertebrae from where they threatened to paralyze him, and deftly bonding them to the bone they belonged to. Wep, who was so close to death only minutes ago, screamed in uncontained pain. Conscious, living pain.

Dad gulped, holding his broken arm, and moved away quickly. He took my arm and led me across to a dark recess of the room, in case anyone dared notice his injury too. I was guessing at this point he planned to bully through without any intervention after watching what was done to Wep.

Mom, noticing us, followed.

Chapter 31-The space before a lightning strike

"Thank God you're okay, Gil." Mom grabbed me and pulled me to her.

My mind was a million places but in this moment I felt guilt mingled with my own pain. "I'm sorry I scared you. I got all your messages," I spoke into her shoulder. "But only a few days ago."

"Oh, honey." She pulled back. "Not even over-protective moms can mess with fate. It's okay." Tears spilled from her eyes. She was just grateful I was alive. "I'm so sorry." I knew she was talking about Alexandra.

She mussed my hair. Dad was still quiet. "I feel like all of this is my fault. I should have gone with you. I messed up the pattern."

Dad shook his head no.

"No. It's me. I was never supposed to get trapped here." He clenched his fists together and paced. "I was supposed to be waiting for you to arrive up there, to get you down here faster."

Anger and frustration were rippling off my normally mild-mannered father. "The Oracle told us to find the pattern from the sky. That it would reveal the path to the Aten. It was supposed to buy you enough time. She said every second counted."

Elaine walked up then.

"She was clear about it." His voice went quiet. "'The space before a lightning strike is all that separates doom from might.' That's what she said. That was my part. Instead, I got trapped here. I wasn't up there waiting! I am the kink." He pointed to the ceiling, to a place nearby in shadows. Another hole. The place he fell through.

"This place is caving in everywhere. All the decoy tunnels are collapsing."

Dad nodded. "I don't know how much that matters, but this, all this is my fault. We found the pattern, but we failed you."

"Joe," Elaine interrupted. "Don't blame yourself. This was all Khonsu's fault. He's the one who changed the pattern. Not you. Not us."

"What did ... did that animal do?"

"He pretended. He's like a chameleon." She dropped to her knees in front of me, her expression serious. Her dark brown hair was cropped short with military precision and her eyes were sharp and focused. "He came on the dig as a student and charmed his way into our circle. We thought he had such potential! But then I caught him with my computer going over the Bau traces we mapped and I knew. Of course he ran, but he had on a Bau tracer. We followed, and Joe and I we saw him duck into the Jaguar Temple. The rest, it seems, is history."

"We got lost," dad finished. "We fell out here. Then we got too close to the Aten and it trapped us for whatever reason. And we weren't up there to do our part like we were supposed to."

My mind felt numb.

This was all too much.

"It was Khonsu." Elaine said it again. "He led us astray. He changed the path. He is guilty of all this," she swept her hand around the room. "And more."

We were quiet then thinking of Alexandra.

And Wep, he was finally quiet too.

■■■■■

I shielded my eyes from the sun as we emerged out the door of the jaguar tunnel. The staunch old temple had finally served its purpose. It could go on crumbling away now if it wanted to. All its secrets were being exposed to the light, one by one, as they emerged from its front door. Ra and Isis shook as they emerged into the sunlight. Time had destroyed much in their millennia underground. She had entered a pristine temple. The one she exited was falling down.

They took each other's hand, took a deep breath, and walked away from it all – walked away from their long imprisonment, away from treachery, away from death, away from entropy, away from time. They followed the path away from it all, downstream toward the main temple group at Palenque.

The scenery had changed somewhat since we were here too. The mega-storm had flattened trees along the path, leaving them snapped in half and jagged. We climbed over them carefully. Wep did it gingerly. He was weak, but he was alive.

Ryan tapped on his watch as we approached the clearing where Neter dropped us off. It was on a rise, so it offered a clear view of Palenque below. Ra and Isis stood gazing at it all. It was still beautiful here. The cyclone had spared the ruins but so much else had changed here in those long years.

"There's nothing for us to go back to, is there Ra?" Isis asked.

He shook his head no with realization. Their Egypt was like this too. I patted him on the back. "There is no going back," I stated flatly. I saw Alexandra's face in my mind. "Now, we can only move forward. It's not Egypt, mind you, but we have our own little Oases Earth."

"I hope you like horses," Ryan said absentmindedly and pressed a button on his watch.

The cylinders fell down from Neter.

"We live in Montana now."

■■■■■

We stayed in Palenque one more week, tending to Wep and making sure no one would ever discover Isis' chamber thanks to some seriously scary purple bombs Neter had been concealing in a secret hold. Purple was the color of Oasen war, Ra told me before the first went off. Remind me never to go to war with them, okay? Those bombs will seriously vaporize you.

We spent the remainder of the week watching the president and other world leaders try to explain away the events of the last month with cryptic details involving massive solar flares, planetary alignment and shifting weather patterns. The frozen tsunami was the most difficult to explain, but it was melting slowly now, so that was the story and not its originations. If anyone was trying to figure it out, they were doing so behind closed doors. I suspect we had stirred up some serious suspicions with people higher up, but the bourgeoisie was blissfully ignoring it all to go back to a semblance of normal life. The desert was returning to the desert and the arctic had frozen over again. Things were back to normal.

I felt oddly detached going about the motions of life. Alexandra felt just out of reach, like I might be able to pull her back to me, but I wasn't bourgeoisie. I couldn't ignore what happened. I knew the truth. Her blood had pooled around her.

I shook off the memory and touched the locket around my neck. The Aten hung quietly there like it was nothing but mundane metal. Ra would look at it from time to time and furrow his brows, but that had been all. He kept silent, leaving the thing shrouded in mystery, much to my dad's discontent. I was happy to leave it alone for now myself.

When we finally left to follow the others home, Neter made the arch in the sky to the place where the Earth curved and showed her splendor. We stopped there to say our goodbyes to Alexandra.

Morty let me say the words. "After all, you had blue sparks kind of love, and that counts for something," he had told me with tears in his eyes.

"Peace be to her."

"Peace be to her," they echoed and we fell back down to Earth.

Ra and Isis stood at the window, surveying their new home as we approached.

"It's not the pyramids," I said trying, "but I imagine log cabins are much cozier."

"Anything's better than the knot," Isis said quietly.

■■■■

Neter put down at the top of her tunnel.

"Don't you want to park inside?"

Alexandra would have asked it too, with just as much sarcasm, so I had to instead.

For a computer, she was oddly perceptive. Purple eyes sighed and answered expertly. "I do not need to be garaged. Thank you very much."

I smiled weakly at the exchange and stood waiting for the hatch to come all the way up. I felt like a caged animal that needed to be freed.

I was home.

I couldn't imagine ever returning to Redding now. Too much had happened. I was an Oasen. This was my Oases now.

An old gray-blue van was meandering toward us from the main compound. It was so odd to live in this half-world of aliens and humanity – a world where starships and passenger vans worked in tandem. But that was what my life was now. I was a halfworlder– half in and half out.

We boarded the van, throwing our bags in the back, and drove silently down to the cabins. Exhaustion set in as we pulled up to the Big House. Apparently we were never going to get a solid moment of quiet though. There was yelling coming from the porch.

"Great," I said to Ra on my left. "What is wrong with Ben and Kos now?" They were a mess, those two – always in a rumble. Ra grinned widely. He had learned their habits quickly back in Palenque. We even had to send them home early in the planetary vehicles.

I peeked out the window trying to get a better view of what was going on this time. I squinted and caught my breath. Unstrapping, I tripped my way from the back of the van over several people to get out. Barreling out the door, I ran.

There, sandwiched between Ben and Kos, was Simon Stillwell screaming about aliens and the end of the world and who knows what else. He rambled frenetically. His movements were jerky, frantic and absent-minded. Ben and Kos were trying their best to quiet him as if someone might hear him and take stock in his psychosis, but we were in the middle of nowhere.

"How did you get here?" I demanded of him. Ben and Kos held him by both arms two feet in the air. "Oh, I know him. Let him go," I added.

In bewildered stereo, they dropped him obediently. He fell with a smack to the ground. This jogged him some but not enough to break him free of the madness that held him. I knelt and looked into his pale green eyes. It was like staring into a shell. Simon wasn't there.

"What happened to you buddy?"

He kept mumbling and tried to focus on me, but couldn't. He crawled along the ground until he got to his backpack which he had apparently dropped at some point. He jerkily unzipped it and pulled paper after paper from his pack, all of them crinkled and smudged with the coal black of his pencils. The papers drifted through the air and scattered along the ground.

When he was done, he lifted the pack and dumped it, revealing the nubs of 50 pencils. He picked one up, too small to be of much use, and finding one blank sheet scribbled a picture of Alexandra lying bleeding behind the portal, Khonsu kneeling beside her. Simon's fingers were black and cracked and bleeding. He drew feverishly.

I took the pencil from him before he could finish. "Oh, Simon. What happened to you?"

The others had gathered around by now. Amisi knelt and picked up the drawings that blew across the dusty ground. Blades of grass sticking up here and there had caught some of them. There were a hundred probably, maybe more. There was a picture of us riding inside the giant fish mouth; a picture of Seshat falling from the sky; one of me standing alone on the tower before the tsunami.

It was everything that had happened in horrifying detail.

"Simon," I shook him by the shoulders. It was like shaking a rag doll. "What are you doing here, Simon?" He paid me no attention. "What are you doing here Simon?" This time I yelled.

The noise startled him.

A semblance of sanity crossed his face. "Gil!" His pale green eyes focused. He was breathless. He grabbed my shoulders. He was stronger than I remembered. He tried desperately to take advantage of his moment of clarity like he knew it would pass soon. "After the world went berserk, I couldn't turn it off." He pounded his head. "It won't stop. I can't turn it off!" He banged his head over and over and over. "Oh, for goodness' sake, please help me! Please!"

Simon's unruly hair fell in his eyes and he was gone again.

Insanity returned.

He went on ranting and mumbling about pyramids and ancient gods and planetary highways, and the doom coming in the sky.

"Oh, Gil, come on man," he broke into his thoughts intelligibly once again, somehow. "Please," he begged with his eyes as much as with his mouth. "Please, you're the only one who can make it stop. Make it stop!" he yelled. He jabbered again. His hands shook and he motioned in the air, drawing without a pencil or paper.

My mind went blank and I ran for the van. "The Bes amulet. Do you think it will work?"

"You can only try."

Ryan held Simon, trying to keep him from hurting himself. He was almost gone. Almost beyond saving.

How did he even make it here?

I dug in my backpack and found it. I ran for him, opening and clamping it down on his wrist. It spun around and clicked down and

Simon went still. Peace entered his body. He breathed out a long slow breath and his long lashes fluttered up.

What was it about Simon? He wasn't a hybrid. What was he?

"Thank you Gil. I figured you of all people could stop it. You're the most like me I've ever met."

He sat up. "Where's your pretty girlfriend?" He seemed confused.

Amisi was holding the picture he drew of Alexandra. Her eyes filled with tears and she handed it to him. I stood up and walked away, watching Simon stare at the paper in realization. I couldn't take it anymore. I couldn't take any of it. I needed to go scream at something. Be alone for once.

But I jumped at a sudden presence behind me.

Turning around, I couldn't believe who was there.

The Oracle stood gazing at me – plainly amused at her own untimely intrusion.

"What are you doing here now?" Hurt reached my voice. Her timing could be better. Maybe she could have saved Alexandra, like she had Seshat?

But she didn't answer.

The Oracle only walked around, weaving silently through our odd group, each of us standing or sitting still and quiet on the lawn. She who had been the originator of all this. She inspected each of us. Each one who played out the game she set in motion.

Here we were. Raw and exposed.

The mask we all tried to wear fell away in her presence. All our pain came to the surface again. Pain we had pushed down and tried to hide. Here it was again.

She looked on our downcast faces.

She saw the weary set of our shoulders.

She felt the defeat that sat crushing our hard-fought victory.

And she stopped in front of me.

Finally. I was growing weary of her pacing.

Her stone eyes, which should have been expressionless in their native state, sparkled maddeningly. "Such interesting things are always happening here on Earth, young Gilbert Scott."

A curve of a smile hinted on her cold lips. "And I am very interested in what comes next."

There was only the briefest pause, and my cell phone rang.

▪▪▪▪▪

"Hello. Hello, hello, hello," the female voice echoed strangely. The connection was bad. "Is this Gilbert Scott? Is it done? Is she gone?"

My face lost all its color.

"Who is this? What kind of sick joke is this?" I yelled into the phone.

"No joke," she said.

"She's not dead Gil."

The voice was clear. Resolute.

"My daughter's not dead."

Ingram Content Group UK Ltd.
Milton Keynes UK
UKHW020629120623
423291UK00013B/524